OWL

and the

JAPANESE CIRCUS

OWL
and the
JAPANESE
CIRCUS

Kristi Charish

GALLERY BOOKS

New York   London   Toronto   Sydney   New Delhi

G

Gallery Books
A Division of Simon & Schuster, Inc.
1230 Avenue of the Americas
New York, NY 10020

First Gallery Books trade paperback edition January 2015

GALLERY BOOKS and colophon are registered
trademarks of Simon & Schuster, Inc.

For information about special discounts for bulk purchases,
please contact Simon & Schuster Special Sales at 1-866-506-1949
or business@simonandschuster.com.

The Simon & Schuster Speakers Bureau can bring authors
to your live event. For more information or to book an event
contact the Simon & Schuster Speakers Bureau at 1-866-248-3049
or visit our website at www.simonspeakers.com.

Interior design by Lewelin Polanco
Cover art by Fred Gambino

Manufactured in the United States of America

1 3 5 7 9 10 8 6 4 2

ISBN 978-1-4767-9499-0
ISBN 978-1-4767-7867-9 (ebook)

For my spousal unit, Steve.
Hon, we play a lot of video games.

OWL

and the

JAPANESE
CIRCUS

1

EGG HUNT

8:45 p.m., Interstate 15, somewhere in Nevada

I hate potholes. I hate desert highways too, about as much as I hate wearing high heels.

My Winnebago jolted over a bad pothole before I could swerve around it. I scrambled to keep the wheel straight and grabbed for my water bottle before it toppled and spilled across my laptop keyboard.

Too late.

I tried to mop the water up with my map before it seeped through to the motherboard. Captain howled from the back.

"Yeah, I hate Nevada too," I said.

That's one thing that sucks about these nighttime desert stretches of highway. No lights and no cars. You don't see anything until it's right there in front of your barreling Winnebago.

I checked my watch. 8:50 p.m. The Byzantine Thief was due online in forty minutes. Damn it, where the hell was that truck stop? I peered at the road for the telltale green sign. I couldn't have missed the exit yet, could I? Served me right for trusting directions from a waitress wearing fishnets and a pair of bunny ears. If there's one thing I've learned in my line of work over the last two years, it's to look up the chain of command for advice, not down.

"Hey Captain, I've got forty minutes to find that truck stop and get supplies. Pull off to the side of the road and log on, or keep looking?"

The blanket rustled and Captain stuck his seal-point head out. He sniffed the air before disappearing into the back. I heard metal clank and water splash as he upended his food and water bowls.

I took that for, *Keep going, I'm hungry.*

I chewed my lower lip as I peered through the windshield down the highway. Now where the hell was that turnoff?

"Would it kill anyone to have more lights out here?" I said.

Captain mewed. I should have taken the gig in Puerto Rico instead. Can't get lost on an island.

My laptop beeped twice. I took my eyes off the road for a second to check the message. One of my teammates, Carpe Diem, was already online.

You're late, Thief. Get your ass online.

Goddamn it. I completely forgot I was supposed to meet Carpe ten minutes early so we could swap gear. Double shit. This was the second time this month I'd blanked on a pregame meeting.

"Remind me to start writing my appointments on sticky notes," I said. Captain hopped up onto my front seat and chirped before curling up in a ball on my keyboard.

I rolled my eyes. "Thanks, I appreciate your enthusiasm."

You know your sanity is in question when you find yourself in a two-way conversation with a cat. Yet another reason my social life is restricted to an online game. Well, that and my paranoia. But I can't talk to sane people about that anyways. They'd just lock me up with a lot of meds, and I know I'm not crazy, so it's not like it'd do me any good.

If anything, my weekends in World Quest anchor me to reality.

For a few hours I can curl up with a beer and forget I live in a Winnebago, running from, well . . .

Let's just say my line of work doesn't allow for sincere in-person social interactions.

I pulled the wet map up to check for the exit when I caught reflective white on green in my floodlights up ahead. Bingo, exit 15. I could even see the lampposts in the distance. I steered onto the gravel road and pulled up to an old truck stop that reminded me of something out of a 1950s teen movie. It had the prerequisite convenience store and gas pump, which was all I cared about.

Carpe pinged me again at 9:10.

Screw you, I've got ten more minutes.

Fuck you, you still owe me for last week.

I pursed my lips. He wasn't entirely wrong. I did have most of our stolen loot in my bag of holding—hazard of being a World Quest thief. Everyone always assumes you have somewhere to stash stuff.

Picking up supplies. Gimme five.

I closed the laptop to cut the conversation short and scanned the floodlit parking lot. Two freight trucks and a jeep.

I had the door handle turned halfway when a light flickered inside the jeep. I had the key back in the ignition faster than you can say, "*Backtrack*" and waited, my heart racing.

Nothing.

I checked Captain. He yawned, stretched, and settled back into his nap. I scratched him behind the ears and breathed a sigh of relief. If Captain wasn't up in arms, they hadn't caught up to me. Yet. Give them a few more hours though, and one of them would figure out I'd just made a delivery in Vegas. They'd be on my tail until it went cold, and then they'd be right back waiting for one of my jobs to light up their digital switchboard, ready to chase me all over again.

Did I mention I'm really paranoid? Trust me, it's justified.

Better safe than sorry, I rifled through the glove box for my infrared night goggles and checked the jeep again. No one inside or anywhere in the parking lot. Just one warm-blooded red form behind the convenience store counter. I shook my head, took a deep breath, and counted to ten.

I've been in my line of work for two years. The first year was the honeymoon, when all I had to worry about were the feds or the antiquities department catching wind and snooping out one of my jobs. Year two I ran into what I like to call "the scary shit," and I've been checking around corners, using disposable phones, and bouncing my internet off satellites ever since. Even with that, I still can't shake the feeling that one of these days I'm going to pull into a gas station and a nasty gang of Parisian men in expensive cars and designer suits will be waiting for me.

But only a handful of people on the planet even know things like the Paris boys exist, and fewer could do anything about them. As luck would have it, I'm on the outs with the few who could actually do anything about them.

It sucks to be me.

Not today though. If there was one thing I could count on to sound the alarm, it was Captain's spider sense.

I pulled my dirty-blond hair up in a ponytail and tucked it underneath my red flames baseball cap. I tugged the brim lower so it hid most of my face and hopped down into the parking lot. Dust billowed around my ankles, adding another layer of grime to my already dirty clothes. I hadn't had time for a shower in Vegas, and filling up my water tank was proving difficult in the Nevada desert. I took a deep breath and smelled the cool night air. Not a trace of anything except stale grease and gasoline vapors. I shook my paranoia out of overdrive and braced myself for the walk. Only a few feet to the door, a quick trip down the aisles, then back to the road.

Simple.

"Back in a sec with dinner," I said to Captain, and with one last look at the empty jeep I headed into the convenience store.

I spilled my basket full of the Friday night usual across the front counter. Three bags of barbecue chips, a two-liter bottle of diet soda, a six-pack of Corona, an assortment of fluorescent orange cheesy twists, and eight cans of cat food fought for space in front of the cash register. The night cashier, a skinny, redheaded kid who couldn't have been more than sixteen, stared at the pile of junk food and then up at me. A bewildered expression spread over the kid's face as he picked up the first bag of chips.

I shrugged. I didn't feel like explaining my dietary choices to a kid barely into his teens. Instead, I focused on my watch as he rang everything up and deposited it into yellow plastic bags. I still had two minutes left to get back to my Winnebago and log into World Quest before Carpe got pissy again.

I pulled out cash—I almost always use cash—and tossed the bills onto the counter as I waited for the kid to finish bagging.

The door chimed behind us, and I froze. No one else had pulled into the parking lot.

The checkout kid's eyes widened as they fixed on something over my shoulder. He missed the bag entirely, and a can of cat food dropped and rolled across the floor.

Before I could turn around, a heavy hand gripped my shoulder like a vise.

I swore under my breath. The hand squeezed, and I winced as it pinched a nerve.

"Owl," a deep voice said with a slight trace of an Asian accent. "You are a very difficult person to locate."

Yeah, and I planned on keeping it that way. I started to shift my weight onto the balls of my feet, readying to reap the guy's knee, when I picked up expensive cologne tinged with amber. I stopped; it couldn't be the Paris boys.

I turned around slowly and looked up at the tallest Japanese man

I'd ever seen, wearing a pair of designer sunglasses. He wore a tailored suit with diamond cuff links—real diamond cuff links—and matching shoes, but that wasn't what got the kid. A tattoo of a dragon wound its way down the right half of the man's face, the tail wrapping around his neck and disappearing underneath his shirt. It was striking, and a stark contrast to the expensive outfit. It was also a signature.

One of Mr. Ryuu Kurosawa's goons.

I let out the breath I was holding. Not good, but a damn sight better than a pack of Parisian lost boys.

Dragon Tattoo smiled, showing off a perfect set of teeth. "Mr. Kurosawa sends his regards. He wishes to meet with you to discuss your last contract."

I already didn't like where this conversation was headed. I popped a piece of gum in my mouth to cover my nerves and checked the exit while my head was down. Two more of Mr. Kurosawa's lackeys were positioned just outside the convenience store door. No chance to run for it. My Winnebago was faster than it looked, but I doubted it could outrun whatever these guys were driving.

I make it a rule to never meet with clients in person. Ever. Especially after I've finished a job. Not because I cheat anyone—the authenticity of my merchandise is guaranteed, and I've built a good reputation on that little fact. The reason I don't meet with clients is that my services are nonnegotiable. I give you the price with exact specifics of the transaction: certificates of authenticity, photos of the dig site, carbon dating. If you don't like it, hire someone else.

That doesn't mean my clients don't go to extreme lengths to try and negotiate with me . . . another perk of staying off the grid.

I could see my weekend of Corona and World Quest exploits waving good-bye in the store's mirrored glass. OK, deep breaths. There had to be a quick solution to this, preferably one that didn't involve me getting paraded into the Japanese Circus or beaten to a pulp right where I stood.

"No insult to your boss, but my courier delivered his piece this morning. If he has a concern or question about the documentation, he can call or email—Ow! What was that for?" I said. Dragon Tattoo had pinched my shoulder, *hard*. I couldn't clench my fist.

"To help you understand the seriousness of Mr. Kurosawa's request and help you make the right . . . *decision,*" he said, and smiled.

I winced. Somehow I doubted there was any decision here for me to make. I sure as hell don't like being bullied though.

"Look, I have a strict policy on not meeting face-to-face . . ."

Dragon Tattoo slapped me right between my shoulder blades. My gum shot over the counter and into the register. I mouthed, "*Sorry*" to the kid, who looked like he was trying to decide whether to press the alarm or pull out a shotgun. I caught his eyes and just shook my head. The last thing I needed was a dead kid on my conscience. Hell, running is my go-to, and even I knew better than to run from these guys.

The kid glanced once more at Dragon Tattoo before ducking into the back room.

Smart kid.

Mr. Kurosawa's goon lost no time steering me out and past the parking lot floodlights, while the other two fell in a few paces behind. I'd expected them to drop me in a car, but no, Mr. Kurosawa wasn't a Vegas casino owner for nothing. I gave a low whistle as the helicopter blades whirred silently overhead. Big, black, and silent. Well, at least I knew why I hadn't heard them arrive.

"You weren't kidding when you said Mr. Kurosawa wanted to see me," I said.

The goon smiled. "I am not prone to exaggeration, and Mr. Kurosawa does not like to waste time in business." He opened the helicopter door and said something in Japanese to the other two goons before climbing in the front. The other two goons "helped" me into the back before sitting across from me, glaring. Way too close quarters for my liking. I nodded over at my Winnebago. "What about my van?" Captain was probably wondering where his dinner was and what the hell I was doing . . . if he was even up, that is.

Dragon Tattoo glanced out the window. "It will be safe for the duration of your meeting," he said, as if my prized possession were an afterthought. It also begged the question, what would happen to it after our meeting? Best not to think that far ahead. I was already well out of my "experience to deal with" zone. And I doubt I could argue the value of an abandoned Winnebago with Kurosawa's goons.

Shit. I hoped to hell they at least planned on giving me a ride back.

The engine started to rev and the chopper lifted. "Hey, what do I call you guys?" I said, raising my voice over the engines. Dragon Tattoo lifted an eyebrow at me over the back of his seat.

I shrugged. "Any name has gotta be better than goons one and two. For instance, I've been calling you Dragon Tattoo in my head for the last ten minutes."

He almost smiled—on second thought, it could have just been an illusion caused by the tattoo. Another flurry of Japanese passed between my captors, then Dragon Tattoo said, "You may call me Oricho. My associates you may call 'goon one' and 'goon two.'"

I rolled my eyes as the two across from me chuckled and tossed me a black hood. I pulled it over my head. I hate this espionage shit. That's why I'm into antiquities. More money, and I get blindfolded a lot less.

I ran over my last acquisition run for Mr. Kurosawa to keep my mind off the buffeting helicopter—flying is worse when you can't see. What the hell had gone wrong? I knew I'd sent him the right egg—I'd excavated it myself, right out from underneath the terra-cotta warrior dig. I'd even done the tomb translation myself, just to be sure I hadn't been getting an ancient replica. Carbon dating, authenticated translation—I'd even had it run under an electron microscope to make sure the metal folding had matched. Hermes, a courier I used for my US deliveries, better not have scratched it during delivery. If that egg was so much as dented . . .

By the time I ran and reran the details through my head without finding a flaw, the helicopter dipped and bumped onto a tarmac.

Someone grabbed my arm and steered me down the steps. I couldn't see a thing, so it wasn't a surprise when I stumbled and landed three feet down, hard on my knees. Angry Japanese yelling later (Oricho, I think), I was helped back up—*gently* this time. From the wind and the distant roar of traffic, I guessed I was on a roof.

On the bright side, no one had hit me yet.

The hood came off. This roof had a small garden and what might have been picnic tables. It was hard to tell with next to no lights. I also didn't have a chance to get a good look before I was maneuvered towards the one and only well-lit area: a pagoda-style doorway, intricately carved and painted in red and gold. I glanced at the surrounding buildings before I passed underneath to get my bearings. I could make out the Bellagio and the airport in the distance. I was on the Vegas strip.

"May I ask why they call you Owl?" Oricho said. I glanced over my shoulder. Goons one and two had disappeared. I must have looked confused at Oricho's sudden conversational offering—he hadn't said a damn word since the hood had gone on—because he added, "It seems a strange name for a thief."

I lifted the rim of my hat. "Because I have such big eyes."

An eyebrow arched on the tattooed side of his face. "Is that all?"

I shrugged. "That and I can turn my head around backwards. Does that count?" I deadpanned.

It earned me a trace of a smile before Oricho opened a wooden door carved in the same style as the pagoda. "After you." I peered down a flight of poorly lit stairs. Keeping with the rest of the roof's theme, the stairway was also wooden, and looked like it could belong in a mountain resort at the bottom of Fuji, not a Vegas casino.

"Jeez, you'd think your boss could afford to light this place," I said, Oricho following close behind. When we reached the bottom step, a red lacquered door with the image of two entwined dragons in black ink blocked our way.

Oricho opened the door. I covered my mouth and stifled a cough as smoke billowed out. Oricho inclined his head, not quite a bow, but close, and stepped to the side. "Mr. Kurosawa is through there," he said and added, "good luck."

"Luck has nothing to do with it," I said, and took a deep breath before entering the smoke pit. I knew I'd done due diligence—dotted my i's and crossed all my t's. The goods I'd delivered were well worth my salary. Hell, Mr. Kurosawa had gotten a deal.

I just had to keep my wits about me. It's not like I didn't have bargaining room: Mr. Kurosawa had a penchant for ancient Japanese artifacts, and I'm a bitch to replace. Especially if he pushed me off the roof.

I stepped past Oricho into a high-ceilinged ballroom with red tiled floors. The door slammed shut behind me. As my eyes adjusted to the dim LED ceiling lights reflecting off the clouds of smoke, I realized I'd entered a private casino that brought to mind images of an evil, enchanted forest—only filled with slot machines instead of trees. Like most casinos, there were no windows, and I had a hard time making out the boundaries. But the maze of slot machines was what got me. Row upon row filled the ballroom, everything from late 1800s original Feys through to electronics. As far as modern antiques go, it was a good collection—eclectic and haphazard, but good.

I headed down the widest and most well-lit aisle. I noticed that the shelves lining the wall sported rows of Cho Han bamboo bowls, which were used in a feudal Japanese dice game. If they weren't authentic, I'd eat my tool kit. There were so many of them that they obscured the walls, all but hiding the gold and black reliefs painted from ceiling to floor. Yet for all these machines, the room was silent—and empty. I shook my head and readjusted my cap. Well, at least Mr. Kurosawa had gone for original decor. I stifled another cough, wishing I had my gas mask. Ventilation, anyone?

The slot machines opened to a bar, complete with mirrored table and white leather couches that formed a plush alcove. A pretty Japanese woman wearing a kimono fashioned like a minidress and a loose interpretation of Kabuki makeup made her way out from behind the bar, stilettos clicking against the floor in rapid succession. She offered me a plate of drinks without a word, or smile.

"Owl?" I heard Mr. Kurosawa say from the couches, his back towards me. I shot the woman a questioning look. She stepped aside. Taking that as permission, I grabbed a glass of champagne and slammed it back—damn right I needed a drink. Say what you will about tombs and ancient burial sites, a deserted casino outcreeps them any day of the week.

Ryuu Kurosawa, a Vegas mogul known for his Japanese Circus–themed casino, looked up from a white couch and smiled that business smile you come to expect from professional sharks. Not the ones who take your money, the ones that eat you while you're still screaming. I sat down and noted his expensive suit, acutely aware how underdressed I was in my red flames hat, blue jeans, and hiking boots. I shrugged the sentiment off; it wasn't like they'd given me the option to change.

"Thank you for coming to see me on such short notice," he said in crisp American English. I'd spoken to him a few times on the phone and seen interviews on TV, and never once had I heard a trace of an accent or glimpsed a break in the Western businessman demeanor. In person though, the thing that struck me the most was how red and waxy his face was, dim lights or not. I shelved that little observation for later—it's not every day you see something like that.

I crossed my hands to stop them from fidgeting and waited, and for half a second I wished I'd grabbed a second drink. Mr. Kurosawa's smile didn't falter as he waved the Kabuki fashion girl over. This time, instead of drinks, she was carrying a wooden box with a puzzle lid, which she deposited on the mirrored table before me.

I recognized the box—I'd packed Mr. Kurosawa's egg inside it just this morning, before transferring the money into my offshore account and burning my trail. The trick lid had seemed appropriate, since Mr. Kurosawa is known for his love of puzzles. It's the personal touches and attention to detail that distinguish the professionals like me from the hacks.

Mr. Kurosawa removed the contents, an ancient silver egg, with his flushed, waxy red hand and placed it in front of me, the smile not faltering. Without a word I picked it up, carefully, and examined it. Everything looked in place. Smooth and etched with characters that hadn't been used in at least five thousand years, the egg was already an artifact when the emperor buried it in his own personal mausoleum. I turned it over and checked the bottom where the gems were supposed to be. They were all there too. It was the same artifact I'd packed this morning. More importantly, it was still in perfect condition. The confusion on my face must have been obvious, because Mr. Kurosawa's shark smile got a lot more vicious real fast.

"Miss Owl, please do not waste my time. Where is the rest of it?"

I did my best to hide my confusion and rolled the egg over in my hands, checking one more time for missing jewels. The metal was colder than it should have been; I remembered that little observation from the dig site. I'd noted it in my files as something you don't see every day in ancient metals.

I handed him back his egg and shook my head. "Mr. Kurosawa, it's all there, exactly as I excavated it from the emperor's tomb." I indicated the folders and documentation I'd sent along with the box, also on the Kabuki girl's tray. "From initial excavation to delivery, everything is documented. If there's a gem or piece missing, I'm sorry, but that was absolutely all there was at the site. Take a look at the photos and video footage. I'm thorough."

He took the egg back and stared at me. I stifled a shiver. There was something sinister about the way his eyes fixed on my face. That and the way his waxy red skin reflected the casino light.

Memories of the dig rushed to the forefront of my mind: images, details, a misunderstanding with the Chinese authorities . . . as if someone was sifting through my thoughts, pulling and tweezing. As I narrowed in on Mr. Kurosawa's face, I noticed how the pupils had widened, eating up the whites until there was nothing left. An unpleasant thought occurred to me . . . really bad. Really, really bad. Of course, it's only now I notice all the dragon imagery around the room.

The shock on my face, or on the surface of my thoughts, must have been transparent, because Mr. Kurosawa smiled. His teeth turned black before my eyes and extended into dagger-like points.

Ryuu, Kurosawa, even Dragon Tattoo's name, Oricho . . . fuck, I'd been buying for a Japanese dragon.

And he didn't like what I'd brought him.

Mr. Kurosawa laughed, low and guttural. "So you did not steal my treasure," he said, as his eyes began to glow black and his skin turned bright red. "Lucky for you, little Owl. I eat thieves."

As a rule, dragons aren't very good at holding other forms. Mr. Kurosawa was holding the rest of his form pretty well, but I figured the only reason he hadn't done the full dragon in front of me was the ten-thousand-dollar suit he was wearing. Dragons really love their treasure—more than eating humans, I hoped. I squirmed and couldn't help myself from checking where the exits were. There weren't any. Shit. If I got out of here alive, I'd have to look up whether there had been any interesting missing persons files around the casino. I could see the appeal to a dragon to set up shop here. No shortage of thieves with "dragon food" stamped on their foreheads in Vegas.

Mr. Kurosawa laughed, and smoke streamed from his nostrils. Well, at least he was enjoying himself. I held up my hands and chose my words very carefully. "My sincerest apologies, I didn't mean to insult you with damaged goods, it was a complete accident on my part. You can keep the egg and I'll even return my fee. I don't want there to be any . . . bad feelings—"

He cut me off with a laugh so grating I winced. Was it just me, or was the room actually getting hotter?

He held out the egg and pressed three small pinholes in succession. The egg clicked and opened into three sections, like orange slices. I hadn't even realized the egg was a puzzle box. There hadn't been any mention of it in the inscriptions.

Still chuckling, Mr. Kurosawa exposed an empty chamber for me to see.

"You misunderstand my intentions, Owl. I'm not angry with you for bringing me what was agreed upon—now that I am sure you did not steal the contents of the egg." His eyes glowed red for a moment. "I wish to arrange a new contract with you to find the missing contents." He must have seen my face turn white. In fact, I'm positive he saw my face turn white, because this conversation was heading into territory I was already way too familiar with and had had enough of to last me three—no, make that five—lifetimes.

I have a strict policy. No magic, no monsters, no supernatural clients. Ever. I stumbled into what I like to call "supernatural shit" on my third job. Completely by accident, I might add. If you were wondering what drove me off the grid into living in a Winnebago, using disposable phones and hijacked satellite internet, *that* was it.

The only reason my "magic check" hadn't come back positive on this one was that someone else had beaten me to it a thousand or two years ago . . . wait, that was it.

"Mr. Kurosawa—"

"Please, Owl," he said, indicating a fresh flute of champagne proffered by the Kabuki girl. "So rarely do I . . . entertain, so to speak," he finished, and grinned.

I took the new glass. I wasn't worried it was poisoned; easier to just eat me. I was having a hard time not cringing every time he smiled though. I started again. "Mr. Kurosawa, whatever is supposed to be inside that egg was stolen a few thousand years ago, maybe more. I don't even know where I would start—"

He stopped me with his hand, now sporting claws. Three-inch black claws. He passed a folder to me across the mirrored table. "I believe this will help you decide where to start."

I chewed my lower lip and opened the folder—it's not like I had a lot of options. Inside was a list of locations: China, Japan, Korea, and a few places in Indonesia. I knew all of them. I'd turned down jobs in each and every one because they were supernatural hot spots.

I closed the folder and passed it back. If I hadn't been sitting in front of a dragon, I'd have thrown it as far away as humanly possible. "Look, Mr. Kurowsawa, I'm really sorry, but I can't—"

"Are you happy with your existence?" he asked.

That caught me off guard. "Ahh, if you mean am I fond of living, yeah, I'm pretty attached to it."

Smoke billowed out of his nose as he reclined against the white leather, his glowing black eyes boring into me. "The running, hiding, evading, knowing no one would ever believe you—doesn't it get tedious?"

"Ummm, no offense, but that's why I don't do supernatural jobs—"

Mr. Kurosawa's smile shifted from sinister to mocking. "And how has that been working out for you?"

I didn't say anything. What was the point? He was right.

He laughed.

Dragon or no, he was starting to piss me off. Besides, this was turning into a lose-lose situation, and I'd rather be eaten by a dragon than chased down by vampires. For one, the dragon didn't have a grudge. "Look, I have enough trouble with vampires right now, and I don't need any more supernatural problems, and that," I said, pointing to the open egg, "is a supernatural problem."

"What is it worth to make your problem go away?" Mr. Kurosawa asked.

That got my attention.

"No more running, no more checking over your shoulder." He leaned in. "No one hunting you down."

The chance to go back to my place in Seattle, actually use my bank account without worrying a vampire or its lackey was going to jump out of the next alley I passed by . . .

"What's the catch?" I said.

On cue the Kabuki girl handed Mr. Kurosawa a third bloodred folder that matched his ever-reddening skin. He removed a single sheet and slid it across the table.

My throat went dry. It was a contract written in bright red ink. The kind of contract you can't break.

"As per our previous arrangements, payment will be given on the delivery of the missing contents of the egg into my possession. As a gesture of good faith I will negotiate a truce with the parties currently searching for you, from this date onwards."

"I don't do supernatural," I said. Even I didn't convince myself.

"My dear, you do not have the luxury of deciding that, not if you intend to keep your current hide intact." He smiled and flashed me those black dragon teeth again. "You're rather famous in my circles now. Accidently bathing a vampire superior in sunlight during an excavation will do that. Though I still haven't decided yet whether you're brilliant or miraculously stupid for managing to deliver the sarcophagus and collecting your pay. In the meantime, you've evaded their agents and completed seven contracts, five of them for me. I'd wager you're about as deep into 'supernatural shit' as you can get. Besides that, you're greedy." His eyes took on a black glow. "And greed is something I can work with."

I held the contract. *Yes or no?*

"And," Mr. Kurosawa added, glancing at his Rolex watch, "this offer will quickly expire."

The Kabuki girl handed me a sealed envelope this time. Three photos were inside, all time-stamped a few hours before. It was the Paris boys; I'd recognize Alexander anywhere. They were in Vegas.

I had two choices: deal with Mr. Kurosawa, or take my chances with the Paris boys. Either way, odds were good I'd end up dinner. I thought about accepting for a minute. But that thought only lasted a minute. Supernatural shit got me into my Winnebago mess in the first place. Stacking a dragon on top of vampires was a stupid idea. I stood up and shook my head. "Sorry, no deal. I'm not working for you."

"Are you not afraid I will kill you?"

I shook my head and shrugged. "You or the vampires. I'm not making the same mistake again," I said, and started walking back towards the maze of slot machines.

"This one job, Owl. You need never see me or their ilk again."

I glanced over my shoulder and he flashed me his black teeth, the height of Japanese fashion a few thousand years ago.

"Just this last contract, and I will deliver on my promise to intervene with the vampires. What do you have to lose?"

"I'd be off their hit list permanently?"

He nodded, once.

I rolled it over in my head. All I had to do was find the contents and I'd be rid of the vampires. It wasn't digging myself in deeper. It was a way out. "One job, and only the one . . . ever," I said.

Mr. Kurosawa smiled.

"And I have conditions."

Another puff of smoke trailed out of Mr. Kurosawa's nose, but he didn't stop me, so I trudged onwards. Shit, what the hell was I doing, bartering with a dragon? "First, no eating me. *Even* after this contract expires or you terminate it. Second, you bankroll the equipment."

"Agreed. I assume there is a third?"

I braced myself. "The vampire clause stands, even if I can't deliver."

His lips curled up at my last condition, and I wondered for a moment if I'd pushed dragon patience too far. I didn't actually prefer being eaten to working for a dragon—not if he could get the Paris boys off my case—but I also wasn't diving headfirst into a doomed wild-goose chase.

Mr. Kurosawa considered me from the plush couch. "Is that everything?"

"I want it in the contract."

Three long seconds passed, during which I held my breath.

"Lady Siyu," Mr. Kurosawa said. The Kabuki girl produced a red lacquer pen with a very sharp tip.

Oh hell no.

I went to shove my hand into my pocket, but she was too fast; a blur of red-tipped fingernails snatched my wrist.

I yelped as she pricked me with a needle and held my finger until a drop of blood fell on the page. She was strong for such a small woman. Lady Siyu said something in Japanese, and my conditions appeared on the bottom page. Just like that. Then she flipped the pen over and handed it to me. I kept her and Mr. Kurosawa in my sights as I signed. I thought I caught a glimpse of a slit eye as I passed the signed contract back to Lady Siyu. If she was human, I was a dancing unicorn.

"How does a dragon get vampires to back off dinner anyways?" I said.

Mr. Kurosawa frowned, as if my question was in line with what he'd expect from a four-year-old.

I held up my hands. "Just curious. They were pretty pissed off the last time we spoke in Egypt." Thinking about my Egyptian run-in with the Paris boys was enough to give me nightmares for a week.

"There are courtesies and etiquettes to follow," Mr. Kurosawa said. "If not, I've been known to eat the occasional vampire."

I believed it. Dragons trump vampires in the supernatural food chain. Which only strengthened my conviction that I was completely and utterly out of my mind for even contemplating this job.

"So, just so we're clear, tomorrow I can use my Visa and no one will jump out of an alley and try to kill me?" Oh yeah, vampires were loving the digital era.

"I suggest you set yourself up in Vegas to start, but yes. I've taken the liberty of having Lady Siyu check you into one of our suites. Your van was retrieved and is in the parkade."

Lady Siyu passed me a receipt for my Winnebago, along with the red dossier. She turned on her spiked heels and motioned for me to follow.

Mr. Kurosawa regarded me. Even halfway to a dragon he still

looked every inch the rich businessman. "Words of caution, Owl: do not let yourself lose track of Lady Siyu in my private casino. People have a way of getting . . . lost."

I scrambled; I was not about to get lost in a dragon's lair—den—whatever you call it. But my business side took over. I glanced back over my shoulder at Mr. Kurosawa before Lady Siyu entered the maze. "How do I contact you?"

"It's all in the dossier." He got up to leave and had almost disappeared amongst the slot machines, but I couldn't help myself.

"What would have happened if I'd said no?"

He flashed his vicious, razor-sharp smile once more. "Those Paris vampires offered an awfully large reward for you. *And* I eat thieves."

With that, he was gone, and I ran to catch up to Lady Siyu, now almost at the end of the nearest row of slot machines. She hadn't waited for me. My head was spinning—I was working for a *dragon*.

Lady Siyu led me through the maze of machines, and I kept my head down, not wanting to be distracted by the neon lights. After she'd turned down too many corridors for me to keep track of, she pushed open two heavy gold doors with old Japanese characters etched deep into the metal.

I didn't realize how tense I'd been until we stepped into the hotel corridor. With just the brush of our feet against the plush carpet to indicate anyone was here, she stopped before a black unmarked door and opened it with a gold key card, which she handed to me.

I wouldn't call it a room. Luxury designer condo was more like it. I whistled as Lady Siyu followed me in. I hadn't been in a real room in over four months—not counting student and hostel dorms. It'd been camping or the Winnebago. I couldn't wait to see the bathroom and take a shower—damn, I could soak in a bath.

Lady Siyu was about to leave when I remembered something. "Ummm, this might sound odd, but I have a cat . . ."

Lady Siyu turned and inclined her head, slowly. She had green, slitted eyes that reflected the light.

Yup, definitely not human. "Umm . . . yeah . . . I just wasn't sure whether I was allowed a pet in here—"

"It's not a problem," she said with a perfect British accent. It took me aback; it was the first time I'd heard her speak. She glided over to my desk. French, Louis XIII, I'd bet on it. In fact, the room was full of antiques—I shook my head. I was *not* stealing from a dragon's hotel.

She picked up a notebook and wrote two numbers down. "You may contact room service here, and secure internet access is available with this network and password. You will have to search for it—it is very secure. Everything else you need is in the file, along with your terms of employment. If you have any questions, contact me at this number. Please do not leave the hotel or casino this evening, as Mr. Kurosawa needs to . . . 'negotiate' your immunity. Will there be anything else?"

"Umm, no. That's all I need."

Lady Siyu bowed—barely, I noted. With a click of the door, I was alone.

On the corner chair someone had deposited my weekend supplies, complete with yellow bags. I pulled out one of my now warm Coronas and put the rest in the fridge. I sat on my bed and took everything in: vampires, contracts with a dragon, whatever Lady Siyu was. How the hell was I going to track down something that was stolen three thousand years ago?

I just had to keep telling myself this was better than running from a pack of vampires.

— m —

I cracked open my third Corona and pulled my wet hair into a ponytail. I was wearing only a casino bathrobe. After the shower, I couldn't stand to put any of my old clothes back on. They just all seemed so dirty. I'd have to go shopping tomorrow. It wasn't like I didn't have the money. I was sitting on over ten million dollars. A significant downside to my run-in with the Paris boy vampires a year ago was that I hadn't had the chance to spend any of it.

Captain picked the middle of the bed to take a nap. I was going to have a bitch of a time getting him off, so I opened up my laptop and logged into World Quest. Time to face the music.

There was a flurry of messages from my team telling me to eff off. Touching, close-knit group that we were. There was a series of messages from Carpe Diem asking if I was OK. I opened up a private chat window before entering the game.

Hey, Carpe—I'm fine, I wrote.

A moment later his reply scrolled across the screen. *What happened? You disappeared.*

Emergency business, couldn't be helped. I'm back for the weekend— beer in hand, room service on the way.

There was a delay in Carpe's response. *Out of your realm of behavior. Had me worried.*

I'm touched.

Wouldn't be hard to find a decent thief. Next time get a message off.

Had to admit, it got to me that my World Quest friend even cared—or maybe it was beer number three talking. *Roger Wilco. What's the schedule?*

Five more hours, then a seven-hour break. Halfway through a dungeon. Get your ass online and I'll port you in.

Room service knocked. I opened the door and could smell the steak instantly. They'd even included a bottle of red wine. I started salivating. I hadn't had a steak in months, let alone a decent bottle of red wine.

I slid back into the hotel chair, and Captain, smelling the steak, hopped up onto my lap. There was one more message from Carpe Diem on the screen.

By the way, sorry about all your stuff.

Fuck.

I pulled up my inventory screen. It, and my bag of holding, was empty. To top it off, my character, the Byzantine Thief, was standing in all her skivvy computer-generated glory. "Motherfu-ow!" I said as Captain chirped at my sudden movement and dug his claws into my leg.

Well, this would be interesting. I'd never entered a match with my birthday suit on before. Son of a bitch.

Carpe Diem, resident team sorcerer that he was, ported me. A flurry of in-game comments on my character's relative nakedness greeted me. For the next few hours the only dragons and monsters I had to worry about were the ones the rest of the world worried about—the ones in a game.

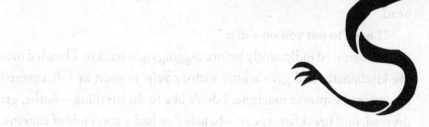

2

THE TROUBLE WITH VAMPIRES

Noon-ish, the Japanese Circus

Something rough scraped against my face, interrupting my sleep. It smelled like fish.

I groaned and rolled over in the incredibly comfortable hotel bed, pulling the thick duvet over my head. Captain fell off the bed with an indignant chirp, and I sealed myself under the covers while I still had the chance.

That bought me all of five seconds before he started to dig.

"I'm so brushing your teeth," I said.

I swung the covers off and checked my watch. Noon. I rubbed my eyes and got up. Not fast enough for Captain, who had bypassed me-owing and gone straight to death howls. Well, five hours was better than nothing.

"Screw off," I said, hoping to avoid tripping over him. Damn it, why do cats always wind around your legs in the morning before you've had any coffee?

He followed me over to the stack of cans and didn't let up until I dumped the contents into his plastic bowl. He dug in, and I shook my head.

"I need to put you on a diet."

He meowed indignantly before digging right back in. I headed into the kitchenette and gave a little victory yelp as soon as I discovered the stocked espresso machine. I don't like to do anything—bathe, get dressed, find breakfast, speak—before I've had a good jolt of caffeine. I loaded a capsule into the holder. While it spit out my coffee, I got a second capsule ready. I like my caffeine.

By the time I was downing my second, I started putting together my strategy for the day. First, find out from Lady Siyu whether I was going to be dodging vampire lackeys; second, find breakfast. The second condition prevailed regardless of the outcome of the first, but if I was still being hunted, my options were going to be limited. That and I could get a few more hours' sleep.

I picked up the room's phone, an off-white enamel number as ornate and expensive-looking as the other antiques in the room, and dialed the number Lady Siyu had left me.

After two rings her crisp British accent answered, "Yes?"

I rolled my eyes. In one word Lady Siyu managed to convey both irritation and a perceived superiority.

"Hi, ah, just checking in to see where things were at—"

"Mr. Kurosawa has completed the negotiation of terms," she said, cutting me off. "You may leave the casino and make travel arrangements accordingly."

And with that, the line clicked dead.

Well, that settled that.

I showered, dressed, and went online to start getting my life back in order and test my new immunity. Digitally transferred funds and a few phone calls to the bank later, I was good to go. It felt weird, seeing my bank account balance for the first time in months, and the idea of actually spending my money—like a normal person. It had been a while since I'd felt anything close to normal. Ever since I'd become an antiquities thief. Well, if I was honest with myself, not since I'd started grad school, but it wasn't until after I'd left grad school that things had gone to hell in a handbasket.

The main draw to my line of work isn't getting dirty on archaeology digs or breathing in corrosive acid fumes while restoring thousand-year-old artifacts. It also isn't the hours of eyestrain on the computer stalking museum and university archives. If that had been it, I'd have tried a hell of a lot harder to stay in archaeology—not by much, but I'd at least have put in a token effort.

It's the money. A *lot* of money. And lower risk than being a real thief. Truth be told, most governments don't really care what happens to their artifacts—not enough to arrest anyone . . . or shoot. Except for Egypt, that is, but with the right palms greased, it's a moot point. After three revolutions, the tourism industry is shot and they're hurting for cash.

Another perk is I actually get credit for the work I do—not screwed over by some talentless dick of a postdoc who spends more time trying to stare down my shirt than dig . . . OK, off that train of thought—I try *not* to have anger management issues nowadays.

My very first paycheck I spent on a condo in Seattle, which I haven't stepped foot in for months now due to the vampires camping outside. I had sources tell me they hadn't torched it, just rifled through everything and broken a few Roman vases. The vases had really pissed me off; I'd had buyers lined up.

The only money I'd been able to spend since the Paris boys started trailing me was on computer and gaming equipment online, and even then I had to use every dirty trick in the book to stay stealth.

Speaking of online shopping . . . I picked my cargo pants and over-sized surplus military jacket off the arm of the chair by the kitchen table. Both were caked in dust and had old coffee stains on them. On a hunch I held them under my nose. Funny how three weeks living in a Winnebago with a cat numbs your sense of smell. My clothes didn't need a wash; they needed to be thrown in a landfill.

There was no shortage of shops on the Vegas strip, but a scene from *Pretty Woman* came to mind—the one where they refuse to serve the hooker in a designer store. Switch out hooker for homeless woman and that would be me. Nuts to that.

I ordered breakfast from room service and pulled up the online stores for Chanel, Versace, and Ralph Lauren, which all had locations in Vegas. My best friend, Nadya, who could pass for a fashion model on a bad day, gave me a piece of advice after I showed up at her club in Tokyo wearing a number I'd picked out myself: next time, shop out of a catalogue. Apparently fashion sense isn't one of my talents.

I checked out Versace first. Time to get my Visa out and test this truce.

I dialed the Vegas number.

"Hi there," I said, "do you guys by any chance have the snake-skin leather jacket and matching leather boots in a small and a size seven and a half? You do? Great, I'm going to need that and a few other things brought over to the concierge at the Japanese Circus—" I flipped to the next page on the screen and checked my watch. 12:30. Six and a half hours until I was scheduled to meet Carpe back online. Plenty of time to get dressed, get food, and do some research on Mr. Kurosawa's egg.

———— w ————

I ordered a bagel and my third coffee of the day at the hotel casino's garden cafe before grabbing a seat poolside. I'd spent an hour and a half researching leads for Mr. Kurosawa's egg and missing scroll while I'd waited for my new clothes to arrive. I wasn't any further ahead than if I'd spent the time playing World Quest. Every mention I'd found of puzzle boxes and scrolls found in the emperor's tomb, or from the same period, had been dead ends; not one shared characteristics with the puzzle egg or the strange inscriptions.

Sitting by the pool and fresh out of any leads, I decided to hack into the University of Tokyo's archaeology server. I remembered a talk a few years back by a Japanese postdoc—Yoshi? He'd spent a few years in the Bali catacombs, and I vaguely recalled him mentioning foreign tablet inscriptions, found in two of the antechambers, that had been untranslatable. On the off chance there were similarities with the inscriptions on Mr. Kurosawa's egg, I dug up the Bali thesis. There's a lot of porn on the university server to sift through, in case you were wondering what Japanese profs and students store in their personal accounts.

The only mention of the tablets and inscriptions was a small footnote, with no picture. I sat back and weighed the possibilities. I knew the postdoc had shown photographs of the tablet in his talk, so the only reason they'd have been omitted from the thesis proper was if there'd been a supernatural link discovered after the fact. The International Archaeology Association would have insisted the Japanese bury it; first and foremost, they had to keep those pesky bits of supernatural proof out of the public's delicate hands. Heaven forbid anyone actually knew there were vampires, dragons, and other assorted monsters out there, just waiting to eat them. . . .

Without an actual image of the tablet in front of me though, I couldn't be sure . . . And there'd been no mention of scrolls anywhere in the thesis . . . but then again, it was supernatural, so maybe the university had buried that too.

I rubbed my eyes. Between the vampires and Mr. Kurosawa . . . How did I get myself into these messes . . .

However long a shot, the tablet and inscriptions from Bali were the only leads I had.

I had to go to Japan and talk to Nadya's contact in the university. If my hunch was right, the egg and missing scroll weren't Chinese artifacts at all but much older pieces.

I pulled up flights to Japan. There was one that left at 11:00 p.m. I checked the time. 2:15 p.m. I'd still make World Quest and be able to sleep on the plane. I emailed Nadya and let her know I was coming for a visit and needed to crash at her place. Code that I needed her to get her contact ready for me . . . and that I'd be crashing at her place.

With five hours to spare, I pulled my new Versace sunglasses down and leaned back to enjoy the poolside sun and people-watching.

Not ten minutes passed before I realized I was being cased. If I hadn't been watching the boys from down under hanging out across the pool, I'd never have caught the greasy rock star wannabe lurking a few tables away.

Stringy dark hair, black eyeliner, leather pants, open white shirt—without the build to pull it off, I might add—and a pair of dark boho sunglasses. How the hell did heroin ever become chic?

I usually suck spotting supernaturals in a crowd, but even I know a vampire's lackey when I see one, and this one was low end. Think slumming it, for vampires.

As soon as he realized I'd spotted him—my look of pure contempt and disgust probably gave it away—he stopped the pretense and creeped around the other tables and suntanners towards me.

I took another sip of my coffee and waited. If I was going to run into one of Alexander's thralls sooner or later, I might as well deal with him now. In the back of my mind I couldn't help worrying Mr. Kurosawa had double-crossed me. But that would be a lot of trouble to go to when he could have just eaten me last night. Out of reflex I cased the rest of the pool for more vampire lackeys. Apparently this guy was solo, though I did catch Oricho and two tattooed guards standing off to the side.

Interesting.

Vampire lackey strode right up, crossed his arms, and smirked down at me. "Well? Have anything to say for yourself, Owl?"

I crinkled my nose—cheap cologne was dripping off him. From how far gone he was, I'd wager it was to cover residual rotting lily of the valley from his vampire master. Damn, where did vampires find these guys? I glanced once more at Oricho, who stood like a statue by the door. Well, time to see what this truce was worth.

"Yeah. Fuck the hell off before I call security."

That caught him off guard. He placed both hands on my table and leaned in, the smirk twisting into a sneer that showed heavily stained teeth.

I leaned back—not out of fear but in disgust. "The least the vampires could do is offer you lapdogs decent dental. Bad teeth ruin the ominous dark messenger effect. So does the cheap perfume. I could still smell you across the pool." That pissed him off.

"There's a bounty on your head. One I plan on collecting." His white shirt slipped to the side, exposing a hidden handgun.

I hate guns. You'd think with all my running away from vampires I'd have a gun or two lying around, or a stake at the very least. My experience is that as soon as you start keeping a gun in your glove compartment, the bad guys manage to beat you to it. A gun is predictable—you point and shoot. Not having a gun means I have to think outside the box, and I've escaped more tight situations that way than I can count. Same thing goes for stakes. I do keep garlic water hidden in a perfume bottle though, for up close emergencies.

I glanced back towards the garden cafe door. Oricho was nowhere to be seen.

I frowned. So much for dragon protection. I guessed human vampire lackeys didn't rate interference.

"You realize there's a truce? I'm not on any hit list," I said.

He smiled, showing me those stained teeth again. "Not officially, but I bring you in, I get made."

"You break a truce your bosses bartered with the dragon running Vegas, and you figure Alexander is going to reward you publicly and make you a vampire? You're dumber than you look," I said.

His smile wavered. Trusting your vampire bosses only goes so far—even for the stupidly devout. But this guy was a fanatic. He shook his head. "She wouldn't do that to me. The others might have caved to the dragon, but she still wants you dead."

It took every ounce of control to keep myself from smiling. *Now* we were getting somewhere. Not having a gun means people subconsciously keep talking—even when they start telling you stuff they shouldn't. My guess is their subconscious figures you'll be dead any-ways, so why bother with the filter? It's not like these guys have a lot of brainpower to spare. *She* told me a lot. For one, it said that against all odds, Alexander and the Paris boys were playing ball. None of them were female. Which meant this was either someone they'd hired or another, unknown female vampire I'd pissed off.

"Don't be stupid. The only reward you'll be getting is a pine box—the kind you don't crawl back out of," I said, hoping to talk some reason into him—not completely selfishly either. His vampire boss would kill him to cover her tracks.

I could see in his eyes though that the blind devotion was back, and I heard, more than saw, the safety click off. Amazing the things you start to hear when someone's about to kill you. I did another vi-sual check: not only were Mr. Kurosawa's big muscles nowhere to be seen but the regular guards had disappeared as well. Along with any guests who had been in earshot.

I sighed. It's always nice to know where you fall in a list of priori-ties. Image, guests, and then probably property damage well above my well-being—just like my archaeology days.

The lackey's eyes glazed over with the apathy people get when they're about to kill another human being, and he aimed the gun at me. I gripped the arms of the chair. I wasn't going to keel over and die just yet. I'd have to time it right, but if I could just keep him talking . . .

"You're making a big mistake. This vampire chick isn't going to let you walk away from starting a turf war with a dragon. She's using you as a scapegoat. You'll be her rogue human who killed the girl after she explicitly told you not to, and then she'll present your severed head. This stuff happens all the time. You're just another pawn to be thrown under the bus—"

"Enough," he said with the fervor only a rabid vampire lackey could show. "Sabine would never do that to me."

Sabine. I had a name. I had no idea who this Sabine vampire was, but I had a name, and a name can do wonders in the digital age.

Now all I had to do was keep myself alive. The lawn chair had some weight to it and acted as an anchor as I leaned back and inched my Chanel boot towards him. If I timed it just right, I'd catch his foot with my heel and reap his knee before he got a shot off. I doubt he'd see that coming. I planned to throw myself to the side and take a bullet to my shoulder, just in case.

"You know what I hate most about vampire lackeys?" I asked, hoping I could distract him so he wouldn't catch the last precious inch I'd slid my boot towards him.

"What?" he growled.

"You guys never think ahead of your next fix," I said as I caught his shoe with my right heel and kicked out my left leg at his knee.

I didn't connect. A tattooed arm reached around my torso and lifted me clear over the back of my chair as I yelped. Mr. Kurosawa's boys apparently weren't as indifferent to vampire lackeys running around their hotel as I'd summarized.

Vampire Boy was nowhere near as lucky as me. He never knew what hit him. Oricho had him by the throat and lifted him up until his feet were dangling off the ground. Vampire Boy's eyes went wide, and he started grasping at Oricho's hands. Oricho didn't squeeze, or threaten, or sprout fangs, or anything else I'd expect from a supernatural working for a dragon. He pulled the quivering lackey in close, and all I could make out were his lips moving quickly as he whispered in my would-be assassin's ear.

At first nothing happened. Vampire Boy looked more confused than anything else. But a half breath later the expression turned from confusion to terror as he began to twitch. The twitching escalated into full-blown convulsions, and white foam began to spew out of his mouth.

Oricho let him fall to the concrete as if he'd been dropping a sack of trash off at the corner. The vampire lackey twitched and choked for a good long minute, until he lay still in a pool of his own vomit.

I took a step back and whistled. "You guys don't mess around," I said. Off the top of my head, I didn't know of any other creatures who could kill that subtly.

Oricho regarded the body and shook his head. "Drug overdose. So sad in one so young."

Yeah. Real sad. And a perfectly plausible junkie's death with no witnesses to say otherwise. As professional a cover-up as the International Archaeology Association ever orchestrated.

I made a mental note to err on the side of caution when dealing with these guys in the future.

"Umm, not that I don't appreciate you guys stepping in and all, but if you weren't planning on letting him shoot me, why not step in sooner?"

Oricho turned his attention to me, and I tried to keep from fidgeting. He'd been wearing sunglasses before, and this was the first time I got a glimpse of his unnatural green eyes.

After a moment of regarding me he said, "Starting a war on a conversation and an argument is not wise. It was more profitable to let him act. Besides, this assassin talked too much," he added, almost cracking a half smile.

I nodded. Yup, that rang true, which reminded me: "He wasn't with Alexander and the Paris boys. Apparently they're respecting Mr. Kurosawa's truce. Have you ever heard of a vampire called Sabine?" I nodded to Vampire Boy's corpse. " 'Cause that's who threw him under the bus."

"Perhaps. I will consult with Mr. Kurosawa. If there is anything of note, Lady Siyu shall contact you. In the meantime, do not leave the Circus's grounds."

I noticed the only people who seemed to be left in the vicinity were the outback Aussie boys, except now they were carrying cleanup equipment.

I arched an eyebrow back at Oricho. He just raised one right back at me. I know when to pick my battles. "Yeah, about that, I need to be on a flight to Japan tonight."

For the first time, Oricho's face betrayed a trace of surprise.

"You've located it already—?"

I shook my head and picked up my laptop. I was done with the pool. Besides, up in my room Captain would smell any vampires before they reached the door. "I've got a lead and it leads to Japan, so I'm on a flight to Tokyo tonight—or at least I'm booked on one."

He frowned and shook his head. "It would be better for you to wait until I have identified and spoken to this *Sabine*," he said, rolling around the name as if it was something distasteful. "The Paris Vampire Contingency was satisfied with Mr. Kurosawa's arrangement and removed their agents and selves from Las Vegas last night."

He nodded at the vampire lackey as two of the Aussie boys lifted the body into a giant metal garbage can. "We noticed him around the casino this morning, but there has been no trace of a female vampire anywhere in Vegas. I promise you I will find her," he added as I opened my mouth to argue.

"Oh, I have no doubt you'll find out who she is, it's the me being alive part I'm worried about," I said.

Oricho smiled at that. "I promise you were never in any danger."

The Aussie boys rolled the garbage can away. They were way too cheerful about it. I'd have to look into what they might be before I spent any more time ogling them poolside. "Yeah, well, danger or not, if you plan on me finding your boss's scroll, I need to be in Japan."

Oricho frowned and tried to stare me down, but I held my ground. I wasn't messing around with this job. Finally, he took his cell out, and after a brief discussion in Japanese that was well over my head, he turned to me and said, "Go to Japan. There will be no problems."

"What—How?" I said.

Oricho raised an eyebrow. That expression was starting to grate on my nerves.

"A minute ago you were insisting I hang around," I added.

"You said it was necessary to go to Japan and I cannot watch you in Japan, so I called in a favor. Do not worry, they will not interfere with your investigation," he added, as if reading my thoughts.

Without another word Oricho and the rest of Mr. Kurosawa's

men headed back inside the casino. One of the Aussie boys, the blond wearing a cowboy hat who'd helped dispose of the body, smiled and waved before making a beeline for me.

Smile fixed, he stopped less than a foot away and handed me a worn black leather wallet. I took it—I mean, what was I supposed to do?—and checked the ID. It was Vampire Boy's: Sebastian Collard's, to be exact. Collard . . . the face wasn't ringing any bells, but the name . . . I flipped through and wrote down the Social Security and credit card numbers before handing the wallet back to the Aussie—or whatever he was.

"I'd give that to Oricho, but thanks for letting me look at it," I said.

He tipped his hat and headed back towards the pool bar without ever saying a single word to me. *Creepy.*

I grabbed my laptop and headed back upstairs to order room service and pack. If I was really lucky, Lady Siyu might even have some info on Sabine. Lady Siyu—that gave me an idea. I opened the door to my room and endured Captain's inspection before he let me in. Like I said, he can smell vampire. I cracked open a Corona and punched Lady Siyu's number into the phone.

"Yes?" came the bored reply.

"Yeah, hi—" I had to balance the Corona as Captain lugged himself onto my lap and launched into a motor run of purrs. "Listen, there was an incident downstairs—"

"I am aware it was taken care of." Her voice turned up at the end, insinuating the unspoken question of why the hell I was bothering her.

"Yeah, that's not why I'm calling. I was hoping if I sent you some details on the assassin, you could find out some information I don't have readily accessible."

There was a pause on the other end. "Send the details and I will see what I can do."

"Thanks, I appreciate it—"

"And Owl?"

"Yeah?"

"Please get to the point in future correspondence." And the line went dead.

I fired off an email with the info I had copied from Sebastian's wallet, along with a list of what I was looking for. Financials, employers, home address, work history, had he checked into the hotel with anyone . . . stuff that would take me a week I didn't have and a lot of bribes. I figured Lady Siyu and Mr. Kurosawa had a lot more pull and resources.

I settled in and logged into World Quest an hour early, heading straight for a dungeon to start making up for lost time. Did you know you can sell World Quest treasure online? For real money?

An hour later Lady Siyu still hadn't returned my email, but the coordinates for my next quest rendezvous, courtesy of Carpe, blinked across my chat window.

"Time to be social, Captain," I said, and ported the Byzantine Thief into Dead Orc Soup, a World Quest pub with a sense of humor and a reputation for buying as many orcs and goblins as we could kill.

I'd worry about Sabine when she popped up again. With my luck she'd rear her head sooner rather than later.

3

TOKYO ROSE

6:00 p.m., Tokyo time, and 10,000 feet over the Pacific Ocean

Tokyo is possibly my favorite city in the world. It never shuts down, and Captain and I can sleep in a locked cubbyhole with only one entrance if need be. More importantly, the vampires in Tokyo have nothing to do with vampires in the rest of the world.

"Miss Owl?"

I looked up from my file as the flight attendant offered me a tray with a mixed array of orange and bubbling flutes.

"Would you like a champagne or orange juice for takeoff?" she said.

And this is why I fly first class. Well, that and the legroom . . . and I can actually get out of my seat to go to the washroom. The waiting lounges are nicer too.

"Thanks," I said with what I hoped passed for a charming smile as I took one of each.

She didn't seem to mind, but she did politely glance down at Captain's carrier. The other reason I fly first class: they let us bring our pets on the plane.

"Oh, he's fine in there. Won't make a noise. Promise," I said, and offered her my best charming smile. Personally I think it sucks—and Nadya seems to agree—but the designer clothes and the fact that I still look like I'm in my early twenties buy me a lot of leeway.

The flight attendant moved on to the next passenger, and I downed my orange juice and opened up the file on Sebastian Collard that Lady Siyu had delivered before I'd caught my cab. The cab ride from anywhere on the Vegas strip to the airport is short, so I'd only had a chance to flip through the first few pages. What I'd seen had worried me enough that I'd been flipping through it ever since.

I can't sleep on planes. Never could. So I usually block time for naps before and after and use the flight itself for research and planning.

On the first page alone there was enough to make me very happy I was taking Captain to Japan with me.

Up until six months ago, Sebastian Collard had been a run-of-the-mill antiques dealer in Florida, specializing in colonial and pre-colonial pieces from the Caribbean. Once that registered, I knew where I'd seen the name. Someone from his shop had contacted me about a year ago and offered me money to fetch a piece from Cuba. It had been right around my run-in with the Paris boys, and I'd needed cash, badly. ATMs and banks in general had stopped being my friend by that point.

Anyway, I'd backed out of the job last minute and had stopped returning emails when local authorities had started investigating Sebastian's company on forgeries. Talk about small world.

However, the man in the mug shot was a far cry from the vampire junkie mess who'd pointed a gun at me. He'd been a respectable . . . well, looking at least . . . businessman. No family, no real friends. After the forgery charges, the shop had closed and he'd vanished from the real world.

Yeah, hanging out with vampires will do that to you.

The more I looked through his earlier business records, a sinking suspicion started to needle me.

People who collect antiques love second-opinion appraisals. Unless Sebastian had been some kind of superpowered master forger, there's no way he could have stayed in business for almost ten years with the steady volume of high-end pieces he'd been moving. It just doesn't happen. Someone would have stumbled onto the forgeries years ago and he'd have been demoted to selling 1960s kitsch. It was starting to look more like an expensive frame job than a forgery bust.

What did I say about vampires hitting you where it hurts?

Whereas Lady Siyu had been able to find all sorts of information on Sebastian, Sabine remained an enigma. Sebastian had checked into the Paradise hotel—a lower-end resort for gambling habits and families on tight budgets—with a young woman, but the trail ended there. I hadn't managed to find anything online either in reference to a vampire named Sabine. I'd have to wait for Lady Siyu to call with more information once she contacted the Paris boys to find out if this Sabine was one of theirs. I wasn't holding my breath. I locked the folder back up in my satchel. No sense obsessing over it until I had something better to go on, and there'd be plenty of time for that once I landed in Tokyo.

Captain gave a *mrowl*. The blond businesswoman sitting across the aisle shot me a dirty look, then flicked her magazine open.

I have this theory that there's a black so deep and bottomless only lawyers dare wear it. I call it lawyer black. They must ask for it by name when ordering suits. The blonde was dressed head to toe in it. I stuck my tongue out and mentally patted myself on the back for the look of pure shock on the woman's face. The things I get away with wearing Chanel.

"Come on," I said to Captain, and held out his harness. He crawled in with minor complaints, and I walked him up the aisle to the bathroom. Those videos that claim they can toilet train your cat? Totally true.

The two Japanese Harajuku teens sitting near the front ooohed and ahhed over Captain and his red harness. Captain rolled over for them, sopping up the attention. It made up for the cat-hating lawyer.

Once I had Captain back to our seat, I checked the time. Two hours left until landing. I rested my head against the back of the seat. What I really needed now was to plan my steps for when I got off the plane, which meant going over my dig notes and the few lines I'd gleaned from the Japanese thesis on the Bali site. I pulled my laptop out and waved the flight attendant over.

"Do you by any chance have a couple of Coronas back there?" I said.

—⁂—

Captain and I breezed through customs. Best ten grand I ever spent was bribing a doctor to prescribe me an "assistant pet" to deal with my "debilitating anxiety and panic disorder." I think they have padded rooms and an assortment of colorful pills set aside for people who tell their therapists they need an assistant cat to help them evade vampires. Ten grand it is, thank you very much.

I breezed past the baggage carousel and through the exit, and hightailed it to the nearest washroom. I had everything I needed in my oversized Chanel purse. As a general rule I try to never check luggage. Lucky for me the washroom was empty. I picked the farthest stall from the entrance. No sooner had I closed the stall door than Captain started to complain he had to go, so I let him out of the carrier while I changed.

I pulled my Chanel jacket off, reluctantly I might add, and replaced it with a hooded Ralph Lauren canvas jacket I'd picked up along with a few other things on my shopping spree. Next were the high-heeled boots, which I replaced with a pair of flat leather riding boots. I zipped the boots up over the Chanel jeans and checked that the bottom of the jacket hung long enough to hide the label. I packed the clothes and purse into a canvas Ralph Lauren backpack I'd rolled up and hidden in the bottom of the oversized purse. Last but not least, I wiped off my eyeliner and red lipstick, replaced them with sporty bronzer, undid the wraparound French braids, and beachified my hair.

Once I was satisfied I looked like your run-of-the-mill, respectably fashionable university student, I pulled up the canvas hood, popped Captain back in his carrier, and headed for the exit. Why all the trouble? People can ask drivers where the girl in the expensive Chanel jacket and designer purse was dropped off, and the driver'll probably remember and be more than happy to tell said person for very little cash. The boho student with the canvas backpack hopping on the train? Who cares.

I navigated the crowded platform until I located the train that would take me to the Shiyuba district, where Nadya lived. Not until I was sitting on the train and relatively sure no one had followed me did I turn my cell phone back on.

Two messages blinked into existence on my screen; one from Oricho and one from Nadya. I checked my email—yeah, international data plans—and still nothing from Lady Siyu yet (or Dragon Lady, as I referred to her in my phone address book, where she'd never see it). I checked Oricho's message first. All he said was that it was important, and to call him. Shit. Why bother leaving a message if you don't leave any details? Why not just text? Nadya's message was a more efficient use of long distance; she was going to be at the club late, so I was to just meet her there.

I put my Bluetooth earbud in and called Oricho. He answered on the first ring.

"Oricho? It's Owl—please don't tell me a pack of vampires are hot on my tail. If they are, so help me—"

"Lady Siyu has successfully contacted the Paris Vampire Contingency on Mr. Kurosawa's behalf and requested that I contact you with the information," he said.

Well, it wasn't completely bad news. "Why the hell didn't she just call me herself?"

Oricho paused for a moment. "Lady Siyu does not deal well with inefficient phone conversations," he said carefully.

"Oh, you got to be kidding me," I said, just as the train pulled up to the next station. I checked the name printed in big black letters on the tile wall through the window; still six more to go. "Fine, well, what information did she get on Sabine?"

Another pause. Not good.

"She said they were less than forthcoming with any relevant information."

"That's it? I thought you guys could make them talk?"

"Though they were evasive throughout the entire conversation—eventually falling on the fail-safe that they couldn't possibly keep track of every vampire in Paris—Lady Siyu is convinced they were attempting to obtain as much information from her as she was from them."

A chill went down my spine. Sabine was independent. "Fuck," I said, drawing a few sideways glances. I could picture Oricho arching an eyebrow. For someone with so many visible tattoos, he sure as hell was prim and proper. "I don't think I can stress how really not good this is."

"I've already arranged—"

"No, you don't understand. If she's not with the Paris vampire pack—" I cupped my hand around my cell as a couple of other passengers glanced over at me. I lowered my voice. "If she's not with them, then that means she's independent."

"We did not agree to negotiate any other truces with other parties you've entered into disagreement with. That would be a separate agreement."

That kind of tunnel thinking pissed me off, and right when I'd started not hating Oricho. "You soooo aren't getting it. I have no outstanding disagreements with any other parties. The Paris boys were it." Well, and Egypt . . . and an assortment of antiquities departments spread over the world, but they've got no idea who I am. I took a deep breath. Where to start explaining? Damn, this is why I work alone and under the radar.

"OK, Sabine is a vampire who a *major* vampire organization wants info about. I'd never even heard of her until her vampire flunkie antiquities specialist showed up in your casino and accosted me. *Right* after I agreed to retrieve the egg scroll—to *try* to retrieve the scroll contents," I corrected myself before continuing. "I don't think this Sabine cares two tail feathers about me. I think you've got another tomb raider after the scroll that was supposed to be in that egg, who happens to be a vampire."

The more I thought about it, the more it made sense. I'll bet Sebastian hadn't had any plans to shoot me. He'd probably been there to grab my notes and deliver me to Sabine. The fact that the Paris boys have been looking for me was just a convenient cover and the obvious conclusion we would jump to.

I was still pissed off, so I took the time to slide another jab in . . . while I was far away from Vegas. "*And* since we're talking about what we agreed to, *I* agreed to try and retrieve the scroll for Mr. Kurosawa in exchange for getting rid of my vampire problem. Nowhere in that agreement does it say I need to deal with *your* vampire problems." Geez, when I say it like that, it sounds like vampires are some kind of infestation. I wonder if there's some kind of high-tech vampire exterminator? I've never found one, but I've seen stranger. I was about to suggest it to Oricho, when he jumped back into the conversation.

"How certain are you of this assessment?"

I thought about it for a second. My reputation rests on transparency, after all. "Let's just say if I had to bet my life on motivation, that would be it."

There was another measured pause on Oricho's end. I didn't blame him. If I found out a vampire was messing around with a business transaction . . . I imagine it's a bit like finding out from a maid that the hotel is infested with bedbugs.

"I will appraise my contact in Japan of our new situation and brief Mr. Kurosawa and Lady Siyu of your assessment."

A lot of good that was going to do me. She probably just thought I'd pissed off another vampire. "Fine, do that. Just don't deal with it too late. Otherwise you're going to need another antiquities specialist—"

"In the future I will refrain from assumptions concerning the transparency of your business dealings. I recommend you do the same, and do try to be careful." And with that Oricho hung up.

I held the phone out for a moment. Damn, that had almost been an apology. I checked the name of the upcoming stop: Harajuku Station. My stop. I tossed my phone back in my pocket and grabbed Captain's carrier, ready to push through the crowds waiting to get in. The door to the train slid open and Captain growled and crammed himself up against the carrier's mesh. I froze. The faint rotting lily of the valley hit me. I held my breath.

A Japanese woman in a pink Chanel suit stood in front of me. She glanced down at Captain, who was putting new meaning into the expression hissy fit, and then back at me. She smiled, revealing the slight points of her canines; nothing a normal person would notice, but I'm not normal. I swallowed, and it took every ounce of self-control not to bolt for the exit.

People were getting restless on either side. Ignoring Captain, the vampire slipped around me into the train as I stood frozen. I forced myself to step onto the platform. I knew I should keep going and not look back, but I'm not known for making wise choices under pressure. I glanced over my shoulder. The vampire in the pink suit was standing by the open train door.

She smirked at me. "Nice cat," she said in perfect English right before the door closed.

I shook my head and headed upstairs. "Just a local vampire," I whispered through Captain's carrier screen. "Nothing to worry about, but nice catch," I said, and tossed him a cat treat from the stash in my pocket.

Still, the incident forced me to take stock of the station. In the young crowd, a mix of club kids and exhausted university students, nothing seemed out of the ordinary. Taking advantage of my adrenaline shot, I darted up the steps through the crowd of Harujuku girls showing off their outfits, then took a left. I kept track of everyone I passed; Ochiro had warned me to be careful, and coming from someone who worked for a dragon, that scared me. Three blocks down, past the noodle and clothing shops, I reached the blue neon signs above the flight of stairs for Nadya's club, Space Station Deluxe. I took in the neon lights that decorated the building like psychedelic sci-fi Christmas decorations. In spite of everything, I was looking forward to catching up with Nadya, something I hadn't had a chance to do in months.

I climbed a flight of steps to where two large Japanese doormen stood manning a black door. I didn't recognize either of them, and from the glares they shot me, there wasn't much hope they were going to let me in. I wasn't in the mood to argue, so I pulled out my cell phone. Nadya could deal with it; she practically ran the place anyways.

Come get me outside. I need to change.

Nadya knew me well enough to get the picture. In fact, I could imagine her cursing in Russian as she read the text.

The two doormen crossed their arms, continuing to glare at me. I waved and smiled. "Hi," I said as cheerfully as I could muster.

The doormen exchanged a glance. The larger one took a step towards me and nodded down the steps—told you I can't pull off charming. I shoved my hands in my pocket, retreated three steps down, and watched the passersby. There was nothing out of the ordinary; still, I couldn't shake that raised-hair feeling on the back of my neck that says someone—or something—is watching you. With vampires, dragons, and who knows what the hell Oricho and Lady Siyu were, who could blame me?

Nadya's head poked around the door. She was sporting a neon red bob, which looked fantastic on her. Nadya had always been a head turner; she was from Moscow and had the height and looks of a brunette Russian bombshell, though she rarely wore her natural hair color and was a fan of colored contacts. Her eyes narrowed as she caught sight of me and took in my appearance.

"Hi!" I said, adding a cheerful wave.

Nadya frowned even more and pursed her lacquered lips. "Would it kill you to dress appropriately? Once?" she said, her Russian accent light.

I gave her a big smile and held up my backpack. "Halfway there. Give me five minutes and I'll fit right in."

Nadya tsked. "Get in and get changed fast. I'm trying to run a business. Broke university students are bad for business." She waved me past the two doormen and into Space Station Deluxe.

I gave a low whistle. "I knew you were redecorating, but damn," I said, taking in the new blue track lights. They were set into the ceiling, walls, and floors, creating swirled patterns. It reminded me of being underwater, like walking through a glass tunnel at an aquarium. The blue tinge gave the place an almost daylight feel.

The dance floor was hidden between the far wall and a sheet of blurred glass that hid the band as well, out of view of the door. It was set up that way because the local laws prohibited dancing past eleven. Though the law is rarely enacted, you can never be too careful. Space Station Deluxe wasn't packed yet, but give it a few hours and it would be. Out of all the renovations, the new bar was what really got me. Before, it had had a 1990s *Star Trek* vibe, with embedded lights and that halogen feel. In fact, the whole place had reminded me of a cross between the bar on the *Enterprise* and the bar in *Star Wars*, minus all the monsters.

The new bar was the centerpiece of the club, its oval shape complementing the swirls of track lights. It was a single, thick piece of glass with a blue ombré tint, darkest blue on the bar side, fading to a light blue on the outside. The whole slab was a lamp and added to the underwater feel.

I followed Nadya past a table of young Japanese businessmen, who all followed her with their eyes as she passed by and greeted them in Japanese. They politely ignored me.

Nadya pushed open the door to her office and gently shoved me inside. The rest of the bar might have changed, but the office hadn't. A neat, minimal desk was still wedged into the corner, an open laptop computer on top and, I assumed, a couple of safes still tucked underneath. The only decoration in the room was a lava lamp on the corner of the desk—a birthday present I'd given Nadya back when we'd still been sharing a dorm room.

Nadya leaned against the open doorframe as I dropped my bag on the chair. "How's business?" she asked.

"Gimme twenty minutes and a beer and I'll tell you all about it."

She raised a bright red eyebrow, dyed to match her neon hair. Damn, I wish I could pull that kind of stuff off. "That bad?" she said. She tried but couldn't hide her concern. Usually my answer was much more predictable and monosyllabic. *Crap, better*, or *dig my grave now*.

"Depends on how you look at it," I said. I started to close the office door, but Nadya wedged her spiked Louis Vuitton pump in between.

"Oh come on, really?"

"Not a chance in hell," she said, and snapped her fingers, the red nail lacquer reflecting the halogen lights. She held out her hand for my outfit. "Friendship only gets you so far with me."

"Barely in the front door, apparently," I mumbled. I pulled out my Chanel jacket and matching boots for her inspection. Nadya was a perfectionist; she'd want to make sure my outfit passed muster for the club's dress code, even if I was only there for a few minutes. She gave her approval by silently handing them back.

"You suck at dressing yourself. I'm just glad you finally took my advice." She opened Captain's carrier and led him out. We'd left the red harness on. Captain knew Nadya, but more importantly he knew she babied him. Nadya didn't bother with the leash; she scooped him up and carried him towards the bar.

The baby talk drifted back. "Did she feed you? Come on, sweetie, Nadya has something for you."

"Hey! My cat gets a free pass but I get the third degree?"

"Captain always looks nice and clean, don't you, Captain?" Nadya said, then turned her attention back on me. "*You* can't be trusted to put the same-colored socks on."

"Great to see you again too, Nadya," I shouted as I closed the door. In my defense I'd never seen the point in matching socks—I mean, who sees them?

I exchanged my student disguise for my black boots and leather jacket and checked my handiwork in the office mirror. Well, no one was going to mistake me for one of Nadya's girls, but I was as presentable as I was ever going to get in a five-minute window or less. At least the bouncers wouldn't throw me out . . . I hoped.

I opened the door and headed back out. The things I do for a job . . .

4

RYNN AND THE GAIJIN CLOUD

11:00 p.m., Space Station Deluxe

I swirled the beer in my glass. It looked really cool over the lit bar. If—when—I got back into my place in Seattle, I'd have to put one of these in. It'd double as a super night-light.

"So?" Nadya said, waiting for me to finish my explanation of the last few days.

"So basically I'm on edge till I find out who this Sabine is," I said, and downed the last bit of my beer.

Nadya shook her neon red bob and passed me a second Corona, along with a shot of Grey Goose. "I think you're crazy," she said.

I took the beer but pushed the vodka back. "No hard liquor." The seven shots of Grey Goose from my last trip to Tokyo, and the catalogue of hazy memories, were still fresh in my mind.

Nadya tsked and pushed it right back. "No, you need a good few shots of vodka in you. Maybe it will kick-start your common sense."

I grumbled but downed the shot. With Nadya you have to pick your battles. This wasn't one of them.

"I'm not crazy. What I am is a hell of a lot better off than I was three days ago," I said.

Nadya sniffed. "Three days ago you weren't working for a dragon and who knows what else. What did you say this Lady Siyu looked like again?"

"No, three days ago *vampires* were trying to eat me."

Nadya leaned over the bar, the blue light giving her face a ghostly cast. "Have you ever heard the phrase 'out of the frying pan into the fire'? Besides, didn't you say this Sabine was a vampire?"

"Yeah, but as far as I can tell she isn't trying to eat me. I think she's just trying to get to the scroll and steal it before I do. Still an improvement." I needed to change the subject, so I pulled out my sparse file on the Bali dig and passed it over to her. For all my bravado, Nadya was the voice of reason.

"How's business?" I said, yelling over the karaoke that a group of hostesses had started up. The businessmen were pouring in for the evening now, and Nadya's servers had their hands full passing out drinks.

She shrugged. "Not so bad, could always be better?" She leaned across the table, adding, "And I'm not so easily distracted by idle conversation."

I sighed. "Look, you're right, I'm in way over my head, but besides 'roll over and die,' I don't have a lot of options here. Now," I said, tapping the file, "can you help me or not?"

She tried staring me down, and for a second I wondered if she was going to say no. Nadya knows when to bail. She can smell trouble—some kind of sixth sense. I, on the other hand, am a trouble magnet. It's one of the reasons I got so screwed by the university and ended up a thief.

Nadya and I met in the same archaeology program, the one that stole two years of my research, handed it over to the up-and-coming postdoc, and hung me out to dry. Nadya had seen the ship sinking six months before me and had taken off while she'd still been able to afford the plane ticket. It's occurred to me on a number of occasions that I'd be a hell of a lot happier if I followed Nadya's advice more often.

If she said no though, I wasn't only screwed; I'd probably be dead. Not that I'd blame her one bit . . .

I nursed my beer as I held the stare. Finally, Nadya swore in Russian, broke off, and snatched the file from the bar. She took her time flipping through each page, until a table behind started to call her by name for drinks. She fixed them with a smile, yelled she was coming in Japanese, and slid me back the closed folder. "I can do it, but it's tricky this time. And more expensive."

I coughed and had to cover my mouth to stop from spewing Corona all over the bar. "What do you mean, more expensive? It couldn't be easier. Call the dirty old man and tell him I have cash." I pulled a clip of cash out and slid it across the table so she could count it—and so she could see I was serious. Nadya was a good friend, but business was business.

Nadya shook her head as she popped the cork on a bottle of champagne and poured four flutes. She handed one to me, downed the second, and sent the third and fourth with a waitress to the table. She wiped a drop of champagne from the corner of her mouth and shook her head. "Nuroshi heard about the Paris boys. He raised his price for working with you."

"So? Tell him me and the vampires settled our differences."

She snorted. "And omit the dragon, I suppose? Not likely." She stepped around the bar to deal with her "privileged table"—basically the drinks cost the men extra in exchange for even more of Nadya's particular brand of standoffish aloofness and verbal abuse. I began to pour my champagne on a plant.

"Drink!" I heard Nadya yell over her shoulder. "You need better alcohol tolerance."

"That's the last thing I need."

Nadya whirled on the heels of her spiked stilettos as if they'd been ballet slippers, just so I'd have the benefit of seeing her glare.

"Drink it! We're going out after this."

I shot her a dirty look before she turned her back on me. Well, I'd worry how to get out of that later.

I pulled the folder back and opened it to the pages that referenced the Bali tablet chamber. I still hadn't worked out exactly why the file was so sparse—I mean, obviously to hide something supernatural, but there were none of the usual hints dropped for archaeologists as to what.

It was a dual thesis project, meaning it had been written by two individual students from different faculties; in this case, physics and archaeology had teamed up. I'd bet the physics PhD had been brought on to do some fancy carbon dating, maybe even some fancy laser imaging of the rooms. Nothing more fun than pissing off old archaeology professors with hard, scientific facts. Used to be one of my favorite stunts. But if that was the case, where the hell was the carbon dating? And pictures of the dig site?

I closed the file. If anyone could tell me, it was Nuroshi. The old man reminded me of a turnip; sickly white, rotund, with puffy eyes that constantly watered. Whereas most men go bald from the center out, Nuroshi was balding from the outside in. All that was left now was a tuft of black hair. Like I said, turnip. He was also a low-level curator for the Japanese Museum of Antiquities, attached to the University of Tokyo. High enough up the ladder to have privileged information and access to the storage rooms, old enough and close enough to retirement not to garner any attention. He also knew his stuff, even though I had a hard time stomaching his particular brand of dirty old man antics. Nadya had dug him up when a few of her high-end clientele had found out she'd been an archaeologist and subtly hinted they were interested in "acquiring" pieces.

The Space Station Deluxe kept filling up as people got off work for the day. A handsome businessman in a really nice suit took the barstool beside me, smiled, and said something in Japanese. It took me a moment to realize he'd mistaken me for one of Nadya's hostesses. I felt my face flush red. The last thing I needed was someone asking me to make them drinks in Japanese. I try not to speak foreign languages—ever. I have a knack for saying the wrong thing. It's somewhat embarrassing. I can read and write ten languages, including Japanese, fluently. Two of them are even dead. I just can't speak or understand a word of any of them—except English, in which my spoken fluency is debatable.

I shrugged and smiled at the businessman, attempting to convey my obliviousness. I then tried to catch the attention of one of Nadya's girls as she dipped behind the bar to grab drinks. The desperation on my face must have been bad, because she dropped what she was doing and seamlessly took over. I let out a breath and kept my eyes down and on my champagne, hoping the customer caught on I wasn't an employee. My presence sucks and I know it. Plus Nadya would kill me if I messed up business.

As far as hostess bars go, the Space Station Deluxe is on the lighter, younger, more fashionable end of the spectrum. For instance, the staff, from the girls Nadya hires all the way up to the house band, knows how to throw one hell of a party. But the seedier, sex work stuff, like creepy old men chasing girls young enough to be their granddaughters? Let's just say Nadya discourages that. The men coming here are paying to be in Nadya and her girls' presence. You want something more? Go find the nearest soap club.

"You haven't been in Tokyo for a while," Nadya said, coming up beside me.

I sipped the champagne; I could feel the alcohol dulling my brain, and it was an effort to keep my face blank. "Only three months."

"That's a long time for you. Someone was asking about you."

I kept on staring at my champagne. "I'm sure someone was, and I'll deal with that. Tomorrow night." I downed the rest of my drink and pointed to her cell. "Call Nuroshi?"

Nadya tsked but dialed the number and stepped into her office.

Hostesses kept moving bottles of champagne across the floor, and the music picked up. Captain yawned and stretched out on the bar.

"Good thing Nadya keeps cat food," I told him.

Nadya returned a moment later with her coat thrown over her shoulder and Captain's carrier in the other hand.

"Nuroshi's going to meet us here tomorrow at noon," she said.

"See, I told you—"

"And it will cost you double."

"Shit." Don't get me wrong, it could have been much worse. He could have said no. Still . . . "If he was worried about vampires, he should have mentioned something before the last three jobs I gave him."

Nadya blew kisses at her "special table." "Come on, I'm off. I feel like partying." Somehow Nadya drew distinctions between the partying she did at work and off work.

I coaxed Captain back in his case with minimal mewing, grabbed my Chanel bag, and scrambled out the door and down the flight of stairs after her. It had started to drizzle, and I wished I'd have thrown my RL hooded jacket overtop. "Umm, about that, can we leave the partying until tomorrow night? I figured I'd settle in and—"

"No."

"But Nadya—"

Nadya spun on me and stamped her foot on the damp pavement. "You can't wait until tomorrow night to visit him. It's rude, not to mention cruel."

I took a deep breath. I knew the tone; it was the same one she'd used on me when I'd tried to turn down her help after my program funding had been pulled out from under me. There was no arguing with her. "All right. We'll go."

We dropped Captain and my stuff off at Nadya's apartment, and I let Nadya fix my hair and makeup. In the mirror, I examined the braids and the light, almost orange-red lipstick Nadya had paired with otherwise minimal makeup. Credit where credit is due, Nadya could do wonders with a hairbrush and ten minutes.

We headed back out to club Gaijin Cloud.

Damn it. I was going to have to talk to Rynn tonight.

I followed Nadya into Gaijin Cloud, a bar that took up half the tenth floor of a Shiyuba district business building. It hadn't changed much since I'd last been in, except they'd also installed a night-light bar, a red one.

"Talk about keeping up with the Joneses," I said to Nadya.

Nadya frowned and shot me a quizzical look.

"The same night-light bar you have," I said, and pointed. "Theirs is red."

She rolled her eyes and headed for the bar.

I hung back while I scanned the floor. The usual mixed international crowd was in attendance, both foreigners and young Japanese, the kind who spend most of their time overseas. It was packed, and the lights were dim enough that I couldn't make out faces very well. When I realized Rynn wasn't manning the front bar, I let out the breath I was holding and joined Nadya.

She tsked as I ordered my Corona.

"Hey, let me suspend belief a little longer. Isn't that the business model these guys work on? Waking up from your dreams is bad? Let me dream Rynn isn't here a little longer."

"You're impossible," Nadya whispered.

The Gaijin Cloud wasn't a host or hostess bar, or even a Western bar. It occupied some strange, nebulous place in between the three. The men and the women working there were gorgeous and there to entertain everyone—for a price. And that's where the nebulousness starts and ends.

The host and hostess bars in Japan get a bad rap, but there's a practicality and efficiency to them . . . and, when it comes down to it, honesty . . . that Westerners always ignore.

Just think, anytime you head out to a bar in the Western Hemisphere, you expect that maybe you'll talk to someone, maybe you'll have a good time, or maybe everyone will just ignore you and you'll head home feeling worse than if you'd just sat on your couch playing World Quest. A hundred bucks later.

Well, what if you could take that hundred bucks, double it, and guarantee you'd have a great time talking to someone who was interested in what you had to say for a few hours? It's an interesting question.

Anyway, Nadya loves Gaijin Cloud and tries to go at least once a week, more often twice. It's not the most popular, since it caters to a mixed crowd, so it's not obvious it's a host bar at first. When I was kicked out of grad school and effectively homeless, Nadya let me crash with her in Japan for a few months. She insisted on it, even sent me the plane ticket. While I was trying to figure out what the hell to do with the rest of my life, Nadya dragged me out almost every night to Gaijin Cloud. That's how I met Rynn.

I'd just been fired. Well, no, that's not entirely accurate. In exchange for saying, "No, I was wrong, none of the data in that report was falsified, the postdoc and supervisor still remain god apparent, I'm a bad grad student," I had been verbally promised funding for the next four years and a coveted transfer to the lost city dig site in Ephesus, Turkey. Right after I'd signed the paperwork that had legally absolved the university and my supervisor of any wrongdoing, all my funding had been terminated and my transfer had disappeared.

University departments have no soul.

Anyway, out of misguided passion for archaeology and love of academia, I'd decided to stick it out, even when I'd known the postdoc had been falsifying data to hide a supernatural mummy from our supervisor. Lesson learned; don't ever be a whistle-blower. . . . I really need to follow Nadya's advice more often.

I'd met Rynn right after I'd screwed myself over in Paris with the vampires and had been doing my best to drink away the memories of screaming Frenchmen with fangs and a vampire vaporizing into dust. I'd not been in the mood to party. Rynn had been the new bartender. You see a lot of blonds in Japan, Japanese and Caucasian, but you

OWL and the **Japanese Circus** 57

don't often see good-looking blond Caucasian men working behind the bar. It was an anomaly, and I'd been halfway to drunk.

"Wow, you've got to have an edge on the competition in here," I'd finally said as he'd stopped by to refill my glass. I'd lost count by that point.

He'd shrugged. "Some. Though you'd be surprised how fast the novelty wears off. Not a lot of regulars." He'd nodded towards Nadya, who'd been flirting with a cute Japanese boy who'd managed to get his hair dyed fire-engine red. "Friend of yours?"

I'd nodded.

"Is she one of the regulars?" he'd asked.

"Wow, you really haven't been working here long," I'd said, and drained half my glass.

Rynn had given me a once-over. "You've gone through half a five-hundred-dollar bottle in less than twenty minutes."

"Damn, I'll have to catch up."

One of his blond eyebrows had shot up. "You've either had a bad night or you're planning on running out on a tab." He'd leaned over the bar and given me one hell of an evil eye. "Bad things happen to people who run out on my tabs."

There was a faint accent, noticeable when he spoke full sentences. My money was on Russian. I'd raised the glass, pulled out five hundred dollars plus tip, and counted it out in front of him. "Now please be a dear and bring me my bottle so I can finish getting drunk."

He'd disappeared and brought back my champagne. I'd been ready for a refill, so he'd obliged.

"I'm Rynn," he'd said, and offered me his hand.

"Owl."

Instead of saying something about my unusual name, he'd said, "You know, I'm a good listener."

I'd laughed and shaken my head. "Look, Rynn, no offense, but no one is that good a listener, and the last thing you want to hear are my problems."

"Try me."

I'd looked at him from under my eyebrows and noticed how blue his eyes were, dark blue, almost navy.

He'd shrugged. "It was a good tip, and I'm cheaper than a therapist."

I'd been drunk enough to consider it. "What the hell, all you can do is tell everyone, and they already think I'm crazy."

"Won't happen," he'd said.

Something about the way he said it, or the look on his face, more likely the booze in my head, I believed him.

"You believe in vampires?" I'd asked.

To his credit, Rynn had just shrugged. "Don't know. There's a hell of a lot I can't explain. I suppose anything is possible."

"Well, that's a better start to this conversation than I could have hoped for, because a whack of them over in Paris just took a hit out on me." I'd held my champagne glass up by the stem. "Hence, I'm getting drunk tonight because chances are good I'll be dead by the end of the month."

Rynn had glanced down at the bar, a concentrated look on his face.

Figured. Another drunken lesson: don't put much faith in an earnest face and a pair of pretty blue eyes. "I think this is where you're supposed to tell me I need real help—the kind that involves pills and padded rooms, or just think of it as a great story to tell your friends when the bar closes. The crazy chick who believes vampires are out to get her." I'd started to get up and move over to where Nadya was doing her best to pick up the redhead, when Rynn had stopped me.

"Just hold on," he'd said, the pensive look still on his face. "How the hell did you manage to piss off a pack of vampires?"

I'd reeled and had to steady myself on the barstool. Drunk, remember? "Whoa, wait a minute . . . you believe in vampires? Seriously?"

Rynn had shrugged. "I work as a bartender in places that are open all night."

And that was the start of our friendship.

Besides Nadya, Rynn is about the only other person I consider a friend. He's also the best therapist anyone could ask for, and better looking. Fifty thousand yen, roughly five hundred bucks, gets you a few hours of chitchat and, better yet, comes with a bottle of champagne. I'm not great with people, and I don't make friends easily. Nadya and Rynn had been my sanity anchors.

Up until three months ago, when Rynn had kissed me . . . and I'd decided the best course of action was to avoid Japan and thereby him for three months. Have I mentioned I suck with people? If I was honest with myself though, I missed talking to him. He's the one person who doesn't give me a lecture every time I bring up vampires.

I downed my Corona and glanced again at the crowd. I liked Rynn a lot; it was hard not to. But therein lay the problem.

Rynn's job was to make people like him.

It goes with working at the Gaijin Cloud. I had no idea if he'd kissed me because he liked me or because I'm a client that drops five hundred bucks a night. I had no idea where the gray line blurred for the staff, and I didn't want to ask. I *really* didn't want to talk about it. But Nadya had a point. If I wanted to keep being friends with Rynn, I might have to.

Buzzed, I had enough liquid courage coursing through my brain that I could have a conversation with Rynn without turning into an awkward mess. I put the empty bottle down and waved for another. "Back in a minute."

"Good luck," Nadya said.

"Screw you." I grabbed Corona #2 and left her flirting with a blond who bore a striking resemblance to a character out of Final Fantasy.

I headed through the crowd towards the back. Gaijin Cloud had a number of theme rooms, nothing kinky . . . except one, but the leather and chains were more of a fashion statement than anything else. I started with those. I stuck my head in each one; Rynn's blond hair and assortment of leather jackets was pretty distinct. I couldn't find him. In the last room before the stairs that led to the rooftop bar and patio, I found a bartender I did recognize—Kitu, a redheaded woman who was constantly perky, like a Japanese version of a cheerleader.

"Hey, Kitu," I said, wedging myself up to the bar. "You see Rynn anywhere?"

She leaned over and flashed me a smile worthy of any Japanese RPG heroine. "Hi, Owl. Long time no see." She scanned thoughtfully around the room before shaking her head. "Hmmm, I thought I saw him in here earlier . . . does he know you're stopping in?"

I shook my head. It occurred to me he might be with someone. If I couldn't actually find Rynn, I might get off easy tonight, though now that I'd worked up the courage, it didn't feel like quite the coup it should have been.

I took one more look around the main room and decided I needed some fresh air. This time of year I doubted many people would be out on the patio. I could check my phone for any emails or messages and breathe for a minute. Living in a Winnebago had lowered my tolerance for crowds.

The night was cold and the drizzle still fell, dampening the air and ground. No one else was outside, so I staked out a seat by the summer bar, where there was some cover, and pulled out my phone.

"Leave it to you to find the most exclusive seat in the house," Rynn said from the doorway.

You know that feeling when someone takes you by surprise and your insides try to tell you it's a good one, but your brain disagrees? Yeah.

"Hey, Rynn," I said, keeping my voice as even and neutral as possible. I swiveled my chair around. Damn, just when you think someone can't get any better looking . . . *Focus, Owl, Focus.* "I tried to find you inside."

He sidled up beside me at the bar, two beers in hand. He passed one to me. Good timing, since I'd finished Corona #2.

"Hmmmm, I can imagine that conversation now. What does someone say to a friend they've been ignoring for three months over club music in a crowd of people?"

OK, this was a lot more neutral than I'd imagined, though Rynn was a bitch to read on a good day. Even after a year, I still had no idea where the hell he was from. If I believed all his innuendos, he'd lived just about everywhere.

I let out a breath. "OK, I'm going to get the apology out of the way before this conversation goes any further, because I'm pretty sure I owe you one . . ."

"Oh? Really? Whatever for?" he said, the sarcasm now obvious.

So maybe not so neutral. Still fixable. I just had to figure out what to say . . . I opened my mouth, but Rynn stopped me.

"Just came outside to say hi and refill your beer," he said. He touched the top of his forehead in a mock salute and headed back for the door.

Shit.

I could feel my heart pounding. Nine times out of ten I say the wrong thing under stress, and the only person besides Nadya who's been able to look past that—and my complete reluctance to engage in personal conversations—is Rynn.

"Rynn, please come back so I can apologize." I crossed my fingers before saying something that was closer to the truth than even I liked to admit. "I'd really, really hate it if my delinquent people skills screwed up our friendship."

Hand on the door, Rynn spun around to face me. "And?"

I closed my eyes. I hate having these kinds of personal talks. They only ever set you up to get totally screwed over or hurt. How bad did I want my friendship with Rynn?

"You made me nervous the last time I was here. I didn't know what to make of it, and personal conversations make me uncomfortable, so I did something stupid and decided to avoid you." I ran my hand through my hair. "I'm a hell of a lot better with inconsequential conversations about vampires and RPGs," I added, hazarding a look at him.

He was still watching me and sizing me up from the doorway. Then he walked back to the outdoor bar and took the seat beside me. "All right," he said.

"We can go back to talking about RPGs and my vampire problems?" I said, maybe a little too hopefully.

"No. We can have the conversation you didn't want to have three months ago, and then I'll decide whether I still want to be friends with you."

Ouch. All right. I maybe deserved that. I took a deep breath. "Fair enough." There was no easy way to broach this; best to just blurt it out. "When you kissed me, was it a host/client thing?"

"Why?"

"Because as much as I'm totally OK paying you to talk about my problems—and trust me, it's worth every penny—I don't . . . want our client/host relationship to go that direction." I bit my lower lip. "I'm sorry, Rynn, but it's creepy. That's my line in the sand."

I'd kept my eyes on the bar, but I glanced over at him now.

He was watching me like a hawk. His face was unreadable. "If it wasn't?"

Another big breath. "That's an entirely different can of worms. It'd be next to impossible not to have some feelings for you, considering how much I talk to you."

Rynn took a sip of his beer, his forehead knit in thought. "So just so we're straight about everything, you disappearing for three months was because you liked me kissing you?"

"OK, well, that's paraphrasing, and cutting down an awful lot . . ."

He held up his beer to stop me from babbling. "Yes or no?"

He was going to make me say it. I swore under my breath. Rynn was really pushing me here. "Sort of—OK, more or less."

He sat back, staring at me as if I didn't quite make sense to him but he was trying to figure it out. I had no idea what was going through his head. Then he leaned in towards me. I almost leaned in, part of me wanted to, but the price of playing this game was going to be way too high. I sat back. "Rynn. I can't."

He sat back and crossed his arms. "Why not?" he said, not meeting my eyes.

I didn't answer. What was I going to say?

"Owl, I work at a bar that caters to people's dreams, and part of my job is to fulfill them—to a point." He looked up at me with those dark blue eyes. "It doesn't mean I don't have feelings."

"I know you do."

He frowned. "That's funny, because I'm getting the distinct impression you assume everything about me is a show."

I bit my lower lip. "Honest answer?"

He inclined his head, and I took a much-needed swig of my beer. "Just that kiss."

Rynn's frown deepened, and he let out a sharp breath through his nose. "So what? Someone like me can't possibly have genuine feelings for someone?"

I closed my eyes. This was exactly the part of this conversation I'd been dreading. "No. That's not it at all. I know you care about me, and even though I pay to come in here and talk to you, I consider you a good friend."

"But." It was a statement, not a question.

I locked eyes. "I'm not in a spot where I can risk getting hurt by you. I'd rather keep you as a friend. If you haven't noticed, I don't have many."

The only thing I heard for a few minutes was the cacophony of traffic and voices from the street below and the bass drifting up from the club.

"Rynn, can we please still be friends?"

He watched me, unreadable as ever. For a moment I thought he was going to say no. Then he looked away.

"We're OK, Owl." He slid off the chair and offered his hand. The relief on my face must have been obvious, because he put his arm around my shoulder and steered me back towards the door.

"You know, you could have just said you weren't interested. I think that might have been kinder."

"Yeah. I thought about it. But stacking little white lie upon little white lie is what usually gets me into trouble."

He inclined his head. "You do seem to have a habit for attracting trouble. What is this I hear about you evading your vampire problem?"

Shit. Rynn had a natural knack for getting people to talk when they shouldn't. "What did Nadya tell you?"

He shrugged. "Surprisingly little."

I took a deep breath. "What if I told you I found someone— something—that can take care of my vampire problem?" And with that I filled him in on my run-in with Mr. Kurosawa, including the part about him being a dragon.

He studied my face until I was done. "You're right," he said, shaking his head. "You should be locked up in a mental institution."

I smiled. Rynn's voice had an amused tone to it. "So I finally found where your belief suspends itself. Dragons."

He glanced over at me before opening the sliding door, a single eyebrow arched. "Let's just say regardless of what I think about the existence of dragons, it's the part about you not knowing when to quit I find disturbing."

We headed back into the warmth and crowd of the club. When we reached the second floor, Rynn pulled me into a corner and up against him. His arm wrapped around the small of my back before I got over my surprise.

"Rynn—" I said, warning in my voice.

He leaned in and kissed me. It was as good as I remembered, and I couldn't bring myself to push him away or otherwise stop him. This was not helping me get over my crush, but this close, his breath on my face and the smell of his cologne . . . I wrapped my fingers around his neck and kissed back.

Rynn took it as encouragement. I gave out a little gasp as he moved on to my neck. I knew I should break it off, but it felt too good.

After a few moments Rynn stopped kissing me, but he didn't let go.

"I figured I'd take one last chance to change your mind. I promise I won't do that again until you ask me."

I nodded. I wasn't in any condition to say anything. Damn, *that* was why I'd stayed away for three months. I remembered now.

Rynn walked me back to the main room. Nadya saw me immediately and waved from the bar.

"You coming back in before you leave Tokyo this time?" Rynn asked, almost as an afterthought.

I shook my head, still recovering. "Ahhh, I don't know—it depends on how things go tomorrow with a contact. Might have to hop on a plane fast."

He gave me a quick kiss on the cheek. "Just let me know you're alive this time."

"Yeah, I'll do that." Rynn headed back into the crowd, and I rejoined Nadya.

"How are you feeling?" Nadya asked as soon as I sat down.

I shook my head. "Don't want to talk about it."

Nadya patted me on the back. "My good deed is done then. You're welcome. Old Russian saying—"

"Let me guess. 'Sometimes what your friend really needs is a good shove under a moving bus'?"

She shrugged her coat on and shot me a smile. "More or less."

We headed outside in the drizzle. It was refreshing after the crowded Gaijin Cloud.

At a stoplight I pulled my phone out to run over the Bali files I'd accumulated and noticed a new text message along with a new contact entry. I did a double take as I saw the name. Rynn.

Remember. Call me.

"Son of a bitch."

Nadya frowned at me, and I held up my phone. "Rynn. I don't know how, but he got into my cell phone," I said.

Nadya's smile turned into a Cheshire grin. I glared back. "Goddamn it, he could have asked," I mumbled, and then it buzzed again.

BTW, who's Dragon Lady?

I shook my head. *Guess. New boss, sort of—I'll fill you in later.* In all honesty, I had no idea what I was going to do about Rynn. Things just seemed so much more confused and jumbled up than they had been a few hours ago. "Just when you think you know someone."

"Hmmm?" Nadya said.

The stoplight turned green. "Never mind." I looped my arm in hers. "Come on, I've got work to do." If I was lucky, I'd get through cross-referencing the other Bali temple digs tonight. Fat chance I'd find anything, but it was worth a shot in case the International Archaeology Association had missed cleaning something out.

Rynn had a point. If I didn't find the scroll for Mr. Kurosawa, or at the very least make a damn good show of finding it, I'd be playing hide-and-seek in a dragon's casino very soon.

5

BALI

12:00 p.m., Space Station Deluxe, Tokyo

I closed my eyes and leaned against the plush leather seat, my hangover threatening to push its way to the forefront again. After getting back from Gaijin Cloud last night, I'd fallen asleep on my computer and missed my alarm this morning. I'd woken up to Nadya swearing in Russian at ten to twelve before she pulled me out the door.

Without coffee.

Nadya and I sat in a booth tucked in the back of her bar, across from Nuroshi. Today his skin was particularly clammy, and he kept dabbing at his red, watering eyes. The only things off with my turnip analysis were his brown, stained teeth.

Nadya argued with Nuroshi in Japanese across the blue lacquer tabletop, hopefully bringing down the price. Whereas Nadya wore a black tank top and designer jeans, I'd shown up in my student getup. Nuroshi, lecher that he was, was so distracted by Nadya's cleavage that he kept giving things away. Little nuances, little twitches . . . he lied, that was a given, but today he was nervous, and that worried me.

I was starting to think the morning had been a bad omen, warning me about the day ahead. I tapped the table as the arguing raised a notch. "Hey you two, quit it for a second."

Nuroshi dragged his eyes off Nadya's chest and turned them on me. A strained smile crept onto his face, as if he'd just been made to swallow something unpleasant. I was not Nuroshi's favorite person to deal with; I don't play nice with lecherous cowards.

"Owl," he said, and glanced back at Nadya. "Ms. Aleyev and I were just discussing my . . . rate."

Nadya made a guttural noise in the back of her throat. "Go to hell," she told him, and added something unpleasant-sounding in Russian. Nuroshi just smiled, flashing his brown teeth. "What Ms. Aleyev so eloquently puts is that we have been unable to come to an agreement that financially takes into consideration the risks of . . ." His red, watery eyes regarded me. ". . . associating with you."

"I got rid of the vampires," I said.

He laughed and started to stand. "Somehow, coming from you, I do not find that at all settling. Ms. Aleyev, Owl, I wish I could say it's been a pleasure—"

I cringed; I hate being on the wrong end of negotiations, and that was happening a lot lately. "I'll double what I usually pay," I said. Nadya made a frustrated noise beside me, but Nuroshi sat back down.

"I'm listening," he said. I slid a white piece of paper with the transcribed inscriptions of the egg's carvings across the slick lacquered table. The less Nuroshi knew about the egg itself, the better. "Can you translate this?"

Nuroshi examined the inscriptions. After a moment his eyes flicked up and he regarded my face as he weighed his answer. "Yes, but it will take time. I'm sorry to say I'm not familiar with this text. How old is it, and where did you find it?"

"What, just because I had a vampire problem you figure I fell off the stupid truck? Just translate it." I took a deep breath; now for the million-dollar request. "I also need to access an old student project online."

"I find that difficult to believe. All theses are public access. Call the university, you hardly need my services."

"Yeah, but I want the good stuff," I said, sliding the thesis title page and bad PowerPoint image of the tablet, which I'd lifted off a video recording I'd seen, over to him. I watched him take the blown-up, pixilated screencap in his clammy, fat fingers. "I want everything there is on the dig site this came from."

He warily glanced up at me. Recognition and greed flickered across his face, as if I'd passed him a coveted Christmas present or a picture of Nadya. "Ahh, now I see. I can do you one better. I'm already familiar with the thesis it came from. This tablet," he said, tapping the image, "is from a dig site in Bali, and the location will cost you."

I choked, and Nadya made a similar noise beside me. "Nuroshi, me paying more for the location is about as likely as you getting a job as a hostess."

His eyes narrowed, and he spit inches away from my feet. Then he leaned across the table and smiled. "Alix Hiboux may be the most infamous archaeology student to uncover something she shouldn't have, but she is not the first or last."

The hairs on my neck bristled, but I kept my temper in check at the sound of my old name.

His smile spread, and I clenched my fists under the table. "However, in Japan we prefer to bury things like this to save everyone's face, not feed otherwise promising students to the proverbial wolves."

I folded my hands on the table and gave Nuroshi a smile, though I'd much rather have slugged him.

After I'd been "dismissed" from academics and decided on my career change, I'd paid a bright young hacker to trash any and all digital records of my old existence he'd been able to find. As far as the powers that be were concerned, Alix Hiboux didn't exist and never had, though I'm sure there are a handful of people at my old university to this day who claim otherwise, especially after several artifacts went missing. What? I'd excavated them, technically, and after they screwed me over, they owed me those pieces. Many people knew what I looked like, and people like Nuroshi who were in the world of academics guessed. Throwing it back in my face was just low.

I would have preferred to throw Nuroshi out. Unfortunately I was pretty sure he was telling the truth. I glanced over at Nadya. She drew a deep breath and looked up at the ceiling as if she was weighing the options. She caught me looking at her and nodded towards the empty bar.

I snapped my folder shut on Nuroshi's fat white fingers before he could rifle through my notes, then retreated with Nadya to the bar and out of Nuroshi's hearing range.

"What do you think?" I asked.

Nadya shrugged. "It's a supernatural temple. If it was me, I'd give back whatever money I'd been paid and tell them to find someone else."

I shook my head. "Don't think the dragon will take kindly to that. Do you think he's lying?"

She snorted. "Lying? Not about Bali, but without a doubt he's not telling us something." She shook her head as if to emphasize the point. "And before you go anywhere, I want to see the dig notes myself."

I let out a breath and glanced over at Nuroshi, who was sitting patiently at the booth, sipping his water. I felt like I was walking into a mousetrap, an ancient, magical, booby-trapped temple of a mousetrap, but a mousetrap all the same.

There also wasn't a hell of a lot I could do, but I did have one idea to get ahead of Nuroshi. I pulled out my phone and checked for flights to Bali. There was one scheduled to leave before nightfall.

Nadya's brows knitted as the airline webpage flashed onto my screen. "What are you doing?"

"I'm booking a flight, what does it look like I'm doing?"

"Are you nuts? Nuroshi could be lying—"

"Which I'm hoping you can check out for me—and if it isn't a wild-goose chase, I'll already be there. If it is, I'll turn around and be on a flight back."

Nadya swore in Russian. "You don't attract trouble, Owl, you dive into it like the shallow end of a swimming pool."

No arguing there.

I slid back into the booth, took out half the fee, and placed it on the table. "All right, here's the deal. You bring Nadya and me those folders with dig site details and that translation by tomorrow morning, and we'll give you the rest."

His usual leer twisted into a sneer. "Everything up front or no folders," he said, but he reached his puffy hand across the table to snatch the fold of bills.

I was faster. "Not a chance. You know I'm good for it. Either you bring us the dig folder tomorrow morning, or we go somewhere else." I gave him my meanest glare. It doesn't work on most people. Let's face it, I'm just not that scary, but Nuroshi is a coward, through and through. He cringed back.

"Do we have a deal?" Nadya asked.

Nuroshi glanced between Nadya and me, calculating. "Only because I'm feeling generous to two such beautiful young ladies who have been such excellent customers."

That much was true. We had been excellent customers, but if he thought for one second I believed he had any kind of loyalty to us, well . . . I think Nuroshi would as soon sell his own grandmother to turn a quick profit, and if you know much about Japanese culture, that's saying a lot about him.

He reached his hand across the table to shake and I grasped it, trying hard not to think of what was under his fingernails. "Deal," he said.

I relinquished the money, which disappeared into Nuroshi's jacket. He stared at Nadya once more before heading out the door.

She said something in Russian under her breath as the door swung shut behind him. "One of these days I'd like to lock the leering fat turnip in a barrelful of water and nail the lid shut."

"How 'bout right after we find out what he's not telling us?"

"Sounds swell," Nadya said.

I checked my watch; I needed to leave for the airport soon, and I still had to swing by Nadya's to grab Captain and a change of clothes.

I pulled out the pages I'd gathered on the two PhD students who'd excavated the Bali site. I'd managed to glean a bit more information off them, current residence, clubs they were known to hang out at . . . remember, I said I'd made friends with a talented young hacker.

I passed the sheets to Nadya. "I don't know about you, but I've got no intention of waiting for Nuroshi to bring us those folders. Think you can get those two talking by tonight? Jaded archaeology student to jaded archaeology student?"

A smile spread across Nadya's face as she looked over the information. "Oh, I think that can be arranged. The owner of this snack bar is a friend of mine. He owes me."

"Save your favor, just tell them you're Alix Hiboux."

She gave me an even stare; it's not often I use my old name. I shrugged. "You heard Nuroshi. Those two were shafted nearly as badly as I was. Tell 'em you're me and see if they'll fill you in on the site so I can avoid falling into some ancient booby trap."

"What if Nuroshi is setting you up?"

That same thought had occurred to me. Between Sabine and the Paris boys—I still wasn't 100 percent sure they'd really backed off—I wasn't thrilled about heading to Bali. "Let's just hope all he's trying to do is cut a deal and turn me in to the authorities. Besides, by the time he brings the site details in, I'll already be in Bali, and hopefully you can get directions off those two students tonight. Waiting for those folders tomorrow morning is my backup plan. If there's something else funny going on, hopefully I'll miss it."

"He didn't tell you which site," Nadya said. "How many dig sites are active there now? Six?"

I shook my head. "Five, but only two are old enough and big enough to house tablets that old. I'm betting on the pre–Majapahit Sanur site."

Nadya crossed her arms. "And what if it's Besakih?"

"Let's just really hope it's not and maybe I'll get really lucky," I said.

Nadya snorted derisively.

I was already headed for the door. I'd need ten minutes on my computer to call in a favor Stateside. As an afterthought, I yelled back over my shoulder, "Can I borrow your windsurfing board and beach clothes?"

"Go ahead—and Alix?"

I paused, halfway in, halfway out of the club. Nadya held up the folder on the students. "I'll see what I can find out tonight, but something smells off about this whole thing. Don't do anything stupid until I call."

"Thanks, I owe you one—"

"You owe me a lot more than one, *plus* my usual cut."

I smiled. "Just get a barrel ready. I've never tried to drown a turnip," I said, and left.

—⁓—

Nuroshi might not have given me the exact location, but I hadn't become infamous for nothing. Archaeology in Bali boomed about six years ago when five ancient catacombs had been found, two of them dating back to before the eighth century; old enough to hide something, but young enough to possibly reference Mr. Kurosawa's egg and scroll, which had been buried in the tomb of the first emperor of China around 210 BC. Even if the Bali tablet didn't mention the egg or China, it would give me more writing to go on than what was on the puzzle case. One set of catacombs, the Sanur Caves, was sitting nice and cozy on the coastline a little north of a beach resort town called Sanur. The Sanur Caves were accessible two ways. From the road you had to go through gates with a handful of guards. The other way was through underwater caves, which I don't recommend for the run-of-the-mill tourist. Even if you managed to rappel over the overhanging cliff or anchor your boat without crushing it on the rocks, you'd still have to navigate and crawl through unmapped tunnels.

As tricky as that sounded, I really hoped Nadya would call and say it was Sanur, because the second set of catacombs posed more problems; they were under the Besakih Temple.

Captain howled under my chair as the plane pulled into Ngurah Rai airport.

"Quiet, we still need to get through customs," I whispered through the carrier screen. I reasoned that even if Sabine had tracked me to Japan, there was no way in hell she could get to Bali in time, but better to be safe and bring Captain than end up vampire chow.

I did one last flip through my emperor tomb dig pictures and checked my ID badges for the site, as well as the most up-to-date Google images I could find of the Sanur catacombs and tide tables in case I had to rappel my way out. I double-checked that I had everything I needed before closing my carryall case. Nuroshi's fidgetiness still had me on edge, and the sooner I was in Sanur and back to Japan, the better. I stood up with the other passengers and filed off the plane and through customs. Today I was dressed as a student, my hair brushed up in a ponytail, and I'd only worn enough makeup to give me what makeup artists like to call a "natural boost." Just your run-of-the-mill girl next door with her cat. Yup, that's me, along with the passport that said I was a Canadian archaeology student named Charity Greenwoods. I mean, Charity Greenwoods—the name reeks of wholesome goodness. No one is going to stop Charity Greenwoods at a security checkpoint, at the airport *or* at a middle-security dig site.

I picked up Nadya's windsurfing board at oversized baggage and claimed my backpack before heading into the warm Balinese afternoon. The sun was only nearing the horizon, so I had a few more hours to plan. Perfect. I'd arranged for a surf hostel pickup to Sanur, and the driver, Kato, had emailed me a photo of him and the jeep to keep an eye out for. The jeep was bright orange, and so was his hair; shouldn't be hard to spot.

While I waited outside with my windsurfing board, a slew of Australian students on holiday passed by me, probably on their way to Kuta, Bali's surf and party destination. One of them whistled, and I gave him the finger. I planned on avoiding Kuta like the plague while I was here. Considering how many temples were crowded into the small Indonesian island, there was enough cumulative magic floating around to make it a death trap, and Kuta attracted all sorts of nasty supernatural messiness.

As I headed out into the sun to wait for my ride, I found two texts on my phone, one from Nadya, which simply read, *On schedule*, and a second from Rynn.

The last person I wanted to talk to right now was Rynn. I was working. I opened the message anyway.

Call me.

Damn it. I'd told him I was going to Bali before stepping on the plane, what more did he want from me? I texted back: *No. I'm working. Back tomorrow afternoon—call you then.*

Next, I called Benjamin, my contact in Toronto. Benji was a nice archaeology boy who'd had the misfortune of running into a supernatural dig site a few years back. He was a nice, normal kid who'd grown up in a nice, middle-class home. He was a bit geeky in an indie rocker, wears corduroys and black-rimmed glasses kind of way, but he'd gotten into the kind of trouble that requires advice from someone like me. He'd had the sense to follow it—and he still owed me, big time.

He answered on the third ring. "Yeah?" he said in a hesitant voice.

"Benji? How's it going on your end?"

I heard the sigh, likely for my benefit. "I told the team I'm sending down a friend for a tour."

Benji wasn't on this dig, but half his supervisor's students were. The team was staying in a Sanur hostel, and Benji had organized for them to take me—Charity—with them to the catacomb dig site tomorrow morning. As I said, it's all in the name.

"But listen, Owl, that's it. Anything else, I can't help you."

I sighed and rolled my eyes at Captain. People are real happy to make friends with you when a two-thousand-year-old mummy knocks off half their team, but returning the favor always pisses them off. No one likes to pay up out of the goodness of their heart; that's why I usually get cash up front. I'd just felt sorry for Benji and figured I could leverage some access later on, the ungrateful little . . .

"No good deed goes unpunished," I said to Captain.

As much as I wanted to tell Benji exactly where to shove his whining, I didn't. All he wanted was to go back to pretending the supernatural didn't exist. Run, hide, and forget it ever happened. I was putting a severe kink in that game plan. I couldn't blame him for being afraid, either—it was healthy, smart. "Look, Benji, I know you're not happy about me calling in a favor this close to home—"

"If anything happens that can be traced back to me, and I mean anything—I'm not stupid, I know you take stuff out of sites—"

"Nothing will happen. I wouldn't have contacted you if I didn't need your help and if I wasn't one hundred percent certain you couldn't be traced." And here I go with the white lies. Oh well, I didn't think Benji needed to hear that I was almost certain I wouldn't be traced back to him. The last thing I needed was him chickening out and calling the local authorities or his team.

There was a pause on the other end. I got the impression he hadn't had a lot of sleep. "I could go to jail," he said.

No shit. Welcome to my world. My understanding, Good Samaritan patience was up. "Yeah, well *I* could have gone to jail for helping you cover up those South American mummies who decided it was time to get up and kill a few people. Hell, I didn't even have to help you out. If you screw me over, you realize there are photos . . ."

He sighed, "No, I appreciate it, I still do. But the stuff you do . . ."

I didn't bother adding anything where he trailed off. His distaste in associating with my types could go screw itself.

"Your university has teams at all five catacomb digs and I need access to all five if need be," I said.

"OK, I emailed the group. They know you're there for surfing and might want to go check out some of the sites. They're letting you stay in the building they've rented from the hostel for their research. But you promise no one will know—"

"They won't have any idea I've even looked through their work. Now, badges? Permits? Lock codes?"

"I'm emailing you what I have. I don't have the gate codes though."

"But everything else?" Things were going better than planned.

"Yup, on its way." There was a slight pause. "Are we square yet?"

"I helped you bury two South American mummies, their slaughtered victims, and then scuttle the research."

"You mean forge and destroy the data."

"Sweetie, you want to go tell your committee you found real mummies and they killed your still-missing coworkers, go right ahead. Hell, I can help. I've got a buddy who can retrieve the data for you," I said, leaving the hint of blackmail in the air. Necessary, but it still left a bad taste in my mouth. Oh, don't get me wrong, I'll do it, but it's the principle that bugs me.

"No, no. I just wish I could forget stuff like that ever existed, you know?"

"Get in line." I felt bad for Benji. He was a good archaeologist . . . too good, and that had been his problem. He'd stumbled into something he hadn't been able to handle, and his own integrity was eating him up inside. I could relate. Hell, that's partly why I'm here and not at a nice cushy university. Benji was not cut out for my line of work. I still felt like I had to throw him hope.

"One more dig site over the next two years and I promise you we're square. Anything else after that, you can turn a profit or tell me to go to hell. Your choice."

He sighed. It had that defeated quality to it. "OK. Good luck with whatever you're after. Can you do me one favor?"

"What?"

"Give me a heads-up if you're ever coming within a hundred-mile radius of a dig I'm on so I have time to get the hell out."

"Benjamin, I'm hurt. Can't I just have a vacation and visit a world-renowned archaeological site?"

He snorted. "And the guy standing in the Mexican whorehouse is just visiting his sister."

Damn, I'd have to remember to use that later. "Thanks, Benjamin," I said, and hung up. No sooner had I gotten my phone back in my pocket than it chimed again. I wrestled it out of Nadya's surf shorts. DRAGON LADY flashed across the screen.

"I thought you were making Oricho make your calls for you?" I said.

"Oricho was not available." From the tone of Lady Siyu's voice, I imagined she was none too happy about that. "Kindly listen, answer my questions, and refrain from babbling."

I sighed. "*Fine.*"

"You believe the scroll is in Bali?"

"No," I said, and thought how to most concisely put it. "But the trail points to two sites there, so that's where I'm off to." There was a pause on the other end of the phone.

"Are there no other options?"

"No, there aren't a hell of a lot of references to unknown dead scripts and two-thousand-year-old thefts from China lying around, though if you find any, I'd love to hear about them—"

"You're babbling again," came her clipped response.

I was about to end the call, except she was still talking. I put the phone back up to my ear. "Furthermore, you will refrain from travelling to Bali until I get back to you—"

"Too late."

"Pardon?"

"I said it's too late, I'm already here and I've already arranged to check the sites—"

"Neither I nor Oricho authorized that—"

Man oh man, if one of my days could work out, just one . . . "Look, I didn't know I needed to ask your permission before getting on a plane. My understanding is that I either retrieve the scroll for Mr. Kurosawa or I'm dragon bait, so, no offense, I plan on doing anything

I bloody well like that gets me closer to getting whatever scroll was in that damn egg—"

"A scroll with a case."

"Pardon?"

"A scroll case. Mr. Kurosawa has confirmed that the contents of the egg chamber should contain a silver scroll case with matching inscriptions."

It took me a second to recover. "And you couldn't have given me that information a little sooner?" I'd have to text Nadya pronto.

Lady Siyu didn't bother answering my question—that wasn't on the agenda. "I am booking you on a plane back to Tokyo, where you will meet Oricho's contact—"

"OK, no offense, but I've had about enough of your interference. I'll get on a plane after I've got what I came for."

"Oricho has arranged help for you in Tokyo. There is no one in Bali, and there are other . . . arrangements . . . I need to make—"

"I'll be back in Tokyo first thing tomorrow morning," I said, and hung up. I was already antsy about Bali, and Lady Siyu was not helping. Damn it, if I didn't need to see the inscriptions and site for myself, did she really think I'd be over here?

I noticed the surf hostel shuttle pull up, and I threw my surfboard in the back and hopped into the front seat beside the neon-orange-haired driver. I sent two emails off, one to Oricho with Lady Siyu cc'd, letting them know I was in Bali, and the second to Nadya, letting her know about the scroll case, with a note to mention it to the two archaeology students, Aeto and Shinobi, who had written the thesis and done the excavation. As an aside, I mentioned she should try them on the egg case inscriptions we did have. I thought Nuroshi was our better bet; unfortunately the old turnip was a genius with dead languages, so it was worth a shot.

"Plan on doing some surfing?" Kato said, and I did a double take. He was a lot younger in person than his photo had led me to believe. I wondered if all Balinese looked young for their age, or if Kato was an exception.

"Windsurfing, actually . . . are you old enough to drive?" I said.

"I'm old enough for a lot of things," he said, flashing me a very white smile.

"Stick to driving, kid," I said. "Hey, could we swing by the liquor store first? I so need to pick something up for the team. They're letting me stay with them for free and all." Nothing wrong with working the broke student angle.

"Sorry, lady. No stops."

"I'll throw in twenty bucks."

He looked at me over the rim of his sunglasses, trying to look cool. Geez, he couldn't be more than thirteen. "Where you want to go?" he replied.

"Oh good, we speak the same language." Kato fixed his eyes on the carrier, and Captain decided at that moment to let out a meow.

"That's a cat."

"So?"

"Cat's extra."

"Like hell it is. I'm already giving you twenty bucks to take me to the liquor store."

He smiled. "Another twenty for the cat or no liquor store."

I leaned over and beckoned Kato with my finger. Smiling, he took the bait. My windsurfing board sticking out the back blocked us from view of the airport. As soon as he was close enough, I grabbed him. "Look, kid, I'm already giving you an extra twenty, and you're going to be happy with that. Otherwise, you're out the entire fare and then you'll have to explain to the archaeologists what happened to me and I'll tell them you left me on the side of the road after taking my money. Do you really want me to do that?"

He gulped. "I'll tell them you threatened me."

It was my turn to look at him over my sunglasses. "Kid, my name is Charity Greenwoods. Look at me—who do you think they're going to believe?"

Kato gulped again but recovered fast. "Twenty bucks it is, lady," he said, and we were off.

Captain mrowled as I shoved his carrier into the back of the jeep. "What, you wanted us to be stranded at the airport?" Apparently not, since he settled down.

It's clichéd, but I let my hair down and enjoyed the salty sea breeze as the jeep wound its way out of the airport and branched off from the rest of the tourist traffic. I had a few hours until sundown. I'd check out the beach, get some surfing in, and give out booze with a little added incentive to go to sleep. Once everyone was passed out in their beds, I'd rifle through their computers and see what I could get. By the time Nadya called, I'd have a complete map of each site.

"Hey Kato, how long till Sanur?"

"Today? In this traffic? One hour." He glanced over at me. "You don't act like any of the other archaeology students."

I had to smile. The kid wasn't stupid.

"Can you keep your mouth shut?" I pulled a twenty out. This was risky, but the kid struck me as smart and picked up fast.

Kato looked at the twenty and then at me.

"No one is going to get hurt, I just want to know who I'm sharing a bathroom with before I get there."

After a second, Kato took the bill from my hand. "What do you want to know?"

"Tell me about the students. What are they like, what do they do for fun? You know, stuff."

"Which one you want to know about first?"

"Start with the smartest, move down the line from there."

I could let myself relax in the breeze for an hour. Tonight I'd be working.

6

SANUR

I peeked over my shoulder at the redheaded kid passed out and snoring on the couch. Balancing my flashlight in my mouth, I kneeled down in front of the locked office door and pulled my makeup bag out of my purse.

Lock-pick kits are almost universally illegal—unless you're travelling somewhere like Syria. Go figure, countries don't like people to visit them with state-of-the-art lock picks. Mine double as makeup brushes and won't trip a metal detector. I pulled the eye shadow brush out, twisted the black lacquer end off, pocketed it so Captain wouldn't eat it, and inserted the titanium pick into the door lock.

The lock clicked open and I twisted the door handle carefully, so as not to make too much noise. Piece of cake. I stepped through.

"Ow! Son of a . . ." I bit back the last word and flicked the light switch on. Captain darted across my feet and hopped up on the windowsill on the other side of the office. Someone had left their dig kit in front of the door. Figures, lazy grad students . . .

Captain chirped and batted at a giant moth fluttering its blue wings against the window, trying to make its way in.

I glared at him. "You could have warned me instead of chasing after a butterfly—"

I stopped as I heard shuffling footsteps in the living room. Shit. I turned my flashlight off and peeked around the door. The redhead was sitting up and rubbing his forehead. Double shit.

I ducked underneath the desk and had to cover my mouth as I stubbed my toe again, this time on the kit pickax. Goddamn it, I *hate* messy archaeologists.

It was Saturday night, and most of the dig students had headed into Kuta to party with all the other foreign tourists. Only two had been at the hostel when I'd arrived, and they'd been more than happy to drink my beer. Note to all you broke students out there: never trust generous offerings of beer from another broke student. There's a string attached. I'd added a little something—something that Nadya used to use on troublesome bar patrons in Moscow, way back when she'd been bartending her way through university, long before we met. Strong enough to put you to sleep, but nowhere near strong enough anyone would suspect you'd drugged them.

The girl from Britain, Kylie, had made it up to her room before passing out, but the American kid, Mark, who Kato said stayed up too late watching sports on YouTube, had curled up into a ball and passed out on the couch.

I heard Mark pad across the bamboo floor. I made out his silhouette in the moonlight as he ducked his head around the office door and flipped on the light. My heart started to pound. Shit, shit, shit . . . maybe I could claim I'd passed out under the desk . . . couldn't find my bed . . .

I didn't breathe, though I'm sure my heart was making plenty of noise all on its own. His face scrunched under the fluorescent light as he checked the handle, turning and twisting it three times and jostling the lock. Thank God I'd had the good sense to do a decent job and not rush the lock pick. Pays to be careful.

He stepped through.

Worst-case scenarios involving a Balinese prison flashed through my head. The great Owl, caught stealing from a pack of broke archaeology students. Fantastic way to go down, with no flames whatsoever. I stared good and hard at the pickax right within hand's reach, but somehow I doubted that adding murder to theft was going to help my bargaining power in the Balinese jail cell. Besides, I've never hit anyone before—I'm nonviolent, and I wasn't about to start with students.

"Mroow?" Captain bleated about as loudly as I'd ever heard him. The student swung his head towards the window.

"Hey, were you making all that noise in here?" The redhead yawned and headed over to pat Captain.

Jeez, the kid shouldn't even have been standing, let alone asking my cat questions.

He went to pick him up, but Captain darted through his legs and out the door. The redhead yawned again and shuffled back out of the room. I heard the lock click back into place behind him.

Hunh, Captain was paying off his kibble tonight. I'd have to make sure I threw in an extra chicken treat.

Once I heard the kid head upstairs I breathed a sigh of relief. I waited until I heard his door close before sliding into the co-opted rattan beach chair and booting up the dig laptop.

"Time to see how good these guys are." I punched in Benji's codes and watched as the dig site files loaded onto the screen.

I called Nadya. She didn't pick up until the eighth ring.

"What the hell took you so long?" I said. I could hear fuzzy talking and music in the background. Nadya must still be at the snack bar.

"What do you think? They think I'm Alix Hiboux. They've been trying to pick me up all night, though they thought I should be much shorter."

I snickered. I could just picture the two grad students trying to hit on the statuesque Nadya. If it weren't so important, it would have been funny. "What did your two fans give you?" I said.

"Good news or bad news first?"

"Good news."

"You were right about the Sanur catacombs. Aeto and Shinobi both say the tablet they showed is from there."

I did a silent cheer. I subscribe to the saying "The harder I try, the luckier I get." That doesn't mean I turn my nose up at blind luck.

"Now the bad news." I heard Nadya cup her hand over the mic and muffled Russian yelling before she came back on. "Shinobi is certain there were two tablets, not one, and guess where the second one is?"

I closed my eyes. "The Basuki catacombs," I said, the excitement drained out of my voice.

"The tablets have complementary inscriptions that work as a codex, or alphabet, for the rest of the cavern inscriptions, or that was their best guess. They think you'll need both sets to even attempt a translation."

"Well, don't they have the other set?"

"That's what really worries me. Their project was stopped right after they told their supervisor about the second set of inscriptions in Basuki. All the material was seized by the International Archaeology Association. Guess who pulled the project?"

I closed my eyes. "Nuroshi."

"Alix, that was what Nuroshi was smiling about. Not only did he think you didn't have the dig location, he knew you only had information on one tablet. The little troll is planning on taking your money and sending you on a wild-goose chase. You need both tablets to do anything."

Shit. Nuroshi was a thief, but he'd never tried to screw me quite like this before. He'd always kept it to extra, hidden fees—very Japanese. Try renting there, you'll see what I mean.

"Does anyone else have any idea you're there?" Nadya said, interrupting my train of thought.

"Oricho, Lady Siyu, Rynn, and Benji, but that's it," I said, and did the quick calculation in my head. Rynn knew to keep his mouth shut, and I didn't think Lady Siyu or Oricho planned on blabbing where I was tracking down their boss's stupid egg scroll.

"Good, let's keep it that way."

Something nagged at the back of my mind. When I figured out what it was, I felt a cold chill go up my spine. "Nuroshi doesn't have enough pull to shut down an entire international dig on his own. Who's pulling his strings?"

Nadya was silent for a moment, then swore in Russian as she caught on. "Owl, get the hell out of there."

"I've still got enough time to make the Sanur catacombs tonight and the Basuki site tomorrow morning. I'll still be on a plane before anyone—including Nuroshi—is the wiser."

Nadya swore again. "And call Rynn, he came in asking about you. Said you hadn't returned his messages. He said if I heard from you to tell you it's important."

I hadn't returned Rynn's last text because I hadn't bothered opening it. I was working, and at his best Rynn is a distraction. "I'll message him later. If he bugs you again, tell him I'm working."

Nadya snorted. "I'm not your social planner. Tell him yourself."

I was about to hang up the phone when I remembered that Benji hadn't had the gate codes.

"No wait, Nadya, don't hang up yet—ask them if they have the gate codes." I heard her muffled voice in the background. It wouldn't matter if I had the maps and dig site locations. I wasn't going anywhere without those codes.

"The codes are the least of your problems. Both said they've got armed guards stationed around all the sites right now. Problems with tourists and *thieves* taking things."

"Shit, I hate amateurs." I have a strong aversion to being shot at, so I'd have to find another way in. "I'm sending you the new maps. See if they can point out any changes I need to know about, and call or message me back. And don't worry about the entrance, I'll think of something."

I hoped.

I glanced down at the Sanur dig site map I'd interposed on Google. The only unguarded way into the catacombs was the cliff tunnels. The moon was reflecting off the crystal water. I looked back down at the Google map and zoomed in on the shoreline outside the catacombs. I flipped the image around so I got a nice "street" view of a small cave opening beneath the cliffs. I referenced it to the latest catacombs map, focusing on a small tunnel the guys hadn't bothered exploring yet. The inscriptions had been washed off by rising water, so it wasn't high on the priority list.

Oh, this was too good to be true.

"Hey, Nadya, I just figured out a way around those gates. Your windsurfing board is about to come in real handy."

— *m* —

Saying Captain wasn't happy was an understatement. In fact, if I was any judge of cats, I'd say he was furious.

I zipped up my black wet suit and picked up his carrier. I'd had to trick him in after he'd realized I was heading out without him. He gave me a baleful meow.

"Too bad," I said through the carrier screen and held up the perfume bottle I'd used to drug the beer. "The sooner I get out there, the sooner I get back. You can agree to keep quiet, or the next meow out of your mouth, I'm dumping this down your throat. It works on cats too."

He settled down, grumbling, and I darted out the door with the windsurfing board while the going was still good. 1:00 a.m. I had plenty of time to get to Sanur and back.

I wasn't confident enough to windsurf in the dark, even with the full moon, but stand-up paddleboarding was well within my capabilities. I took to the water and headed down the coast. In forty-five minutes I'd reached the cliffs of Sanur, and fifteen minutes later I found the caves. There were four almost perfectly cylindrical openings, the nearest of which was seven feet above me with the tide out. From the Google pics and my angle, I guessed all four of them were large enough for me to crawl through without too much trouble . . . provided they didn't narrow halfway up. I found three jagged rocks jutting out from the water that were close enough together to stow Nadya's board and the paddle I'd borrowed from the hostel shed. The tide was still ebbing out, so I shouldn't lose them to the currents.

I scrambled up onto the largest and flattest of the rocks and pulled my cell phone out before sliding my backpack off. Thank God for waterproof casing. I checked the time. Ten past two. I had four hours before I had to get back. By the time the students woke up, it'd look like I was just out for a morning surf, and I'd be there in time to tag along to Basuki. With any luck, by early evening I'd be back on a plane to Tokyo with two full sets of inscriptions. If I had any real luck, I'd be able to piece together a codex and come up with a translation for the egg chamber. If I was really lucky, I'd find mention of the egg itself.

No messages from Nadya were waiting for me; I'd been hoping to confirm my route through to the site, but it could wait until I was back in cell phone range. It had to come back in a little ways up—I couldn't imagine this troop surviving a whole dig day without mobile games and email.

I slipped my spiked sneakers on and removed a flashlight, climbing rope, hooks, and drill from my Gore-Tex pack. A girl like me never travels unprepared. I hear grappling hooks are a popular tool in movies—I wouldn't know, I spend most of my spare time in World Quest. What I do know is that grappling hooks are a great way to get yourself killed—either by gravity or guards who hear the insistent tapping of your failed attempts at catching the ledge. No one hears my fancy hook drill. That's what sets me apart from amateurs . . . like the tourists playing Indiana Jones for the day and ruining Bali for the rest of us.

I climbed up the rocks, balancing my flashlight between my teeth. The cliff jutted out over the water, so I had to use five hooks to reach the first cavern opening. The edges of the opening were polished and smooth to the touch, so much so I wondered what kind of water flow could have eaten through the cliff like that. I was surprised geologists hadn't gotten in on the action.

The opening was high enough for me to crouch without getting claustrophobic. I pulled myself in over the lip and was happy to find that the cavern flattened out before heading in an upward trajectory into the cliff. It reminded me of a dried-out waterfall.

I pulled my rope up and removed the two hooks in range on the cliff face, in case I needed them up ahead. I inched up the cave tunnel on all fours until I reached a spot where it inclined steeply enough for me to stand. I shone my flashlight up and watched the beam bounce off the loose network of tunnels, moonlight filtering in through small openings far above. The tunnels were connected, all right. Score one for amateur geologist me.

With my flashlight I checked how far the tunnel ran upwards before changing direction towards the catacombs. From the looks of it, it was a good eight or nine feet. I sighed, put my flashlight back between my teeth, and primed another hook in my drill. Good thing I had four hours and chalk.

Forty-five minutes later I still hadn't reached the catacombs. On a positive note, I hadn't gotten stuck. All the tunnels had a surprisingly uniform width and smoothness, like polished stone. What they did do was branch off every which way. Even with a compass I still managed to make three wrong turns and spent half my time backtracking and erasing my colored chalk marks and notes. I'd started off with a generic "this way back," but after the fifth wrong turn, my notes deteriorated to "you idiot, you made another wrong turn, didn't you?"

By the time sixty minutes was up I was worried I'd made yet another time-consuming wrong turn. The tunnel widened and opened into a cavern tall enough to stand. I pulled out my phone; still no reception. I opened the map I'd taken from the team's laptop and checked my point the old-fashioned way. They'd never made it all the way out to the water, only speculated like everyone else that's where the tunnels lead, but they had noted smooth caverns at the bottom of the catacombs with old pictograms on them. I edged over and started to check the cave walls inch by inch. I was just about ready to start backtracking yet again when I found a cluster of pictographs. It took me another few minutes to match the exact ones on file, but finally I was in the right place. And I had a trail of chalk to lead me back to the water. Figured that a fifteen-minute walk took me just over an hour.

The cavern was roughly the size of a small apartment with two offshooting alcoves. All I needed to do was figure out which one led to the catacombs. I walked around, careful not to loosen any rocks with my feet, and checked where the catacomb entry point should be on the map.

What the . . .

I shone the flashlight directly on a set of pictographs wedged underneath one of the outjutting rocks. Unlike the white relief images the archaeologists had documented, these were done with a vibrant red paint and depicted a woman surrounded by snakes. Lots of snakes. It looked new . . . and wet. On a hunch I leaned my face as close as I dared and sniffed. The unmistakable metallic scent of blood overwhelmed me. I covered my mouth and nose against the unpleasant smell and took two steps back. Even though they looked and smelled fresh I doubted the images were recent, since as far as I could see, the students had stopped short of reaching this section of tunnels. From the undisturbed cliff face, I found it just as unlikely anyone had come from the water. It dawned on me this was ritualistic magic, the kind that stands the test of time.

I closed my eyes. I'd really hoped I could avoid supernatural shit tonight. Checking out the tablets and getting the hell out of here were now my top priorities. Snakes and ritualistic magic are not a good combination.

I turned my attention back to the alcoves. Both led upwards and back into the cliff. They both ran so close together in the same general direction that I couldn't tell which one was more likely to take me where I needed to go—not without the PhD students' notes. Sometimes you just have to work with what you have . . . and hope to hell you don't stumble into some ancient booby trap. I really didn't need to get lost again. I shook my head and drew another arrow on the floor with my chalk. Well, on the bright side, if the map distance was accurate, I was only ten minutes away from the catacombs.

I decided to go left, mostly because I'm left handed. Four feet in, the light dimmed and I needed my flashlight once again.

A pebble skittered and clicked down the cave wall, then rolled to a stop by my feet. I froze. Adrenaline took over my senses, priming them to react as I listened for other sounds—like the hiss of pressurized acid or other assorted ancient booby traps. I don't put much faith in coincidence. For the first time, I noticed the faint taste of mold in the air, like stale water left in a rock pool too long. There's something really eerie about getting an image like that out of the blue.

I took slow, deep breaths and waited, ears strained for anything out of the ordinary. For a ten count of me trying not to hyperventilate, there was nothing, and then something slid against the rocks above me. I looked up and saw a series of interlaced caverns; smooth and polished exactly like the tunnels that led out to the ocean. I stood still and waited for what I hoped was a giant bat or lizard to pass by . . . hell, even a crocodile was preferable . . .

Something hissed, above and to my left. I swore and fumbled my flashlight as I aimed the beam at it. A patch of rock began to move and wind over itself, glistening in the moonlight. It took me a sec to make the connection. Scales. Giant white scales.

Adrenaline hit me so hard I froze. I stumbled over my own feet, twice, before I regained my balance enough to bolt. I scrambled up onto a ledge as the very large snake dropped to the ground behind me.

I ran, and I didn't give a flying rat's ass who the hell heard me at this point.

In the words of a famous archaeologist, "I hate snakes."

Less than fifty feet down, the tunnel ended and spilled out into the catacombs. Rule of thumb: never look over your shoulder when running from monsters. Keep running, fast. Especially where snakes are concerned. Think all those Medusa stories.

Instead, from the tail I'd glimpsed winding through the tunnel lattice, I could well imagine the giant white snake hurtling towards me. Apparently it had decided I was tonight's dinner theater. I swore and kept running, convinced with each hiss that it was gaining on me. I think I even blew right by the tablet.

I recognized this section of tunnels from the maps and pictures I'd studied. Instead of keeping left and heading farther into the catacombs, I took a sharp right, straight for the main temple. If I was lucky, the giant snake was bound as a guardian in the temple proper, meaning if I passed by the temple threshold I'd be out of the snake's range . . . or have more open ground to run on. Either way I'd be better off than if I kept running in the catacombs. . . . One giant snake mousetrap.

My feet hit the tiled floor of a temple side room. Halfway across, I hurdled over an altar in hopes the slab of granite would slow the snake down. In a matter of seconds I was across the chamber and out a doorway that led to a flight of stone stairs cut into the bedrock. I was breathing heavily now—maybe I should cut back on the World Quest and Corona—but the stairs went up, and up meant I'd be heading towards the surface.

I pushed my lungs to reach the flight of stairs before the snake caught up. My legs quit taking orders and I tripped over an uneven step, landing hard on my wrists and knocking the wind out of myself. The stone altar broke behind me. Not daring to look back, I scrambled back up, ignoring the sharp pain in my left wrist. Damn it, that was the one I used. At the top of the stairs was a wooden door, not the original but a good replica, complete with a slab bolt. As soon as my foot touched the top step, I slammed the door behind me and dropped the metal rebar into place, bolting it shut. The snake crashed into the door, but the hard wood panels held. For now. I had no illusions how long a few slabs of wood would hold up against a three-hundred-pound snake. Anything that opted to crash through a granite altar rather than slide around it would have no problem with a wooden door. The rebar only bought me a few more minutes. Time to hide.

I took fast stock of my surroundings. I was in a larger temple room roughly the size of a baseball diamond with vaulted ceilings and Balinese statues lining the walls. From the style and structure, I could tell this had been built after the lower catacombs, probably by a few hundred years, give or take, and a cool breeze carried fresh air here.

I was right under the surface; all I had to do now was find the exit. I wracked my brain and tried to remember where the exit had been on the map, and where I was.

Crack!

The wood door splintered along the length, bending against the rebar as the snake smashed into the door again. Who cared about the exit—a giant snake was about to eat me. I heard the door splinter again behind me and a hiss echoed through the temple, bouncing off the walls, as if in an amphitheater.

There were six statues, three on each side of the room. I ran by the second pair and skidded to a halt; I'd almost blown by an escape route, a set of narrower, steeper stairs built into the wall on my left and leading up to a ledge that ran along the perimeter. I made a sharp left for the stairs, hoping and betting that the snake couldn't climb.

If it can ever be said that there is a golden rule of archaeology, it's this: "Always keep an eye peeled for ancient booby traps."

Why the hell can't I follow my own advice?

It sprung after my foot landed on the tenth or twelfth step. I swore as the stone slabs collapsed underneath me into a slide. This part of the temple had a lot of foot traffic, so either the giant snake or I had triggered something . . . something the damn student archaeologists hadn't found or bothered to disarm yet. I scrambled to wedge my fingers and toes into any cracks or crevices, but the ancient Balinese had thought of that. I slid right back down to the temple floor and came to a stop below one of the statues, an Apsara to be precise, a female Balinese muse of gaming and fortune.

Figures.

The rebar shrieked and I couldn't stop myself from staring at the door. It looked more like a balloon now than the laws of physics gave it any right to. A balloon ready to burst. Flat on your ass, you notice things—like the snake imagery woven into the stonework and statues . . . A sickening thought struck me: I didn't think the ancient Balinese had designed this place for getting away from the snake.

The collapse of the ancient slide and the snake obliterating the door were also just the right amount of noise to get the guards' attention . . . if you were wondering what it would take to get the minimum-wage night shift to put their drinks down and do their job. I heard two male, middle-aged voices echo from the far end. They worried me less than the snake—they'd run as soon as they realized it was supernatural. No sense risking them seeing me here though.

I scanned the room, but hiding spots weren't exactly jumping out at me, and the ledge recessed around the ceiling seemed to be it— designed for priests and spectators, I'd wager.

The only things in the temple left to climb were the statues. I gauged the one closest to me; it stood nine, maybe ten, feet in a classic pose, one arm raised towards the heavens and the other extended down towards the earth. Though the tip of its headdress didn't reach all the way to the ledge, it was a hell of a lot closer than I was now. I hopped up and latched on to the extended statue arm. I winced as a sharp pain shot up my injured left wrist, but I ignored it with a mental reminder of guns and snakes. I pulled myself up onto its shoulders.

There was a commotion at the far end of the hall—the guards, and closer than they had been before. From the sound of it, they were arguing, probably about whether to come in or not. It stopped and footsteps began again, coming towards me. I frowned. Why hadn't they turned back yet? The hissing alone should have sent them into supernatural mode—wasn't the IAA training these guys anymore? *Hiss* and *Crash* don't mean "Go look for intruders"—they mean "Run! Run now!"

I stood up, a foot on either shoulder and knees balanced against the headdress. To say the recess was a bit of a jump from the statue was an understatement. It had looked a hell of a lot closer from the ground. I was glad I had my spiked shoes on; I'd need them to help catch the ledge.

I leapt.

A yelp escaped me as I slammed into the recess. My right hand latched onto the ledge, but my injured left one grabbed a jagged piece of rock. My reflexes took over and my left released in a wave of fresh pain. I managed to get a fingerhold in a carved relief with my right, but it wasn't good enough, and I began to slip. My shoes scraped against the ancient carvings. Great, now I could add ruining priceless artwork to what I'd accomplished this trip.

The fingers of my right hand started to go numb. I looked down at the floor—why do things always look so much higher from above? If I didn't get hold of the ledge now, I'd fall, or the guards would shoot me . . . or the snake would break the door and eat me after I fell . . .

In a last-ditch effort I began to swing my body side to side to create momentum. The guards were getting closer, and for some reason the snake had ceased its onslaught on the door, which worried me.

Having gotten as much momentum as I dared, I shut my eyes and swung my legs up. With a colossal effort from my out-of-shape abs, I shimmied my leg over the ledge and pulled the rest of me over. I lay flat so that only my head peeked over the side while I caught my breath. The temple amplified every sound, so I slowed my breathing and tried to keep as quiet as possible as the guards entered.

My phone buzzed.

I screamed silently as I fumbled it out of my pocket—silent settings on phones are a joke.

Where are you? read the text from Rynn.

I swore. I was starting to wish he'd never gotten hold of my number. *Not a good time.* I started to put my phone back in my pocket, when it buzzed again.

The guards heard it this time and started to look around, guns out, when the snake began to beat up the door again. Instead of running like they should have, they turned their guns on the door. Jeez, how stupid do you have to be? I checked the message.

Call me. Now.

I turned the phone off—except it wouldn't power down. What the hell? *You're going to get me shot—stop texting.*

I checked back on the guards, who now flanked the door. Oh, this was going to be bad. I bit my lip. On the one hand, I didn't favor being shot at; on the other hand, I couldn't *not* warn them. I didn't have much faith in their bullets doing damage.

I stuck my head over the ledge and cupped my mouth. "Hey, you idiots—run, there's a—*shit!*" I ducked back down as the first two bullets careened into the stonework. Of course the guards hadn't listened to a word I'd said—easier to just open fire.

My phone buzzed again.

CALL ME. CALL ME RIGHT NOW OR I AM NEVER SPEAKING TO YOU AGAIN.

I swore. The guards were far enough away that I figured a phone call would be faster than writing. Rynn picked up before the first ring.

"Goddamn it, Rynn, I'm trying not to get shot by antiquities guards here—" Another set of bullets ricocheted above me.

"Where are you?"

"Where do you think? Ass deep in a Bali catacomb trying to steal something." I was actually trying to copy inscriptions this time, but usually I'm stealing something.

"Owl, listen to me very carefully. The guards aren't the problem. There's something else there you need to worry about. How well are you hidden?"

I snorted. "If you're about to tell me to watch out for a giant snake, you're a little late. Found that one already—in fact it's about to eat the idiot guards. So if you wouldn't mind—"

"You know, I'm beginning to see why the vampires were willing to chase you halfway across the globe for a year. You're only half right about the snake. Sanur has a resident naga."

"Shit."

Nagas have the torso of a woman and the tail of a snake. They're

smart, more so than your run-of-the-mill giant snake. They're territo-
rial and covered in a thick hide that's hard to cut through. They also
have a nasty, nasty temper. I'd read somewhere they had venomous
fangs, but reports varied on that one.

"Well, what the hell am I supposed to do about a—" I stopped
midsentence. There weren't any bars on my cell phone. I had one of
those chilling horror story moments.

And I hadn't mentioned to anyone except Nadya the set of catacombs I was headed for.

"Rynn, how the hell are you even calling me? And how the hell do
you know where I am? Did Nadya tell you?" Or for that matter what a
naga was. Rynn was a pro at suspending disbelief, but I'd never gotten
the impression he had an interest in the supernatural.

My train of thought was interrupted as the rebar gave a final shriek
before buckling and the guards screamed. "Gimme a sec," I said, and
peeked over the ledge.

The naga's torso was as white as the tail I'd glimpsed in the tunnels
and offset by a crown of black hair that reflected a green sheen under
the lamplight. Her features were that of a beautiful Balinese woman—
except for the two white fangs that extended over her red lower lip. I
realized that she bore a striking resemblance to the Apsara statue I'd
scaled, complete with ornate headdress.

Her eyes were golden and shone as she glanced at the guards. They
stopped screaming, stopped everything in fact. She had both of them
in some kind of trance. She glanced up in my direction. I dropped and
closed my eyes tight. Never look snake monsters in the eye.

"Owl, what's happening?"

I didn't answer. On the one hand, I could maybe make a run for it
while the naga was busy with the guards . . . on the other hand, they
didn't stand a chance against her. As much as I disliked the idea, I
wouldn't sleep well if I let her eat a couple of minimum-wage hacks.
Besides, she'd come straight for me after finishing them, so it was in
my best interest to keep as many of us alive as possible; more people

to outrun. Added bonus, I wouldn't dream about two hapless guards being rended into pieces by an ancient Balinese snake god.

Gave new meaning to "death by minimum wage."

I took a deep breath. I hate making choices like this. They'd been shooting at me, for Christ's sake.

"Rynn, gotta go. That naga is about to turn the guards into snacks."

"Stay hidden and I'll be there in less than a minute."

"*What*? How? This isn't a game—"

"Just don't do anything stupid," he said, and hung up.

"Who, me? Wouldn't think of it," I said to myself. This evening was already weirder than I'd ever imagined. I couldn't contemplate what the hell Rynn was doing here, or why, but I knew I sure as hell didn't like it. This is what I get for stepping back into the supernatural world. Everything goes to hell in a handbasket in five minutes flat.

The naga hissed and slithered towards the frozen guards. How to get her attention? I searched around the ledge, found a loose stone in one of the carvings, and wedged it out. It would do. I inched back to the ledge and peeked over. The naga was a few feet away from the guards, her tail stretched out past the entrance behind her, about ten or eleven feet. She was taking her precious time. I took the rock and aimed.

"Hey, snake lady! Over here," I yelled.

It hit her square between her shoulder blades. Her head whipped around, and I swore she looked straight at me, even though the ledge hid me from sight. The gold eyes started to shine . . . sooo pretty. I shook my head and shut my eyes.

With the naga's lapse in concentration, one of the guards must have broken free, because the next thing I heard was a gun go off and the naga shriek. I just hoped the guards had enough sense to run like hell. Even a little of the naga's stare left me dazed. It took me half a minute before I trusted myself to open my eyes. I peeked over the edge. Both guards now flanked the naga. Of all the stupid things . . . points for bravery though. I needed another rock. Not finding one, I searched through my bag. Flashlight? No. Drill? No. Empty water bottle? Bingo. I hurled it towards the naga's head this time. It struck the side of her headdress before she could get either of the two men back under her spell. Unfortunately, one of the guards saw me. In no time he had his gun trained and was shooting. I edged back from the ledge as the bullet struck the recess below.

"Hey! I'm on your side. Shoot the giant snake monster!" I yelled.

Another bullet hit the ledge.

I frowned. That's gratitude for you.

I heard one of the men scream. Bullets or no, I edged back to the ledge and got ready to throw the flashlight.

The naga had one of them wrapped in her tail. She raised the struggling and screaming man up to her mouth and bit into his neck before I could throw. He immediately went limp in her arms. She dropped the body unceremoniously and struck like a cobra at the second. Before she bit into his neck, she glanced up at me and hissed.

I was a sitting duck.

Something metal bounced and clinked. An innocent-looking silver ball came into view as it rolled across the ancient tiles towards the naga and her prey.

My phone buzzed. *Close and cover your eyes.*

"Shit." I dove backwards and buried my face in my backpack.

There was a pop, and the naga screamed as the room exploded in a burst of light. Even with my eyes covered, I still got a residual flash. A good UV grenade will do that.

I pulled my head out of my backpack to answer my ringing phone. "Rynn, it's a giant snake woman, not a vampire," I said.

"They're dazed, aren't they? Where are you?"

"Up here." I stuck my head up over the ledge and waved.

The remaining guard was out cold, and the naga writhed on the floor.

Rynn nodded at me. "Are you all right?" he said, and pulled what looked like a high-powered rifle off his shoulder to aim at the naga. He fired a small dart into her tail.

Tranquilizer darts. Damn, I wished I'd thought of that.

"Owl, I'd hurry up and get down from there. I used a horse tranquilizer, but I have no idea how long it will last."

Getting down proved a lot easier than getting up. I walked over to the collapsed set of stairs and slid down.

Rynn was waiting for me. I had to do a double take. It was a completely different image from the one I was used to at the bar. He was dressed in some sort of modern black motorbike armor. Besides the tranquilizer rifle, he had two different guns holstered on his belt, both with what looked like silencers. If Rynn hadn't been as good looking as he was, I'd have sworn he was some kind of black ops.

"Ahh, not that I'm not really grateful and all, but what the hell are you doing in Bali, let alone dressed like an assassin?"

"Mercenary," he said.

"What?"

"I used to be a mercenary," he said.

"Oh, I got that part—I'm just not sure I believe it, regardless of the getup. Serving drinks to pretty girls and shooting people don't exactly go together."

He rolled his eyes. "I owe Oricho a few favors, and he asked me to keep an eye on you. I've had a hell of a time tracking you since I landed."

"*You're* the backup he was talking about?"

Rynn was the last person I'd imagine toting a gun. A martini glass or beer, sure, but . . .

Rynn frowned. "This is exactly why I didn't say anything to you in Tokyo. You'd never have believed me."

I looked him over and nodded. "You're right. Not if I hadn't seen it with my own eyes. Even after seeing it with my own eyes I'm having trouble with it. And what kind of mercenary carries around a tranquilizer rifle?"

"The kind of mercenary who runs into supernatural things every now and then."

As strange at it sounded on the surface, it actually made sense. Rynn had hinted he was from Eastern Europe, though I still hadn't figured out where exactly, and parts of Eastern Europe were supernatural hot pockets. Transylvania, anyone?

"How did you go from mercenary to host/bartender?"

"I'm taking a break," he said, and started to head for the exit. "I got tired of people shooting at me."

Well, it was something I could relate to. I nodded at the naga. "Think we have a bit of time?"

Rynn shrugged. "Hard to say. I've never tranquilized a naga before. I wouldn't bank on more than half an hour, an hour max. Why?"

I jogged towards the stairs that led back down into the catacombs.

"Where are you going?" Rynn called after me.

"The snake—naga—started chasing me before I could copy the tablet and photograph the walls."

"After all that, you want to go back in there?"

"You can come with me or stay here with them," I said, and nodded towards the two guards and the naga. "I'm not leaving without those pictures." I noticed that the guard who'd been bitten was turning a purple color. I was sorry for him, but then again, I'd tried to help. I was still miffed they'd shot at me.

Rynn was one step ahead of me. He checked the poisoned guard first, then turned the second one over. He groaned but didn't otherwise move. Rynn pulled out one of the smaller guns on his belt and aimed.

"You don't have to kill him—"

Rynn raised an eyebrow at me as the dart pierced the guard's leg. The guard stopped moving immediately.

"Never mind," I said.

Rynn shook his head, tossed the rifle over his shoulder, and, to my relief, followed. After all, there might be more nagas. There were an awful lot of tunnels.

I couldn't help but be impressed by how silently Rynn moved. It's a thief thing. Even with no one around I still can't stand making noise when I don't have to.

I glanced over at him. He raised his eyebrow and I shook my head.

"Even seeing the whole mercenary thing with my own eyes I have a hard time believing it," I said.

He smiled. "Guess I'm full of surprises."

I realized I hadn't actually thanked him. Hell, I wasn't used to anyone coming after me. This was new . . . and awkward. Come to think of it, there were more questions, now that I was running this whole scenario over in my head.

"How did you know where to find me? And how did you get my cell phone to work?"

"Between Oricho and Nadya, I was able to figure out which of the two temples you were heading to. I used your cell phone signal to triangulate you partway along the coast, but by the time you were at the cavern entrances, I lost you. I found the students in Kuto and talked one of them into bringing me along. Once I was there, I was able to get the location and paid the kid with the jeep to bring me here." He held up his phone with a black case on it. "This creates a cell line so I could patch into your phone. By the way, you owe the kid a hundred bucks."

I swore. "Why the hell do I have to pay him?"

"You're on Kurosawa's payroll. Write it off as a business expense."

"I'd have at least bartered. He overcharges."

"Saving you fifty bucks and being late would have been self-defeating. Especially for you."

I guess I couldn't argue with that.

We found the chamber with the tablet, and I wasted no time photographing it. The tablet, two feet by four feet, lay on a slab of rock cut into the wall. First I made sure I had enough to make a 3-D reconstruction of it once I was back. The room itself was the size of a small bedroom, with a low ceiling and inscriptions covering the walls. Those didn't interest me; they were classic Balinese.

"How did you know about the naga?" I asked.

"Lady Siyu and Oricho. Apparently she tried to warn you—"

I snorted. "Warning me would have been, 'Whoa, wait, there's a naga living in the temple catacombs.' All she did was order me back on a plane."

Rynn shrugged.

I switched to an infrared filter and shone the light on the tablet. I often use multiple filters to screen artifacts. Ritual and supernatural sites tend to be etched with different light patterns, if you know what to look for. Which I do.

The tablet was exactly what it seemed. The walls, however . . . There was a set of inscriptions lying right underneath the carved images. I photographed them, and on a hunch ran through the rest of my filter wheel. I found four more layers of different inscriptions superimposed on one another.

I whistled and showed Rynn the readout on my tablet. "These guys didn't mess around. They either were going to be really thorough, or they really didn't want anyone to read this . . ." I swore. There was one more way to hide an inscription. It was rare, but I'd already seen that kind of magic hinted at in here once already.

"Do you have a knife?" I asked Rynn.

He looked at me quizzically but removed one from his belt and passed it over. I pushed down my squeamishness by reminding myself of the casino maze Mr. Kurosawa would chase me down in if I didn't get his damn egg scroll back, then winced as I made a shallow slice in my left palm. The blood pooled in my hand. Rynn's eyes widened.

"Stand back," I said, and pressed my blood up against the writing on the wall.

A pattern emerged, like leaves budding at warp speed. I breathed a sigh of relief. I'd been worried it was a weaker spell and I'd have to cover the whole thing. A lot of people think this kind of ritualistic blood magic needs an incantation. It probably does to set it—I've never seen an actual ritual in practice and have no plans to. But looking at it is a totally different thing. This stuff was pushing two thousand years old, and it still took less than a second to activate. Someone had known what they were doing.

Rynn drew in a quick breath and took a few steps back, a frown etched on his face.

I smiled at his uncomfortable look. "Bet you've never seen that before?"

"I've seen blood reliefs, just never seen one activated quite like that. Owl, was that wise?" he said, not bothering to hide his worry.

I shrugged. "My supervisor once told me they could combust, but I've never seen it. Frankly, I think the IAA made it up."

He shook his head, not quite buying my explanation.

"Normally I'd use diluted chicken blood in a spray bottle, but I didn't bring any," I said. "It's not something you run into that often."

I got my camera out, balancing it with my uninjured right hand, and started snapping before the blood faded. This set looked different from the others. I had a sneaking suspicion this was a different language, or maybe some kind of codex.

Midpicture, Rynn tapped me on the shoulder. "Why is it doing that?"

I looked up from my lens. Sure enough, the blood relief was flickering, like a fluorescent light switch about to go out. I'd never seen that before . . . I caught the whiff of what smelled like charred hair.

The lines of the relief ignited where I'd first touched my blood to the wall.

"Run," I said. I grabbed my bag and bolted out of the catacomb, Rynn following closely. We'd only gotten a tunnel away before the explosion knocked me hard on my knees.

The whole cliff shook, showering us with pebbles.

Rynn pulled me off the ground and half dragged me towards the entrance. Another reverberation shook the catacombs as we reached the lower temple room. Rynn caught me before I could fall and pushed me through the shattered door and up the stairs. We both hit the main temple at a run as the entire building rocked again. I heard something crack above me.

"Run faster," Rynn said. We jumped over the tranqued naga and

I skidded to a stop. Both guards were still prone on the floor. Though I highly doubted the purple one was still alive, the tranquilized one was. I thought about trying to help, but Rynn pulled me along.

"No time," he said.

I ignored him and grabbed the tranqued one by the collar. Rynn swore but returned to help me.

Halfway up the steps outside, another tremor rattled the temple. I glimpsed back in time to see one of the Apsara statues topple over and shatter. I winced. So much for not trashing a two-thousand-year-old archaeological heritage site. Benji was going to kill me . . . Maybe he'd buy that it was geological coincidence.

We exited the temple and spilled out into a surprisingly tranquil night sky. We dropped the guard by the entrance gate; the morning shift would find him when they checked in. My good deed was done. I crouched down and stopped to catch my breath. The orange jeep was parked just outside the road gate, about fifty feet away. Kato stood up and waved when he saw us.

I glanced up at Rynn. "So what happens now?" I said.

Rynn removed his padded jacket and pants to reveal a tank top and beach shorts underneath. He frowned at me and glanced back at the now collapsed catacombs. "The IAA made exploding blood reliefs up? You could have gotten us killed!"

I held my hands up. "I'm sorry. I *swear* I've never had one do that before. Ever."

He snorted and stuffed his gear into his bag. Next he was packing up his guns in a surfboard case, of all things. It didn't escape my notice that he jammed one of the smaller guns into the back of his waistband.

"Well?" I said, after an uncomfortable silence. "We can't stay here all night," I added as Rynn glared down at me.

He shook his head again. "We head back into town, try to get an hour or two of sleep, and I'll come with you to Basuki to make sure you don't get yourself, or me, killed." He finished by ruffling his blond hair.

I opened my mouth to argue but thought better of it. I wasn't keen on having backup, but having Rynn with me if I ran into another naga wouldn't be bad.

"It's a little frightening how quickly you go from mercenary to beach bum," I said instead. I wasn't close to having caught my breath yet, but I got up and started towards the orange jeep.

Kato flashed me a big grin as I tossed my bag in. "Hey, lady. You owe me two hundred bucks."

"You said it was a hundred," Rynn said, before I could open my mouth.

The kid smiled. "You want to walk back to town, mister?"

"And what the hell makes you think I have two hundred dollars?" I said.

Kato shrugged. "If you have a hundred bucks, I figure you have two. Not like you have a lot of rides waiting."

I turned on Rynn. "See? This is exactly why you barter. Now he figures he can walk all over us."

Rynn had his back to me, so I grabbed the small tranquilizer gun I'd seen him place in the back belt of his shorts.

As soon as it was in my hand I pointed it right in the kid's face. Kato's confidence deflated as he stared down the barrel. It was my turn to smile. I knew it was a tranquilizer, but the kid didn't. "Kid, I've had a bad night, so here's what's going to happen. You're going to drive us back, I'm going to give you a hundred bucks like he," I said, pointing to Rynn, "promised, and you will never mention this night to anyone. Ever. Otherwise I'm going to shoot you, leave you here, and drive the jeep back myself. Do I make myself clear?"

The kid swallowed. "I was just kidding, lady."

I handed Rynn his gun and hopped in the back. He was shaking his head as he hopped in beside me.

"I can't believe you just pulled a gun in a kid's face," Rynn whispered in my ear.

I shrugged and gave his beach bum outfit a once-over, a new

problem forming in my mind. "We'll need to figure out a way to get you on the dig tomorrow morning."

"No need. I've already got an invite."

"What—How?"

"You'll see," he said. He leaned his head back against the seat rest and closed his eyes.

There was something about his smile I didn't entirely like. I was about to ask for more details, but there was a crash behind us and the ground shook. The outer catacombs were collapsing under the cliffs. I leaned against the back of the driver's seat and tapped the kid on the shoulder. He looked about ready to jump out of the car and run.

"Drive, kid," I said. Without any more prompting, the jeep set off like a bat out of hell down the gravel road and back towards Sanur.

I glanced over at Rynn, who was relaxing. There was something else bothering me. "You lied to me. About why you believed me last year about vampires. You'd run into them before."

He opened his eyes and gave me a measured stare. "I didn't lie. You'd be surprised how often I see a vampire in the bar. I just . . . omitted a few details. Don't tell me you've never omitted a detail or two about your line of work?"

I didn't think I'd ever made that big an omission, but I wasn't ready to bank on it.

I'd be damned if I knew what to do with this new development in our relationship—friendship, that is. I wasn't entirely sure how I was going to get this to gel with the box I'd already slotted him into. As we wound down the hillside, my phone found reception. There were a lot of messages, mostly from Lady Siyu. I started with Nadya.

"Alix?"

"Nadya," I said, fumbling my phone and trying to get my voice to carry over the wind rushing through the open jeep. I hoped she wouldn't be too upset about her surfboard. "Do you want the good news or bad news first?"

7

THE DRAGON CATACOMBS

7:00 a.m., the Basuki Temple, Bali

"Shit!" I jumped up as my coffee seeped through my shirt when the jeep hit another pothole.

Well, there went my caffeine fix. I sighed, finished the last sip, and took my first look at the Besakih Temple.

I'd nodded off for a few minutes—hence the spilled coffee—so I'd missed most of the winding road. My first impression of the temple was all the more striking for my impromptu nap. It looked like something out of a Southeast Asian fairy tale. I let out a low whistle.

Besakih is the oldest and most famous of the Balinese Hindu temples, dating back to the eighth century. Located at the base of Mount Agung—a volcano, if that doesn't provide a few hints—at the north end of the island, it's also known as the "Mother Temple" and is one of Bali's most photographed sites. It really does look like something of a fantasy novel . . . like the palace the evil wizard lives in.

Less known is the fact that the epithet "Mother Temple" didn't come into use until the fourteenth century, when the last great Balinese

Hindu empire, the Majapahit, moved in. For six hundred years before that, the temple was called Basuki, or "Dragon Temple," dedicated to the dragon god, Naga Besukian.

And don't ask me how the hell you get "mother" out of "dragon." Some little old priest's sick, twisted idea of a joke . . . or maybe being sacrificed to the "mother" temple met less resistance than being fed to the "dragon": six-hundred-year-old propaganda.

I tried not to glance at Rynn as the jeep bounced over another pothole on the dirt track.

I hadn't gotten much sleep last night. As soon as Rynn and I had gotten in—and gone our separate ways—I'd had to deal with both Nadya and Lady Siyu on the phone. Nadya had not exactly been thrilled about her surfboard, namely that I'd left it behind. Lady Siyu had been even less impressed with my run-in with the naga. Apparently barging in on another supernatural's territory without going through the proper channels was a no-no in her book.

Oops. I'd glazed over the falling statue and collapsing temple.

Once I'd cleared the Basuki catacombs with her, there'd been a particularly terse message from Carpe Diem, since I'd blown off game time.

By the time I'd finished dealing with the three of them—Carpe and Lady Siyu duking it out for most bitchy—I'd had less than an hour to sleep before getting into the jeep.

Some days you just can't win.

I glanced down at Captain, who was out of my cat carrier backpack and on his leash, curled up under Rynn's feet.

"Traitor," I whispered.

Captain yawned.

Rynn sat beside me in the backseat. The tension between us had been palpable ever since we'd gotten back to the hostel earlier this morning. I was still having trouble with the whole mercenary thing. You think you know someone . . .

Don't get me wrong, I was grateful he'd gotten me out of Sanur.

What really had me pissed off was how he'd managed to get an invite to the Basuki catacombs.

Rynn leaned in close enough to whisper, "You're ignoring me. Why?"

I didn't miss the irritated edge in his voice. "I'm looking out the window so I can see where we're going," I whispered back.

"What are you mad about?"

I turned and ended up staring right into Rynn's blue eyes. OK, I'd try honesty. "I just can't believe you snuck into the camp picking up one of the dig girls."

There. I'd said it. I'd been honest.

He frowned. "It's not like I had a lot of options. You refused to answer my messages, I couldn't track your cell phone, and Nadya didn't exactly have an explicit itinerary of your activities."

"OK, noted," I said. I nodded at the California blonde with her hair in surfer braids sitting beside the redheaded driver, Mark, from the hostel. I'd taken to calling him Red. "But her?" Bindi. A name that comically fit the hippie girl image.

Rynn shrugged. "I was short on time," he said and leaned back, folding his hands behind his head. "Besides, she's cute."

"She's an *idiot.*"

"Good thing I don't plan on having any long, drawn-out conversations with her."

I sat back. What the hell was I supposed to say? "I can't believe that was the best idea you could come up with."

He threw me a half smile. "Never pegged you as the jealous type."

I glared. Rynn laughed.

"I still can't believe you were a mercenary."

"And I already told you I'm retired. This is a special favor. For Oricho."

"Great. Good to know Oricho is paying you well enough to pick up university students and babysit me."

His brow furrowed. "I said favor, not job. You know, for a thief you have one hell of a judgmental streak."

I was about to comment on Rynn's general level of sincerity in dealing with women when Captain got up and started straining to get his nose in the wind. I swear that cat is three-quarters dog.

Bindi turned around in the front seat and gave Captain a once-over.

"I've never seen a cat on a leash before," she said. I got the distinct impression she didn't like cats. Or maybe it was just Captain. He has that effect on some people. It's never fun coming face-to-face with a house pet who's smarter than you.

Bindi flashed both Rynn and me a big smile, but she lingered on Rynn. I forced back a cheerful smile. "Derrick" (aka Rynn) and I were supposed to be complete strangers.

"Charity, Derrick, we're almost there, but we're about to hit a rough patch of road. I'd put your shades on if you have them." She winked at Rynn, and I caught him winking right back. My notice didn't go unnoticed either.

"Role playing," he mouthed at me.

I shook my head. He was pissing me off on purpose and enjoying it way too much. "I know exactly what you're doing. You're manipulating me. It's not working."

"Funny, from here it looks like it's working spectacularly." He winked and pulled his sunglasses down. "What can I say? I play to my strengths. I'm flattered you're this jealous. I didn't think you had it in you."

Goddamn it. I switched topics. "So, Kuto at night, all by yourself. I'm impressed. I'm not that brave."

A whisper of a frown crossed his face. "What exactly is that supposed to mean?"

It was my turn to frown. "I mean Kuto is a supernatural hot spot. There are more succubi and incubi per square inch than there are in Ibiza."

He faced me and lifted the mirrored aviators. "Really? I hadn't noticed."

"Whether you noticed or not, Kuto's crawling with them. Count yourself lucky you didn't run into any."

"I'll have to keep that in mind next time," he said offhandedly. He was silent for a moment. "You ever run into one?"

"Hmm?"

"Succubi and incubi. Have you ever run into one?"

I shook my head. "Nope. Vampires, dragons, naga, mummies, werewolves, whatever the hell Oricho and Lady Siyu are, vampires—"

"You said vampires twice."

"That's because it bears mentioning twice. Vampires are the supernatural cockroach." I paused before asking, "Have you ever run into one?"

"Vampires? Who hasn't? You said it, they're like cockroaches."

"No, succubi or incubi."

Rynn shrugged. I couldn't see his eyes behind his mirrored aviators. "Once or twice."

I sat up a little straighter. "Well?"

"Well what?"

"Well, what happened?"

He shrugged. "There's not much to tell."

"Rynn! You can't just tell me you've run into them and hold all the details."

He shrugged again, his face unreadable. "Didn't strike me as particularly dangerous."

I snorted. "Yeah, and that naga just wanted to say hi."

I could see the lines forming in Rynn's forehead. I'd said something that had gotten under his skin. Good, it was about time the tables were turned. He'd had me unsettled since our reunion in Tokyo.

He turned towards me, his mouth set in a terse line. "For someone who supposedly hates the supernatural, you do an awful lot of business with them. And ask a lot of questions."

"It's not my fault every supernatural creature I've ever run into has either tried to kill me or threatened to do so if I don't hop, skip, and jump for them. What's not to hate? You can't blame me for trying to be prepared."

Rynn shook his head. "I just think you dismiss your choices as necessity a little too haphazardly." And with that he changed topics. "So what's the plan once we're on site? Oricho didn't give me many details besides 'expect vampires' and 'try to dissuade her from anything that might get her killed.'"

No doubt Oricho used those exact words. "There's a second tablet like the one we saw last night in Sanur. I'm guessing there are a few layers of inscription in the room as well. I'll need a few minutes to transcribe. The two students who worked on the tablets are convinced I need both to get a working codex—a translation." I hoped there might be some mention of this scroll's theft from the emperor's tomb or hint as to what it did. It was a long shot, but it was the only trace of the same language written on the egg that I'd found.

"I hope you don't plan on repeating that explosion. One cave-in is enough for one day," Rynn said.

I shook my head and opened my bag, exposing the hairspray bottle full of chicken blood. "I did some checking. Bad idea to use human blood on those ancient diagrams. Learn something new every day."

Rynn snorted. I pictured him rolling his eyes behind the aviators.

"So . . ." I started, not entirely sure how best to broach the subject. "How do you know Oricho? And what is—"

Rynn grabbed the headrest of the seat in front of him and stood up. "Nope. Oricho will kill me," he said.

Before I could add anything else, Rynn hopped into the front of the jeep right beside Bindi. He wrapped his arm around her shoulder and whispered something that had her giggling like an idiot.

He raised a blond eyebrow and smiled back at me.

I shook my head. He wasn't impressing me this morning.

I watched the road and kept an eye out for the temple. I was here to work, and there was no way I'd let Rynn get to me on a job.

Choices with the supernatural. Hah, like I had any. Roll over and die is not a choice.

Bindi hopped out of the front seat as Mark the redheaded American from the hostel pulled it to a stop. He was looking worse for wear this morning after my beer cocktail. Bindi was one of those girls who'd mastered talking to two people when she was really only talking to one, i.e. Rynn. She went right into "bestest little surfer girl tour guide mode." A big part of me was pissed, but if Rynn kept up the distraction, I might have an easier time "getting lost" once we were in the tunnels.

I noticed Red head off towards the temple proper. He'd been quiet the whole way over. I wouldn't have talked much either if I'd been navigating the potholes hungover.

"Aren't you coming?" I asked him.

He shook his head and tossed his dig pack over his shoulder. "Naw, I've got work to do. Besides, I don't think I want to watch Bindi hit on that blond guy for the next few hours."

"Yeah, join the club."

He laughed. "Be glad you don't live with her." As an afterthought, said, "Benji didn't say much about how he knew you."

OK, Red wasn't as dumb as he looked. I smiled my best sweet-girl smile. "I helped him out with some data analysis a while ago. We've kept in touch."

He watched me as if not quite able to decide what box to stick me in. "Benji never struck me as someone who needed help with data analysis."

I smiled wider. "I'm better with ancient forensics. He was having trouble with cause of death of a few Chilean mummies."

"What was cause of death?"

"Decapitation by ritual axe," I said as cheerfully as if I'd been reciting a cookie recipe.

Red looked like he was about to say something else, then shook his head. Smart move. Trust me, he didn't want to know the real details.

"Look, I'm hungover and I've got to finish my excavation by the end of the week or my supervisor will have my hide. Benji said you were interested in catacomb inscriptions, yes?"

I nodded.

He motioned for my copy of the "official" dig map—without the newer side tunnels. He drew a handful of lines off the main tunnel with a red marker. "Bindi is planning on taking you guys down this main run. You want my advice? Take the third catacomb to the left, not one of the other ones. We don't have them mapped out yet, and the ceilings aren't stable—not by a long shot." He marked a spot farther down the third hand-drawn tributary. "About five hundred meters down it forks—don't go any farther. Both those tunnels get too close to the lava. A lot of water runoff comes back through fissures as steam. Trust me when I say it's scalding. Instead, head up into this side tunnel."

"Hey, Charity?" Bindi yelled.

I glanced back over my shoulder. She and Rynn were halfway up the hill.

Red nodded to me, slid his baseball cap on, and started heading up towards the temple. "Check out the side tunnel," he said.

I threw Red a smile and caught up to Bindi and Rynn in time to catch the tail end of her history lesson.

". . . archaeologists who uncovered the catacombs five years ago called them the Basuki, or dragon, catacombs for two reasons. One, they run under a volcano, and two, in a lava-sealed chamber they found a hoard of treasure."

I had to stop myself from rolling my eyes at her high-pitched voice. If she hadn't figured out by now it was a dragon lair, I had a lovely bridge to sell her. She could put a little toll booth on it and everything. Where was the IAA finding these idiots?

I feigned interest as Bindi looked me over. I didn't have to pretend for very long, since she focused right back on Rynn.

Ever get the feeling someone is going through the motions pretending you're a person?

As far as I could see, Rynn hadn't done a thing today except flirt. He was supposed to be helping me find the tablet, not making a date.

Between keeping an eye out for the tunnel and an eye on Rynn and Bindi, I tripped over a groove in the tiled floor and stumbled, almost falling flat on my face.

Bindi glanced back at me. "You really need to watch where you're going in here. Try to keep your eyes on the floor."

Rynn snickered.

I frowned. That was it. Time to forcefully insert myself into the conversation.

"So Bindi, what happened to all that treasure?" I asked.

Bindi looked surprised, as if it hadn't occurred to her that my mouth might move and sound might come out. "I'm not sure. My guess is the local museum—the Balinese are big on keeping their national treasures in Bali nowadays."

Hmmm . . . really . . . now that *was* interesting.

Rynn must have caught the look on my face, because he shook his head and mouthed, "*No*" at me.

I rolled my eyes and shrugged back. Yeah, yeah—I was here for inscriptions, not treasure. I had bigger issues on my mind, like how to exit Bindi's tour. I kept my eyes out for the tunnel entrances Red had described.

"These carved images over here are meant as a ceremonial instruction to people who worshiped Naga Basukian. Explaining the kinds of worship through the seasons . . ."

I had to stop myself from snickering. It was an instructional all right, on how to pick whom to feed next to the mountain dragon. Even a third-year archaeology student would know that.

"And these over here—" Bindi's phone went off, and she checked the screen. "Excuse me," she said. "I've got to take this." And with that she ducked off into a side tunnel a little ahead. Leaving Rynn and me alone.

Rynn didn't miss a beat. "You aren't here to steal national treasures."

"It doesn't hurt to ask. Besides, if I'm lucky, I'll finish early."

Rynn frowned and crossed his arms. "As soon as we finish, I'm throwing you back on a plane for Tokyo."

"You'll have to catch me first," I said, only half joking.

Rynn moved faster than I could react. His arm wrapped my neck in a rear naked choke and he lifted me off the ground as I kicked out.

"Rynn, knock it off!"

He put me down, still wearing a dark, pissed-off look on his face. "Mercenary, remember?" he said.

I regained my footing. It hadn't hurt—unless you counted my pride. "Yeah, fine, no stealing from the Balinese Museum. Got it. When the hell did you grow a conscience? And what the hell was that for?" I said, pointing to my throat.

Rynn propped his hand against the wall and leaned over me. "I like you, Owl. A lot. That doesn't mean I'm stupid. I don't like what you do for a living, and I don't plan on helping you while I'm here. You can come back to Bali on your own time, not mine and Oricho's."

I snorted. I couldn't help it. "You're one to talk." I nodded in Bindi's direction. "What? Thieves like me are bad guys, but leading on girls like her is totally in your green zone? You're supposed to distract her so I can sneak off and find the tablet, not pick her up."

Rynn's frown deepened. It struck me that this was a new pattern in our conversations. Pissing each other off. "Is that what you think? You don't know anything about her. If you'd done any research, you'd know she picks up a different surfer every weekend in Kuto. I'm just another notch on her glorified surfboard to write home about."

I was wading into sore territory. I should have stopped, but I didn't. Instead I threw up my hands. "So what? This is a job, so that makes sleeping with her OK? I wonder why I'm even surprised. You're already halfway to being a whore back in Tokyo." I couldn't keep the spite out of my voice. It surprised even me. As soon as I said it, I knew I'd gone too far. Way too far.

Rynn's face twisted in a pained expression, and he leaned in until he was an inch away from my face. "I'm not here on a job. I'm here because after talking to Oricho I was worried you were in over your head—and you *are*. And for your information, I didn't sleep with her. If I'd slept with her, she'd have gotten rid of me already. I'm putting up with her idiotic advances because the idea of you being killed by your own stupidity and recklessness would be worse." He spread his hands out and gave me a mock bow. "But at least now I know what you really think of me."

I stood there, stunned. I didn't know what to say. Hell, I didn't know what I felt. Mostly I couldn't believe I'd just called Rynn a whore. That was low, even for me. I'm an international thief, for Christ's sake. Who the hell am I to be judging what people do for a living?

I closed my eyes. "Look, I'm sorry. I didn't mean that—"

"Which part? That I'm a glorified whore serving drinks, or I have no conscience?" Rynn was good at hiding his emotions, but I'd hurt him. A cold lump formed in my stomach. One of two people in this world I trusted and cared about, and I couldn't go two days without saying something horrible to him, all because of a little jealousy. Damn it.

I took a deep breath and tried again. "I'm sorry. I didn't mean it. I don't think that of you . . ."

There'd been a grain of truth in there, and Rynn knew it. What should I have said? That I cared about him and that fact bothered me more than I wanted to admit? That I was a little unnerved and scared that he cared enough to chase me into Bali?

Even one of those would have helped. Instead I feigned pushing my hair out of my face so I could look away. "Rynn, what can I say? I'm sorry. How often do you want me to say it?"

Lame, I know, but I've said it before and I'll say it again: I'm not good with people.

He just stared at me. "Save it. Or at least try meaning it." He nodded at Bindi. "Go get your tablet inscriptions. I'll keep her distracted."

"I really didn't meant it—"

He was almost to the room. "Funny, from here it sounds like you said *exactly* what you meant." And without another glance at me, he stormed off after Bindi.

Captain, who'd been cleaning himself while we'd argued, glanced up at me and meowed.

"Yeah, that was an all-time low for me." I felt sick to my stomach, worse than when I'd been thrown out of grad school, and that is my all-time low benchmark.

I hoisted my pack and jogged towards the tunnel, Captain on my heels.

"I wouldn't be surprised if he stayed mad at me either this time."

------⟋⟍------

I jogged past the first and second tunnels in my rush to reach the third catacomb entrance Red had marked on my map.

Why run? Always good policy to save time when you can; never know when you'll need it later.

The tunnel made a sharp right turn. The air turned heavy, with a musty, metallic taste. I wondered what could have caused it when I skidded on slick rock, almost falling on Captain. I did a quick check of the walls and ceilings with my flashlight. Thin trickles of water reflected the light back, making the wall look like it was covered in zebra stripes. I ran my fingers along the matte black. It was malleable and crumbled off with a bit of applied pressure, confirming my suspicion. The entire tunnel was dug through porous volcanic rock. Would have been nice if Red had mentioned just how much water was in here.

"The good news, Captain, is an explosion and cave-in probably won't kill us. The bad news is it's gonna get wet."

The puddles deepened as we continued. Captain kept his nose to the wind and took his time finding the driest spots to jump between. Better than watching a cat on a hot tin roof.

About twenty meters in, the tunnel walls smoothed out and the first pictograph relief came into view.

One thing about the supernatural is that it never ceases to surprise me. I guess if I was desperate for a positive thing to say about the supernatural, that might count. The relief was painted in white—maybe a faded light blue, but with my flashlight I couldn't tell for sure. It depicted a dragon rising out of the ocean in a crested wave towards a circle of nagas holding a sacrifice—read: victim.

A water dragon in a volcano. Well, that explained all the damn water.

I followed the pictographs with my flashlight, keeping my eye out for any hints of booby traps, ancient pits, pressurized hydrochloric acid, as well as the fork Red had mentioned. With the uneven flooring in the dark, a fork would be easy to miss.

Besides the usual "Beware, trespassing in dragon's home," there wasn't anything that jumped out. Why wasn't I worried about running into a dragon? Since the archaeologists who found the tunnel aren't dead, I'm betting dragon Naga Besukian is long gone . . . or dead. I prefer to think it moved out; however, I didn't favor the thought of stumbling into something that could kill a dragon in a narrow passageway.

Out of nowhere, Captain laid back his ears and hissed. I swung my flashlight around as the scent of fermenting lily of the valley hit me.

Vampire.

Sabine? How the hell had she found me so fast?

I dropped my backpack and dug out my gas mask, the kind that heavy-duty painters use and makes you sound like Darth Vader.

I fastened the catch around my head and checked the seal, when the hackles on Captain's back shot up and his warning growl morphed into a battle howl.

"Captain! Stay—" I whispered as loud as I dared and reached out to grab him before he did something stupid.

But he darted down the tunnel before I could grab hold of his red harness. I checked my phone to see if I could get a message off to Rynn or Nadya. No reception again. Talk about déjà vu.

I powered on my UV flashlight and pulled out a squirt gun filled with garlic water. Why do I always carry a squirt gun filled with garlic water? Because I'm paranoid.

I don't carry stakes for the same reason I don't play with guns. Unless you happen to be Buffy the Vampire Slayer—and if you think you are, I strongly suggest you get help—chances are very good the vampire will take said stake and ram it through *your* heart. I hear they get very touchy around people who carry stakes.

Captain yowled up ahead—the sound cats make when another cat makes the mistake of crossing into their territory. I shoved the squirt gun into my pants and flipped my UV flashlight onto flood before running after him.

The tunnel made a series of S turns. As soon as I caught sight of Captain's flicking tail, it disappeared around the corner ahead of me.

Shit, he was going to get us killed.

Captain was in hunt mode and well past listening. I swore and sped up. I should never have let him off his leash; if he got hurt, it was going to be my fault.

Egyptian Mau cats are bred to smell vampires, which makes for a fantastic warning system. Unfortunately they've also been hardwired to hunt them, and once they pick up the scent, it's next to impossible to get one to stop and think. What worried me was that they'd been bred to hunt in packs, not take them head-on like Captain was trying to do.

The tunnel straightened out and my flashlight picked up the fork. Captain had stopped, his nose in the air, trying to pick the scent back up. There was also an opening in the ceiling, roughly five meters off the floor, reminiscent of the naga burrows in Sanur. I skidded to a halt and pressed myself against the wall.

"Captain," I whispered.

But he'd picked up the scent again and didn't give me a second glance as he leapt up the wall like a mountain goat and shot through the opening. His growls echoed in the chamber above.

I readied my squirt gun and waited. Nothing moved up ahead,

so I continued on until I was a few feet away from the naga burrow. I half expected Sabine to drop down any second. A little closer, a little closer . . .

A sharp shriek that could only be from Captain echoed through the catacombs above, about ten feet away, I'd guess.

I tried not to breathe—mostly because of the raspy sound the mask makes—as I aimed the flashlight up where Captain had disappeared. Still no Sabine. I stepped into a foothold and pushed myself up, edging the flashlight around. The burrows were only wide enough to crawl through. Great for a cat, but not me.

I slid down and crept along the right fork, where Red had indicated the tablet was. It was also where I'd heard Captain howl. Sabine must have gotten there ahead of me and laid a trap. Well, she clearly didn't know me very well, because she was about to get one hell of a garlic UV surprise . . .

It was a dead end. And there was no sign of the tablet. And where the hell was she?

Something hard and heavy slugged into my left calf, more than enough to knock me off my feet. I grabbed at the wall, but it was too slippery to get a grip. I landed on my ass in a puddle, my flashlight rolling out of reach. Rough hands reached under my arms and pulled me up. A man holding a baseball bat and wearing an expensive suit and even more expensive leather shoes stepped out from a hidden alcove and retrieved my flashlight as if it were a distasteful piece of trash.

I swallowed at the sight of his shoes. These were vampires all right . . . and far too familiar to be Sabine's. The one holding me under my arms half carried/half dragged me down the left fork—the one Red had warned me about. A shove sent me stumbling into a side cavern. Another shove from behind forced me to my knees. Trying not to fall flat on my face, I scrambled to the far wall as fast as I could in order to put as much distance between me and the vampires as possible. My efforts only brought on laughter. In spite of the situation, that pissed me off. I pushed my back against the wall and slid my hand to where my water gun was. Laugh it up, boys, just makes it funnier when I soak you in garlic.

There are a few misconceptions about vampires. Whenever people think vampire, they think of some superstrong, enigmatic, romantic, gorgeous monster that drinks blood and only wants to fall madly and tragically in love with the first pretty high school girl who swoons their way. Sunlight, garlic, holy water, and wooden stakes burn them up into a pile of ash. A more accurate image is a moth careening into a flaming blowtorch. Vampires are the blowtorch. They aren't nearly as susceptible to light and garlic, but I'll get to that in a sec.

Another vampire approached from the side, wearing the same expensive shoes, his face hidden in the shadows. It dawned on me that they were fencing me in. He crouched down in front of me, his face peeking out from underneath shoulder-length brown hair. Alexander smiled as I recognized him, and two tiny fangs peeked out. He still didn't look a day over twenty. He was still beautiful, except for the thin scar that ran from just under his eye to the corner of his mouth. Alexander grabbed the front of my gas mask as a handle so he could tilt my head back.

Meet the Paris boys, vampire Eurotrash extraordinaire at its finest. Alexander was the ringleader and my least favorite of the bunch.

I stayed where I was and checked the cave out of the corner of my eye. There were three vampires, two guarding the exit and Alexander.

The third vampire stepped into view and said something in French to Alexander. I noticed the scratches down the side of his face and the shredded front of his suit, then caught my breath. He was dragging Captain's limp body behind him like a spoiled brat drags a stuffed toy he doesn't care about. I straightened and had to stop myself from pulling my water pistol out right then and there. If I wanted to get us out alive—*if* Captain was still alive—I had to wait for my best chance.

Alexander smiled, showing off his incisors again. Most people miss them completely; the supposed size of vampire fangs is overblown, one of those bigger-is-better things . . .

Alexander was all smiles for me today. I smiled back through my mask and did my best not to look at Captain. Why the hell hadn't I kept him on the leash? I knew exactly why; my guard had been down because Rynn was here with me. I hadn't been thinking in survival mode, and it had cost me.

"So kind of you to join us today, Owl," he said with the slightest trace of French accent.

"Go fuck yourself. We've got a truce."

The smile on his face faltered for a second before turning vicious. He pressed his face up against my mask. "That's only a problem if we are caught—and if they find your body."

I refused to look him in the eye. He unclipped my gas mask, and I took the last clean breath I'd get. I made it a good one and held it as my mask was pulled off.

"Though I think it will be much more fun to turn you into my next lapdog. Hmm? How do you like that, Owl? Clip your wings, so to speak?"

I kept holding my breath and glared at him. Come on, Alexander, look away at one of your stupid cronies, just for one second, that's all I need . . .

He did it. He couldn't resist the audience. Thank God I knew Alexander.

I spit in his face and, when he looked back, unloaded my water pistol in his eyes. It feels good to watch a good-looking vampire scream as his face has one hell of an allergic reaction. He grabbed his eyes, dropping my gas mask in the process. I slid it back on and set my sights on the two remaining and very surprised vampires.

Vampires really are like cockroaches. Bug sprays are supposed to work, but in reality they're just mildly irritating and piss them off. Same with garlic, holy water, and sunlight on vampires. Sunlight only has the cool vaporizing effect on the really old ones. In reality, they're little more than glorified thugs that drink blood and excrete that lily of the valley narcoticlike pheromone. They aren't even that pretty or strong—it's the pheromone talking, a potent aromatic that hits you with euphoria akin to heroin and weakens you everywhere so you can't lift a finger to resist. They heal a bit better than we do, but a stake through the heart works as well on vampires as it does on people. So does an AK-47. The old ones get powerful, but they also have to deal with the spontaneous combustion thing. I know; I've seen it firsthand. The point is the garlic wouldn't down Alexander for long, so I had to move fast.

Next on my radar was "Vampire stupid enough to hurt my cat." I unloaded the rest of the water gun into his face, grabbed Captain— still warm, which was a good sign—and tried for my pack. But the vampire who'd been holding Captain was down, not out. He growled something in French and held onto my pack for dear life. I cut my losses and grabbed my UV flashlight by his feet, turning it on Euro-trash vampire #3. He didn't go up in flames, but he screamed as I gave him second- and third-degree burns. As soon as he huddled in a fetal position to escape the light, I bolted down the fork.

And slammed right into Red's six-foot frame.

"Kid, run, run now," I said, recovering from the impact.

He smiled but didn't make a move.

A sick feeling hit my stomach. Red had set it up from the start. I shook my head and took a step back. I only had a minute tops before the vampires were back on their feet.

"Out of my way, kid. I don't want to hurt you."

"Or what? You'll shoot me? With your water gun?" To make his point, he swung his dig pickax at my head. I ducked and felt the air stir above as it bit into the wall.

I took another step back, my precious escape window disappearing. Then I remembered Captain concentrating on scent in the jeep: vampire traces, of course.

"You don't want me on your bad side, and you've got no idea what those people are capable of doing. I do. Out of my way and we can both walk out."

Red just smiled wider and shook his head. I could hear the vampires regrouping behind me. I'm lousy with French, but the words I recognized were not indicative of happy captors. Maybe I could knock Red over. Captain stirred and I folded him into my jacket. I made ready to rush Red. Better the pickax than the vampires.

I faked to either side, and just as Red spaced his legs apart to stop me ducking around him, I kicked up. Really, really hard.

I hopped over him and broke into a full-out run. I didn't know where this tunnel led, but if I could get ahead, even without my backpack, I was better off in here and better equipped . . .

I sailed a foot into the air as I tripped over the trip wire and landed on all fours. At least I didn't crush Captain. The wind knocked out of me; it took me a second to stand.

That was all the vampires needed. Before I could get back into a sprint, I heard a growl and was yanked back by my jacket collar.

Funny thing, even though technically I'm a criminal, I've never actually been in a fight before. In my life. I've always run—*really* fast and *really* far.

Physical altercations are something I've always dreaded. I get roughed up occasionally, it goes with the job, but I've always managed to make myself scarce by the time people start throwing punches or firing guns.

It was worse than I imagined.

Someone delivered a boot to my head and my mask went flying. Two thoughts ran through my head as I passed out. The first was to cover my mouth with my hand to cut down on the pheromones I'd breathe in. Not useful if I'm passing out. The second was that I'd been so mad at Rynn that I hadn't bothered setting up a meeting time or plan if I didn't show up. I had no way to warn him about the vampires . . . Shit.

And this is why I don't let people come on jobs with me.

8

COCKROACHES, VAMPIRES, AND OTHER ASSORTED PESTS

My face was wet, and I hurt.

Everywhere.

And it smelled like flowers that had been rotting in a pond for a few days. . . .

Bali, the catacombs, vampires—everything flooded back to me like a bad hangover. I lifted my face out of the puddle and groaned. Even with my eyes closed, the world was spinning. I barely had enough strength to hold my head up.

I coughed, and someone prodded me with a sharp stick. Captain wasn't tucked into my jacket anymore, and a wave of panic hit me. I hoped they hadn't killed him; vampires like Alexander don't kill things mercifully. I had to know, so I forced my eyes open and batted the stick away.

My hand connected with it, and a chill crept over me. A wooden stake. Shit.

"I remember hearing that you assholes had a thing for stakes. What, vampire S&M?" I said.

Laughter.

Well, if I kept entertaining them, maybe they'd keep me alive long enough to figure something the hell out.

I propped myself up on my forearms and gritted my teeth through a wave of nausea. My arms wouldn't hold me up and I fell right back down, face-first, into the puddle.

More laughter.

I started to drift off again, and I forced myself to snap out of it and stay awake. When they'd knocked me out, they must have given me a concussion. Not good. No more drifting off. I had to stay awake, or I might not get up ever again.

Alexander's expensive leather shoe moved into my line of vision. I noticed it came as close as it could without touching the puddle, followed by Alexander crouching down. I made eye contact, and a flicker of euphoria washed over me. Shit, that meant I'd been breathing in the pheromones for at least half an hour—maybe more. Well, it explained why I was so weak and sick.

I hoped to hell Rynn had started looking for me.

One of Alexander's goons grabbed my wrists and pinned them behind my back, *tight*. There was no sign of my water gun or backpack. One thing I've got to give Alexander is that he learns.

Alexander leaned in close enough that I could smell the blood on his breath, like raw ground beef left on the counter for a few hours. I cringed. From the smile and peek of fang, I think Alexander got off on it.

"Alexander," I managed, holding my breath. "Why don't you come a little closer so I can puke on your shoes?" Oh God, I hoped to hell he stopped breathing on me soon.

"Owl," he said, giving me a little more glimpse of fang. "Fancy meeting you here."

"Go fuck yourself," I said as another rotten lily wave hit me. Yup, that's me with a concussion and high on vampire pheromones. Eloquent.

Alexander just smiled and adjusted his angle so he could get a better look at me without getting mud on his suit. I wished I had something in my stomach so I *could* puke on his shoes.

He took a cell phone out of his pocket—my cell phone.

"Exactly who is this Rynn person? He keeps messaging you. Should we go after him next?"

I kept my mouth shut. If he didn't know Rynn was in the tunnels with Bindi, I sure as hell wasn't going to enlighten them.

Alexander continued. "Every time I see a message come in, I wonder to myself, 'What would the great Owl say in reply?' Shall I be coy? Offensive? Or 'smart-alecky,' I believe you Americans like to say."

Something must have passed over my face, because Alexander smiled and nodded. "Yes, I think offensive is more your style, is it not?"

He started to click at the tiny keypad and recited each word back to me. " '*I'm still busy. Go to hell. I will let you know when I'm done.*' Yes? Does that sound enough like you? I would hate to misrepresent you in your own personal dealings." The smile turned sinister. "Now let's get down to business, shall we? Maybe then I won't need to hunt down every one of your friends, so conveniently listed in your device."

The way his goon held me, all I could see was Alexander. Vampires have a talent for staging if nothing else.

Alexander stood, and the lily of the valley hit me like a wave; part chloroform and part elation. With enough exposure, the pheromones that vampires excrete from their skin can be more addictive than heroin. I nuzzled my mouth and nose into my shirt collar so I'd have a marginal filter at least. I needed to fix a lock on my gas mask straps.

I didn't trust myself to say anything coherent, so I spit where it would hurt him. On his shoes. Alexander wiped it off on the front of my jacket and backhanded me.

"Always such a pleasant young lady. Now, why don't you tell me what you are here looking for?"

I shook my head, twice, I think, but it could have been more.

"None of your fucking business," I said . . . I think. I was still trying to get a grip on the way his words warped into my brain. I closed my eyes and pushed them away, concentrating on my bruises, the wet ground, and the bloody meat breath that was still there.

"I'll decide what is and isn't my business. What is so important that the dragon bartered you away from us? My employer is very curious to know this," he said.

Even through the euphoria—for obvious reasons I've spent the last year building up a resistance—I noted the "employer." Not "we," not "the council," but his "employer."

I looked through the haze that was my head. "Who the fuck are you working for now, Alexander?"

"Why, I'm loyal to the Paris Contingency, of course."

"Bullshit." I took a gamble. "When did you jump ship to work for Sabine?"

Alexander stood, laughing, as if I'd made a joke.

" 'Jumped ship.' You Americans have a way of making everything sound so crass. I've made a new friend is all. You might want to try it sometime," he said, and kicked me. "It might keep you from ending up in situations like this."

It was my turn to laugh. "When the Contingency finds out you broke their treaty with a red dragon, I somehow doubt your new friend is going to be much help—"

He sneered, but his eyes told me I'd spooked him. He was scared of Sabine, whoever the hell she was. Whether *of* her or that she'd hang him out to dry, I wasn't sure.

"You assume they will find out. But enough talk about me, let us talk about you. Apparently you are still not ready to cooperate. That makes me sad, as we must now come up with another way to persuade you."

I winced as a stake dug into the side of my lower back.

"I hear humans are quite fond of their kidneys. I've also heard they are quite the delicacy. Shall we try out those theories?"

I bit down on my lower lip, hard, but didn't make a sound. As soon as I told Alexander what he wanted to know, he'd kill me . . . or worse.

The tip of the stake dug in further and broke the skin. I yelled.

"No, Owl? Still not willing to chat? What else can I do to loosen your tongue, hmmm?" Alexander held up his hand in mockery of an epiphany. "Wait, I have an idea."

The pressure on my upper back eased slightly as the stake was lifted. Alexander flicked his hand. The vampire holding me dropped my bound hands and grabbed my neck like a vise so I couldn't turn my head.

A new vampire—that made four in total now, this one looking even younger than Alexander—stepped in front of me. My heart jumped up in my throat.

He held a struggling, fully awake and bound Captain. They'd pried open his mouth and gagged him with a medieval-looking bit and ball. With his paws trussed up, he looked like a pig at Christmas. Captain was doing his damn best to get free, but it was no use. With the vampire pheromones coursing through me, I couldn't stop myself from crying out.

Alexander placed a hand on Captain's head. "I remembered this cat from the last time I had the pleasure of your company in Egypt, but when he did this . . ." Alexander stroked the thin scar that ran the length of his cheek from under his eye to his mouth. " . . . small inconvenience, I did not think of him as much more than a nuisance. Imagine my surprise when the scratch did not heal." I couldn't do anything but watch as Alexander's grip tightened around Captain's neck.

"Even more so when one of my superiors told me, 'But of course, Alexander! The Egyptians bred Mau cats to hunt us like animals. They attack on sight! Their claws are full of venom.' " Alexander's smile turned into a sneer. "I am so disappointed you would be so cruel as to sic him on me, little bird."

Actually, that had been luck . . . and complete coincidence. Captain had just happened to be crawling around the same tomb as me when Alexander had caught up. Captain had attacked Alexander on sight and bought both of us time to get out. I'd taken Captain with me, reasoning that any animal with that much of a grudge against vampires deserved better than starved mice for dinner.

"You can imagine my excitement when I found an attic full of contraptions, like this one, all to deal with this particular breed." He tightened a strap, and the ball wedged further into my cat's mouth.

I lost it. "You son of a bitch, I swear to God, Alexander, I'm going to wring your scrawny vampire neck and feed you in pieces to my cat—"

"Tell me what I want to know and maybe I'll only kill you and let your cat go." He'd been playing the gentleman, but he dropped the act now and just looked like his vicious self.

The goon holding me gave me a shove. I landed on my side and, while they were laughing, noted something cold and cylindrical against my ankle.

They'd missed my UV laser pointer hidden in the cuff of my boot.

Adrenaline picking up and overriding some of the pheromones, I slid my bound hands into the cuff while I pushed myself back up onto my knees and palmed it into my sleeves. All I had to do now was get out of the rope. Not as hard as you think—big wrists, small hands. I just had to buy some time.

I nodded at the vampire holding Captain by the scruff of his neck as I worked the ropes. "Let the damn cat go and I'll tell you everything you want to know, including what Mr. Kurosawa has me after."

He smiled. "Tell me first and you have my word I'll let it go."

I stopped myself from snorting. Yeah right. Alexander would "let" Captain go, and then proceed to shoot him. Then turn me into a vampire junkie like Sabine's poor flunkie who'd been killed back at the Japanese Circus.

Anyways, I didn't plan on telling Alexander anything. Even dead I had a reputation to maintain.

One of my hands slipped the ropes. As soon as it did, I aimed the UV laser right at his face.

Shock, then pain shot across it as he screamed and clutched his eye. It wouldn't kill him, probably wouldn't even blind him, but man, would it hurt like a son of a bitch for the next few days. Miraculously, the other two vampires didn't hit me. I think they were too shocked I'd managed to cause yet another problem.

No one ever accused vampires of being smart.

While Alexander rolled on the floor clutching his eyes, I hit the three remaining vampires in the face, making sure to give the one holding Captain a third-degree burn. That one shrieked as he dropped my cat.

I scrambled up onto all fours. It hurt, but I did it. I was weak and had trouble seeing straight, but I reached Captain before any of the vampires got up. I didn't know how long it would take before the pheromones were out of my system, but I could still make a run for it.

There were two exits to the cave, each leading in the opposite direction. Damn it, I kind of wished I'd stayed conscious for the trip down. I opted for the nearest—and the one that didn't involve going around the downed vampires.

I couldn't run yet, but I stumbled away as fast as I could. If the vampires caught up to us, I had no illusions about my chances of surviving a third encounter.

I almost tripped in a puddle as the catacomb tunnel wound like a snake downward. I couldn't remember seeing a section like this on my way in or on my map. Alexander had dragged me into the unmapped tunnels. I just hoped I was headed out and not headed deeper into the mountain. I swore as I slammed into a wall, and I cursed myself for not hiding a better flashlight than my penlight; in fact, my night-vision glasses would have been damn useful right about now. If I got out of here alive, I was sewing a pair in my jacket lining.

Five, maybe ten minutes later, I needed to catch my breath—and take a look at Captain. Up ahead was dim light. I slowed down and felt where I placed each footstep, careful not to disturb any rocks. As I neared the lit area, I relaxed. It was sunlight filtering in from the catacombs above. I ducked into an alcove and surveyed Captain's limp body for damage.

I drew in a sharp breath. It was worse than I'd expected, and mentally I'd readied myself for pretty bad. First I undid the headgear, careful not to rub the small, pinlike spikes in any more than Alexander and his goons already had. As I cleaned him up, my emotions spun like a pinwheel in a windstorm: fear, sadness, anger. Anger was so good, I kept spinning back to that one.

What kind of sick bastard designs a torture device for a cat? I mean, I know vampires are sadistic, but even for Alexander this was pushing it. My heart dropped a little as I found two spots of red-stained fur on Captain's back where one of the vampires had bitten him. Captain opened his eyes and tried to twist around. I wiped away my tears— they sure as hell wouldn't help—and zipped him into my jacket.

"I should have given him more than third-degree burns," I said when Captain mewed at me.

I pulled my thoughts off the vampires and studied the network of tunnels overhead. They went a long way up and resembled an uneven spiderweb. On top of that, even from down here I could tell it was a lattice of volcanic rock. I'd have to be careful. And slow. And quiet.

I cleared my head and let out a long breath, trying to shake the pheromones. Either Captain and I would crawl out, or Alexander would catch up and accidently kill me in a fit of rage . . . or we'd fall to our deaths onto the cavern floor.

Any way I looked at it, dead was still better than being turned.

I sure hope Rynn had escaped.

I made sure Captain was secured under my jacket, then surveyed the lattice above me. All the branches within arm's reach looked brittle. I grabbed the first branch and eased myself up, careful not to make too much noise or hold the lava rock too tight. I felt naked without my backpack.

The branch held, and I was on to the second when I heard the rock scuff below me. A tall silhouette stepped out of the shadows.

Red. In all his scruffy, grad student glory.

What with Alexander and Captain, I'd forgotten all about him. He'd lost the worn red baseball cap, but his pickax hung loosely at his side.

Just great.

He sneered and set the pickax in a lazy swing. I was already out of his reach.

"Listen, Red, I don't know what these guys are paying you, but trust me, it isn't worth it. They're bad news—"

"Funny, that's exactly what Benji said about you," he said, taking a step towards the wall. He let the pickax fly on the lower branch, and I felt the reverberation in the lattice I was standing on. Shit.

Numbness, that's the best way I can describe what raced through my chest. "What do you mean?"

Red laughed. "Benji said, and I quote, 'If you want to be neck-deep in supernatural crap for the rest of your life, go right on ahead and let her wander around. Hell, she'll probably ruin your career as a freebie.'"

I shook my head and tried to focus. The pheromone was starting to work itself out of my head, but it would still be a few hours until I was back to good old, respectable me. "You're lying. I saved Benji's career—"

"He said if he knew you'd hold it over his head for the rest of his life, he'd have pushed you off a cliff in the Andes when he had the chance."

I'd thought better of Benji than this—not that I haven't been screwed over before. I should have known . . . Was I upset, betrayed? Hell yeah. Funny how when people's lives are in ruins, they're more than happy to associate with the likes of me. It's after I fix everything that they suddenly recall I'm treacherous, unconscionable me.

I shook my head. "No good deed goes unpunished," I said more to myself than Red. No sense being pissed off about it now—Benji would get what was coming to him . . . if I survived. "Did you even send me into the right cavern?" I snapped.

Red laughed. "Of course not. You think I'd let Owl run loose in a real archaeological site if I could help it? I'm not letting you steal anything."

"I'm not here to steal anything—"

He nodded behind me. I heard the first growl, a cross between a man and a rabid dog. "That's not what they say—and they're funding my project for the next three years." He let the axe fly again. The lattice I was on cracked down its length. The whole thing was so fragile that one more hit would send the entire branch crashing to the floor. I was really starting to hate Red's pickax.

The inhuman growl was followed by a second. The vampires were recovering and starting to move out. What little lead I'd had was gone. I readied my UV penlight. No way in hell was I in any condition for round two . . .

Red angled himself away from me so that even if I dropped right down in front of him, my foot-to-the-nuts trick wouldn't work a second time. I tried one last time to reason with him. "You have no idea what you're dealing with. Do yourself a favor and get the hell out."

He hefted the pickax over his shoulder and readied to swing. "You're not the only one of us who deals with the supernatural. Difference is, the rest of us know where the line is."

I couldn't believe what I was hearing. I snorted. "There is no way you're that stupid . . ." I hadn't paid much attention before to the bags under his eyes, writing them off to grad student lifestyle. But he was an addict. Worse, he probably didn't even know it and wouldn't realize until it was too late.

If I dodged at the right time, I might get by—or get my head smashed in. Unless . . .

I palmed my UV laser pointer. Wouldn't burn him like the vampires, but it'd blind him for a few seconds at least. "Red, you've got no idea where the line is. If you run now and get on a plane, you can still make it out—make up some story about looters. Hell, tell them you ran into Owl. Just run now—I promise I won't stop you."

Red smiled and readied the pickax. "I'm not letting you ruin my career."

I shook my head. "Buddy, you don't need my help—you're doing that all on your own." I aimed the laser pointer at his eyes. It surprised him enough that he froze with the pickax raised. It was all the time I needed. I dropped down and slammed my fist into his nose.

"Ahh!" He dropped the axe and doubled over, covering his eyes.

I looked overhead. I didn't have enough time to climb up again, not with the fractures Red had caused. I shoved him into the wall, and while he was on the ground I wrapped him in a choke hold, cutting off blood flow to his brain. I held it until he shuddered and passed out. After that I bolted.

I could feel Captain stir inside my jacket. He chirped and pushed his head out of my collar, blocking my view of the tunnel and putting me off-balance. I skidded to a stop.

"Watch it, I can't see!" I pushed him right back in; with this many vampires floating around, I wasn't about to let him out.

One of Alexander's goons stepped out and blocked the tunnel up ahead. Captain started clawing at my jacket. I swore as I battled to keep him under wraps and the vampire in my line of sight.

Growling and hissing, Captain pushed off my chest. I dove to catch him and grazed the fur on his tail.

Shit.

In three bounds he reached the vampire, who was smiling with his arms wide, as if readying to catch a football. Clearly he'd never met Captain before; I almost felt sorry for him.

Captain launched at the vampire's throat, and I wasn't sure which guttural growl was whose. The vampire snatched Captain midleap, holding him out as he hissed and slashed, a furry ball of fury.

Alexander's goon smiled. He wasn't the one I'd burned badly; he'd probably hidden in the corner.

"Anything you want to say, Owl, before I eat your cat?" the goon said.

"Yeah. Now I have a flashlight." I pulled the UV flashlight out of my jacket and inched forward, keeping the beam on his face. He sizzled and edged down to his knees, but he wasn't old enough for the light to set him on fire. I should have grabbed Red's pickax while I'd had the chance. Captain hissed and went for the vampire's throat before I grabbed the scruff of his neck. "Come on, you stupid cat, let go." He growled, but let go. I placed my boot on the vampire's neck and pressed down just so he wouldn't get any ideas.

The vampire snarled as I passed the beam over his face again. "Sabine is going to have your throat for this," he said.

"The only throat at risk right now is yours. What the hell do Sabine and the Paris Contingency want with Mr. Kurosawa's artifact?"

He sneered, giving me a good look at his tiny yellowed canines. "Who says it's just the artifact?"

I frowned and put more weight on his throat. "Kurosawa brokered a truce. I don't care what your boss says, the vendetta against me is over."

His sneer widened. "You should be more careful who you piss off. Maybe steer clear of the supernatural for a while—"

Before he could say anything else, his eyes fluttered and rolled up.

Shit, I'd overdone the UV light. I kneeled down and pulled up his eyelids. Nothing. Damn it.

"Well, there are other ways to get information," I said to Captain, and started to rifle through his jacket. Wallet, no ID, a couple hundred bucks—I pocketed that, no sense letting good, hard cash go to waste—a piece of paper with a Stateside number scribbled on it . . . I pocketed that too . . . and, last but not least, a cell phone. I flipped it open to check recent calls when an ice-cold hand reached under the cuff of my cargo pants and snaked around my ankle. I glanced back down at Alexander's vampire. Faded gray eyes stared back at me.

"Boo," he whispered.

Then the pheromones hit me. Breathing them is bad enough, but skin-to-skin contact? It's a wonder I didn't pass out right then and there. As it was, my arms and legs turned to jelly and everything started to spin. I dropped my flashlight.

The vampire moved fast, grabbing me by the throat and lifting me off the ground. I barely registered more than a warm, fuzzy feeling as he slammed my back into the pumice wall. Captain growled and readied to pounce. The vampire's neck wound was turning an angry purple, which was probably why he was bent on killing me now and either didn't hear Captain or didn't care. Yeah, well, his mistake. I tensed what muscles I still had control over and braced myself for the fall. As soon as Captain hit him, that would be my last chance.

The vampire leaned in and smelled the skin on my neck. "Sabine never did say what condition she wanted you in."

She'd have to wait a little longer.

Captain shuffled his hind end one last time before launching onto the vampire's back. He screamed and let go of my neck in favor of getting my cat off him. My knees caught the brunt of my fall. I found my flashlight nearby and used the tunnel wall to stand. Captain still rode the vampire's back, and more purple welts were appearing where Captain hit his mark.

OK, Owl, you need a plan. Use the flashlight, grab your cat, and stumble out of here as fast as your motor skills can handle.

My hand wavered as I aimed the flashlight. *Come on, Owl, focus . . .* I braced my arms and got ready to turn it on. One good shot was all I needed . . .

I registered the thwack against the wall somewhere from behind my vampire-induced haze. I searched the wall for the source until I registered the flickering blue LED light attached to a thin, silver tube lodged in the wall a few feet above me. It took me another few seconds to register that the light was speeding up, like a strobe light . . . shit . . . that couldn't be good. Well, there went my flashlight-cat-grab plan. I closed my eyes, covered my face, and clenched my teeth. I had a sinking suspicion this was going to hurt.

Even with my eyes closed, I registered the UV flash—or my retinas did. And it hurt. I think I screamed, but I couldn't be sure if it was me or the vampire. The flash just about knocked me out cold. I slid down the wall to the floor, forcing myself to keep conscious.

Chances were only fifty-fifty I'd wake up from a second concussion in one day.

Cool fingers turned my chin from side to side.

"I'll say this. You have a certain knack for finding the bad guys," a familiar voice said.

I opened my eyes.

Rynn.

I opened my mouth to speak but ended up wincing as his flashlight passed over my face. Enough pheromones in your system will make you sensitive to light and garlic.

He crouched down to get a closer look at me. I thought he frowned, but it was hard to tell with the world spinning so fast. I tried to say, "Nice of you to drop by," but it didn't come out as anything intelligible, at least not to my ears.

"You're about as high as I've ever seen anyone on vampire sweat before," Rynn said after he finished examining my face. I wished he hadn't taken his cool fingers away. I tried speaking again but my tongue wouldn't work, and I was freezing. If I could have strung words together, I'd have said, *Get the damn DMSO—now.*

Lucky for me this wasn't Rynn's first vampire rodeo. DMSO, or dimethyl sulfoxide, was a readily available sulfur compound that neutralized the effect of vampire sweat in the blood. Anyone who's ever dealt with vampires carries a vial or two around. A sharp prick in my bicep and a stream of ice shooting up my arm later, the use of the muscles in my neck returned. That was followed by a dull pain radiating through my back from where I'd been slammed. Yeah, that was going to hurt tomorrow.

A sliver of a frown touched Rynn's mouth. "Your pupils are still dilated. Just how much did you take?"

"A lot. And not voluntarily," I said. I didn't need a lecture right now, thank you very much. If anything, the UV flash had made things worse. "Not that I don't appreciate the assist, but I'd have been better off without the UV."

"Seriously?"

I held my flashlight up and almost dropped it. "I had it covered. We were on our way out."

To his credit, Rynn didn't push. "Can you move?"

I tried my legs out before nodding. "Yeah, just don't ask me to jump, climb, or run." Using the wall, I pushed myself to a shaky standing.

Rynn steadied me. "Sorry it took me so long. I had the girl to deal with. She tried to knock me out with chloroform but didn't know what she was doing."

I closed my eyes. They'd both been in on it. How could I have been so stupid? "Benji has some explaining to do. And so does Mr. Kurosawa," I said, and filled him in on what both Red and the downed vampire had told me.

Not one bit ashamed for using Rynn for balance, I glanced back at the tunnel. And took a step. A wave of nausea hit me. "Come on," I said. "Alexander and Co. will be right behind us, and they're pissed." Rynn arched his eyebrow and I added, "I hit them with a UV penlight. Red won't be out much longer either."

Rynn stopped me and shook his head. "We've got some time. I came across them on my way here. I set trip wires outside the cavern. UV grenades and a little something for localized cave-ins." He crouched down beside the vampire and began to fasten silver-coated plastic ties around his wrists and ankles.

I shook my head. "They'll just take the UV hit and dig themselves out, it won't buy us much time—"

He winked. "That's why I added silver shrapnel. Should keep them busy for a day or so. How far back is Red?"

"I dropped him under the lattices. Maybe twenty feet?"

Rynn nodded and headed back down the tunnel. He returned a moment later dragging an unconscious Red by the feet. Red's ankles and wrists were bound with the same plastic ties Rynn had used on the vampire.

"Owl, who the hell is this Sabine?"

"The vampire whose lackey got the drop on me in Vegas. She's managed to rope Alexander and some of the Paris boys into working for her."

"I know that, I mean who is she?" Rynn said. "More to the point, what the hell does she want with you?"

I shook my head. "The same scroll that Mr. Kurosawa wants, apparently. My best guess is she figured she'd let me do the groundwork and then get the jump on me."

Rynn frowned. "Maybe. But this was personal. This Sabine knows you. How?"

Yeah, that was what Red had said too. And I sure as hell would like to know where Alexander and the rest of the Paris boys fit into all this. They wouldn't go against the Paris Contingency unless there was a damn good reason. "No idea," I said, and nodded at the unconscious vampire. "But I'm hoping he has a few answers—Why, you son of a bitch! I turn my back for one second—"

Captain lifted his head up from the vampire's hand and mewed. He was doing his best to turn the hand into a pincushion. I pulled him off the swollen, purple hand and refastened his leash, which thankfully was still in my jacket pocket. I then crouched to pick up the vampire's wallet and phone. Except for a few scratches, it had survived the fall.

I tossed it to Rynn. "And I'm willing to put money on this giving me a few answers."

He glanced through the numbers. "What do you plan on doing with them?"

I shrugged. My head hurt too much to think that far ahead. "I don't know. Start calling and see who answers?"

Rynn slid the phone into his jacket pocket.

"Hey, I didn't say keep it."

He rolled his eyes at me. "You've had two concussions in as many days and enough vampire sweat to bring down a horse."

"So?"

He crossed his arms and peered at me. "Have you ever heard the term 'train wreck'? You might want to look it up."

I made a grab for the phone and immediately regretted it as I lost my footing. Rynn caught me.

"Damn it, why did everything have to go sideways today?" I said.

Rynn didn't answer, but he didn't let go of me either. "I have someone back in Tokyo who can trace these, probably get you a location—*before* you start making random calls. It's called a plan; you might want to try it sometime."

"I always have a plan," I said.

"Really? Is that what you call this?" he said.

Truth be told, I'm an awesome planner . . . I just hadn't foreseen vampires finding me this fast or having archaeology flunkies. Besides, pressed up against Rynn, the world wasn't spinning as much. I didn't rush standing back up.

"Hmmmm . . . you smell nice." Yeah. Eloquence, that's me.

Rynn gently untangled me and held me at arm's length. I remember his blue eyes, really blue, peering at me. He swore in Russian . . . I think.

"You're still higher than a kite, and I can't give you any more DMSO," he said.

Now that I wasn't pressed up against him, the world started spinning again. He was probably on to something.

Captain had inched his way over to the unconscious vampire. This time Rynn swore as he took the leash from me and reined an angry Captain in.

"You realize you have to train Mau cats?" he said to me as Captain turned on the leash and did his best to sever it with his teeth.

"Yeah, well, we're working on it," I said. I wrapped the leash around my hand. Captain quieted somewhat.

Rynn shook his head as he knelt down by the vampire and started to pull tools out of his pack. "Train wreck."

"Only on a bad day." I leaned against the wall. "All right, for the past year. But you're not exactly one to judge."

"No. No, I'm not," he said quietly. For a second, he looked like he was about to say something else. Instead he turned back to his pack.

I might have been high, but I didn't like his resigned tone. I pushed. "What?"

"Hmmm?"

I got better footing and found a rock to rest my shoulder against—my own personal weight-bearing rock—so I could watch what he was doing. "I'm out of it, not stupid. You were about to say something else."

"Just that it's your life. I'm the last person to try and tell you how you should go about ruining it."

"I call it surviving, not ruining. And I don't have a choice."

"You keep saying that."

"And you're starting to sound like Oricho."

Rynn shrugged. "When two different people say the same thing, usually I start to listen." He rolled me a bottle of water. I hadn't realized how thirsty I was until it was in my hand. "Surviving this long doesn't count for much when the end result is still dead." He nodded at the vampire. "Or worse. But then again, what do I know? I'm just a glorified whore."

I closed my eyes. Shit, Rynn was still pissed about that. Oh well, yet another thing to fix. When I came down.

I focused what little attention I could muster back on Alexander's vampire, still out cold on the stone floor. I cringed. Now that the DMSO had stripped some of the pheromones out of my blood, the vampire looked more like an emaciated heroin addict in expensive clothes than a Calvin Klein model. It takes a jaded heart like mine to remember what I'm looking at through that euphoria.

Damn it, if Rynn hadn't shown up when he had, there's a chance I could have been joining them. "Rynn, if—"

Rynn whistled to get my attention and held up a heavy glass syringe. "What's your preference, garlic or silver?"

I was about to push out my apology and thought better of it. Whatever reflective mood he'd been in had passed. Probably for the best.

I shook my head. "No point. All they'll do is irritate them. It's like hitting cockroaches with bug spray."

The corner of Rynn's mouth turned up in a smile. "Clearly you've never shot up a cockroach with bug spray before."

I didn't know if I should be impressed or a little horrified that Rynn had better toys than me. Under the circumstances, I went with impressed.

"And what do you want to do with him?" he said, and nodded at Red.

I chewed my lip and glanced at Captain, still growling at the vampire but resigned to squat on the floor. I'm not a vindictive person—well, not as a general rule at least. Unless it's self-defense, I stop short of hurting humans, especially ones like Red—an addict who doesn't even know it . . . but the son of a bitch would have strangled my cat.

"Throw him and Bindi together and keep them separate from the vampire."

"Why separate them?"

It was my turn to smile. "You've never seen a vampire junkie desperate for a fix, have you?"

Rynn opened his mouth to say something, but a sharp crack echoed from behind us, towards the caverns where I'd escaped Alexander. I cringed. My head was in no condition to take loud noises. It was followed by distant snarls and screams.

"UV grenade?" I said through clenched teeth.

"One of them. I imagine they'll trigger a cave-in next." Rynn grabbed an ankle tie in each hand and started dragging Red and the vampire down the tunnel. "Come on," he said. "This loops around back to the temple proper."

"How did you find that out?"

"The girl."

I snorted and used the wall for balance as I followed him. "What did you have to do to get her to give that away?"

He threw me an innocent expression. "I'm charming and persuasive."

9

GET ME THE FUCK OUT OF BALI

Vampires are predictable.

Across from the main chamber of the temple proper was an old kitchen with an old fire pit built into the wall, or, as I like to call it, ancient vampire storage unit. Rynn only had to show him the syringe filled with silver and Alexander's vampire—his name was Charles, we found out—folded. He didn't know a hell of a lot. Apparently Alexander was keeping all his goons out of the loop. Whether it was so they could feign innocence to the Contingency if everything hit the fan or because Alexander didn't trust them was anyone's guess.

As I said, vampires are predictable.

People . . . not so much.

And Bindi was a whole new level of batshit crazy.

Rynn frowned and leaned in over her. "All I want is for you to tell me where the tablet is. That's it. Then we'll let you have the vampire tied up in the other room. You give me something I need, I'll give you something you need."

Back up in the temple proper, I let my head rest against the wall. I was still hazy, but even I knew what she'd say next. She'd been going in circles for half an hour.

Bindi licked the sweat off her lip and eyed Rynn hungrily. "Sabine is coming back for me, and when she gets here she'll give me anything I want." Her eyes glazed over, not unlike some young vampires I'd seen. Not quite there yet, but give it a few more months. "Even you," she told Rynn.

Rynn clenched his fist and his mouth drew into a tight line. I gave him less than a minute before he lost it. On the one hand, I was tempted to sit back and watch things explode; I'd never seen Rynn come this close to losing his temper. On the other hand, Bindi was as indoctrinated as any vampire groupie I'd ever seen. Over the past hour her skin had turned a clammy yellow, and her surfer braids and clothes were soaked with sweat. The eyes really got me though; they were so sunken and rimmed with red that I couldn't help but feel sorry for her.

Red looked up as if seeing me for the first time, and with renewed interest. He hadn't said much since waking up. He'd left Bindi to scream the vampire propaganda at us.

My head was a bit more lucid, so I pushed myself up off the floor and stepped in. "Rynn, you're wasting your breath," I said. "Neither of them is scared of pain. Or you."

Red wasn't nearly as far gone as Bindi was, and part of me wondered if that made him worse. Red was lucid enough to know what he'd gotten himself into. Part of me hoped watching Bindi come down off her fix would be a good lesson for him.

". . . and you," Bindi said, turning her snarl on me, "can't imagine the horrors my mistress has in store for you . . ."

"Save it, princess. I'm not buying," I said. Yeah, I felt sorry for her, but not enough to listen to the rhetoric. I tapped Rynn on the arm and nodded to the hallway. He sighed and, after ramming a gag into her mouth to damper down the obscenities, headed out.

Red glared at me accusingly. "You can't just leave us tied up like this," he yelled.

"Watch me," Rynn yelled over his shoulder.

I just shook my head. "Don't blame me, kid, you should have run when I told you to." I followed Rynn out and slammed the wooden door. But he would blame me. Another archaeologist whose career and life I'd supposedly ruined. Damn it, I hate being a scapegoat.

Even with the door closed I could hear Bindi kicking and struggling against the restraints. I took a deep breath. "You're approaching this all wrong. She's batshit crazy."

"Really? Funny, I hadn't noticed—"

I held up my hand. Yeah, his usual cool demeanor was just about done. "Let me have a go at her. I've got experience dealing with vampire junkies, and my head's cleared up enough. I think."

He gave me an incredulous look. "You *think*?"

I shrugged. "Well, we don't have a lot of options right now, do we? I mean, we can't just stay here indefinitely. We either leave now without finding that tablet, or you let me have a go at her."

Rynn sighed. "All right." He stepped aside for me. "Lead the way."

"Lesson one. Vampire junkies are scared of only one thing," I said, grabbing my mask, a Ziploc bag, and a pair of latex gloves from my pack and ducking into the ancient kitchen. I walked right up to Charles the vampire, right where we'd left him, tied up and cowering in the brick oven. Captain was exactly where I'd left him too; tied to his leash just out of striking distance. I figured the more he got used to them, the less likely he'd be to charge in every time he smelled one.

Captain mewed, and Charles's eyes widened as he focused past my cat on me.

"Relax, I just need something," I said, as I ripped out a chunk of his greasy brown hair and slid it into the Ziploc bag. Rynn stayed at the doorway, but he raised an eyebrow as I headed back in to see my rapidly derailing archaeologists. "Watch and learn," I said.

I crouched down in front of Bindi and removed the gag. She tried to bite me, but I was ready for it. Like I said, I know my vampire junkies.

"You two are dead, mark my words, as soon as Sabine finds me," Bindi said, her teeth bared.

Taking my time, I opened the Ziploc and waved it under her nose.

With the first whiff, her eyes sharpened and she shut her mouth. She breathed in deeper, shivered, licked her lips, and lunged against her restraints. I waved the bag one last time before sealing it shut. She fixed hate-filled eyes on me, but her lip curled up in a frightened snarl.

"Noooww we're getting somewhere," I said, and placed the sealed bag on her lap. "Here's what's going to happen. I'm not going to threaten you, like Rynn, and I'm not going to barter with you. Because we both know you need what's in that bag." I tapped it for effect. "Now, if you tell me where the tablet is, I *might* be persuaded to open it back up and leave it here."

And just like that, the screaming indoctrinate was gone. I don't know if she looked more crazy, angry, or scared. Maybe some middle ground she'd found in a burst of lucidity. Her eyes didn't leave the bag though, and she kept licking her lips.

What can I say? I'm good with crazy.

"She'll kill me if I say anything," Bindi finally whispered.

I nodded. "You're right, she'll probably kill you. What I do know is I won't open that bag unless you tell me what I want to know, so it's up to you." I crossed my arms and leaned back against the wall.

A minute dragged into two with only the sound of my gas mask grinding in the background.

"Time's almost up. What's it going to be?" I said.

"All right," she said, and licked her lips.

Red, who'd been silent up till this point, pulled against his restraints. "Bindi, you can't tell her," he said. Rynn silenced him with a blow to the head. But it was pointless. Bindi couldn't see or hear anything except the bag.

"It's at the back of the room," she whispered. "Behind the curtain there's an alcove. We hid the tablet under a canvas sheet before you arrived."

They'd moved it.

"What about the bag?" Bindi screamed as I ran to the alcove and pulled the canvas off. Sure enough, there was the matching tablet I needed.

"Shit."

Rynn came up behind me. "What's wrong? That's the tablet, isn't it?"

"What's wrong is I'm *fucked*." I ran my hand through my hair, and I swore again as it caught on a bad knot. I so needed a shower. "They pulled it out of its setting."

"So?"

"I expected the room the tablet was housed in to have inscriptions on the wall like the one in Sanur."

"Then get the images you need off this and we'll find the cavern."

I shook my head. "Once you take the focus object like this," I said, kicking the stone tablet, "all the arcane symbols fall away fast. I might still get the inscriptions off the tablet, but I doubt I could get an imprint off the room anymore. And everyone says *I'm* the one who ruins archaeological finds." I threw the canvas sheet across the room. I wanted to scream, but that wouldn't help me and would probably just get Bindi riled up.

I strode back to her, the adrenaline making up for any of the haze still left over from my giant dose of vampire pheromones. "When did you remove that tablet?"

She looked up at me with desperate eyes. "You said you'd open—"

"The deal's changed."

Her bottom lip quivered. "But—"

I picked up the bag and started to walk out of the room.

"Three days ago!" she screamed.

I stopped.

"Sabine called us and said to copy the inscriptions and take it out."

Three days ago . . . Sabine hadn't followed me to Bali; she'd laid a trap. She'd known exactly what I was looking for before I'd even taken the job. I glanced over at Rynn. He hadn't missed that either.

So what the hell did Sabine need me for if she'd already known about the Bali link?

"What did she want with me? Come on, it's important."

Bindi shook her head. She was losing it fast. I wouldn't get much more out of her. "She called us when you left Tokyo and told us to give Alexander whatever help he needed to capture you. She never told us why she wanted you, only that you had to be alive." She nodded at Rynn. "They didn't say anything about him though. It was only supposed to be you."

"Why the hell did you try to chloroform me, then?" Rynn asked.

"She figured you'd make a good vampire flunkie," I said. I turned back to Bindi. "Am I right? Let me guess, a few days ago Sabine said keep a lookout for good-looking men?"

Bindi's eyes widened, but she nodded.

I glanced back to Rynn. "That's when Sabine's old flunkie jumped me at the Circus. She'll be looking for a replacement," I told him. Rynn just shook his head.

Bindi whimpered. "I've told you everything I know, *please*."

I doubted it. Still though, I had just about everything I needed, so I opened the Ziploc and watched her bury her face in it. I had a much bigger issue to worry about. Two, in fact.

"She's a step ahead of me," I said.

"Superficially," Rynn said. "If she knew where to go next, she would have already. She thinks you know something she doesn't—or can figure it out, I'll wager."

It was the same conclusion I'd come to. If Sabine could find the scroll on her own, she would have by now.

"There's something else bothering you about this, isn't there?" he asked.

I nodded. "How did they get my flight and travel plans? I only told three people: Nadya, Oricho, and Lady Siyu. I didn't tell you or Benji until I was already on the plane."

"It wasn't Nadya or Oricho," Rynn said, seeing where I was headed.

"Why so certain about Oricho?"

He shrugged. "It's not his style. Besides that, he's meticulous. He would have known I'd be tailing you, and this," he said, looking around the room, "is sloppy."

I nodded. Funny that *Oricho isn't the kind of person who'd kill his employees* wasn't one of Rynn's reasons. I'd shelve that tidbit for later. "That leaves Lady Siyu," I said. I had no problem believing she would hang me out to dry.

Rynn wasn't convinced. "Oricho is very careful who he works with—it could be that a message was intercepted or she had a spy tailing you."

"Maybe." But I wasn't convinced. I used some pretty high-tech encryption. I'd paid enough for it.

I ran my fingers through my hair again, gave up on the tangles, and pulled it back into a ponytail. "This whole trip is turning into a disaster."

Bindi, high again on pheromones, laughed. "You have no idea."

I rolled my eyes. Great, another junkie who got brave and delusional. "What is that supposed to mean?"

She laid her head against the wall and looked up at the partly restored ceiling. "Sabine made a plan in case Alexander failed. All you're going to see is the inside of a jail cell. They'll have found the bodies by now."

I snorted. "The vampires are still in the catacombs, probably for another day. At least. And you two won't even be missed until your buddies at the hostel figure out you haven't come home. They don't seem the brightest bunch, so I wouldn't count on that happening until tomorrow—"

Her maniacal laughter just got louder and grated on my nerves. I didn't like that smile on her face. "What the hell is so funny?"

"Who do you think Sabine had us kill?"

I froze. "You wouldn't. It's stupid and pointless—"

Bindi just laughed. "Who do you think they're going to pin all the dead bodies on? Little old me, or the renowned international antiquities thief? Sabine thought of everything."

I lost it. I grabbed her by the neck and slammed her head against the wall. "What dead bodies?" I yelled. Even as I said it though, I knew. It made me sick to my stomach, but I knew.

She spat at me, and even though I had her by the neck, she was grinning madly. "It's too late," she said. "We poisoned them. They were dead before we left this morning." She leaned forward. "Go ahead, strangle me, you know you want to."

They'd killed the only other people I'd had contact with in Bali. The four other archaeology students staying at the hostel.

I let her go and stepped back, shaking. I'm used to crazy, a safe level of crazy . . . but everything had just left my comfort zone at warp speed. Thefts, a few maimed supernatural creatures . . . *that* I could marginally deal with, but a trail of dead bodies and a crazy, hopped-up serial killer were totally different.

I took another step back. "Rynn, I'm out, I'm so out—hell, we need to get out of Bali, now." I pulled out my cell phone and started to dial. "Maybe Nadya can pull a few strings—I've got an extra passport on me, I can head back to Tokyo under that . . ."

"That's not going to help," Rynn said.

"Fine, I'll head to Australia this time . . . I don't think dragons like Australia, and there are more than enough places to get lost in the outback—"

Rynn grabbed my hand before the phone connected. "Owl—"

I spun on him. "Don't 'Owl' me, Rynn. This stopped being a job thirty seconds ago. We're questioning a goddamn serial killer. Two serial killers," I said as I realized both of them had been in on it.

Rynn shook my shoulder, snapping me back to the present. "This isn't your fault."

I stopped fighting him. He was right. I hated it, but he was right. I took a deep breath. I hadn't actually pulled the trigger. If I'd never accepted the job or come to Bali, the four students at the hostel would still be alive, but these two had carried out the murders, not me.

"Somehow that doesn't make me feel any better about this—"

"*Please.* Deal with the tablet. That's your specialty. This is mine."

I didn't want to. I wanted to run, to get the hell out while I still had a very small and disappearing window to escape. And tell Oricho and Mr. Kurosawa where to shove their lousy job.

"Please," Rynn said. I looked up at his face and into those incredibly blue eyes.

I hate it when people look at me with that much sincerity . . . I pinched the bridge of my nose and nodded.

I don't know why I agreed; it went against every single instinct in my body, every single one of them screaming at me to run for it . . . hell, that was what I was good at.

But Rynn was asking me to trust him. Some small voice in the back of my head told me I owed him that much. A very small voice, mind you—never underestimate my instinct to run and hide, it's big and loud—but a needling one nonetheless.

I gave Bindi one last glance. She was smiling. She'd killed four people for no reason except to try and frame me, and she was pleased about it. I shook my head and forced my thoughts to the tablet.

"I need five minutes, Rynn," I said, and headed to the antechamber to work.

The tablet was lying exposed on the alcove. I assembled the filters I needed and started shooting pictures.

The first thing I noticed was the sloppy job they'd done removing the slab. It looked like they'd taken their pickaxes to it instead of taking their time to pry it out of the floor relief. That worried me. Arcane inscriptions are more fragile than real ones. Cracks and faults made in the stonework can cause inscriptions to unravel, depending on how intricate and delicate they are. From what I'd seen in the Sanur tablet, these were very delicate.

When I slid in the first filter and saw the fuzzy results, I knew they'd damaged the sets. Whether I'd be able to read or translate was another thing entirely. I kept taking pictures and switched the filters. Each arcane set had been disrupted by different micro fractures in the stone edges when they'd removed it. Shit.

I pulled out my last tool—the diluted chicken blood, which I'd left for last on purpose. I figured that with the symbols already this fragile, the blood would probably unravel all the others.

As soon as the first drop of chicken blood hit the tablet, it lit up like a short circuit. I shielded my eyes until I was relatively certain the flash was gone. Once I opened them, I saw that the tablet was intact but charred.

"What was that noise?" Rynn yelled from the main temple.

"Not an explosion," I said. Well, it hadn't been.

The arcane blood symbols were glowing, some of them fuzzy and offset by the charred bits, but there. I started taking pictures. Not my best work, but pretty damn good, considering what I'd been given to work with.

I got down on all fours to check underneath the tablet for any markings I might have missed. If I hadn't, I wouldn't have seen the black computer bag. I pulled it out and checked the name. Bingo. It was Bindi's. I knew she'd been holding out. The laptop was small and light, so I slipped it into my backpack along with my camera.

Rynn was standing right outside the curtain, waiting for me. He blocked most of my view of the room, but I glimpsed Bindi and Red propped up against the wall, looking peaceful, serene . . . lifeless . . . Shit.

"What did you do to them?" I said and tried to push past.

He stopped me and steered me into the hall towards the temple kitchen, where we'd left Charles. "I only wiped their memories and planted some suggestions," he said. "They'll wake up tomorrow and confess to killing their roommates over drug money."

"Really? You can do that?"

He shrugged. "Either they'll turn themselves in or go on another killing spree."

"Rynn!" I started back for the temple room.

He spun me back around. "I'm kidding. They'll turn themselves in. I've never had it backfire before."

"Are you sure?"

He nodded. "Positive."

I glanced back anyways to make sure they were in fact breathing. They were. "Jeez—where do I get whatever you shot into them?"

"Trade secret, can't share."

"Can't or won't?" I pressed.

He shrugged.

Damn it. I slid my gas mask on before we entered and glanced over at Rynn; I hadn't seen him put on a gas mask once. It unnerved me.

He caught me looking and said, "I don't need the mask. I've got a chemical inhibitor I use instead."

My jaw dropped. "Oh, come on, you have to share that one—"

"I told you, trade secrets."

I snorted, though it sounded more like Darth Vader coughing than me being derisive. "I think I might join a mercenary band when this is over."

Rynn smiled and shook his head. "You wouldn't like it. The emphasis is on mercenary—not stealing."

He had a point.

Charles was still tied and gagged where we'd left him, with Captain curled up, licking his paws.

"What do we do with him?" I said.

"Feed him to your cat?" Rynn replied.

Captain perked up and stopped grooming. Charles mumbled through the gag and started to struggle and wedge himself further into the fireplace.

"Tempting, but can we just knock him out for a few hours? Maybe you can use that chemical memory trick again?"

He shook his head. "Doesn't work on vampires." He removed another syringe and held it up for Charles's benefit. "Horse tranquilizer mixed with a heavy dose of morphine should knock him out for half a day though."

I nodded. "Good."

Even though Charles was tied up and terrified of getting in

Captain's striking range, Rynn still had to pin the vampire down in order to inject him. Charles's eyes rolled up as he passed out.

"You surprise me. I thought you'd want to kill him," Rynn said, putting his syringe away.

It caught me off guard. I shrugged. "Just because these idiots want to break a truce with a red dragon doesn't mean I want to be stupid too and go right ahead and nullify it. Besides, Alexander doesn't slaughter people. He just wants me dead. Killing one of his vampires just escalates things somewhere I don't want to go." I was going to add, *I'm not a cold-blooded killer,* but that was a little close to the whole mercenary thing. I'd pushed enough of Rynn's buttons in the last twenty-four hours.

"Even when he wakes up, he'll still need to get through the ties," Rynn said. "You just don't strike me as having a soft spot for the supernatural."

I shrugged. I wasn't about to give him all my deep, dark secrets. My actions had led to death twice in my career. The first was a vampire—by accident, I might add. The other—well, that had been a person, and it'd been less killing and more self-defense by inaction. At the end of the day it'd been an accident too, one I didn't think about—or tried not to. I wasn't OK with it then, and I'm still not OK with it. I get self-protection—Oricho knocking off Sebastian hadn't caused me to loose a wink of sleep—but this was different. Charles wasn't a threat right now; he was pathetic.

"I draw the line at executing living things. Besides," I said, and nodded back down the hall where Bindi and Red were out cold, "those two are the only ones who actually killed anyone in the last forty-eight hours. If I were going to kill anyone, it'd be them. Come on," I added, needing to change the topic. "I need to get out of here."

Before I accidently blew up a second temple in as many days.

I grabbed Captain's leash and bent down to scratch his ear. "I'm so way in over my head," I said. He mrowled, and to my surprise he followed me instead of straining to reach the vampire. Maybe desensitizing him was working . . .

He feinted back and pulled on the leash in an attempt to break my hold and get back to Charles. Nope, not desensitized. Getting better at manipulation.

"Did you get what you needed?" Rynn asked as we exited the temple. Damn, but the sunlight felt good on my face.

"From the tablet?" he added.

"I don't know. Hopefully I can find something useful. Without the placement though it's going to be incomplete . . . maybe I can figure out a patch in the inscriptions from the other piece, pick up patterns . . ." If I could get a translation out of Nuroshi.

Rynn put a hand on my shoulder, and I brushed it off.

"It sounds like you've got enough to keep going," he said.

"That's not what's bothering me." I sighed. "Benji and Red are right. I'm bad news. Just by showing up in Bali I got four people killed. I never thought I'd hear myself say this, but I think I was better off running away from vampires." I slid my gas mask off and started looking for the jeep. Goddamn it, Red had the keys. Shit.

"I should never have taken this job," I said.

"Finish the job and you won't be thinking that," he said, his face softening.

"Yeah, well, explain to me why the more I tell myself that, the less I believe it?" I closed my eyes and took another deep breath. "Come on. Let's get the hell back to Tokyo." I caught sight of Red's jeep by the side of the temple and made a beeline for it . . . and noticed the second bright orange jeep. Kato popped his head over the backseat and waved.

"Hey, lady!"

"Seriously? Again?" I asked Rynn.

"Well, we can't take the jeep we came in," he said.

I didn't bother arguing. I was out of arguments today. I threw my bag into the backseat and hopped in with Captain.

"Where to, lady?"

"Kid, just get us to the airport," I said.

Rynn hopped into the front seat. "Extra if you get us there fast."

"You got it," Kato said. He peeled out and down the mountain faster than a bat out of hell. I gripped the seat, though I doubted it'd do me any good. I kicked the back of Rynn's chair. "I'm blaming you if he rolls the jeep."

"He won't roll the jeep."

It wobbled as Kato took a turn without slowing down.

"I'm holding you to that," I said, and rested my head against the seat.

Captain complained as I eased him into his carrier. "Yeah, you said it, this whole trip has been a complete disaster."

What the hell had I gotten myself into?

—⁓—

We reached the airport in record time. I couldn't get out of the jeep fast enough. I handed Kato fifty bucks. "Nice knowing you, kid. Do yourself a favor and stay the hell away from any archaeology students. Bad for business."

Rynn handed him a hundred-dollar bill. "And if anyone ever asks, you've never seen us."

Kato lifted his shades and eyed Rynn. There was something funny about his eyes . . . something off-color and old . . . but he pulled the shades back down before I could get a good look.

"It's a deal, mister. Just keep your side of crazy the hell off my island." He pointed at me. "And that goes double for her. She's more trouble than she's worth."

"Hey!"

But Kato had already peeled out of the airport.

"What the hell was that about?" I said to Rynn.

Rynn couldn't quite wipe the grin off his face. "You really do have a blind spot for supernatural things, don't you?"

I spun on my heels and almost fell over. "Shit—him?"

Rynn laughed. "An Apsara-Balinese luck demon."

I rolled my eyes and made for the line. "Get me the fuck out of Bali. And stop laughing."

"You have to admit, it's a little funny."

I shot him a dirty look and pushed past him to the check-in counter. "The sooner we get back to Tokyo, the sooner I can have a shower and a beer. Make that four beers."

I had been about to say, *So things could go back to normal,* but I'd have been lying through my teeth. Both of us knew damn well normal wasn't ever going to happen.

10

NUROSHI, THE AMAZING TURNIP

10:00 a.m., Space Station Deluxe, Tokyo

Rynn dropped me off at Space Station Deluxe straight from the airport and made me promise to stop by at Gaijin Cloud that evening, after Nadya and I dealt with Nuroshi. I would rather have slept, but as he so helpfully pointed out, not with two concussions. Would suck to escape a naga, a pack of vampires, and psycho serial killer grad students only to die in my sleep.

I tied my hair back and breathed in the coffee fumes from the cup Nadya had brewed for me. Now that the adrenaline had worn off, I was feeling the bruises from my beating. I wanted to crawl into bed, concussion be damned. At least I'd had a shower. I'd leave the beer until after I finished with Nuroshi.

Nadya placed her hands on her hips. "She was with one of the Paris boys, no?"

I savored my first sip before answering. "Not that simple. Alexander was freelancing, and he was nervous this time. I don't think this has anything to do with the Paris Contingency. It's got something to do with Mr. Kurosawa's scroll. They're not telling me something." I opened my laptop with the pictures of both tablets and placed Bindi's laptop on the bar. "I'm hoping these shed some light on what the hell all these supernatural assholes aren't telling me."

Nadya paused as she sipped her own coffee. "Alix, you're avoiding an important detail. This woman has something personal against you. Who have you pissed off that much—besides the Contingency—that would want you dead?"

"Vampire, not woman," I said. "And your guess is as good as mine."

Nadya lowered her head and looked at me.

"Nadya, really. I have no idea who this vampire is or what the hell I did to piss her off."

She shook her head. "All right, but none of this fits—or not completely. For example, how does she know Alexander if she has no ties to the Paris Contingency?"

"Easy. Don't vampires have some kind of hotline or something . . . a dark bar where they all go and plot the enslavement of humans?"

"Come on, you know as well as I do it doesn't work like that. They've got a very complicated social and political structure—"

"I know, I know, like a superhive of cockroaches."

Nadya pursed her lips. "More like ants, but yes. The point is, their connections are complicated. He has to know who she is—probably how she knows you."

"Yeah, I'm not exactly on speaking terms with them, so that's out . . . wait a second." I fished into my pocket for the cell phone I'd taken from Charles the vampire. I still had it. I scrolled through the contacts until I found Alexander. I dialed and put it on speakerphone. An angry male voice answered, and I let him go on for a few seconds before interjecting. "Slow down, Alexander, my French sucks."

I heard a hissed, drawn-in breath on the other end. "*You.*"

"Hey, how's it going? You guys out of the catacombs yet?"

He paused. "No, your trap was well set. We are still, how do you say it, killing time." Hmm . . . even better. He didn't realize there'd been two of us. Only Charles knew that, and he was upstairs.

"Hunh. You guys are slow."

"Much as I am enjoying this impromptu chat, I hope you didn't call simply to mock me."

"As much fun as that would be, no. I want to cut a deal."

"Interesting. I would need to speak with Charles first."

"No can do. I don't make a habit of kidnapping vampires. He's upstairs in the temple, tied up. He let me borrow his phone though."

"How do I know you are not lying? That you didn't just execute him."

"You don't until you go upstairs and find him and the murdering Bobbsey Twins tied up in a room. You know, Alexander, you guys are really slipping with your flunkies. That girl is a real piece of work. I expect more from you."

"Don't insult me, she isn't one of mine." Hmmm, that had pissed Alexander off—yet another useful tidbit. The vampire was losing his edge; he was letting all sorts of stuff slip. "What is it you wish to barter?"

Alexander was trying to sound aloof and bored. It was an act.

"I'm not going to waste time playing games, so here it is. You tell me everything you know about Sabine and why the hell she has it in for me. In return, I'll leave you out of my report to my boss, the dragon who threatened to eat all of you if you touched a hair on my head. I'll even leave out this lovely little cell phone, with all the names, numbers, and addresses of all your associates. No one will ever know you betrayed the Contingency."

"A generous . . . offer . . . but what you ask for is impossible—"

"Did you know that I can triangulate the location of all these numbers? I mean, a friend was just telling me yesterday. Who knew?"

"Owl, you are not being fair, what you ask is impossible because—"

"Or I could just start dialing random numbers. I think this one means 'boss' in French; shall I try that one?"

"*Merde*, will you listen to me, you reckless sewer rat? What you ask is impossible because I do not know."

"How the hell can you be working for a woman—vampire—you

don't even know? You're not that stupid . . ." I started to laugh. "Holy shit, first you let me get away, then you let some vampire chick blackmail you? You're losing it. Damn, maybe I should just screw all this and head back to my apartment in Seattle if this is what your standards have dropped to . . ."

"Listen, you worthless piece of peasant trash, I don't know who she is, but I am willing to tell you what I do know. Will that satisfy you?"

"Tell me what you know and I'll tell you if we have a deal."

There was a tirade of French expletives—or I think that's what it was—on the other end. I hung up the phone.

Nadya stared at me with her mouth agape.

"He needs a minute to think about it," I said.

"You enjoyed that."

I took another sip of my coffee. "Damn straight." The phone started to ring with Alexander's number.

"Aren't you going to pick that up?" Nadya asked me.

I shook my head and let it go to voice mail. "He'll just yell some more." The phone rang three more times. After it fell silent, I picked up and dialed.

"Owl." Alexander's voice strained with forced control.

"Hey asshole, you ready to deal yet?"

There was a sharp intake of air on his end. "What I should do is wring your neck and hand you over to a meaner vampire—"

"Wrong answer." I went to hang up the phone, but Alexander stopped me.

"*Since* you leave me with no other choice, I will tell you what I know. She goes by the name Sabine, and she appeared on the vampire club scene roughly three months ago. She is old, older than I. She has a need for other vampires to help with daylight tasks. She also has a perverse pleasure in making the kind of human companions you saw." He sniffed. "She uses them up quite quickly. Very distasteful."

I rolled my eyes. Leave it to an aristocratic vampire to try and justify making thralls. "*Right*. Controlling the doses you give your thralls somehow makes it all OK."

Alexander ignored my snide comment. "Sabine approached me about an archaeological site in Romania. I connected her with an archaeologist I know, and we did some mutual business. She had a connection in Florida, and I had a buyer for Caribbean artifacts."

Sebastian, Sabine's old flunky. I'd jumped to the conclusion that he'd been selling forgeries, like the news articles had reported, but if he'd been selling pieces to Alexander, what were the chances he'd been running supernatural pieces? If the IAA had gotten wind, they would have made it look like forgeries. Same downward end to Sebastian, different and more complicated cause.

"So how did she become interested in Mr. Kurosawa's egg?" I asked.

"I do not know. Initially her interest was mostly with you. She has a personal grudge. She approached me about it, since I have some knowledge of how you . . . work."

"You mean you've been hunting me like a dog for the past year."

"You always have to be so crass."

"Get to the point. How'd she rope you into this mess after the truce? You're slimy, but you aren't stupid."

"None of your business—"

"Ah, ah, ah—I'm going to start calling through the contacts, one by one, alphabetically. Tell me, who is Anajoulie? Is she important? 'Cause I can give her a call—"

Alexander swore. "Through our dealings, Sabine uncovered how one of my elders met with the true death. The one from Ephesus I paid you to bring to Paris." There was a hell of a lot of venom in his voice.

Shit. I'd have felt bad for Alexander—if he wasn't evil. He'd hired me a year back, and at the time I'd had no idea he was a vampire—I'd just thought he was some hot, rich French kid obsessed with the occult and in possession of more money than sense. I really do suck at spotting the supernatural. Maybe that's why I keep bloody well tripping into it . . .

I'd had a sinking suspicion Alexander had lied to his bosses about what happened to the vampire I was supposed to deliver to Paris from Ephesus, the one I'd sent up in flames—accidently, I might add. I had no doubt the ancient vampire would remain "missing" until Alexander could drag me in, the proverbial lamb to slaughter. It's a shame our working relationship had gone south after that, because his checks always cleared.

"Alexander, I've said this before and I'll say it again. That was an accident. I'm sorry. I didn't mean to kill your Grand Poobah vampire. If I had known there was an actual real vampire in that case, I never would have opened it."

"I told you explicitly it was a vampire—"

"And I thought you were nuts!" Actually, I'd thought there'd been treasure he'd been trying to hide from me. When someone tells a budding antiquities thief, "Don't open a box, there's a monster inside," surprise, surprise, the first instinct is to open the box. "All right. So Sabine has you by the short and curlies. If she tells them you were responsible for the fuckup, they punish you."

"It's a far cry worse than punishment—"

I rolled my eyes again. There was that indignant tone I'd grown to hate. "*And* if they find out you're working for a rogue vampire, you're just as screwed."

"*Correct.*"

I let out a breath. "All right, out of the goodness of my heart— and the fact that I feel really sorry just how pathetic you sound right now—I'm going to give you advice."

He snorted. I continued anyways. "Either way, you guys are fucked. If you get out and Sabine keeps you going after me, my boss will find out, and either he'll eat you or you'll be on your boss's hit list. *If* you get out and don't work for Sabine, she'll tell them exactly what happened to your Grand Poobah vampire."

"*He was not a Grand Poobah—*"

"*Then,* the Contingency will call you in for a 'fate worse than death.'" I didn't add that under those circumstances I'd still get off scot-free because the Contingency wouldn't want to piss off Mr. Kurosawa. I have a remedial understanding of when to pull my punches. "Am I right?"

"Correct."

"All right, so here's my advice. Stay buried a few days. Say there was a cave-in and it'll take some time to dig yourself out. I'd head upstairs though and grab Charles. A bit of good faith advice here, Sabine is making some twitchy thralls. I wouldn't want to leave him with that girl too long."

The other end was silent for a moment, then I heard, "An interesting assessment of my predicament."

"You're welcome." I went to hang up the phone, but Alexander chimed in.

"A good faith piece of advice, Owl. Sabine has a rat in Tokyo. And, if you go back on your end of the deal, even one breath—"

He hung up.

"Son of a bitch." I hate vampires; they always have to get the last word in.

Nadya caught my expression. She'd been listening the whole time over speakerphone. "You know who she is?" she said.

I shook my head. "I've got no clue, but I do know what she is. She's an old vampire, older than Alexander. That puts her over three hundred, and she's interested in antiquities, with at least a partial archaeology background."

"You stepped on her toes," Nadya said.

I nodded and pulled out my laptop. "All we have to do is go through my jobs list and figure out where we missed the supernatural clue. Once we find out what I took from her, maybe we can arrange some kind of barter—"

Nadya nodded. "At the very least we'll be able to open a dialogue. It's worth a shot."

"Any dialogue is going through the dragon. You heard Alexander. Sabine is some kind of pheromone sadist, and coming from Alexander, that's a new crazy kind of scary." I turned my attention back on Bindi's computer. "I'm hoping we can get something off this. I haven't been able to crack into it yet. It's got some pretty hefty encryption."

Nadya opened the laptop and frowned at the start-up screen. "Let me take a look at it."

"Be my guest. If you can't get anywhere, I've got someone online who can do it, but they might be busy." Or in jail.

She took the laptop into the club office and shut the door.

My phone rang. DRAGON LADY flashed across the screen. I swore and answered. "Lady Siyu? Good news. I've got copies of both the tablets. As soon as I get a translation up and running, I'll be able to figure out more about this language and where to look next—"

"*Stop. Babbling.*"

I shut up and listened as she drew in a deep breath. "You are to be on a plane tomorrow afternoon back to Las Vegas. Oricho will meet you at the airport. You will *not* miss that plane. You will not make *any* changes to the reservation. If anything arises, you are to call myself or, preferably, Oricho immediately. *If* you do not follow these directions to the letter, you will have me to face, and you do not want to see me angry. Do I make myself clear?"

"Crystal."

"Your travel arrangements are in your inbox," she said, and hung up.

I finished my coffee and checked my email.

I opened the one from Oricho first. It was a warning that Lady Siyu wasn't used to dealing with individuals who deviated from her plans, and also asked what my progress was. I drafted a quick letter and gave him a heads-up about Sabine and the translation. A minute later he replied, telling me that he would contact Rynn concerning my safety.

I'd have to have a talk with Oricho as soon as I touched down about keeping me in the loop on things like Rynn from now on.

I checked the clock. 11:00 a.m. Still plenty of time. I opened up my emails from Carpe next. There were four.

You're late.

This isn't funny.

OK, now I'm worried. There is some strange stuff going on with your account—get in touch.

Byzantine. Please call me when you get this.

This last one was followed by a phone number. I looked at it, trying to decide whether I wanted to break my World Quest tradition.

What the hell. Everything else had gone out the window lately. I dialed.

"Yeah, who is this?" The male voice that answered was familiar but lower than the one that came over the mic—lower than I'd expected for a computer geek—and slow, as if he'd just gotten out of bed. Shit, I probably should have checked the time zone.

"Hi, Carpe. Wow, so you're actually a guy. What's up?"

"Byzantine? Is that you?" The groggy tone vanished. His voice was hesitant; I'd say scared if there hadn't been a confidence behind it. *Wary* might be the best description.

"Yeah. Listen, I hope I didn't catch you at a bad time. Your message just said call."

"It's fine, I'm up." A pause. "Your voice is different than I expected."

Hmmm, maybe this hadn't been such a good idea. "Look, Carpe, I just wanted to give you a shout and let you know I was OK—your message sounded worried . . . and you said something about my account . . ."

"Please don't get me wrong. I just expected the voice of Owl the antiquities thief to be more . . . refined."

I went cold. OK, calling strangers you meet over the internet is in fact a bad idea. "Nice talking to you. Bye." And I hung up. And blocked his email address. I was about to block him on my World Quest chat, when my phone rang. Same area code, different number. I ignored it and fired off a chat message. *Leave me alone.*

The phone in Nadya's office rang next.

"Don't answer it, Nadya," I yelled.

"Yes, one moment," I heard Nadya say.

Too late.

Nadya stuck her head out of the office, confused, phone in hand. She passed it to me, frowning. "It's for you."

I jumped off my barstool and grabbed it. "Look, I don't know who you are or what you want—"

"Relax, will you. I've been watching your account since after you disappeared. I thought you would want to know about some strange worms being dropped in. I chased them down, but they were pretty high-tech—not cheap. When you didn't get back to me, I did some searching. You cover your tracks pretty well. Tell your guy he needs to cover manually scanned reports and images better than he has."

Shit.

Carpe laughed. "I wouldn't worry about it—it took me a while to put together a search program. Not just anyone could do it."

I didn't say anything. I really wanted this situation to go away.

"Look, Byz, I didn't mean to scare the shit out of you. I'll do the fix myself, for free this time—"

"Why?"

He paused. "I know we haven't met in person, but I consider you a friend. Let's leave it at that."

"Who are you? Really?"

He hung up.

"Son of a bitch." I was getting sick and tired of people hanging up on me. I handed Nadya the phone. "I'll explain in a sec."

An encrypted message from Carpe appeared in my inbox. How

much did I trust him, really? I thought back to all the hours we'd spent dungeon crawling and writing messages back and forth. I opened it. A picture of a comic book with the name "Sojourn" written across the top appeared on my screen, then vanished, along with the email.

I closed my laptop. Holy shit. My campaign buddy was a hacker. Sojurn—a famous one.

"I can't make normal friends," I told Nadya. "I am not physically or mentally capable of connecting with people who aren't as fucked up as I am." Then I filled her in on Carpe.

Speaking of connecting with people of a pathological nature, I called Rynn next. For someone who was supposed to be my convenient friend, he'd certainly injected himself into my day-to-day life as of late.

He answered on the fifth ring. "Whore of the Orient. How can I be of service?" he said, sounding like he was still in bed. I wiped that thought from my head fast.

"Knock it off. I was wrong, I was mean, and I don't want to fight about this anymore."

"And I said don't apologize again unless you're sincere. What did you wake me up for?"

At least he got to sleep. I was still on awake duty for the next twelve hours, damned concussions. I filled him in as quickly as I could about what Alexander had told me about Sabine.

"Do you think he'll stay out of things?" Rynn asked when I was done.

"Well, he's a vampire. And he would prefer me dead. Normally I'd say he'd help Sabine out of principle, but this time Alexander has a hell of a lot on the line."

He sighed. "All right. Come by my place as soon as you can—"

"No, I'll meet you at the club early tonight. Nadya and I are going to go corner Nuroshi first."

"No. It's too dangerous."

"I've thought about it, and it's not."

"I'll call Lady Siyu," Rynn threatened.

I bit my tongue, took a deep breath. "It's the middle of the day. Alexander said Sabine was older than three hundred, which means she can't go outside. If we're lucky, we'll catch Nuroshi in his office. And even if she's there, she'll have to be asleep in a box or closet."

Rynn paused, probably to calculate the likelihood I'd run into trouble. "All right. I've got some business I need to attend to before tonight's shift, and if Nadya's with you, at least she has some common sense. Call if anything changes, and take your damn cat leash."

"Hear that, Captain?" I said, and brought out the leash for him to crawl into.

"Be careful and keep your phone on," Rynn said before hanging up.

Nadya locked the laptops in the office while I grabbed my bag and Captain's carrier. Thankfully Nadya had brought my student outfit from her apartment. I changed and ducked into the washroom and fastened my rat's nest into a loose ponytail. I would have left it at that, but I decided to add some bronzer and light makeup. Bali had left me paler than I was comfortable with. I did one last check. Yup. Trendy and forgettable.

Nadya ditched the cocktail dress and high heels for flat boots and jeans. A strawberry-blonde wig had replaced her neon red bob, but her signature red lipstick was nonnegotiable.

She was waiting by the door. "You haven't said anything about Benji."

I shrugged my jacket on and grabbed my backpack. I handed Nadya Captain in his carrier. "What is there to say?"

"Alix," she said in a warning tone.

"Don't worry. He'll get what's coming to him, he's just low on the list of priorities right now. Besides, I doubt he's heard back from his buddy Red yet. I like the idea of him sweating it out for a while before I say hi." I held the door open for her. "Come on, time to skin a turnip."

—⁂—

The university was a quick half-hour trip by subway from Harajuku to Nezu. It was Sunday, so Harajuku Station was packed, and neither of us fit in with the weekend cosplayers. The university itself wasn't deserted, but it was mostly students studying on their weekend. Except for the expected glances foreigners always merit, it was less pronounced once we reached campus.

How did I know Nuroshi would be at the university on a Sunday afternoon? Simple. Nuroshi was a thief, like me. More importantly though, he was a lazy thief that didn't like to take chances. His main source of income was the university archives. If I was him, I'd be living there on weekends. Doubly so since it was more secure than his home. I'd want to be somewhere with good security if I had a crazy, sadistic vampire breathing down my throat.

We entered the archaeology museum and headed for the upper floors. There weren't any guards, as the building was completely key card–controlled, which in my mind translates to, *Please, take a look around and help yourself.* You'd think it'd be harder than that, but key cards from one university tend to be interchangeable with other university buildings. Has to do with lack of funding . . . and the fact that people usually aren't trying to break into university archaeology buildings—drug development, OK sure, but not archaeology.

We headed up to the third floor; Nuroshi's office was next to the washrooms. Even his colleagues didn't have much respect for the slimy old rat.

As we got closer, I realized that Nuroshi's door was ajar. "Damn it," I said, and sped up, expecting the worst.

His office was piled with boxes, no shipping addresses. A white folder was open on the empty desk. I flipped through it as Nadya booted up the computer—the one item that wasn't packed up.

The first page I looked at was an official archives catalogue, printed and left for his supervisors. I imagined it was a hell of a lot lighter than a day or two ago, though no one would be able to prove it.

"Nothing on here. He's gone ahead and wiped the hard drive," Nadya said.

Smart. Even if they suspected he'd lightened the museum of a few items, Nuroshi would have disappeared by the time they'd checked the original paper files, provided he hadn't shredded them.

I dropped the folder and headed for the elevator, but Nadya grabbed my arm and pointed to the stairwell. "The museum archive has a bell that sounds whenever someone enters. We'll take the stairs."

The archives were in the lower basement, five floors down. I think they put them there because they were able to make it earthquake proof, far safer for a sealed airtight room filled with expensive scrolls and fabrics. I'd never been down there. In general I don't like B&E's (breaking and entering)—I prefer dig sites; there are more exits and opportunities to improvise if things go wrong. Museums remind me of dungeons, and every time I'm tempted to sneak in, I get this image of crawling through a smelly ventilation shaft or sewer. Perfect place for Nuroshi though. Somehow I didn't think either of those options bothered him.

We reached the bottom of the stairwell and very carefully—and quietly—opened the door. I cringed the whole way, expecting it to squeak any minute and give us away. It didn't though, and we entered a short, floor-lit hall, no more than ten feet long: the archive's back entrance. Just wished it didn't look so damn much like a dungeon. The end of the hall took a ninety-degree turn—good in that no one inside could see up, bad in that we couldn't see them either.

I could hear shuffling nearby, like someone was moving boxes around and crumpling packing paper. Something metal clanged and rolled across the floor. Nuroshi swore.

"Bingo," I whispered to Nadya.

We reached the end of the hall, and I peeked around the corner. Nuroshi was standing on a chair, bent over a large box, packing the metal plates of a samurai suit. The helmet was what had rolled across the floor. Five more similarly sized boxes were scattered around the room. The turnip was sweating through his shirt, clammier-looking than usual. I peeked at Captain. No noise, no agitation. "We're clean for vampires," I whispered to Nadya.

Nuroshi didn't realize I was there until I tapped him on the shoulder. The old man screamed and spun, falling off the chair and into the box.

"How convenient," Nadya said, leaning over the half-packed crate. "Look, Owl, we've caught a large rat. One who sells out clients to vampires."

His face turned a deep shade of purple I wouldn't have thought him capable of. "You! Get me out of here now."

"Ummm, no? You tell me why you sold me out to a *vampire*. Then maybe I'll help you out and let you finish stealing from the archives."

"You stupid, stupid girl, I haven't got much time left, she'll be coming—"

"All the more reason for you to tell me what she offered you. A cut of the artifact I'm after? Money? I'll believe either one, I'm just curious."

He spit and missed. It fell back and hit him on the face. "I'm in enough trouble as it is. I won't have anything more to do with you."

Nadya sighed. "Nuroshi, come on. We don't have all day, and you clearly don't have all day, so why don't you tell us what we want to know and you can go back to stealing?"

He said something in Russian. I didn't get all of it, but I'm pretty sure I heard the word for "whore" in there somewhere.

Nadya shrugged and looked at her nails, and when he finally finished, she said, "Well, have it your way. What we're really here for is to recoup our costs . . ." She strode over to the nearest packed box and tapped the lid. "How does this one look to you, Owl?"

I whistled. "I don't know, better open it and rifle around first."

Nuroshi swore and scrambled amongst the armor in the box.

"Get your filthy hands away from those, thieves."

Talk about the kettle calling the pot black . . . or whatever that saying is.

I laughed and pushed him back in. "No, you had your chance." I opened up a second box and pulled out a vase. "Hey, Nadya, what do you think this will get me?"

She glanced up at it. "Twenty thousand if it's first century, ten thousand if it's more recent."

"Better take both," I said, and pulled a second one out.

"Oooooh, matching set, I have a buyer," Nadya said, and held up a sealed scroll tube. "What do you think?"

"Hard to say, better open it up."

Nuroshi managed to scramble out this time. His jaw dropped when he saw the two vases I was holding. Add to that the scroll Nadya had found, and I think we just about gave him a heart attack.

"Harpies, give that back!" He launched at Nadya first, and she tripped him. He rolled on his back and I pinned him down with a chair. I held both vases in my hand.

"Now, answer our questions and we'll leave." I tossed up the vases and caught them as Nuroshi made a guttural noise. "I can do this all day, and I'm sure I can find more. Have fun cleaning up our mess and getting out in time."

"You don't understand what you're dealing with—"

"Try me," I said.

Nuroshi swore. "The woman vampire came and found me shortly after you did. She said she needed information. I told her what I told you."

"You mean you fed her the same lie you fed us?"

He swore and spat at my feet. "I didn't lie. You only asked about one tablet. I was deciding which one to send you to when she arrived."

"What happened?"

"She already knew there were two, and suffice it to say that she was not happy with me. She 'requested' the files and translations."

"So you handed them over?"

Nuroshi shook his head but didn't say anything. I pressed. "Come on, spit it out."

"Let an old man up!"

"No. I can't trust you."

He said something in Japanese I didn't understand—probably wasn't very nice. "She took the computer with my files, but once she opens them she will not be happy. I couldn't translate them. A translation key for the language used does not exist. Why do you think I was planning to send you after them? On the off chance you might stumble over something I could work with to translate the two I already had. I didn't give you the site right there and then because I had to review my notes and determine which gave you the best chance. Be glad I did, or that crazy vampire would have found you sooner."

I rocked back on my feet. That . . . made sense. It was exactly the kind of below-board stuff I expected from him.

"So . . . why the hell are you running? I would have brought the tablets back here if you hadn't sent a vampire after me. The least you could have done was send a warning."

"You don't understand—"

"What? That you got beaten up by a vampire? Join the club. This is overkill—"

"Too late, she's already killing everyone who knows about the site. When the police showed up this morning, both Shinobi and Aeto were found dead in their apartments, their room sacked. The police say it was a robbery, but only the computers were missing. Now get off me and let me finish running before she comes back and finishes me off as well."

I got up. Shit. More bodies.

I looked at Nadya and she nodded, looking less confident than a moment ago. I stashed the vases in my backpack, and Nadya stuffed the scroll in her jacket.

"I told you what you wanted, give those back—"

I waved with my free hand over my shoulder. "Good-bye, Nuroshi. Good luck."

"Nice doing business with you. Don't call," Nadya said.

And we headed for the stairs.

Nuroshi swore after us, but the swearing turned to a gurgled cough. Captain hissed.

Both Nadya and I turned around to see Nuroshi a foot off the ground, clasping the head of a spear now sticking out of his neck, surprise on his face. Behind him stood a tall woman in a black hooded jacket and expensive shoes. Her face was obscured by the hood.

Sabine; it had to be.

"Run," I said to Nadya. The two of us bolted down the hallway, Nadya's longer legs putting her ahead. Captain was hissing up a storm, but it wasn't until he gave a death wail that I realized she was right behind me. She had me by the hair and pulled me back. I screamed and tore at her hands. She laughed and spun me around to face her.

At first I couldn't say anything; it's not every day you see a ghost from your past. "No, you're dead . . ."

The woman pushed back the hood. No, there was no doubt about it. Marie, an old associate of mine—a *dead* associate, by all accounts—was here, in front of me . . . and had just speared Nuroshi.

She smiled, exposing the telltale hints of fang. "Hello, Owl. So nice to see you. It's been a very long time, too long, I think."

I swallowed. "You've—you've been busy, Marie."

"Alix!" Nadya yelled, then covered her mouth with her sleeve while she fished in her pocket for her gas mask.

The scent of rotting lily of the valley washed over me, and I followed suit. Shit. Marie was a vampire. Even though I was seeing it with my own eyes, I barely believed it. How?

"Alix, watch out!"

My fingers worked the straps on my mask, but I wasn't quick enough. Marie moved fast, faster than I'd seen Alexander move, and he was two hundred years old, at least. She lifted me off the ground—what the hell was it with vampires grabbing me by the throat and picking me up lately?

Her hand was like an ice-cold vise through the collar of my jacket, cutting off air and blood to my brain. I ignored it and tried to fix the mask in place. If not for my collar, I'd have been out from pheromones by now.

Marie's breath slid over my face, heavy with raw meat. Everything was blurring, including the straps of my mask. I threw it over my face while I still could and took a breath. Things cleared up somewhat, but with Marie holding my neck I had no idea for how much longer. One of the vases pressed against my back. I winced at the waste, but I was running out of options. I slammed it into her head.

It shattered and didn't affect her a damn bit.

She tsked. "What's the matter, Owl?" she said, her French accent tinting the words. "I'd think you'd be happier to see a friend?"

"Marie," I said, focusing on her green eyes and barely holding onto consciousness. "You've really let yourself go."

She didn't like that. Not one bit. Her smile faltered, like cracks at the edges of an old painting. She slammed me into the wall.

What have I said before about vampires being predictable? Grabbing your throat, slamming you against a wall . . .

I dropped Captain's carrier to wrench at the hand around my throat. "Nadya, run!" I yelled.

Nadya hesitated. "She's not going to kill me," I said, adding, "she needs me—for the fucking translation, isn't that right?"

Her fingers dug in. "And you have a bad habit of pissing people off."

I laughed. "What? Did Sabine decide to make you her vampire bitch? Must have been right around the time you tried screwing me over at Ephesus. You should be dead."

She squeezed harder. "You're only half right. I am Sabine."

What? My mind whirled through the vampire pheromone haze. Marie was Sabine? How the hell had that happened? The last time I'd seen Marie, she'd been on the wrong side of a closing door beneath the ruins of Ephesus. I'd thought she was dead—hell, I'd felt guilty about it ever since, even though it had been self-defense. If I'd known she'd ended up a vampire . . . I didn't have time to mull it over.

"Do you think I like being a vampire?" She smiled sickly sweet, much like the look I'd seen on Bindi.

"You seem to have taken to the crazy part just fine." No matter how much I pried, her fingers wouldn't give. Just how the hell had she gotten so strong? She'd only been a vampire for a year.

"Don't worry, I plan on sharing the whole experience with you. Isn't that what friends are for?"

"Not possible. You can't turn me in one bite." Vampirism wasn't all or nothing, it took multiple bites over days' worth of pheromone exposure to set in. The problem was, after one bite you'd crave more. I tried loosening her fingers and failed. Damn it, why couldn't vampires have lousy grips?

"You'd like to think that, wouldn't you?"

Marie was settling in, getting confident. I needed to shake her. "I hear from Alexander you're into some really kinky stuff—going through flunkies like a pack of cigarettes. You need to watch it, or you're going to wear yourself out before your time—"

"Vampires are evil pests, I'm just playing the role. What's the matter, dear? Bring back fond memories?"

She pressed her face up against mine and licked the bottom of my cheek where my gas mask ended. I resisted cringing. "You don't like being a vampire? Too bad for you. Not my fucking fault—not my fucking problem."

"That's where you're wrong."

She opened her mouth and pressed her teeth up against the crook between my shoulder and neck. I'd never been bitten by a vampire. Oh sure, they'd threatened to do it, and Alexander had come real close in Bali, but none of them had actually managed to sink their teeth in yet.

Sabine/Marie; whatever she called herself now, her breath was cold on my skin, as frigid as an air conditioner. I closed my eyes and braced for her fangs to pierce my neck. If I was ready for it, maybe I could even fend some of the euphoria off, at least until the first wave of pheromones was in my bloodstream . . . if I didn't pass out first . . .

Instead, Marie drew in a sharp breath and tensed. I opened my eyes in time to see Captain launch himself at her face, only this time he hadn't announced himself with his usual hissing fit. Marie raised her arm to fend him off, and Captain was more than happy to oblige and sink his claws and teeth into her forearm. She was caught completely off guard and shrieked, releasing my neck so she could fend Captain off.

The way she used her forearm to occupy Captain's teeth indicated there was no way she knew Mau bites were toxic to vampires. Besides, she'd "died" before I'd even come across Captain . . .

Hunh, guess Alexander had kept his side of the bargain and hadn't bothered to warn her. Go figure, an occasionally honest vampire.

Without Marie to hold me up, I slid down the wall. My brain was short on blood supply, and standing proved to be too much. Nadya came up beside me and shook my shoulder.

"Alix, are you OK?"

I felt the skin on my neck before nodding. No bite marks—I probably would have been as high as a kite if she'd broken the skin, but it's the kind of thing you're still paranoid about.

"Yeah, I will be. What the hell, Nadya, I told you to run!"

"You're very welcome."

Marie was on her knees, baring her teeth at Captain and trying her best to rip her red, swollen arm out of his mouth. Damn, I'd seen welts on Alexander and his bunch before, but nothing like this. I filed that off for later.

I tested crouching. When the head rush didn't come, I figured it was time to get us the hell out of the archives. "Get ready to run," I told Nadya. "This time I mean it."

My plan? Extract my cat and run like hell before Sabine could get her claws back into me.

She was so busy with Captain I escaped her notice, and Captain, well, he was oblivious to anything but his vampire dinner. Maybe he'd had enough by now.

"Pssst . . . Captain!"

He rolled his eyes towards me and hissed without letting go of Marie's arm for a second.

Well, so much for the careful, cautious way. I waited for the right moment and grabbed him by the scruff of the neck. He howled in defiance and dug his claws and teeth in tighter. Marie screamed. I gave him another good yank.

"I said time to go!" This time I pulled hard enough to dislodge him. He howled, she howled . . .

I dumped Captain into his carrier, spun on my heels, and broke into a dead run. I wasn't fast enough. Marie's hand snaked around my ankle and pulled, hard. I managed to toss Captain's carrier through the doorway towards Nadya before slamming face-first into the floor, driving the edges of my mask into my face. Damn it, that was going to smart later. Before Marie could drag me back, I latched onto the doorway and held on for dear life. Marie snarled. Her eyes were dilated black, and she growled before biting down on my foot. Thank God I never cheap out on leather. She worked her teeth back and forth, trying to shear through.

I caught a blur of black and red run past us.

"Nadya, not a good idea," I said.

Marie lifted her face from my boot to regard Nadya as she disappeared back into the archives; the vampire was like a cat deciding whether to chase the bird or mouse . . . or settling for both. Not if I could help it.

"Screw off," I said, and kicked Marie in the face, two, three, four times before she finally let go.

"How'd you like to see how the other half lives?" she said. In answer, I pulled my UV penlight out of my pocket and aimed. Yet again though, Marie was ready for me and faster. She slapped the penlight out of my hand and across the floor.

"Get me that scroll and maybe I'll only turn you. I might even let your friends live."

"Go fuck a vampire. No, wait, you already did," I said. I tried to kick her again, but this time she caught my other foot. She pulled me towards her and pinned my arms. She smiled and sniffed my cheek again. I turned my face away, glad I couldn't smell anything through the mask.

"Fine, have it your way. After I turn you, you'll be begging to do my bidding. Maybe I'll have you turn all your friends for me. Starting with your Russian friend—" Marie's eyes went wide, but not from anything I'd done. She reached for her gut and fumbled at the spear tip sticking through it. Nadya stood behind her, in her hands the shaft of the spear that'd killed Nuroshi. Nadya didn't wait to see if she'd finished Marie. As soon as I'd scrambled out from underneath the vampire, she leapt past me.

I didn't need a hint. I trailed her into the stairwell, where Captain was howling through his carrier. If it hadn't been for Marie's laughter, I doubt we'd have looked back.

Marie was on her knees, pushing the spear back out. She smiled. What with the blood loss from everything Captain had done, she wasn't looking so good; her eyes were rimmed in red, and her lips were a grayish shade of blue. "Have to do better than that," she said.

"I thought you said the young ones couldn't do that!" Nadya said.

I shook my head, still working the shock out. "They can't."

We both grabbed the handle to the stairwell door and pulled at the same time. One of the security guards must have done a pass and locked it from the other side.

"Shit." I fumbled my lock picks out and took to the door, more brute force than finesse. My fingers were shaking so badly that I bent the first one and dropped the second.

I had half the lock worked with the third pick when Nadya gave my sleeve three sharp tugs.

"What!"

"Work faster," Nadya whispered.

I turned to see what Nadya was worried about.

Marie stood now, the hole in her stomach sealing over. She shouldn't have been able to do any of this. Only the really old vampires could do that, and she'd been a vampire less than a year.

I focused back on the lock. My fingers weren't moving fast enough.

"Good friend you have there, Owl. Bet you haven't told her what happened to me."

I'd had just about enough. Everyone lately was blaming all their worldly problems on me. Not this time. "What's to tell? You tried to backstab me and ended up a vampire."

"You haven't changed," Marie snarled. "Not one bit."

The door clicked and I felt the handle give way. Marie was coming at me. I still had my heavy UV flashlight, so I aimed it at her; she shrieked and jumped back out of the beam as her skin started to sizzle.

I left the flashlight wedged in the door handle, trained on the hallway. It wouldn't keep her back for long, but it'd slow her down enough.

We slid through the door and were about to slam it shut when Marie laughed. Both of us stopped to peek through the door; even Captain quieted down. We knew we should run, but we couldn't help it. If you'd ever heard a vampire laugh, you'd get it. It sounds more like a psychotic bird than any sort of normal laughter, and the only time you hear it is when they're on the verge of losing it.

Nadya swallowed beside me. Marie must have heard it, because she smiled.

"Careful dear, you never know when Owl will need someone to throw under the train." She held out her hands. "Now you've had a firsthand look at what happens to the ones who don't get to fly away."

That was it. Marie was twisting things, trying to get under my skin. "Wow, Marie, taking the high road. Even on the vampire sliding scale of morality, you managed to hit rock bottom. Even in your warped little brain, you don't really believe you're the good guy here. You're just pissed I sold you out before you could do the same to me."

Marie smiled as her eyes again dilated to pure black. Only old vampires—*really* old vampires—are supposed to be able to dilate their eyes like that. "You'll never know for sure."

I shook my head. "Enjoy your pool of blood. You earned every goddamn inch of it." And with that, I slammed the door.

My heart was racing. I had to believe what I'd said. If I didn't, that made me just as bad as her. I went to lock the door and swore; I'd ruined it with my lock pick.

"Son of a bitch. Nadya, I need a piece of metal—now."

"I don't have any."

"Gimme the scroll," I said.

"What? No—"

"Do you want to fight her again?"

Nadya swore in Russian and tossed me the case. I slid the scroll out—carefully. I wasn't sure what to do with it exactly, but I sure as hell wasn't leaving it behind. I tossed it back to Nadya as I fixed the metal case between the door handles and tied them together with the lower half of my T-shirt for good measure.

"I can't believe you just opened that case—"

"I'm not getting eaten so some client gets a premium product."

I tested the door one last time; it seemed like it would hold for a little while.

"Ready to get out of here before security wanders by?" I asked. I pulled my hood over my head and did up the jacket to hide my torn, bloody shirt. Two bona fide fights in as many days. *I* was slipping. I had another problem too, as I looked down and saw Captain's head poking out of a corner of the carrier. He was eating his way out. I let Nadya open the heavy door while I crammed Captain's head back in and did my best to plug the hole. "Get it through your thick cat skull. We're done here."

We headed out. At the last minute we opted not to go through the building proper but to take the back stairwell exit. Slamming into the metal door bar, I almost caught the carrier on the fire alarm. Captain complained.

"Sorry, the hallway's narrow." An idea struck me.

"Hey Nadya, what were you telling me about this building and fires?"

She frowned. "What? That they forgot the floor drains? The

building floods every time the sprinklers go off—" Her eyes went wide as she caught on. "Nuroshi complained when they refitted the archives with automatic sealed doors to protect the storeroom."

I opened the door first and pulled the alarm. The siren started, and I pulled out a lighter. Never leave home without one. I tossed it to Nadya, since she was taller than me and could reach the sprinkler. Captain mewed as water began to rain down on us.

"You attack vampires, but you cry at water? What kind of battle cat are you?"

We were out the door and found ourselves on the side of a hill. It was dark now—we'd been inside longer than I'd thought, but it worked to our advantage. I really didn't want to explain the blood to anyone. There were still people around, but no one paid us any attention. We backtracked through a garden to the train station. Nadya didn't say anything until we were standing on the platform.

"What the hell was she talking about?"

I shook my head. I couldn't bring myself to talk about it right now. Not while I was still processing it. There are a lot of things I'm not proud of, but there's only one I'm ashamed of. "Nadya, I promise I'll tell you as soon as we're at Rynn's."

She gave me a hard stare before nodding. "I need a drink."

We didn't say much—well, anything—while we rode the train back to Shiyuba district and Gaijin Cloud.

Why the hell is it the past always comes back to haunt us in loud, inconvenient, impossible-to-ignore ways? Why can't it ever be a telephone call so I can hang up?

11

SO MUCH FOR STAYING OUT OF TROUBLE

10:00 p.m., Gaijin Cloud

I slid back onto the stool beside Nadya at the glowing red bar and shook my head.

"No sign of Rynn anywhere," I said. I'd done a lap around Gaijin and hadn't caught sight of him.

Nadya snorted and downed her glass of champagne in one shot. "Wonderful," she said, and opened another bottle. "Shit. She really did a number on your face."

I'd hidden the black eye as best I could; I'm thinking the resurgence of heavy navy-blue eyeliner has less to do with fashion and more to do with practicality.

"I'm more worried about these," I said, and tweaked down the collar of my leather jacket to show the strangulation bruises. They'd ripened since we'd left campus.

Nadya shook her head and raised her glass. "You are a walking disaster. Never have I seen someone who attracts so much trouble."

I took a sip of my Corona, only to find it was empty. I waved the bottle at Nadya's host. He nodded but didn't smile or wave like he normally did. Come to think of it, he looked away as fast as he could. Before I could put much thought into it, Nadya pulled my attention away.

"Nuroshi was a rat and a sleazy old man, but he didn't deserve to die." She glanced up from her glass at me, eyes tired, but not from lack of sleep. "A lot of people are dying who don't deserve to, Alix."

What could I say? She was right. "On the bright side, we didn't get shot at."

"Yet."

I didn't have an argument, so I checked my phone. Still no reply from Rynn to my earlier text telling him we were here and to come find us. I'd added exclamation marks to get the emergency component across. I didn't want to admit it to myself, but I was more than a little worried. Doing business with me was becoming hazardous to people's health. Besides, Marie had said she was going to start taking potshots at people close to me. I hoped Rynn hadn't been first on her list.

I just about dropped my phone as a Corona bottle rattled the glass bar under my nose. The host smiled at Nadya but again gave me a nervous once-over. OK, it wasn't my imagination. He wasn't exactly friendly with me, but he'd never been outright rude before.

I turned to Nadya and nodded at her retreating host. "What the hell was that?"

She shrugged. "Maybe Rynn said something to the other hosts."

"Like what?"

She shrugged again. "Like 'Stay away. She's a train wreck and hazardous to your health'?"

I snorted. Figured. I noticed the bartender removing an empty vodka bottle. "Hey, Yukio, right? Pass that over here."

He avoided looking at me and glanced at Nadya instead, as if pleading for her to make me stop.

Just what the hell had Rynn said to them?

"Just give her the bottle," Nadya said. "She won't shut up otherwise." He obliged with the same guarded fear, for lack of a better word.

I measured the opening with my finger. Yup, just the right size. "Hey, do you still keep desiccant on you?"

Nadya pulled out the tiny packets from her purse and slid them over. Yukio's eyes widened.

"That's not what you think it is," I said. He didn't look like he believed me. I rolled my eyes and emptied the packets into the bottle, shaking them around so they coated the glass. Powdered desiccants, the universal enemy of parchment-rotting dampness everywhere. Even a thin coating would keep any moisture at bay. "Now gimme the scroll." Nadya glared over her champagne glass, studying my bottle. It must have passed scrutiny, because she reached inside her jacket and forked it over. I rubbed the remaining packet of desiccant over my gloves and rerolled the scroll before sliding it into my makeshift scroll chamber.

"See? Ancient scroll in a bottle," I said, holding it up. "If you have a buyer, tell them it's added value. They can actually see the scroll. Just don't stick it in direct sunlight."

Nadya took it and rolled it over in her hands before handing it back. "Not bad," she said. "If you don't mind clients thinking you live in a trailer."

I would have said something, but I caught sight of Rynn on the other side of the bar near the entrance. He was facing away and hadn't seen me yet. I slid off my barstool. Thank God he wasn't dead, or maimed, or—I froze.

Shit.

Rynn was with someone. A blond Japanese woman I'd seen hanging around on numerous visits here. Marie wasn't torturing him; he was with a client. That's why he wasn't answering his phone.

I slid back into my chair and stared down at the glowing bar as fast as I could. Partly because I didn't want to watch, but mostly because my face was turning bright red and I didn't want Rynn to see that I'd seen him. OK, so maybe I was a little jealous. Rynn didn't need to know that. It'd definitely give him the wrong idea.

When I glanced back up though, Rynn was watching me. He nodded and held up two fingers. Well, so much for subtlety.

"Found Rynn. He'll be over in two minutes," I said to Nadya.

"About fucking time," she said. She twisted in her seat to scan the floor and started waving as soon as she spotted him.

I grabbed her arm. "What the hell are you doing?"

"What does it look like? Speeding him up," she said.

"Quit that, he's with a client."

Nadya twisted again to stare and reassess Rynn and the blond woman. An evil smile spread across her face. "Maybe we should go say hi. Evaluate your competition."

"Stop it."

She shrugged. "I'm just saying, I bet he'd like talking to you more. There? See, he's coming over!" And sure enough, Rynn was heading our way, and the blonde he'd left behind was glaring daggers at me. Well, good for her. She could get in line with everyone else who wanted me to drop off the face of the planet.

"Shit."

"What's the matter? You like him, he likes you—"

"The problem is I almost got him killed twice this week. I don't need to be fucking up his work too."

"Hmmmm, I could think of worse things for you to fu—"

"Nadya!" I would have added more, but Rynn had reached us and stepped behind the bar. My ears burned, which meant they were as bright red as my face.

"You can thank me later," Nadya whispered.

Rynn leaned across the bar towards me; his face guarded, he picked up my makeshift scroll bottle-case and held it up by the top to inspect it. "Please tell me you aren't fencing stolen goods at my bar."

"OK. I'm not fencing stolen goods at your bar," I said.

He lifted an eyebrow and glanced at the vase resting beside my beer. I couldn't blame him. I wouldn't believe me either.

"Relax, I'm not selling it. Here. And I didn't actually steal it this time. Nuroshi did."

"And somewhere, somehow, deep in the workings of your mind, that makes it OK?" he said.

"If I find something someone else stole, it isn't stealing. It's finding." I took the bottle from Rynn and slid it into my bag. "And why the hell aren't you giving Nadya a hard time? It's her scroll."

"Yet you're the one holding it."

I closed my eyes. "OK, let's can the philosophical discussion of my day job—we've got more important things to worry about," I said, and gave him the abbreviated version of our run-in with Marie. I hoped Rynn would be impressed with all the new information.

"You said you wouldn't be getting into any trouble," he said, glaring, and not bothering one bit to hide he was pissed at me.

"I said I didn't plan on getting into any trouble. Marie shouldn't have been there at all."

One side of Rynn's mouth twitched up. He grabbed my jacket collar and turned it down faster than I could block. Nadya winced at the sight of the bruises, and I scrambled to pull the collar back up. "Not cool," I said.

Rynn didn't say anything, just inclined his head in a disapproving manner. I think that was worse. We'd have to have a discussion about boundaries.

Nadya came to my defense. "Rynn, none of it made any sense. Alix says Marie hasn't been a vampire more than a year, but I could have sworn she was older than three hundred."

I shook my head. "There's no way she's three hundred." I took a swig of my Corona; it was now or never. "I knew her when she was alive."

I only caught the looks Rynn and Nadya gave me out of the corner of my eye. Any other situation and it would have been priceless.

Nadya set her face. "No, you're mistaken—it's not possible she could be that strong and that young—"

"Let's pretend you're right and I'm mistaken—which, for the

record, I'm not. For one, she's nowhere near sensitive enough to light. If she was as old as she is strong, she should have gone up in flames as soon as the flashlight hit her. She didn't."

Nadya pursed her lips. She wasn't giving up that easily. "But she was a hell of a lot more damaged than she should have been for a year-old vampire."

I nodded. "You're right. The whole thing makes no sense, and I don't know enough about vampires to know why."

"Do you know anyone who would know?" Rynn asked.

I frowned. "Nuroshi probably did, but anyone else?" I shook my head and placed my almost empty Corona on the bar.

Rynn grabbed it and pulled it out of my reach before I could have the last sip. "I find that hard to believe," he said.

I glared. Damn it, he wasn't even trying to play the charming host.

"Well, let's put it this way. No one I'm on speaking terms with. You piss a few people off in the archaeological world and all of a sudden you're persona non grata on just about everyone's list, including the people already on the fringe. Unless one of you knows a vampire willing to chat with me—" I stopped talking and pulled Charles the vampire's cell phone out of my bag. It was still active.

Alexander picked up on the fifth ring, and I transferred it to speakerphone.

"What do you want?" came his clipped voice. I got the distinct impression he'd been holding the phone for the last five rings deciding whether or not to answer.

"Hi there, nice to hear your friendly voice again. I'm doing OK. How's that tunnel in Bali treating you?"

"*Owl*," Rynn said, warning in his voice, "that is not what I had in mind." He reached for the cell.

"Just a sec, Alexander," I said, muting the cell and stopping Rynn from hanging up for me. "Relax, they're trapped in the tunnel and they're staying there until this Sabine/Marie mess is over."

Rynn wasn't satisfied. "I said get information. Not bait vampires over the phone."

"Stop worrying. I'll keep it short. You wanted someone who'd know about vampires? Well, who better than a two-hundred-year-old vampire? Besides, serves you right for stealing my beer."

Rynn rolled his eyes and made a derisive noise but otherwise didn't interfere. I unmuted the phone.

"Sorry about that, Alexander. Look, I ran into Sabine—"

"Is she dead?" he said, not bothering to cover the hope in his voice.

I frowned. "Ummm, I'm flattered you think I could kill a vampire—"

Alexander tsked. "I doubt you could kill a dead gerbil. I'm referring to your companion, the blond mercenary."

My mercenary companion—hunh. That meant Alexander had to have spoken to Charles in order to know about Rynn. I pushed back my gut response and went the diplomatic route. "No, Sabine's not dead. She's also not an old vampire like you. In fact, there's no way in hell she's over a year old."

He was silent for a long moment. "That is impossible—"

"It *is* possible, because I knew her when she was alive. Last September, to be exact. You either think I'm really stupid or you're hiding something."

More silence. Then, in a measured and clipped voice, "Who is she?"

My turn to tsk. "You know I don't work like that. You tell me something, I tell you something. Now, I'll give you her real name, hell, I'll even tell you her last known home address and toss in some bank account info, but you have to tell me something first."

"What?"

"How did she do it? How did she get so powerful in less than a year, and why doesn't sunlight torch her?"

I recognized just about every nasty term in French I knew and a handful I didn't. "I *cannot* tell you that—"

I hung up.

Rynn was watching me, now thoughtful instead of angry. I had no idea what had warranted the change, but I'd take it. I nodded at my beer, and he passed it back. I pointed the bottom of the Corona at Charles's cell phone.

"Watch. He'll call back as soon as he's done throwing a tantrum," I said.

"For someone who hates vampires, you're building up quite the repertoire," Rynn said finally.

"*No,* I'm using a resource." I pointed the open end of my now empty beer at Rynn and almost dropped it on the bar. Maybe it was time to cut myself off . . . after the next one. I'd had one hell of a rough day. "Of course, if he has the chance, he'll try to kill me and torture my cat. *Again.* But I'd be stupid not to use him for information while he can't track me down. What's so funny?"

Rynn took the empty bottle from my hand and replaced it with a new, cold Corona. "You referred to the vampire as 'him.' Twice," he said.

"So?"

He shrugged. "Just that I never thought I'd hear you referring to supernatural monsters as 'people' instead of 'things.'"

"They're still things."

"Your subconscious doesn't refer to things as 'he' and 'she.'"

I frowned. "I think I preferred it when you were scowling at me for getting into trouble."

Rynn snickered, and the phone vibrated across the counter. "Fine. Prove me wrong. Stop baiting the vampire," he said.

I made a face and answered, "Pest control. What kind of vermin would you like exterminated today?"

Rynn scowled.

"*Owl*—" Alexander said.

"Oh hi, Alexander, how are you? Spill or I'm hanging up."

I heard him draw a sharp breath. "I will keep this short so as not to waste our time. I cannot tell you anything concerning how Sabine acquired her strength."

"Well fine, I won't tell you anything about Sabine either. We're square, and this conversation is over."

"You are the most infuriating—" I swore I heard Alexander kick one of his vampires. I had to admit, after a year of running from the Paris boys, part of me was really enjoying this.

"What I *am* willing to discuss with you is certain vampire laws that necessitate our compliance."

I snorted. "I know enough about vampire laws to know none of you bother following any rules, unless it's 'Don't get caught.'"

Alexander sighed. "While that is often true, there are a handful that are taken more seriously than others. A few are punishable by death—if one is, as you say, caught."

"All right, I'm listening. Shoot. If it's actually useful, I'll give you what I know."

Something grated; I think Alexander was grinding his teeth. "There are three laws that we may not break. The first is to not kill another vampire. The second, and more serious, is that it is forbidden to feed off another vampire."

I rolled that over in my head. A little too slowly for my liking. OK, maybe I should cut back on the Coronas. "The killing vampires makes sense—though considering you guys multiply like cockroaches, my guess is it only counts if the other guy is bigger than you. What's with the no cannibalism?"

"I do not know for certain, for I have little to no interest in such occult practices. However, I remember one saying to me many years ago it was because the blood of another vampire is poisonous."

"How?"

"I do not know, though madness was loosely hinted at."

"I'm getting ready to hang up—"

Alexander tsked. "So impatient. Even though I had little interest, I always wondered, 'If the blood is poisonous, why make it a law punishable by death?'"

That clicked. In a warped vampire kind of logic, it even made sense. If feeding off other vampires made younger, weaker vampires stronger, it'd be in the upper cockroaches' interest to keep the younger ones from doing it. Hell, the madness thing might even be true; Marie was sure as hell well enough off the deep end to qualify. "Has there been a mass disappearance of vampires lately?" I asked, keeping the excitement out of my voice.

"I am afraid there are none I am aware of. I can tell you though that the Contingency takes missing vampires very seriously. This Sabine would need to be very careful to drain vampires and leave no witnesses. Very tricky, very careful."

"Or just toss a few vampires into a river during daylight," I said.

"Ah, yet that would result in some missing. We do keep track of our own."

"Like overlords in a pyramid scheme?" I said.

Well, it was better than anything I had, but something still bothered me. Curiosity got the better of me. "Wait, you mentioned one more rule. What is it?"

"Ahhh, did I? It is simply that you must acquire permission from the Contingency before making any vampire. Population control, as it were."

That clicked, and all the pieces slid into place. "You think Sabine is making her own vampires and feeding off them until they die?"

"An interesting academic question. If one needed to break one law, it reasons that it would be easier to break all three and leave no witnesses."

I ran that against what I knew of Marie when she'd been human. It still wasn't the smoking gun I wanted, but nothing about this entire job had been easy. "All right, Alexander. You've kept up your end." I glanced over at Rynn and Nadya for their approval. Both nodded, even if Rynn did it begrudgingly. "Sabine's name—or the one she was using before she turned vampire—is Marie Bouchard. I hired her to work the second case you gave me—the volcano over in Finland."

"*You're* somehow responsible for this?" Alexander hissed.

So much for friendly repartee. "Let me finish. If you bothered using your memory, you'd recall I needed help with new import licenses out of Iceland. Your exact response, and I quote, was 'What the hell do you think I pay you for?'" I even added in a French accent. "It was either risk getting caught smuggling my cargo into France, or find a good forger. I put out the word I needed someone, and Marie found me. She was a restoration artist in the archaeological museum, one of those people who do reproductions for tourists. She had a knack for documents and swore she could get past French customs, so I brought her on—*What*?" I said as Alexander snorted.

"I fail to see how this does anything but 'dig your own grave.'"

I rolled my eyes. I'd never thought about it much before, but Alexander had a bad habit of using colloquial American phrases, not always accurately. It annoyed me when I was working for him, and it annoyed me now. Goddamn it, for something that lived over a hundred years, vampires sure picked the strangest hobbies.

"No background? No reference?" Alexander asked, conveying his contempt. I wasn't about to add that it wasn't until later—much later—that I'd found out she'd basically stolen the job posting off someone else. Considering my contacts had been in pretty low places, that said plenty about the kind of person Marie had been stealing from. Instead I offered, "I was under the gun, Alexander—*your* fault. You wanted the goods yesterday, and I didn't have time to check. She said she could forge the customs documents to get your items clear, and she did."

I glanced up at Nadya and winced. She couldn't entirely hide the mixture of surprise and hurt. Guilt hit me. Nadya was my best friend and the only business partner I'd ever trusted. I'd never told her about Marie. I'd been too embarrassed.

I'd started taking supernatural-leaning jobs from Alexander at a low point in my life; I'd been freshly blacklisted from archaeology departments and universities everywhere. Needless to say, no one had wanted to hire me for anything other than trinkets and museum B&E's, and that hadn't paid enough to keep me under the radar. Hiding is expensive in the digital age. Anyone worth their weight as an antiquities thief veers wide of any jobs that even smell of the super-natural, and at the start, at least, I'd had every intention of doing the same . . . but I'd needed cash, and the hostess part-time lifestyle Nadya had in Tokyo wasn't for me. I'd swallowed my pride—and every ounce of good sense—and that's how I'd ended up working for Alexander.

I've been in over my head ever since. It wasn't worth it.

I'd spent almost a year fetching things for him before I'd figured out he was a vampire. He'd been my biggest bankroller. I'd built my career on fetching minor supernatural trinkets. That was why they'd had so little trouble tracing the cash they'd been paying me for almost a year. Right after my world imploded with the Paris boys, Nadya had put me up in Tokyo while I'd licked my wounds. I'd told her every-thing, including how stupid I'd been to take the supernatural jobs. She'd never judged me; she'd just listened and helped me get back on my feet.

But I'd never, ever mentioned Marie Bouchard. Hell, I don't even like to remind *myself* about the details of that sorry fiasco.

I tried to look apologetic as I continued. "Marie worked out re-ally well. For a while. I got a reputation for being able to slide any-thing past customs, and the jobs started pouring in. It wasn't until Ephesus that I noticed the first discrepancies. There were some strange emails to your underlings from me asking for site details any first-year archaeology major should have known, and I hadn't writ-ten them. She'd done it behind my back, and that's when I started digging. Turns out a Marie Bouchard did take art history, but she died in a car accident right after she defended her thesis. I looked up the obituary photos; she didn't look a thing like the Marie I knew. I did find mention of one of her classmates, Nicole Coutard, who had specialized in archaeological art restorations. *Her* class picture bore an uncanny resemblance to my Marie's. To top it off, she was wanted along with three other students in a site theft that went seriously south."

"She planned to steal from you?" Alexander said.

I shrugged. "I figured she was probably trying to get around needing me at all and loot the site behind my back. But that's not why I was worried. The dead bodies piling up in that site theft did."

Nadya swore in Russian. "She killed people at the site?"

I nodded. "The archaeologists died in a landslide, every last one, but the thieves forgot to take the catalogue. When the university realized pieces were missing, they suspected foul play and went looking for the four unaccounted students. They found three of them dead in fleabag hostels across France, each one poisoned and garroted."

Nadya's eyes went wide. Rynn just stared at the bar, his look reminiscent of the one I get when I'm knee-deep in a dig site, trying to piece all the details together.

"The worst part was it made no sense. The pieces they'd taken were in bad condition from weather exposure; broken, cracked, not worth much. None of them would have broken a few thousand. There was maybe—*maybe*—ten thousand total." I pointed to the vase and scroll still resting on the bar. "I won't lift a finger unless I can guarantee myself a profit of twenty."

"Ten thousand is still a lot of money. There are people willing to get their hands dirty for much less," Rynn said.

I pursed my lips. I wasn't explaining it right—or not in mercenary terms. "It's not just the body count. I'm talking about the effort and funds needed to orchestrate the whole thing. Funds need to be fronted, and then you need a guaranteed buyer with a set price—preferably half up front. Considering the pieces they took, I doubt there was a buyer."

Rynn frowned, still not convinced.

"Think of it this way; you wouldn't sell booze for less than it costs, right? But you don't just factor in the cost of the booze, you factor in rent, your time, wages, taxes, and on and on. A well-planned theft is the same thing. There is capital that has to be factored in before you claim any profit."

Rynn gave me a wry glare and shook his head. "Thieves with business plans."

I ignored him. "No one remembered anything unusual, except for some pothead kid cleaning toilets at one of the hostels where one of the guys had died. He told the cops the murdered man had been drinking with a girl. He only remembered her because he was staring at her legs. I tracked him down before heading to Ephesus and showed him a picture of Marie. It was her."

"Then what happened?" Nadya asked.

"I left for Ephesus a week early to try and get the jump on the site, but she was already at the tomb. I surprised the hell out of her and she started making excuses, tried to tell me it wasn't her, it was someone else, a fifth party, who'd been after all of them and used her as bait. I didn't wait around. I ran like hell. Marie was a good forger, but not so good on the archaeology front. She set off a pulley trap while she was trying to get hold of me, and the tomb started to close. I got out in time. She didn't."

The whole fiasco with Marie had taught me one hell of an expensive lesson: Be careful who you work with, especially when you're desperate. I spend a lot of time trying not to think about it; almost getting killed by a psychotic serial killer will do that to you.

I lifted my beer to my mouth, only to realize it was empty. Goddamn it, I thought Rynn had given me a new one. I slid the empty bottle over.

Rynn, the wonderful bar host he was, passed me a glass of water.

I made a face and passed it back. Rynn didn't look happy about it, but he got another Corona out. "Alexander, are we done yet?" I said, a little more tersely than I maybe should have. I wanted this over with.

"You have been most helpful," he said after a moment.

I couldn't decide if that was good or bad.

"But I do have one question. Why do you think she went to all that trouble?" Alexander asked.

"What do I think? I don't know. She's a psychopath who targets thieves? I don't think she had any motivation. I think she's doing what she was doing before, just now she's a vampire, so it's a hell of a lot easier."

"Hmmm. Crass as always. I have another theory," Alexander said. And hung up.

"Son of a bitch." I hate it when they beat me to the punch. I stashed the cell back in my pocket.

Rynn frowned. "They can trace that."

"Don't worry, I have it covered," I said, and swallowed another gulp of beer. Jesus, I was already halfway through the bottle. I held up three fingers to Rynn and raised a questioning eyebrow. He held up five fingers, then drew his hand across his throat. I was about to tell him exactly what I thought about him cutting me off when I noticed Nadya frowning, eyes on her vodka martini.

"Look, I'll get rid of the cell phone first thing tomorrow. I've got a plan," I said.

Nadya shook her head. "That's not it," she said, and looked at me. Not with her usual friendly eyes, but with calculating, "I smell trouble and it's you" eyes. "She never admitted to killing them, did she." It was a statement, not a question.

I shook my head. "She was already in the tomb, waiting for me. I ran, she chased."

"Yet she claimed there was a fifth person, someone else who might have—"

"There was no fifth person," I said, maybe a little too tersely.

"How can you be so sure?"

"Nadya, everyone she'd worked with was dead. I didn't stop and ask a lot of questions."

"You left her inside," she said. There was no missing the accusation in her voice.

I frowned. I had my own resentment and guilt to deal with. I didn't need Nadya's piled on top. "I didn't particularly want a garrote around my neck, so yeah, I left her there."

"Why would someone who was that obviously guilty deny their guilt?"

I shook my head. "There was no evidence of a fifth partner—anywhere. I *looked*. She wasn't even supposed to be in Ephesus. I went a week early. Trust me, when I broke into that tomb to find her already in there, I didn't exactly have a lot of time to think about my options."

"*Exactly*," she said. "You were so worried about saving your own damn skin that you didn't *think*. Alix, that's half you're problem. You *never* stop and think."

It took a second to sink in, but my face showed it as soon as it did. Nadya wasn't done with me.

"You weren't supposed to be there either. She wasn't trying to kill you, she was trying to avoid you. For all you know she was trying to save you from whoever killed her partners."

That . . . had never occurred to me. It set me back. I hate making mistakes. I stared at the red-lit table. "I've said it before and I'll say it again, Nadya: I'm not good with people."

She didn't yell, didn't scream—didn't say anything as she finished her martini and stood.

"Nadya," I said.

She held up her hand. She didn't even look at me as she slid her jacket on. "Not now. If I say anything, I might regret it. You can come by and get Captain tomorrow."

I don't like confrontation, and it usually takes a cold day in hell for me to lose my temper. Maybe it was the beer or the stress of the last week, but my control was wearing lace thin. "So, what? You're mad at me for saving myself?"

Nadya spun on her heels, and I sat back in my chair. I'd never seen an expression like that on her face before; anger, contempt, and, worse, disappointment. "No, of course I'm not mad at you for saving yourself. I'm mad because to do it, you buried someone in a tomb to die. You didn't even try to save her." She shook her head. "The worst part is you don't seem to care. You never questioned yourself or whether what you did was right or wrong. You let someone die. Regardless of whether you were justified or not, somewhere inside, you should be questioning what you did."

I remembered Marie screaming through the stone door, begging me to let her out, that she could explain. I'd spent a lot of time pushing back the guilt, and I sure as hell didn't appreciate my best friend throwing it in my face.

"I wouldn't have left her there if I'd had any other choice," I said.

"But that's just it. You did have a choice, you always have a choice, but you never take responsibility for your actions."

"You know me better than that—"

"Really? Because right now I don't feel like I know you at all."

I was angry, and getting angrier. I hadn't meant to leave Marie in the tomb, and I hadn't meant for her to turn into a vampire, yet my best friend was acting as if it was all my fault. "After the week I've just had, this is about the last thing on the planet I need right now—"

"Fine, have it your way. Nothing is ever your fault, you are *always* the victim of *all* your disasters."

My face heated up. "I am not a victim. Take that back."

"Why, ring too close to the truth?"

"*Take it back.*"

Nadya swiped a neon blue shot off a girl's tray, downed it while the girl stood stunned, and slammed the glass on the bar. Her host, Yukio, appeared beside her instantly and attempted damage control.

"You're right," Nadya said. "I do take it back. You're not the victim, it's your friends that end up victims." She added something in Russian to Rynn, who glanced up from the spot on the bar he'd been staring at while we'd fought. She then headed for the exit, Yukio close on her heels.

It wasn't until her back was turned that it hit me. What the hell had I just done? Nadya was my best friend—my only friend. I leaned my forehead on the bar and pushed back tears before looking up. At least Rynn's face didn't hold the disappointment and judgment Nadya's had.

"What did she say?" I asked, my voice barely a whisper.

He frowned. "I don't think you want a direct translation." He squeezed my shoulder. "Wait here, I'll go talk to her," he said, and left to follow Nadya and Yukio to the door.

He stopped Nadya at the exit, and I watched her let loose a tirade. Rynn stood there and took it, and after she was done, he said something that mollified her. Nadya's shoulders sagged, and the anger radiating off her dissipated like rain. I watched them exchange a few more words, then Nadya threw her head back and laughed. As Rynn walked her out, she was leaning on his shoulder. It struck me that they looked a hell of a lot closer than I'd ever seen them before . . .

I looked away, focused on my beer, and pushed the flash of jealousy away. I knew that if I was starting to consider Nadya and Rynn hooking up, I'd had enough to drink . . . I knew enough about Nadya to know Rynn wasn't her type. Rynn was pretty enough, but he wasn't Japanese. But still . . .

I rubbed my eyes and pushed the thought out of my head. I really had to stop getting jealous every time I saw Rynn chatting with a girl. I'd already said no, and considering I was down to one friend, I wanted to keep the status quo.

A few minutes later Rynn was back. He got two shot glasses out. He filled them with vodka before sliding one over to me and taking the other for himself.

"I thought you were cutting me off," I said, eyeing the drink.

He shrugged and raised his. "That was before you almost lost your only friend. I wouldn't head over there until tomorrow to be safe. Knowing you, you'll talk her right back into never speaking to you again."

What the hell. Things couldn't get worse. I picked up my shot glass. "Thanks. Here's to having one friend who still puts up with my disasters."

Rynn slid into the seat beside me before picking up his shot. "No one's perfect. And you're not as bad a friend as you think—no, you didn't have to say anything. I can read it on your face." He nodded at the door. "I think she's more upset that you never told her."

I looked down at the table. "It was a pretty stupid omission," I said.

We touched shot glasses. It burned as it went down my throat, and I pursed my mouth.

"Are you done backing yourself into deadly corners for the night?" Rynn asked.

I nodded. I felt better, though I wasn't sure if it was the booze or Rynn sitting beside me. I'd had enough to drink that I found myself not caring anymore.

Rynn considered me for a moment, his face unreadable as usual. I fidgeted with my collar. I got self-conscious whenever I caught him studying me a certain way—not a common condition for me.

"Aren't you busy with a client?" I said.

He raised an eyebrow.

"Your blond friend? I don't think she was impressed that you came over to see us." The questioning look didn't leave his face, so I added, "I told Nadya I was going to try my best not to screw up your work."

The corner of his mouth turned up into a mischievous smile, one I realized I hadn't seen in a while. He shrugged. "I sent her home. Your life is way more screwed up and interesting to hear about."

I stared at the bar, hoping Rynn wouldn't notice my flushed cheeks.

He moved in closer, not close enough to kiss me but close enough for me to pick up the vodka on his breath and his light cologne mixed with leather. That's when I made the mistake of looking up. Anytime I look Rynn in the eye, I can't bring myself to look away fast enough. I always end up staring a little too long, wondering how the hell his eyes are so blue.

He reached out and brushed a strand of hair behind my ear. "You're beautiful. If you didn't always run and hide, more people would see it."

I made myself look away. "I do not need that pointed out to me right now," I said.

"Doesn't hurt."

I felt his eyes on me, but he didn't move any closer, and for once I didn't run. We were at some strange equilibrium, like a balance waiting to be tipped. Maybe it was the alcohol, but this time my flight reflex wasn't screaming at me to leave, go, and hide . . .

I breathed in. "Do you really think I'm a train wreck?" I asked.

And that was all it took to tip the balance.

"That depends," Rynn said. He leaned in, and his lips brushed against my cheek. "Still think I'm a whore?"

12

WORST. HANGOVER. EVER.

9:00 a.m., somewhere . . . God, I hope I'm still in Tokyo

Ugh. It was morning, and way too bright. I rolled over onto my stomach and buried my head in the pillow.

It didn't help.

I've only had a handful of really bad hangovers in my short life. This was number four. Oh God, my head was pounding . . . And there was sunlight . . . Why the hell had Nadya left the blinds open? I opened my eyes. They didn't want to open, but I opened them anyways and pulled the cream-colored sheets back over my head.

Cream? When had Nadya changed the sheets?

The fog cleared, and memories of the night before—sketchy though they were—flooded back with a vengeance. I turned my head, slowly . . .

Rynn slept beside me. Whereas I'd passed out, at some point during the night he must have gotten up, because I was pretty sure he hadn't been wearing boxer shorts. His upper body was bare and above the covers, and looked even better in daylight . . .

I shut my eyes tight and tried to will my headache away. All that did was make the room spin. I ran my hand through my tangled hair. I had no reference point to deal with this. What was I supposed to do?

I did what any respectful thief would do. I crawled out of bed, grabbed my clothes, and snuck into the bathroom. What makeup wasn't left on the pillow had smeared down my face. I washed it off as best I could. There wasn't a brush anywhere to be had on the vanity, so I pulled my hair into a ponytail. Not great, but considering my hangover, I'd gotten off easy.

I opened the bathroom door, holding the handle so the catch wouldn't click. Rynn lived in a studio apartment, with an open floor plan and high ceilings. Only the bedroom was set apart by dividers. I'd figured he lived in a nice place, but I was impressed with the size, especially for Tokyo. He must have put some serious cash away from his mercenary days. He had good taste; minimal furniture, more functional than fashionable, and few decorations. Cleaner and less cluttered than my place in Seattle; I had a habit of collecting things and displaying them until I could sell. Suddenly I wanted to pack up some of the clutter back at my place and stick it in storage.

If I ever got back to Seattle.

I stood there, undecided. What was I supposed to do? Sneak out? Wake Rynn up?

My flight response won. If I got out now, I could pick up Captain, head to the airport, and worry about Rynn later. I headed through the kitchenette to the front door and found my bag and sunglasses along the way. Now where the hell had I put my boots? I opened the closet—way too neat for my liking; I have this theory that the neater the closet, the less likely you'll find anything. I got down on my hands and knees, and started rifling through Rynn's neatly arranged shoes. My boots had to be in here somewhere. I couldn't exactly go out into the hall barefoot.

"You know, I don't think I've ever been in the position of having to pin a girl down to stay."

I peeked around the corner of the closet. Rynn was leaning against the kitchenette counter with his arms crossed. He'd found a pair of gray sweats but hadn't bothered to put on a shirt. There are few people who look great without clothes in daylight. Rynn was one of them. He also didn't look anywhere near as tired or as green as I felt.

"Looking for this?" he said, and held one of my boots out to me.

I squeezed my eyes shut. So much for my escape plan. I stood up and grabbed the closet door to stop myself from falling. Hangover head rushes, bad. I could have sworn Rynn covered a laugh as I tripped over my own feet.

"You're not even hungover, are you?" I said.

He shrugged. "Perk of working in a bar. Or not drinking as much as you."

I held up my single boot. "Any chance you know where the other one is?"

He smiled. "The least you can do is have coffee with me. I'll take you over to Nadya's after." He nodded at my boot. "Unless you're set on bolting out my front door barefoot. If you are, try not to run through the lobby. It upsets the doorman."

"Now you're just making fun of me."

"Preempting. You think I'm backing you into a corner?"

"I do not—" I started, my face flushing.

"That reminds me. Before you even start, you know as well as I do you weren't that drunk when you came to bed with me last night, so don't even try it."

What the hell was I supposed to say to that? I let out an exasperated breath and sat down at the small kitchen table. There was no sense arguing with something so obviously geared towards getting a rise out of me. "I was going to say I don't normally do this sort of . . . thing," I said, and waved my hand in the general direction of Rynn's place.

"What? Have fun? Indulge? Let go for a few short hours? Stop me when I hit the right one."

I made a face. We were not going to have this discussion—not now, anyways. That this was all partly my fault didn't help. When we'd left Gaijin Cloud last night, I'd convinced myself I'd only crash on Rynn's couch, since I couldn't go back to Nadya's.

Yeah. Right. Sure I would. Drunk enough my inhibitions had been lowered; sober enough I'd still tried to justify it.

I could smell the coffee from the stove percolator. Just what my hangover needed. Thank God Rynn knew how to make a good cup. He passed me a mug and slid into the chair across from me. I took my first sip and picked up a hint of cardamom. Time to change topics.

"Turkish?" I asked.

He tilted his head in acknowledgment. "Yes. I spent some time there and developed a taste for it," he said.

"In other words, no, you're not from Turkey."

"I'll give you three more guesses this morning," he said.

Rynn had played this game with me a few times before. I'd already ruled out North America and most of Western Europe. That he had no discernable accent made it next to impossible to narrow down. "Ukraine?"

"No."

"South Africa—and it's a good guess, it fits with the whole mercenary thing."

He shook his head and smiled. "You can do better than that."

I pursed my lips. I'd hoped it was one of those. "I give up. Just tell me."

"It doesn't work like that. Besides, the game is most of the fun. You're a thief, you're supposed to be good at figuring things out."

"Archaeologist," I said. "Russia?"

"You're getting closer, but no. And that was your last guess."

I was about to say something about it being too early in the morning for this, but the buzzing on the counter derailed my train of thought. I scanned the kitchen and saw the buzzing was coming from my bag. "Shit, I was supposed to call and report in to Oricho last night." I scrambled across the kitchen and fumbled my phone out of my bag. I winced. There were four missed calls from Vegas. All from Oricho. "Yeah—hi, Oricho?"

"Owl, is everything well?" Oricho said, a concerned edge to his voice.

"Yeah—look, I'm sorry. Some things came up and I couldn't call you back right away." I cringed at my white lie, but it wasn't exactly far off from the truth. I had been too preoccupied to report in—first with Nuroshi, then with Nadya, and last, Rynn.

"I received some disturbing reports that one of your contacts from Tokyo University, Dr. Nuroshi Kabu, was murdered yesterday afternoon, along with two of his archaeology students—"

"I know," I said, and filled him in on our run-in with Marie—glossing over the sordid past together and the part about us lifting a few items. I didn't think my picking up the odd convenient item lying around would be an issue, but with Oricho you couldn't be sure.

When I was done, there was a pause on the other end.

"So you are no closer to translating the inscriptions and finding the whereabouts of the scroll. You have reached a dead end," Oricho said, pronouncing each word carefully, as if he'd been making sure that yes, in fact, Grandma did just die.

"Not exactly," I said, and rushed on so I wouldn't get his hopes up too much. "We recovered a lot more data from the sites than Nuroshi's students ever did. Don't get me wrong, they are—were—good, I just have more levels in dealing with the supernatural."

"Levels?"

Of course Oricho wouldn't get a World Quest reference. "Sorry. I've got a lot more experience than they do—did—" Goddamn it, if I referred to them in the present tense again I was going to start feeling guilty. I already have enough complexes as it is. I took another sip of coffee and pinched the bridge of my nose. *Come on, Owl, concentrate.* "I'm pretty sure they missed one, maybe two, sets of inscriptions. Whatever they and Nuroshi were trying to translate would have been incomplete."

"Like missing words?" Oricho asked.

"Mmmmm, more like trying to read a sentence with two-thirds of the letters removed."

"So you have everything you need to translate the tablet and writing on the egg now? It will tell you where the scroll is located?"

I winced at the rise in Oricho's voice. Time to manage expectations. "Finding the scroll is still a long shot. Even with the full inscriptions, we still have to find a translation key. I think we'll figure it out, I just don't know when. It's a dead language I've never seen before."

"Or supernatural," Rynn offered.

"Or supernatural," I said, and shot Rynn a dirty look. I didn't even want to consider supernatural languages at this point. There's a reason only supernaturals speak them; things tend to blow up when humans try to string a few words, let alone sentences, together. I wasn't about to experiment with what reading one might do.

I waited for Oricho's response, but he said nothing. I took another deep breath and pushed on.

"Look, I know it's not the smoking gun you'd like, but it's a lead—"

"How long will it take you to investigate these possibilities?"

I weighed the variables in my head. "It'll take me a few hours to sift through the images, and another few to search through Nuroshi's and his students' notes for a partial translation key. If it's in there, I should know by the time I touch down in Vegas."

"What about this Sabine?"

I glanced over at Rynn. "It should be fine. I'm with Rynn, and I have the feeling he can handle her." Rynn inclined his chin. "Besides, she's terrified of my cat."

"Your cat?" Oricho said.

"Let's just say vampires have a natural aversion to him." Speaking of which, I had a deal to uphold with Alexander. "Oh, one more thing, the Paris Contingency isn't involved. It's freelancers."

I heard Oricho's breath hiss over the phone. "A pathetic attempt to navigate our agreement and elude responsibility. Luckily Mr. Kurosawa included a clause that requires the Paris Contingency to control their numbers. I will inform him of the infringement. He does not take kindly to broken deals."

I'll bet. "As much as I appreciate it, you might want to hold off. I think I've handled it."

"Are you certain?" he said, uncertain. "Mr. Kurosawa is within his rights to demand satisfaction and the removal of these 'freelancers' and any other vampire that offends him."

I weighed what I said carefully. "No, I'm not sure, but it's less messy than an all-out dragon/vampire war with me caught in the middle."

Oricho paused. "What shall I tell Mr. Kurosawa?"

"Tell him there was a misunderstanding," I said. I held my breath and waited. It wasn't that far off from the truth.

"I will do as you ask, this once," Oricho finally said. "However, if there are any more 'misunderstandings'"—I was surprised at the venom in his voice, hopefully at the vampires and not at me—"there will be no more bartering. Advise me once you have landed in Vegas."

"Wait!" I said, catching Oricho before he could hang up. "One more thing, and it's important. I need you to get me in to see Mr. Kurosawa."

The line went silent for a four count. "That is exceedingly difficult, Owl. Lady Siyu or myself can ask any question you require on your behalf."

"I wouldn't ask if it wasn't necessary. I need to talk to him in person." And see how he reacted.

The line went silent again; this time I counted three seconds. "I will do what I can," Oricho said, and the line went dead.

I looked at Rynn. "He really doesn't like people who go back on deals, does he?"

"No, he doesn't, and you'd be wise to remember that."

I checked my phone as I took another sip of coffee. 9:30 a.m. One crisis averted, now on to the next dozen. If I had any chance of getting back to Vegas tonight, I needed to start moving now. I sent a probing text to Nadya.

SNY? (Systems normal yet?)

No more than five minutes passed before her response.

No. But they're not likely to improve. Come over.

I held my phone up. "Nadya gave me the green light to head over."

"I'll take you," Rynn said, and grabbed his leather jacket off the counter.

He still hadn't bothered to put a shirt on. "You plan on going out like that?" I asked.

The corner of his mouth twitched, not quite a smile but almost. "It crossed my mind." He got up and headed into the partitioned bedroom. Well, if anyone could pull off a bare chest under a leather jacket, it was Rynn.

I started to put my boot on. "Any idea where my other boot is?" I yelled.

"Right here. Come in and get it."

Yeah right. "Just throw it to me," I said.

"Coward," Rynn said. The next thing I knew, my boot was sailing through the air and I had to dodge out of the way. Son of a bitch! I drained the last bit of my coffee and not too gently dropped the cup into the sink. Two people could play it that way.

Rynn reappeared around the corner. He'd switched out the sweats for jeans and wore a black T-shirt decorated with gold paint underneath his leather jacket. "Breaking dishes is a little juvenile for you, isn't it?" he said.

"No more than throwing my boot."

He shrugged. "I expected more originality is all." He closed the distance between us, fast. I took a step back, right into the wall. Rynn was a good head taller, so he had no trouble leaning over me. "Now, why don't you tell me what's really bothering you?"

I avoided his eyes and stared at the floor. "Can we please leave it for now?"

"Look at me."

I channeled every stubborn and defiant thought in my head right into my face before meeting his stare. It was as if he was searching me, looking for something. After a few moments he backed off, clearly disappointed. He shook his head. "Have it your way, Alix. Though why you insist on running away from even those who go out of their way to earn your trust—"

"I'm not pushing you away—" I started.

"Yet you'd leave like a thief in the night rather than speak to me this morning." He touched my check briefly, then turned away from me. "You may want to play this game forever, but I won't. I'm sorry, this is my fault. Bringing you here last night was a mistake."

I closed my eyes. Goddamn it. Why the hell couldn't we just keep our status quo a little longer? I didn't know if I wanted more with Rynn, but, against all logic in my brain, I wasn't ready to shut the door just yet.

Oh well, blurt something out now, or slam a door. I guess I'm like Captain that way. I hate the idea of closed doors . . . maybe that's why people always equate cats with thieves. We'd rather have open boxes than closed . . . I took a deep breath.

"I was going to sneak out this morning because I didn't know what this meant—if it meant anything—oh, hell, I didn't want to be the girl who sticks around and asks where things stand," I said, and waved my hand in frustration.

Rynn crossed his arms and leaned against the counter. Waiting. I took another breath. When I have conversations like this, I find it's better to just get this stuff out in one shot. "Hosting, talking to girls, hell, maybe even sleeping with them sometimes. I care about you, Rynn. And it scares the hell out of me, because making me care about you is a part of your job."

"That's not fair," Rynn said softly.

"There are ten other girls just like me who you talk to, just like that girl last night. I've avoided doing *this* because I'd rather keep you as my friend than end up just another client you fall into bed with. That's why I try so hard to keep things the way they are—so I can still care and not get hurt."

Rynn kept his composure, but I could see frustration building under the surface. "Is that what you think I do? Toy with girls' emotions for fun? By now I hoped you knew me better than that."

This time I had no problem looking him in the eye. "No, I think you're one of the best friends I have. But I make a point of not trusting my own judgment anymore when it comes to people. Especially when I care about them. I usually get hurt."

We stood there for I don't know how long, eyes locked. I held my breath.

"OK," he finally said. His brow was still furrowed, but he uncrossed his arms and took a step towards me.

"OK what?"

"OK, I can work with that," he said, and kissed me. This time, instead of bolting for the escape route, I kissed back. We hadn't figured anything out, but somehow I was OK with it.

Rynn was the one who broke it off. "Come on, let's not keep Nadya waiting," he said, and pulled two helmets out of the closet. I took one and raised my eyebrow.

"We're taking my bike," he said. "I'm dropping you off, then coming back here to pack."

That caught me by surprise, until it dawned on me where he was going. It must have telegraphed across my face, because before I could say anything he added, "Yes, I've arranged to follow you to Vegas. Someone needs to make sure you don't get yourself killed."

I was about to argue. I usually argue, but this wasn't the battle to pick. Instead I said, "Let's go see how much Nadya has really cooled off."

Rynn placed a light hand on my arm as I tried to slip past him into the hallway.

"For the record, I've never met anyone like you."

—m—

Ten minutes later we pulled up in front of Nadya's apartment. I slid off the back, my legs shakier than I would have liked—Rynn's version of driving was what I called street racing—and handed back the helmet.

"You sure you don't want to come with me?" I said.

"You'll be fine."

I shook my head. "You're getting to be a bad influence on me. Left to my own devices, I'd have let this cool for another week, at least."

Rynn removed his helmet, a serious expression beneath it. "Alix, when I get to Vegas, there's something we need to talk about—nothing bad, just important, and not something I want to discuss on the back of my motorbike."

"Honestly, I've reached my serious talk quota for today. Can it wait until after I've gotten all the supernatural creatures off my case?"

He frowned. "I don't think that's likely to happen to you in the near future. I should be in Vegas late afternoon."

I thought about it and nodded. "Make it evening. Oricho's trying to get me to see Mr. Kurosawa."

Rynn wrapped his arm around my waist and pulled me in. My heart rate and body temperature shot up.

"I think you like being difficult on purpose," he said, and kissed me.

I snaked my fingers around Rynn's neck and kissed back. As much as part of me hated admitting it, I liked Rynn, a lot. And If I was being completely honest with myself, I liked kissing him. There was something comforting and calming about Rynn, especially when he touched me. I'd never noticed it like this before, but then, I'd never spent this much time with him. I'd always had an escape route lined up.

I heard the front door to the apartment building open behind us. I broke off with Rynn to see who was there, though Rynn didn't let go of my waist.

Nadya.

Instead of saying hello, I did a double take. Nadya was dressed in pink and black velour sweats and a matching pair of sneakers. Her face was bare of any makeup, and her usually fluorescent red hair was a decidedly natural color and tied in a ponytail. Not the Nadya I'm used to.

I recovered and untangled myself from Rynn. "That's a new look."

Captain appeared behind her, gave me a quick inspection, sniffed the air, and mrowled before sitting beside Nadya's feet and cleaning himself.

I shot Captain a dirty look. *Turncoat.*

Nadya stared at me, her hand on her hip, and gave us the once-over. I did my best to not look sheepish. She raised a perfectly arched eyebrow. The three of us stood like that for half a second, sizing each other up, as if we were still deciding whether we'd shown up to a gun-fight or a housewarming party.

Nadya broke the stalemate first.

"Well? Don't just stand there," she said, and waved a folded sheet of paper. "Owl, stop messing around with Rynn and help me pack. Our flight leaves in four hours."

I glanced at Rynn. "Guess we're not fighting anymore," I said.

He shrugged and passed me my bag. "If I'm right a few more times, maybe you'll start listening."

"Oh, I listen. It's the believing part I have a hard time with."

Rynn yelled something at Nadya in Russian, then gunned the engine. "Be careful this time. Straight to the airport," he said.

I nodded. That one was easy. I had no intention of chasing after a mad, superpowered vampire.

"Tomorrow night, then," he said. He winked, slid the visor down, and took off.

I made my way casually towards Nadya. Captain meowed and stood on his hind legs as I walked by. "Figures," I said, and picked him up. "You'll do anything for a can of tuna."

Nadya wasn't outwardly angry with me anymore. That was clear enough. But it was the subtle changes, the harder set to her jaw and the guarded look she gave me, that told me we weren't past this yet by a long shot.

"Nadya—" I started, trying to figure out what the hell I needed to say to make things go back to the way they were.

She stopped me with a shake of her head. "Save it. You can't fix it this time. Not completely, and not right away."

"I'm sorry. I should have told you about it, but I was so ashamed of the whole thing I just wanted it to go away."

Hunh. Ironic when you look where that got me.

"That's only part of it. Am I hurt you hid it from me? Of course. But you did something I never thought you capable of—me, who's supposed to be your best friend. That scares me—that *side* of you scares me. Not because I can't forgive you but because it's going to get you killed, and I've been to enough friends' funerals."

She was right, about everything. "What do I have to do?" I said.

She sighed. "We move on, and I hope to hell you show me you're the person I always thought you were, the person I know is inside there somewhere. Deal?"

I nodded. "Deal."

Nadya's mood lightened, and she nodded back towards her building. "Now, help me pack. We leave for the airport in two hours. Dish about last night and I'll put it towards calling it even."

"Yeah, what's this about 'we'?"

"Something is fishy about all this." She held up her hand as I started to protest. "Someone has to figure out what the hell is going on while you're running around. Marie is dangerous, and my nose tells me something else is going on besides just an artifact retrieval."

"It's going to be dangerous—" I tried.

Nadya ignored me. "Besides, I have all Nuroshi's old documents and jump drives. I've only scratched the surface, but there's some good stuff in here. You need me. And I haven't been to Vegas in a while."

I sighed. I knew that look. There was no dissuading Nadya once she set her mind to something. A number of Japanese hosts had found that out the hard way. "What flight are we on?"

"Oh, no—your boss is taking this very seriously. We're going on a private jet."

Private jet? Wow. Well, hell, maybe I'd even get some work done. "Provided they have coffee and Corona on board, they can bring me in on the Goodyear blimp."

"By the way, where did you stay last night?" Nadya asked, trying to sound less interested than she was.

"Rynn's," I said as offhandedly as I could.

Nadya grinned as she opened her apartment door.

"What?" I said, following her in.

"Sooo, you finally came to your senses and followed Rynn home?"

"I don't want to talk about it right now."

"Tough, I do," she said, and tossed me a bag of jump-stick hard drives.

I sighed and began sliding them into my bag. I tried to keep them in order with Nadya's color-coded tape. With luck we'd have a chance to get through most of them on the plane.

I searched through the various pockets in my bag. I could have sworn I'd put the scroll and vase in here last night . . . I found a folded note with my name on the front tucked in a side pocket.

It's not stealing, it's finding. I'll return this to the university.

"Son of a bitch."

"What?"

"Oh, nothing. We're just down twenty grand is all," I said, and tossed her Rynn's note.

"You mean you're down twenty."

"What?"

"Your boyfriend, your problem." She shrugged. "Only fair."

"He's not my boyfriend—"

"Close enough."

"Goddamn it. One night and he's already cost me twenty grand."

I headed into the kitchen for a coffee, pulled out my cell, and texted Rynn.

We need to have a talk about boundaries.

It's a date. Tomorrow night in Vegas.

I snorted and wrote back. *Just please say you still have that scroll. Otherwise I'm down twenty grand to Nadya.*

I closed my phone and headed back into the living room. "Everything OK?" Nadya asked.

I sighed. "You know me. I attract trouble."

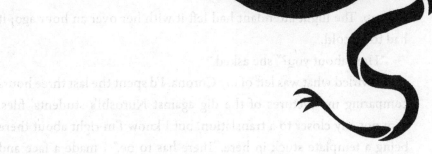

13

FANATICS AND COMPUTERS

4:00 p.m., somewhere over the Pacific Ocean

Fanatics and computers don't go together.

Most people put a couple passwords in and toss in a few extra fire-walls if they're really paranoid.

Fanatics add booby traps.

Nadya swore and shut Bindi's laptop. I glanced up from the binders and pictures laid out in a circle around me. We'd only been at it for six hours, but Nadya had bags under her eyes and looked like she was about ready for a nap or shower or both.

Well, at least the private plane was a nice touch. The seats were comfortable, and there was plenty of room . . . that, and the steward-esses weren't skimping with the Corona. "Anything?" I asked.

Nadya shook her head. "Someone didn't want anyone in these files. I'm terrified to open most of it, because I think there are self-destruct sequences built in, not only to wipe the hard drive—those are in here, too—but also for the computer to explode." She ran her hand through her hair and took a sip from her tea. She spit it back into the cup. The flight attendant had left it with her over an hour ago; it had to be cold.

"How about you?" she asked.

I swirled what was left of my Corona. I'd spent the last three hours comparing my pictures of the dig against Nuroshi's students' files. "I'm not any closer to a translation, but I know I'm right about there being a template stuck in here. There has to be." I made a face and started flipping through a file I'd discarded hours ago. "I just need to puzzle all the pieces together."

Nadya cradled a bottle of water in her lap and chewed her lower lip. "I may have found one thing, but," she said, holding up her hand as I sat up, more alert than I'd been in hours, "*if* it is anything, it is *only* a hint. Some of her emails were left open. It may be nothing, but she keeps referring to a 'device.' It's all ramblings, mind you, but I think Mr. Kurosawa's artifact and this device are one and the same." Then she showed me the emails.

Sure enough, in between the ravings of a Sabine/Marie-worshiping fanatic, there were references to a "device of blood and destruction, a great equalizer" they'd been looking for in all the same places I'd been.

"Any other mentions of this great equalizer?"

Nadya shrugged. "Beyond those emails it's gibberish. As you said, this girl is 'batshit crazy.'"

I couldn't help thinking what Alexander had told me about Marie and what she did to her flunkies.

"It sounds like a weapon more than a device," I said. I really didn't like the idea of Marie, or Mr. Kurosawa, for that matter, getting their hands on any kind of "great equalizer." Something about the mention of blood got me thinking. I opened my laptop and pulled up the blood pictographs from the first site. There was something about them that didn't quite fit with the other sets; they were more picture than writing, if that makes sense.

"Hmmm?" I said. I'd completely missed something Nadya had said. "Do you have something?"

"Kind of sort of." I flipped my laptop around to show her the images. "I need to do some cross-referencing, but I don't think this set is part of the writing. I think it might be the codex. I need to run a search for similar images on the net." I took a closer look. People, or some kind of animal, maybe dancing around a ring . . . or, for all I knew, it could have been a gathering of gods, or a hunt; ancient pictographs aren't exactly known for precision. You'd be amazed how many are horribly misinterpreted. Those cave pictures in France, for example? They aren't chasing the animals to eat them.

I'll let you mull that one over.

I closed the laptop and finished off my Corona. "Regardless, it'll have to wait until we reach Vegas. I need access to online archives, and I need some sleep. Maybe Mr. Kurosawa can even shed some light on what the hell he has us chasing after."

Before I'd stepped on the plane, Oricho had left a message saying Mr. Kurosawa was reluctant to meet me. I'd called back, gotten his voice mail, and left a message. "*Oricho, Mr. Kurosawa can stuff his 'reluctance.' I don't care if you have to move heaven and earth in the next twelve hours, get me that meeting.*"

A half hour later he'd sent me another message, this time saying he "*. . . perhaps had arranged an appointment with Mr. Kurosawa.*"

How the hell do you "perhaps" arrange an appointment?

Nadya glared at me. "Alix, please, I am begging you. Don't mouth off to the dragon. Not while I'm there."

"Depends," I said, and settled back into one of the plush chairs.

Nadya glared. "Depends on what?"

I frowned. Where did they keep the blankets on private planes? In first class they always had them right by the seat. I started looking under the chair. "On how much I think he's hiding. I'm getting sick and tired of vampires and other assorted supernatural creatures trying to off me on this job."

"What about the inside person? The one who is feeding Marie information?" Nadya said.

I let out a low whistle. "My money is on Lady Siyu. I can't prove it yet, but I think she's the one who wants me dead."

"Why would she risk betraying a dragon just to kill you?"

"Wait until you see her. She's a real piece of work, hates humans— Come to think of it, that might be enough. Turning the device and me over to Marie could be a big 'eff you' to her boss for bringing a human onto this job. You don't know these monsters like I do—count yourself lucky. They don't think like us, and the ones who don't think we're food figure we ought to be indentured servants. And they're petty; they spend more time fighting with each other than an '80s rock band."

Nadya shook her head. "I still think it's far-fetched. Why not just wait until you finished your work for her boss and then poison you, or strangle you or something . . . what?" she said when I frowned. When I didn't respond, she continued, "Just because they're petty and think we're insects doesn't mean they're incapable of logical thought."

I shook my head. "I'll have a better idea what's going on after I speak with Mr. Kurosawa," I said, and shut my eyes to try and get some sleep during the flight's remaining three hours.

Just as soon as I'd started to drift off, Captain complained. I groaned.

"You couldn't have asked earlier?" I said. He swished his tail and danced on his front paws. I pushed myself up and led him to the washroom.

"No rest for the wicked," I said.

———— ᨰ ————

7:00 p.m., Vegas.

Oricho was waiting for us at the airport with a black limo.

"Hi, Oricho," I said before tossing my bags in. "Did you get me my meeting?"

He frowned. "With some effort. Mr. Kurosawa and Lady Siyu were not happy with the demand."

"Well, tough. If he wants this job finished, I need to speak with him, not you and Lady Siyu."

"I related as much. Though I caution you to be careful in your treatment of this request. A dragon requests one's presence; they are not accustomed to granting audiences."

"Yeah, I figured as much," I said as Nadya, Captain, and I piled into the back. "I promise I'll try to be careful."

Nadya snorted and rolled her eyes. Well, I'd try my best. Whether I'd succeed or not was a different matter.

We headed through the Vegas strip to the Japanese Circus. Nadya and I didn't say anything on the ride over, just watched all the pretty lights go by. I wondered how many supernatural entities lived here. Somehow I doubted it would hold much appeal for anything other than dragons or vampires, maybe a succubus or incubus. Most supernatural creatures like a sense of history, roots in civilization. Vegas is just a flood of lights and a hell of a lot of people partying.

Even Captain didn't make a fuss on the ride over. Sometimes the universe says silence is the best course of action. When that happens, I try to listen.

It wasn't until we passed the main entrance of the Japanese Circus that I perked up. We headed straight for the underground garage.

"Hey, Oricho, what's going on?"

"Mr. Kurosawa has given explicit instructions for this meeting. We are to use a separate entrance."

"Well, can we at least let Nadya off? She doesn't need to be here."

"I'm afraid that is not possible," he said, all business. The glass partition slid up between us.

"*What's going on?*" Nadya mouthed.

I shrugged. Shit. This wasn't good. There was no reason she had to meet a dragon.

"Oricho?" I tried. But there was no response through the glass.

The car didn't stop until we reached the fourth basement. The lights dimmed, and as hard as I tried to peer out the window, I couldn't make out a damn thing. That the doors were automatically locked didn't escape my notice either. Captain gave a low growl.

"Yeah, I'm not much fond of this cloak-and-dagger crap either," I told him.

"Reminds me of stories my parents used to tell me of the Russian Secret Service taking people away in the middle of the night, never to be seen again. Only they didn't use limos," Nadya said.

I bit my lower lip. Could we make a run for it? Not likely, and besides, Oricho didn't seem to hate humans as much as most of the supernatural world did. At least he had a sense of fair play. We were also too far underground. Better to wait until we were in the casino to make a run for it if we had to . . . if we made it that far.

There were no parked cars on the fourth level. Oricho pulled up beside a black door embossed with the gold lotus designs I'd seen on the roof. The car door swung open. I crawled out first. Captain growled again and raised his hackles. I shoved my hands in my pockets, trying not to look as shaken as I was.

The door opened on its own into a wood-paneled hallway, complete with bamboo-paneled floors done in feudal Japanese style. Only the electric torches hinted at its modernity and lit the walls painted red with black lotus designs. Oricho stood aside and waved us through. I glanced over at his impassive face, and my temper spiked. Here I was, terrified we were going to be eaten by a dragon, and Oricho looked like this was just another day of work.

"I get the sinking feeling I'm being pushed into the thieves' entrance of a dragon mousetrap," I said as I passed him by.

He raised his tattooed eyebrow, the closest I think he came to surprise. "I give you my solemn word that is not Mr. Kurosawa's intent. He feels it safest if no one knows you are here and wishes you to use this entrance."

"Nadya doesn't need to be here though."

Oricho shook his head once. "He wishes to meet your business partner."

I hesitated over the threshold.

Oricho added, "You have my word no unjust misfortune shall befall you or your companions."

"That all depends on what your definition of *just* and *unjust* is," I said. That was about as good as I figured I'd get from Oricho, and he didn't strike me as one who gave his word lightly. Whereas humans could break their word whenever the hell they felt like it with no consequences, the supernatural—with the exception of vampires and a few other bottom feeders—were physically bound to their word. Think genies. I hoped Oricho was that kind.

"Let's get this over with," I said, and stepped into the red hallway, Nadya and Captain close behind me.

My eyes started to adjust to the electric torches, and I did a double take. It was a tunnel more than a hallway, and it was covered with murals in sealed glass cases, all scenes of samurai. Old murals, if I was any judge, like feudal Japan. The colors were beautifully preserved, easily one hundred grand per case, maybe more, depending on whether it was a known artist or rare . . .

I caught Oricho studying me.

"This is my own private collection," he said. "I had this entrance constructed when we relocated ten years ago. The paintings remind me of home—and more comforting times."

"They're beautiful. 1000 AD, I can't place them though . . ." I stopped in my tracks as my eyes fell on the largest painting, a battle scene between an army and a red dragon. Amongst all the paintings, six in total displayed a supernatural element.

"You will not place them," Oricho said, stepping beside me, running a hand across the glass case beside the dragon battle scene. A samurai fighting a green and gold naga . . .

"I made them myself. These," he said, indicating the six supernatural paintings, "are originals. The others are reproductions of paintings burned in a fire outside Osaka more than one thousand years ago." He motioned to a mural of two blindfolded samurai navigating a dragon's lair, the dragon clinging to the rocks above, waiting for them to pass. Both the samurai had half their faces covered in black tattoos. Just like Oricho's. I swallowed hard and caught him studying my reaction.

"Six hundred years ago I led an army of samurai, loyal to the last, even into death. They had the honor of proving it the day a neighboring warlord challenged us to battle." The corner of his lip curled up. "He met us on the battlefield at dawn and within the first hour had decimated half my army. Too late I realized my mistake in underestimating him. Thinking he was honorable, I offered my allegiance in return for sparing my samurai." Oricho's mouth tightened, and his green eyes flared red. "He agreed, but as it turns out, we had different definitions of *spared*. Every last one of my samurai was executed while I watched on my knees. He said it was an honor to serve him in death."

"What was the warlord's name?" I asked, already knowing the answer.

"Kurosawa. He needed another servant to guard his lair while he slept. I was the winning candidate," Oricho said.

I'd assumed he was a voluntary employee . . . not an indentured servant. "Why did Mr. Kurosawa make you bring me through here?" I said.

Oricho inclined his head. "I believe he wishes you to see what happens to those who raise his ire."

"*What* are you?" I said.

He turned his back on me and continued down the hallway.

I was shaken. I followed in silence for another fifty feet. The walls of glass-encased pictures stopped, and the hallway forked into two narrower red hallways. We kept to the right until we reached another doorway. Black lacquer with another gold lotus embossed on it. Oricho opened it this time.

Right back into the dragon's private casino.

I grabbed Nadya's arm as she started to step past me. "It's Mr. Kurosawa's lair, the one I told you about," I whispered. She nodded and fell in step behind me.

I glanced over at Oricho. I was liking the look of this less with each step. "Don't you guys have any better spaces for meetings? Like a boardroom or office?"

"This is Mr. Kurosawa's preference. I have given you my word you will not be harmed. I do not give my word or protection lightly," Oricho said, without a trace of deception on his face.

"Lead the way, and let's get this over with so I can get back to work."

Oricho led the way through the rows of flashing slot machines. Whereas before they'd been silent, now they clinked and chimed all over the room in a warped imitation of an electric orchestra. Nadya squeezed my wrist.

"Stay close and try not to look at the lights," I said. "And whatever you do, don't let Oricho out of your sight," I said as Captain's ears perked up and he began to creep towards one of the machines as it chimed jackpot and coins poured out. I picked him up and tucked him under my arm before he could reach any of the coins. "That goes double for you, mister." Cold air brushed against my skin and sent a shiver up my spine. "I guess cats aren't immune to dragon lairs either," I said.

Oricho cleared his throat from the end of the row. "Perhaps you should put your animal in a carrier."

"We're good now. It won't happen again." It damn well wouldn't with the grip I had on him. I slid the leash on for good measure. He mrowled in protest. "Well, if you'd stop running off, I wouldn't need the leash, would I?"

"It's eerie how the slot machines keep running without any players. I don't like it," Nadya said, keeping her voice low. "It smells wrong, cold, like dark winter." She tsked and shook her head. "It's hard to describe, but there is something off in the entire room."

It hadn't occurred to me until Nadya pointed it out, but with the running machines and cold air . . . "Nadya, not to alarm you, and just so you know, but red dragons collect ghosts." I glanced over at Oricho for confirmation.

He gave me a sad smile. "I told you Mr. Kurosawa and I had differing interpretations of *sparing*. What better spirits to guard his treasure room than that of a loyal samurai army?"

I felt sick to my stomach. Nadya's eyes went wide, and she cursed under her breath. Her grip on my wrist tightened. We both edged ourselves around a narrow corner of the crowded maze. I don't think either one of us breathed until we spilled onto the poker floor.

Mr. Kurosawa sat on the white leather couches by the mirrored coffee table, waiting for us, just like he had before. Lady Siyu stood behind him, a tray of drinks in her hands. Her lacquered red mouth drew in a severe line of displeasure at the sight of me.

Mr. Kurosawa smiled, and I felt Nadya straighten beside me and draw a quick breath. He'd only made a passing effort this time to appear human. His skin was bright red, and wisps of smoke rose off it like rain on hot pavement. His eyes glowed red, consuming his black pupils, and black fangs like those of a tiger protruded over his lower lip.

I think Mr. Kurosawa was more frightening like this than if he'd completed his shift into a thirty-foot-long dragon.

He laughed, though it sounded more like a growl. He indicated the couch in front of him. "Please, Owl and companion. Be seated," he said.

Lady Siyu sidled around the couch and offered us both a drink. Nadya glanced over at me, eyebrows raised and hands clasped in her lap as Lady Siyu balanced the tray in front of her. "Take a drink, any drink," I said between my teeth, and proceeded to take the martini. Nadya reached for a glass, then hesitated.

"Trust me," I said. "If they want to kill us, they don't need poison."

That earned me a shocked expression from Lady Siyu and another guttural laugh from Mr. Kurosawa.

"Well said. Now why don't you explain why you are here and not searching for my artifact? Oricho claims you are getting close."

"OK, that's fair," I said, and placed my martini on the mirrored coffee table. Time to set myself apart from the run-of-the-mill human. I looked straight at Mr. Kurosawa. "Why the hell didn't you bother telling me I was after some kind of supernatural weapon?"

Lady Siyu hissed, and the pretense of a smile faded from Mr. Kurosawa's face.

Oricho stepped in. "Mr. Kurosawa, I apologize. Owl has run into a competitor searching for the same artifact." He gave me a sideways glare. "She must have acquired that information from them—"

I held up my hand. "Oricho, don't bother. I'm sick of being left in the dark on this 'artifact.' You can't possibly expect me to find it when I barely have an idea what I'm looking for, and this bullshit about not knowing, when all three of you obviously do—hell, even Marie knows more than I do, and she's a crazy vampire, and I don't mean their usual brand of crazy, I mean psychotic crazy. You've sent me in completely blind and expect me to perform some kind of miracle retrieval. Well, I have news for you. Either start helping me, or your time will be better spent blackmailing another archaeologist."

Oricho's jaw was clenched. "It is not so simple as you ask—"

I snorted. "If I had a dime for every time a supernatural monster used that line on me . . . what is it with you people?"

"There is no need for that tone," Lady Siyu said, stepping around the glass table towards me.

"Yeah, there is. You think I'm a servant at your beck and call? I've got news for you—I'm not playing. And for the record, the ghosts, the secret entrance? I'm a professional, I don't appreciate the scare tactics."

"You will show respect when addressing Mr. Kurosawa." There was a threatening drop of the *s* in "Mr. Kurosawa," and it came out like a hiss.

I stood up and Nadya followed. "Fine, have it your way." I gave a mock bow to Mr. Kurosawa, who was looking less than pleased with my display.

"You dare go back on your agreement?" Lady Siyu said.

Now that she was mad, I even got the glint of fang. Naga. No wonder she was so pissed about the Bali temple. Chances are I squashed a relative. Hopefully a close one.

"You don't need an archaeologist, you need a hired thug," I said. I turned my back on her and headed for the door.

Oricho blocked my way. "Much as I admire your bravery, I cannot help you if you persist with this course of action," he said quietly, a sympathetic expression on his face.

"Oh, come on. I have no intention of going back on my word, but if you three are bent on keeping me in the dark, then you might as well let us get back to work and hope to hell Sabine doesn't have a translation yet." While my bravery was still fueled by my temper, I grabbed Nadya and Captain and stepped around Oricho.

"What is it you need?" Mr. Kurosawa said.

I stopped and slowly turned around.

The smoke had stopped rising off his skin, and he'd switched back to the well-respected Japanese businessman in an expensive gray suit. I had no idea if that was a good or bad thing. "For one, I need help with this translation."

"What about Nuroshi? You've used him before, and he has been efficient," Lady Siyu said, not bothering to hide her contempt.

"Yeah, funny you'd mention him. He was working for Sabine before she put a spear in his back, so to answer your question, no, I won't be using Nuroshi."

That surprised her. I guess Oricho hadn't told her yet. Well, at least one monster was taking my advice seriously.

"It's coded," I continued, "but nothing I recognize. I think it might be supernatural text."

Mr. Kurosawa snarled. "Unlikely. As a habit, we do not leave such things lying around for humans to stumble into."

"All the same, I'd like you to look. Saves me blowing myself up trying to read it."

Smoke spilled out of his nostrils, but he held out an expertly manicured hand. I passed him the file with all the copies of the language I'd found thus far, including the blood inscriptions.

He took the file and passed it to Lady Siyu. "Anything else?"

"As a matter of fact, yeah. Once I get you this weapon, what do you plan on doing with it?"

"Mr. Kurosawa," Lady Siyu said, her eyes narrowing as she fixed me with a vicious stare, "I understand the necessity of bringing in this *human* for business purposes, but it is beneath you to be performing a servant's tasks by answering *its* questions."

I balled my hands up at my side and took a step towards her. "Why don't you try calling me a servant when you don't have a dragon, Oricho, and a room full of ghosts standing behind you?"

"Enough," Mr. Kurosawa said, his voice echoing around the room like a well-rehearsed parlor trick. Except it was no trick. Lady Siyu stepped back from me, and for once I kept my mouth shut.

"You will have a translation, as best as can be accomplished, by tomorrow," he said. "As for the weapon, my only wish is to remove it from circulation."

"Bullshit," I said.

Nadya gasped. Oricho placed a hand on my shoulder, a troubled look on his face. "Owl, I caution against this—"

"Well, you'll all forgive me if I have a hard time believing you want me to find a weapon for you *not* to use," I said, not bothering to cover my sarcasm.

Mr. Kurosawa smiled at me. It wasn't friendly. "Regardless of what you wish to believe, that is the truth. All you need to know about the device is that there are those of us who are not as satisfied to live in coexistence with humans as I am—"

I snorted. "If by 'coexistence' you mean 'enslave at will,' sure."

Mr. Kurosawa frowned, which added a dangerous cast to his face. His well-manicured fingers dug into the couch. "You will be doing your kind a favor retrieving it for me."

I bit my lower lip. Here was the thing: until I knew more about what the scroll/device did, I had no intention of putting my faith in a dragon's good intentions. *Especially* after hearing about Oricho's samurai. But it was a catch-22. Letting a supernatural weapon land in Marie's hands had to be worse . . .

One step at a time. I'd decide what to do with the scroll once I had it. If it was too dangerous to fork over to Mr. Kurosawa . . . well, I'd deal with that when I got there.

"Just keep me in the loop from now on, otherwise you'll be chasing Sabine for your damn scroll," I said. I turned and started to head for the casino door.

"One more thing we need to discuss," Mr. Kurosawa said.

I glanced over my shoulder in time to see his eyes flash red. Then I was airborne. I heard Nadya yell and Captain howl right before I slammed into the wall, pinned like an insect to a board. I tried to breathe but found the pressure on my chest didn't make it possible.

Shit, I'd made a mistake. I'd pushed Mr. Kurosawa too hard. This was going to be bad.

"Now that I have your attention, Ms. Hiboux, I have a few things *I* wish to say. First and foremost, I take great offense at being referred to as a monster, however indirectly."

The pressure intensified and pushed the remaining air out of my lungs. Captain howled and darted across the room to where I was now pinned, but he couldn't reach me. Nadya started to yell, but her voice was muffled. Out of the corner of my eye I caught Oricho covering her mouth and speaking to her. One point for Oricho, not letting my friend follow in my suicidal footsteps.

Mr. Kurosawa continued, "Secondly, Lady Siyu and Oricho act as my hands. As there appears to be some confusion, let me clarify. An order from them is an order from me."

I nodded against the pain. Something snapped in my chest; I think it was a rib.

"Lastly and most importantly, you are never to request an audience with me ever again. Otherwise, I will run you through my maze and let my ghosts chase you down like the dog of a thief you are."

The first icy blast hit me, followed by a second, third, and fourth. On the assault of ghosts went until my limbs were so cold I couldn't feel them anymore. When I thought I'd just pass out, I heard Mr. Kurosawa's voice cut through the ghosts as if he was standing beside me.

"Have you learned your lesson yet, Ms. Hiboux?" The pressure decreased on my chest and I gasped in sweet air.

Mr. Kurosawa stood below me, flashing his black tiger teeth and waiting for an answer.

The smart answer was yes, but I think by now we've established my character flaws.

"*Fuck you,*" I said.

Mr. Kurosawa stared at me a moment, as if he didn't quite believe I was that stupid. Then he snarled and let out a low growl. An icy hand gripped my throat, and I smelled sulfur as the cold choked off my air once again. I kicked out and tried to draw in a breath; I was suffocating, or freezing to death. I wasn't sure which one was worse.

Like hell I was going to give him the satisfaction of breaking me. A pang of guilt hit me as I realized Nadya and Captain were going to have to watch me die. I hoped Oricho kept up his end of the bargain and got them out. They hadn't been dumb enough to piss off a dragon. Well, at least I'd have the satisfaction of watching Mr. Kurosawa kill his one and only chance of finding his artifact. I glared down at him.

"Mr. Kurosawa," Oricho said, and stepped forward, his head bowed.

The dragon growled and ice shot down my throat, reaching for my heart. I screamed . . . I think. Captain howled below me.

"I beg you, Mr. Kurosawa, though you are justified in your punishment of this mortal, we still need her to reach your goal."

The ice and pressure lessened. The jury was still out as to whether I'd black out.

"I believe this one is prone to unwise outbursts and will regret her actions imminently." I thought Oricho shot me a dirty look, but I couldn't be sure. "I will take responsibility for her and her companions for the remainder of their service."

Three heartbeats later, air returned to my lungs. I slid to the floor and landed hard behind one of the poker tables. Nadya and Captain rushed to my side.

"Alix?" Nadya said.

I tried to focus my eyes and only half succeeded. I got one last whiff of cold sulfur. "I'm freezing," I said.

Oricho appeared around the poker table, and both he and Nadya helped me up, Captain making encouraging noises and pushing my legs . . . at least, that's what it felt like.

As soon as I was upright, I glanced around the room. Mr. Kurosawa and Lady Siyu had already left. Probably for the best.

"Of all the stupid things to do, Owl," Nadya said.

"Can we save it until I'm not frozen? Please?"

"Your companion is correct. That was not an advisable course of action," Oricho said.

I shook my head, trying to clear it, as Oricho and Nadya helped me into the hallway towards the elevator. "What the hell is wrong with you supernaturals?"

"There are certain rules and protocols that must be followed when dealing with humans. One is that they are not to be told our secrets. You already have stumbled over many of our inner workings through your own means. Defiance, while excusable in a lesser human and admirable for bravery, does not work in your favor."

"I'll try to remember that for next time," I said.

The four of us headed into the elevator. My fingers and feet were still numb, but I could move my legs. What I needed was a warm bath.

When we reached our floor, Oricho inclined his head down the hall. "Your companion is in suite 12. Can she attend you until the morning?"

"My *name* is Nadya. And she'll be fine," she said.

Oricho transferred my weight over to Nadya and gave us a quick bow before turning back to the elevator.

"Oricho. What does that mean, exactly, that you're taking responsibility for us?"

"Exactly that. Your trespasses against Mr. Kurosawa are now mine." His eyes narrowed.

I nodded. "Great, I screw up, you get punished. Is that how it works?"

He didn't correct me as he stepped into the elevator.

"Why the hell do you work for him?" I said, and winced as feeling came back into my fingers. Why do thawing fingers always hurt like a son of a bitch? "He's evil. As far as I can see, you aren't."

"Because I gave my word," he said before the elevator door shut.

Nadya helped me into my room and dropped me on my bed. "Are you going to be OK?"

I nodded.

She crossed her arms and glared at me. "Wonderful. Can you tell me what the hell that was all about?"

I sat up. It hurt. "I had to make a stand with them, otherwise they'll never think of me as more than a lowly human servant. Mouthing off"—I managed a shrug—"showed them I wasn't a pushover, and that I'd rather die than cower."

"How does that help you?"

I shook my head and wrapped the comforter around me. Next step, warm bath. "They'll be more careful now. Mr. Kurosawa knows he won't find the scroll before Marie without me." My head started to go dizzy again, so I leaned back into the pillows. "I'd have never have gone that far if Oricho hadn't offered protection when we stepped inside. Otherwise, Mr. Kurosawa would have just as likely punished you and Captain too—what's another human, right? I wanted to warn you, but I didn't want to waste the chance. Sorry."

"I'm not mad at you," she said, pushing her hair out of her face. "Rynn pointed out something to me the other evening, and I'm starting to see that it's true."

"What was that?"

"That you can't help but do stupid things. It's in your nature. It's also what makes you the best at what you do. I'm next door. Let me know if you need anything."

I didn't want to lift my head to nod, so I gave her a thumbs-up. When my head stopped spinning, I called room service.

"Yes?" came a girl's voice.

"A Corona, please, and put a shot of tequila in it."

My phone buzzed before room service arrived. It was Rynn, saying he was running late and wouldn't be in until tomorrow.

I texted back: *No worries—that works out better. I just went a round with the dragon and lost. Will tell you about it later. Right now I need a long nap.*

No sooner had I put the phone down than a call came through.

"Do you listen to anything I say?" Rynn's voice was controlled, but just barely.

"Before you get upset, it was unavoidable. It also went a lot better than it could have. Oricho ran interference before Mr. Kurosawa had a chance to do any permanent damage."

"And *what* was the point of that?"

"Show my dominance?"

Rynn snorted. "Train wreck."

"Whore. Besides, I thought my poor decision-making skills are part of my genius."

"Nadya wasn't supposed to tell you that."

I rubbed my head. I could feel the start of a bad headache coming on. "Look, I'm sorry. But I'm tired of all these supernaturals pushing me around. Haven't you ever wanted to tell them all to fuck off?"

"Not when they can squish me like a bug."

"Yeah, well, I'm sick of it."

There was a moment's hesitation on the other end. "Owl, be careful. Try not to do anything stupid until I get there."

"I'm done mouthing off to dragons and nagas for today," I said.

"It's the morning I'm worried about, when you're feeling better. Call me first thing," he said, and hung up.

I sat there looking at the phone. Maybe it was the near-death experience, but I wished Rynn hadn't been delayed. My reflection was interrupted by a knock at the door. I slid the phone onto my night-stand and made myself stumble out of bed. I swung the door open with about as much charm as a freight train.

The girl outside couldn't be more than eighteen . . . nineteen, tops. I must have looked worse for wear, because her eyes went wide. "Ummm, I—here," she stuttered as she passed me the bill to sign.

"Sorry," I told her, and handed the paper back with a generous tip. "It's been a rough night."

She nodded and retreated down the hall about as fast as she could without actually running.

"Well, I tried, Captain."

He glared and gave me an unconvinced meow.

"Next time I'll make more of an effort not to scare the shit out of the kid, OK?"

That seemed to satisfy him, so I drew a hot bath and climbed in. My feet and fingertips were still numb. The bathtub had a TV, so at least I could catch up on the news I'd missed over the last few weeks. There was a brief mention about the students and professor murdered in Japan, as well as the American students missing and dead in Bali. Both cases were being classified by the local authorities as serial mur-ders, orchestrated and carried out by two highly disturbed and dan-gerous students.

Well, they'd gotten the disturbed part right. Pictures were shown of Bindi and Red. No mention of Nadya, Rynn, or me in either of the cases. Or vampires. I shot back the tequila. That was how the world worked. No such thing as monsters.

Captain crept up on the edge of the tub and tried to get comfortable—or as comfortable as possible, inches away from a pool of water. I checked the clock on the TV. 10:00 p.m. I finished my Co-rona, dried off, and climbed into bed. I set my alarm for 2:00 a.m. and curled up for one hell of a nap.

14

A TRUSTED FRIEND IS LIKE A LIVE ORC . . .

2:00 a.m., The Dead Orc, World Quest

As soon as my alarm went off, I crawled out of bed and checked my email. There were two messages, one from Carpe, and another from our teammate Paul the Battle Monk, both asking me to log in. Paul's was generic; we need a thief to raid a dungeon. Carpe's was more layered.

> **Hope you survived Japan. If you get this, *and* you're still alive, log in—I need a thief.**

I stared at the message and tried to decide how—and if—I was going to respond. "What do you think, Captain? Delete and block him, or let him know I'm still alive?"

Captain stretched and sneezed but didn't offer any advice.

I started to type but only got to *Go to hell.* Did I trust Carpe? Not a chance. He'd broken the golden World Quest rule; thou shall not out other players. That kind of stuff goes a long way with me. If you can't keep a simple rule straight, what else will you do? In the end though, I deleted the message I'd started and didn't block him. Somehow I doubted I'd be able to block an infamous hacker.

Before logging on, I checked my inbox for anything from Mr. Kurosawa. I wasn't sure when dragons slept, so I set my mail to chime alert so I'd know as soon as it came through. I grabbed a soda from the fridge, sent Paul the Monk a heads-up—at least one of my team members could follow simple guidelines—and logged the Byzantine Thief in.

A pleasant chill ran up my back as the screen opened to the Dead Orc Soup and I slid my headset on. Regardless of Carpe's recent indiscretion, I was happy to be back in. With all the vampires, dragons, and other assorted monsters, I hadn't had my fix in days. Maybe I'd get lucky and he wouldn't show up . . .

No such luck. As soon as my thief stepped into the tavern, Carpe's elf ported in. Damn sorcerers and their teleport spells.

"Hey Byzantine, you're still alive! How long you in for tonight?" Carpe said.

"What? No 'go to hell,' 'I stole all your crap,' 'get lost, we replaced you with a chicken'? Either you're going soft, or you plan on throwing me down a dungeon to see if there's a bottom."

"Actually, I was hoping you'd crawl down and save me the throw," he said.

I sighed. "Of course you were. All right, gimme the map and layout."

"So that's a yes?" he asked, a little too hopeful for my liking.

"No, it's a 'gimme the map and layout.' I'll see."

Carpe's dialogue box blinked with a new entry. *Touchy, touchy.*

Oh, we haven't even gotten to your colossal fuckup yet, I wrote back.

A moment later Carpe's dungeon map appeared in my game inventory, along with another dialogue box entry.

What fuckup?

I frowned. As if he didn't know. I ignored the message and opened the map instead.

The map was laid out in four levels, with adjoining pathways and stairs indicated with arrows. Nothing too surprising; obvious spots for traps, might even be a few serious monsters in wait in some of the small mazes or stairways . . . nothing to warrant Carpe's level of niceness.

"What's the catch?" I said.

"Check the last door on the third floor, past the poison arrow traps. And what the hell fuckup are you talking about?"

"You know what you did," I said, and zoomed in on the spot. There wasn't anything noteworthy about the door: big, wooden, typical. I cast my one and only magic spell—Reveal Magic—on the map.

Reveal Magic does exactly what the name implies. You cast it, and anything magic lights up; it's particularly useful on maps. Green usually means it's a good spell—and I want whatever it's attached to— yellow, orange, and red are bad with respectively increasing chances of killing me in one shot. I try to avoid those. Purple and blue usually mean there's some kind of mind-altering spell: love, hate, confusion, possession. I avoid those too.

Usually a Level 12 thief would have four or five spells, but they'd be a combination of useless crap like Light—does it really kill you to carry a torch?—and one or two good ones, like Uncanny Dodge. I saved all my points and spent them on one of the best spells in the game. It wasn't until Level 10 that I was even able to use it, and then only with all the magic skill boost items I stole. As I see it, why bother with the small, crappy stuff when you can be the only Level 12 thief in the game to see—and avoid—all magic.

And yes, I'm probably making up for my inability to see anything supernatural in the real world—even when it's right smack in front of me.

When I cast Reveal Magic, there was the usual mix of yellow, red, and orange spots on the map. The last door on the third level was glowing black.

"Shit," I said. "How'd you know about that?"

"Easy, I stumbled through and died. Didn't even see what killed me."

I made a noise somewhere between a whistle and a laugh. "Wow, sucks to be you. You wasted one of your spare lives. How many do you have left now? Oh, wait, that was your last one."

"It's not nice to laugh at the misfortune of others."

"You want to bet on that?" I said, and snickered. To keep World Quest interesting, when you die in a game, you die. That's it. You can come back with a brand-new character and start over, but once the fat lady sings, the curtain falls—unless you happen to have a resurrection charm on you, and those are few and far between. I'd been playing the Byzantine Thief for a little over a year, and I'd found a grand total of two, carefully stashed away. Carpe had only found one two weeks back.

Add to that the general difficulty of the game and you have a relatively small gaming crowd worldwide—maybe a grand total of one hundred thousand. What drew me in? Well, besides appealing to my being a pathological sucker for punishment, the level of archaeological accuracy was astounding—and the monsters were a pretty big game draw as well. Some of them were even accurate.

I spun the map around and took another look at the floor layout. Way back in my school days, we made the connection that the in-game temples, tombs, and monsters were all based on real ones. My pet theory was that the designers were archaeology school dropouts. It gave me pleasant goose bumps thinking about the misuse of trade secrets going on so publicly.

"Not Egyptian," I said into my mic. "Not Greco-Roman either—not enough maze work—Ooo, wait a minute," I said, and double-checked the angle of one of the shafts and resulting maze work below. The temple was Mayan and belonged to something that would kill you, all right.

"Carpe, I've got good and bad news for you. The good news is I know what killed you."

"Bad news, please."

"You were killed by Ah Puch, the Mayan Lord of Death. The one who gets off on human sacrifice."

I heard Carpe pull his headset off and swear in the background. I smiled and pictured a scrawny computer geek throwing a hissy fit in his ergonomically corrected chair, the kind of chair I imagine hackers use.

"Can we kill him?" he said a moment later.

"Ha—that's funny. Level 20-30, and I'd only recommend trying it with celestial help. If we're still alive next year, we can come back and try it."

"You know, you laugh, but that's only because I haven't told you yet how much of our campaign fund I squandered on that map," he said.

I leaned back in my chair. "Oh, I guarantee I'd be pissed. *If* I didn't know a shortcut to the treasure room."

Carpe was silent for a moment, then, "Please say you're not kidding."

I shook my head and cradled my soda in my lap. On the treasure whore sliding scale, Carpe made me look like a saint. "Why?"

"Because I know a guy in the Blue Beard Inn who will sell me another resurrection charm. I just need enough gold—"

I snorted. "If you think anyone in this game is going to sell you a resurrection charm, I've got a lovely troll bridge I'm willing to part with."

"It's real—"

"You could set up a tollbooth, camp out, collect fares—"

"Byzantine, I've never begged you for anything before, but I'm willing to come close," Carpe pleaded.

"All right, I'll get you in. But I get fifty percent of the pile. And we still need to talk about your royal fuckup."

"Thirty percent. I lost a life first time round finding that trap. And I didn't fuck up. You disappeared off the grid."

He caught me midsip of soda, and I had to stop myself spitting a mouthful over my keyboard. "Fuck me, thirty percent. If you'd sent me the map in the first place, I would've told you there was a demigod sitting behind door number three and saved you the trouble of dying." I added, "And I go off the grid all the time! That's no excuse to chase me down."

"You were kidnapped midgame off Interstate 15 outside Vegas."

I sat up, and my soda careened onto the carpet. I didn't care. Lady Siyu could clean it up. "You son of a bitch, you've been tracking me from day one?"

"I didn't start tracking you until I figured out you were running from vampires. And for the record, I didn't 'chase you down.' I called because I was worried."

"From day one we agreed to play anonymously."

"And you went with that? No wonder you've got vampires chasing you."

I took my headset off and hit the mute button. I didn't want to hear it. I was too pissed. Besides, there's only so much profanity the World Quest filter takes before you get a black spot on your card. When you get to five, you're banned for a week. I was at four again.

The text box lit up with yet another message. *Hey, I was only trying to help—I'm your friend, or at least I thought that's what we were. Before I knew you were the kind of person who'd screw me over for a lousy 20%—*

A bell alerted us that our third party member, Paul the Monk, was entering the game. The dialogue box I had open with Carpe flashed again.

This conversation isn't over, Carpe wrote.

Oh yes it is, I wrote right back before closing the window and putting my headset back on. I checked my email inbox while I was at it. Still nothing from Mr. Kurosawa.

"Hey Byz," Paul the Monk's middle-aged voice rang in my headset. It was the kind of voice I imagined belonged to a guy who spent most of his weekends corralling kids to soccer games in a minivan. "Carpe filling you in on our dungeon?"

"You mean how he wants to fuck us over for a lousy twenty percent?"

Paul laughed. "Told you she wouldn't go for it," he said.

"Oh, don't tell me he's got you roped into this death trap too, Paul? You realize he just wants the treasure because he thinks someone is going to sell him a resurrection charm—"

"He said he has it, and he comes with recommendations—" Carpe chimed in.

"Yeah, from the guys who are going to be waiting outside the Blue Beard to jump you for your gold—"

"Come on, Byz. It'll shut him up. And he agreed to that castle we've had our eye on," Paul said.

I swore under my breath. How could they be so stupid? I needed to find the guys hanging out at the Blue Beard and get in on the scam. If it was this easy to convince people to show up on your doorstep with a pile of gold . . . "Fine, three-way split."

"Come on . . ." Carpe tried.

"One more squeak out of you and I raise my price to fifty percent."

"Deal. Carpe?" Paul asked.

"Not a peep more," Carpe said.

I was still pissed, but I wanted to play. Besides, Paul was there now, so that would keep the game conversation generic. I could berate Carpe later. It's odd that out of the two people I hang with on a more than weekly basis, one of them knew way too much about me, and the other was clueless and probably spent half his game time figuring how to sneak a beer while still watching his kids. Where the hell was the balance in my life?

We headed into Ah Puch's tomb. Paul the Monk stepped on a poison trap, and we ran into a pack of goblins who'd followed Carpe in on his first solo run and set up shop. As a general rule I don't like killing things, even in a game . . . except for goblins.

Besides that, and the occasional text prompt from Carpe (I closed them as soon as they flashed in the lower left corner of my screen), and me checking my inbox for a message from Mr. Kurosawa, 3:00 a.m. passed uneventfully.

At 4:00 a.m. we hit the third level.

"All right boys," I said. "This is where things get tricky. One of you needs to stand on that block while the other two go get the treasure."

"How stupid do you think we are?" Carpe said, sounding like he had a mouthful of food. I'd always pictured Carpe as a scrawny guy, but it dawned on me he could be a fat computer guy.

"No seriously, one of you needs to stand here on that block, otherwise I can't open the secret passage at the end of this hall."

There was silence from the other two.

"Oh, come on. One of you will be with me, and I can't steal all the treasure."

Paul snorted.

I sighed for Carpe and Paul's benefit. I thought about ordering room service; I was going to need coffee and breakfast soon. "Look, guys, decide between yourselves, but one of you has to either stand on that block or go back and grab a hundred and twenty pounds' worth of goblin corpses. I'll be back in a minute."

"Byzantine, this isn't—" Carpe started.

I muted the mic, took off my headset, and picked up the number to dial room service.

"Hello?" answered the prim voice on the other end.

"Hi there, I need breakfast and coffee—preferably something with espresso in it. What do you have?"

After I was done ordering I put my headset back on. "Well boys, what did you decide?"

"I'll stay here. Paul will go with you," Carpe said. He didn't sound enthusiastic about it. I wondered how Paul had won that round. I thought about asking Carpe in our dialogue box, but I decided against it. I didn't want to give him the impression I'd cooled down yet. Son of a bitch, tracking me behind my back.

"Fine. Carpe, stand on that red tile," I said, and used my cursor to indicate the right one. "Paul, you're with me."

We reached the halfway point down the hall towards the door of death. I stopped at the wall and looked for the right set of mosaic patterns, the ones I'd had to memorize from my grad school textbook on Mayan temples and deities.

"Gimme a sec, Paul, I need to solve this puzzle."

It was a series of numbers that had to be entered perfectly to open an adjacent passage, otherwise a fireball would launch from the opposing wall . . . or was it spears? Anyway, if you screwed up, something bad shot out. On the off chance you dodged that, a trapdoor opened underneath. I had no idea what was under the trapdoor. As far as I knew, no one did.

I was on the final sequence of equations when my inbox chimed. A message from Mr. Kurosawa had come in. I stopped midpunch to skim the message.

> **I have looked at all six sets of inscriptions. Though I echo your suspicions that this is derived from one of the languages you so quaintly refer to as "supernatural," it is not a form I am familiar with. In the future, direct your inquiries through Lady Siyu or Oricho.**

"Shit." He couldn't translate it. Any of it. I'd let a dragon beat the shit out of me, and it hadn't gotten me anywhere. I was back where I started. Nowhere. Now what the hell was I going to do?

"Byzantine?" Paul said.

I shook my head and turned my attention back to the game. I did the second-to-last equation in my head and pressed the tile with the Mayan five, written in red ochre. The treasure room door slid open a crack to the right of the Mayan tiles. "Sorry, Paul—out-of-game stuff. This will just take me a few more seconds."

"No worries, I can relate," he said, and chuckled.

I can't, wrote Carpe.

I frowned and closed the text box. Snarky bastard. Another one popped up in its place.

Sooooo . . . how long have you been running from vampires?

Son of a bitch wasn't going to let it drop. *Stop it. I come here to get away from my day job, not talk about it.*

You know, you might be the most famous archaeologist on the planet. You should see what comes up in a Google search.

Will you stop! Someone might read this.

Relax, I've got the line secured.

Smug little bastard. *Don't want to hear it—If I can't trust you to keep your word, how the hell am I supposed to trust you outside, let alone in-game?* I closed the text box as soon as I clicked Send. Another one appeared.

Ummm Owl—Carpe started, but I closed the box before he could finish. Another popped up, this time on my laptop, overshadowing the rest of the screen.

No Owl, seriously, why is Paul casting Monk's Fist?

What the—?

I focused back on the game screen. Sure enough, Paul's monk was getting ready to cast Monk's Fist, a melee attack able to rip out an opponent's heart in one shot.

"Paul," I yelled into my headset. "What the hell do you think you're doing?"

"Sorry, kid, but if I kill you, I get the experience points and the treasure. I'll reach the Blue Beard before Carpe and buy that resurrection charm."

"Oh, not you too—"

"Nothing personal, but I've got a job and three kids. I don't have the luxury of scourging these places all day like you losers."

I couldn't believe it. I'd been playing with Paul for six months, and he'd blindsided me. "You lying, cheating, bigoted son of a bitch—just because we don't have lousy time-management skills doesn't mean we don't have real job shit to do too. Grow a pair of fucking balls and tell your goddamned kids to drive themselves to soccer—" I kept going, but the World Quest PG buzzer went off.

"Son of a bitch," I yelled, though only Carpe and World Quest's version of the FTC could hear me now. It would be a cold day in hell before I let Carpe pick team members again.

I watched as Paul's avatar readied to throw Monk's Fist at my Byzantine. I did what any respectful thief does. Dodge. The fist caught my hood but didn't deliver any damage.

I pulled up the secure message box with Carpe. *Carpe, get your ass teleported over here now. Paul's gone rogue.*

I hit Enter as Paul readied another fist. Damn it, I wish I'd bothered to learn how many strikes a monk had on special attacks . . .

Carpe's voice came over my headset. "I set up a private line."

"Good, 'cause World Quest FTC just booted me out. I didn't even deserve it this time."

"I'll be there in less than a minute. Keep him busy."

"How the hell do you suggest I do that?" I said, as I ran the Byzantine Thief through a series of flips and rolls that placed a batch of poison arrows between her and the bastard rogue monk. Paul's avatar didn't falter as the arrows hit. Instead, he readied his staff.

Shit, monks had poison resistance. I was totally fucked. All Paul had to do was hit me once, that's all it takes to kill a thief. Unless . . .

The secret passage door was ajar, but I still had one more number to press on the tile set for it to slide the whole way open. My guess was that Paul figured he could pry it open after he looted my avatar's body. He was dead wrong.

"I'm going to try something stupid, Carpe," I said into the mic.

I targeted the wall and pressed Enter. Byzantine rolled for the sequence, catching a kick on her leg that knocked my health bar down by a third. My avatar still managed to slam into the Mayan number five instead of the nine.

The game screen began to rumble as pieces behind the tomb walls began to slide. Two large slabs of rock slammed down and blocked off both ends of the tunnel, trapping me and the monk. Poison arrows flew from above, then from the side, in a repeating pattern. Paul's monk looked like a ballet dancer as he dodged them. Well, goody for him. By comparison, the Byzantine Thief looked like a monkey doing a jig as I dodged enough to stay alive. I kept my eyes on the floors and walls, watching for the trapdoor to open.

The hall shook again as the treasure room door started to slide shut. Paul must have seen it too, because the next thing I knew he dove for the opening and wedged his hands between the wall and the door. The monk strained to hold the slab open.

Ha, good luck with that.

"Byzantine, what the hell did you do?" Carpe yelled.

"Sprung the ancient Mayan booby trap—" Out of the corner of my eye I caught the tiled floor start to drop away, one by one, the scraping of the slab drowning out any noise the tiles made as they fell. I swung the screen camera around; Paul was still concentrating on the slab. I couldn't tell whether he noticed the opening or not.

Now or never, while I had a head start. "And do me a favor? Kill Paul," I said.

I held my breath as Byzantine jumped. My view of the torchlit tunnel faded as I hit a steep ramp and slid into darkness. The screen shook as I slid to the edge of the ramp and somersaulted over the lip. I scrambled to grab onto something, and I held, for a second, suspended over a cavern, the light from the torches flickering above like dim beacons. I hit the Up arrow as fast as I could and watched the Thief start to pull herself up. If she could just hold on a few seconds more, just enough to get her back on the ledge, I could ride it out until Carpe arrived.

The Byzantine Thief wrapped her arm around the ledge. I breathed a sigh of relief and started to maneuver her up slowly to conserve her strength.

She slipped.

"No!" I yelled, not quite believing what I was seeing.

"Byz? Don't do anything stupid, I'm almost there—" Carpe said.

The screen jolted one last time before fading to black. I pulled my headset off, not bothering to untangle my hair first, and threw it on the floor. "Son of a bitch."

Captain unraveled from his perch on the windowsill to see what the commotion was about. Only two things in World Quest make the screen go black; when you're knocked unconscious, and when you die.

I picked up my mouse and threw it at the wall; Captain yawned and curled right back up. "Shit." Best-case scenario, I was unconscious. Not much help if something came along and decided to eat me. Death by rat pack, anyone?

Five minutes later a message popped up on my out-of-game screen. *Byz? What the hell happened?* Carpe wrote. *And where are you?*

Jumped down the rabbit hole and got the black screen of death. The turnover was twelve hours. In twelve hours, I could either use a resurrection charm, or my avatar would wake up. *Either way, I'm not playing again for twelve hours.*

Shit. Anything I can do in the meantime?

Yeah. Hunt down and kill Paul.

You know elves don't kill things out of revenge . . . I could maybe drop him in a deep dark marsh or bog though.

Yeah, yeah. Just make sure it's full of zombies, or goblins—or something that'll eat him. I tipped my chair back violently so it banged into the wall, then checked to make sure I hadn't left a mark. I was on bad enough terms with the dragon as it was without breaking his things. I wanted to scream, or hit someone, with Paul at the top of my list. Mostly I wanted out of World Quest.

I'm out. See you in twelve, I wrote, and logged out without waiting for a reply.

I was too pissed off to try and work or sleep, so I grabbed my jacket. I needed to get out of my room. I checked the clock. 6:30 a.m. Maybe the coffee bar was open by now. Once I cooled down I could find Oricho and Nadya, and get back to work.

Between this job and World Quest . . . I shook my head. Trusted teammates were like live Orcs. Eventually one of them was going to jump out of hiding and stab you in the back.

Well, no sense pondering my most recent failures. Otherwise I was liable to throw myself down an elevator shaft.

"Come on, Captain," I said, and held the door open for him. From the trinket table, I took one of Captain's favorite mice and a plastic bag with the vampire pheromone–soaked rag I'd recovered from Charles. "Let's see if we can get your growling under control before people show up at the pool."

15

SO YOU WANT TO PLAY WITH MONSTERS?

7:00 a.m., the Japanese Circus, poolside at the Garden cafe

I hefted the red mouse a few times in my hand to get Captain's attention.

"Stay," I said.

Captain sat back on his haunches. Sort of.

I wound back and launched the toy mouse across the garden's green lawn. Captain lifted his behind off the ground but waited. I counted to five in my head.

"Go get it," I said.

With a noise that was a cross between a meow and growl, he shot after it. I sat back down, and a shiver went up my spine as I remembered my run-in with Sebastian, Marie's first lackey, a few days ago. I pushed the thought out of my mind and focused on Captain.

Besides the pool-boy nymphs, the only other people around the garden at this time were a handful of retirees taking a morning walk before they got back to their gambling. The air smelled better in the morning, crisper and cleaner before the smoke, perfume, and booze spilled over from the casino floor.

I pulled my leather jacket tighter around me. It was cooler than I'd expected, and I was glad I'd had the sense to grab it on the way out of my room. I nodded at one of the nymphs on his way to the pool shed. He smiled and waved but didn't say anything.

You'd think I'd be happy that I could spot a nymph, but out of all the supernaturals out there, they were about as easy as it gets. I'd read once that they had a hard time communicating with language; come to think of it, I wondered if they could speak at all. Whatever they lacked in communication skills they made up for with the sheer volume of charisma that rolled off them. I don't think they could rope it in to save their lives. Made identifying them a piece of cake once you knew what to look for: an incredibly hot mute you just about fell over to talk to.

Goddamn it, I hate my blind side for spotting supernaturals more than I hate my lousy spoken-language skills.

Captain trotted back across the grass and dropped the mouse at my feet with a loud chirp.

"All right, time to up the ante, Captain. Let's see what you've got."

He just stared at the red mouse in my hand, waiting. I pulled the Ziploc bag out of my pocket that contained a white piece of cloth. I held my breath as I opened the bag full of Charles's vampire phero-mones and tossed the mouse in. I gave it a good few shakes before retrieving it and holding it up for Captain to smell.

I grabbed the scruff of his neck and launched the mouse across the garden. He strained and almost fell over trying to go after it. "Wait," I said.

He twisted to face me and gave a baleful meow.

I counted to five, then said, "OK, go get it," and let go. Captain almost nose-planted over his own front legs as he blindly bolted across the lawn.

He just about barreled into a middle-aged woman—from the Hawaiian shirt and sunburn I guessed this was her vacation—as she strolled down the path towards us. As it was, she didn't see him until he shot between her legs with a loud chirp. She yelped and did an unsure-footed dance from side to side. She didn't strike me as the most agile woman, so I was surprised and a little impressed that she held her balance.

She stared after the vampire-killing ball of fury, her mouth open in shock, then shot me an accusatory look.

I shrugged and tried to look sheepish. "Catnip," I said, "he really loves catnip."

She shook her head at me, then turned tail back towards the relative safety of the casino. I thought about the ghosts tied to the slot machines of Mr. Kurosawa's private floor. *Lady, if you only knew. Trust me, it's safer out here with the crazy cat.*

"You might want to tell Captain old people are fragile. Otherwise a few more throws and you're liable to have a broken hip and a lawsuit on your hands."

I turned around. Nadya was wearing a light sweater and balancing a coffee and a stack of folders on her laptop. Her hair was pulled back in a ponytail, and she'd forgone contacts for glasses. Her eyes were rimmed red, and she hadn't bothered to put makeup on. She looked more set for a day on her couch with a bag of chips than poolside at a luxury casino. I don't think I'd seen her dressed this casually since our dorm days, cramming for exams.

"How did you know I was here?" I said. I winced as Captain let out a howl when he reached the mouse across the yard.

"I didn't. I stopped by your room, and when you weren't there, I headed down to the bar—"

"Even I don't drink at seven a.m. Hey!" I yelled across the garden. Out of the corner of my eye I caught Captain crouch down and start tearing into the toy mouse. "Get back here!" Captain bleated in complaint but picked the mouse up and made his way back towards us until he was three feet away. He crouched down again, mouse in mouth, eyeing me warily. I frowned. "I said here, not three feet away. Damn it, he was bringing it back a minute ago."

Nadya tsked. "As I was saying, after swinging by the bar I passed an old couple in the elevator talking about a woman in a leather jacket and boots playing fetch with a cat."

Captain continued to ignore my command and started tearing into the mouse again. I strode over. "Gimme that," I said.

Captain growled and chewed faster.

"Naturally I jumped to the logical conclusion and came out here to find you."

I wrenched the mouse from between his teeth. "Bad Captain," I said. And with that I threw the mouse into the pool.

Captain whined and darted to the edge. He stretched his paw for the floating mouse (they're made of cork after all) but wasn't committed enough to get wet.

Nadya took a seat at one of the picnic tables, so I joined her to wait for Captain to either cool off, or get desperate enough to jump in. I figured it was fifty-fifty.

Nadya sipped her coffee and watched Captain chase the mouse around the edge of the pool, mewing at it every few seconds.

"Why is he so obsessed with that mouse?"

"Because I doused it with vampire pheromones."

Nadya swore and instinctively covered her nose and mouth with the sleeve of her sweater. "Owl, have you gone insane! Get it out of the pool before it contaminates the water, otherwise we'll have a casino full of vampire junkies on our hands."

"Relax, the pheromones are fat, not water, soluble, and even if they could wash off, it's a small enough amount the pool will dilute it. The only thing in this area that can smell them is Captain, and maybe a bloodhound."

Nadya swore. "Why?" she asked.

"I'm trying to train Captain not to go ballistic every time he smells vampire."

She snorted. "How is that going?"

I frowned. "We're making progress. It's just slow is all."

Captain had given up trying to get the mouse out of the pool by himself, and he gave me a baleful whine. I fetched the mouse and held it up. "Now bring it back this time or it goes back in the pool," I said, and hefted it across the lawn, where one of the nymphs was gardening.

Nadya nodded at the nymph. "I thought nymphs always travelled in pairs, male/female."

"They do. The girls are dealing blackjack."

"Smart. No human is going to be able to stay mad at a nymph, even when they're on a one-way streak for the poorhouse."

I took in Nadya's appearance again. She wasn't just tired. She was worried. "Did you sleep at all?" I asked.

She shook her head and pulled out one of the files.

"Couldn't. Not after I found this," she said, and slid it across the table. It was a compilation of ancient accounts in Europe about a weapon, all in Cyrillic. An unmistakable diagram of the egg I'd fetched for Mr. Kurosawa, with inscriptions, was in the side margin.

I grabbed it. "Where did you find this?"

"Russian archives. One of Nuroshi's cryptic notes hinted there was something there." She shrugged. "They still don't have the security there they should, so my old passwords still work."

"Shit, Nadya, they'll know it was you who logged in and was sniffing around—"

She waved a hand dismissively. "It was worth the risk."

Captain returned with the mouse and took up a position under my seat. I rewarded his obedience with another throw, and he waited until I gave the signal to chase it. Captain might be stubborn, but he sure as hell learns fast.

"I know what it does," Nadya said, the same flat edge in her voice she used when throwing out unruly Japanese men from her club. She slid the top file across the garden table, her mouth drawn in a hard line.

I leafed through the edges. It was a collection of photocopied pages from old Cyrillic texts. I leaned back in my lawn chair. Captain trotted back under the table and dropped his mouse by my feet, swishing his tail. I packed it back into the plastic bag and slid it into my coat. Sensing playtime was over, he didn't push, and instead curled up.

"I'm guessing this doesn't say it's the equivalent of a 'dragon happy meal' toy?" I said.

She shook her head. "Direct translation?" she said, and removed the first page. "Here they call it 'Devil's Vengeance.' Owl, this isn't some minor magic weapon, it's a bad one." She tapped the text. "This is a page from a collection of known magic, written by a priest from an offshoot Christian cult popular in Russia during the ninth century. The priests and friars used to entomb themselves and starve to death for penance. The priest who wrote this, Cervac, was the only one who ever came out alive. He was anointed a saint by his followers."

"Vampire?" I asked.

Nadya shook her head. "No, vampires weren't common in Russia then—too cold. Besides, there's no mention of avoiding the sun or drinking blood. More likely a skin walker or genie possessed him and decided to have a little fun. There were lots of them buried in the tombs and caves throughout Russia and Mongolia, just waiting for someone to break their cages. We used to have to watch out for them—not always bottles either, more often half-cracked ossuaries. Just try moving one of those."

I cringed, glad I hadn't spent my first year of grad school crawling around Russian dig sites. The Americas had their share of demons and mummies, but nothing as dangerous as genies or skin walkers. No wonder Nadya was so good at spotting supernaturals; first-year grad school in Russia weeds everyone else out.

"The history of magic and supernatural creatures Cervac wrote down is mostly accurate, which is why I lean towards genie. After three or four days, skin walkers start to smell bad, like ammonia or old urine, and besides that, they aren't much for writing, more like finger painting with blood."

"So what does the scroll do?" I asked.

"From what I can tell, it's a spell that when cast sends a sheet of magic in a radius of about a kilometer, give or take. The one holding the spell is fine, animals are fine, buildings are fine, but anyone in that kilometer radius disappears, like they never existed in the first place. It's like a localized extermination. And all anyone needs to cast it is the scroll."

"Shit." That was just what a psychotic vampire like Marie didn't need. A magic atomic bomb. I also didn't know how crazy I was about handing it over to Mr. Kurosawa either. The lesser of two evils? Maybe. But as fond as he was of his Vegas empire, I didn't hold much hope that he'd think twice about blowing up a rival's city, repeatedly.

"What about destroying it? We could accidently light it on fire," I said.

Nadya shook her head and flipped to another page. "They tried that. It can't be done. The scroll went untouched, but a nearby castle and town were leveled." She leaned across the table and lowered her voice, as if afraid someone might overhear us. "I don't know what's worse. Finding it or not finding it."

I shook my head. As tempting as it was, not finding it was out of the question. A supernatural like Marie or Mr. Kurosawa reading a spell was bad enough, but a human? In general, when humans try to read written magic, the best you can hope for is an explosion. The worst? Well . . . let's just say that if a human stumbled across the scroll, they were liable to blow up more than a city center. And what if a fire or bomb went off where the scroll was hidden? That could be just as bad. Either way, supernatural or human, it was lose-lose.

"I really don't like the idea of handing it over to either Marie or Mr. Kurosawa. And I'm not crazy about leaving it for someone to accidently trip over."

"Are you certain?" Nadya said. "Once we go after this, there is no changing your mind."

I thought about it. "Yeah, and not just because Mr. Kurosawa would eat me. He _might_ blow a few cities up with it, but I guarantee Marie is planning to use it. And leaving it under a rock doesn't solve anything. Besides, I'm not convinced we can't figure out a way to torch this thing."

Nadya furrowed her brow but nodded. "I made the same decision. I just wanted to make sure you reached the same conclusion as well. We both have to live with the consequences." She opened her laptop. "And I think I found it."

I sat up straight. "And you didn't think to mention that first?"

She shrugged and spun the screen around. "I wanted to make sure you understood the consequences first." On the open page was an advertisement for a museum exhibit of the Dutch East India Company going on in San Francisco. "I think our ancient thief did bury the scroll in the Balinese temples. Remember I said the inscriptions on the egg were familiar, but I couldn't put my finger on it?"

"I figured you saw it where I did—the image of the Bali tablet in the students' talk."

"I thought so too until I came across this." She pointed to the Dutch East India Company exhibit. "I remembered I saw this exhibit in Moscow years ago. It's mostly spices and records of the trading company as it established its presence in Asia, but there was a small section on items taken by Dutch traders in the early seventeenth century from the Indonesian islands, particularly the Besakih Temple." She zoomed in on one of the images. "There was a series of scrolls recovered from Aruba and Curaçao in the Dutch Caribbean. I remember them because one was out of place. It didn't have any of the native languages on them. The seal had the same kind of symbols as the tablet and the inscriptions. I think the Hindu priests found it in the catacombs when the temple was rebuilt in the eighth century and placed the scroll in the temple proper. The Dutch found it and thought it was treasure, not realizing what they had."

I went cold. Sebastian, Marie's first thrall, had been an antiquities dealer in the Caribbean. He'd specialized in items from the British

East India Company, but he'd dabbled in items that had made their way to the Caribbean from the Dutch traders as well. I stood up.

"Shit, I think Marie knows more than we thought. We need to get to the Berkeley exhibit, now."

"Considering they're moving the exhibit to Los Angeles tomorrow, that would be wise. They'll start packing it up at four, when the museum closes for the day."

I stood up and turned into a well-muscled, bare nymph chest. I swore under my breath and muttered, "Umm, sorry, I didn't see you there."

He just smiled a perfect set of white teeth and handed me a manila envelope with my name scrawled across the front in black ink, reminiscent of calligraphy. I took the envelope with a good idea who it was from. "Umm, thanks," I said. The nymph winked and without a word headed back to the pool house. I shook my head and waited until he disappeared inside before opening the envelope. "Man, that unnerves me," I said to Nadya, and started to tear open the note inside. The paper had a heavy, weighted feel. Expensive. I have an aversion to people sending me expensive things. There's usually a catch.

"Beautiful men who smile and don't speak? Only you would find something to complain about."

I glanced up from the envelope. Nadya was watching the remaining pool boys with a renewed interest and energy that hadn't been there a moment before.

"Down, Nadya, it's a nymph. All the pretty pool boys are nymphs."

"I know he's a nymph—I don't have your blind spot. And I've never heard of a nymph killing anyone, only fu—"

"Not now." I opened the seal and unfolded the paper. Even the glue was expensive. As I'd suspected, it was a summons from Oricho. Well, technically a request for us to meet him inside, but I took "request" as a euphemism.

"Well, at least Oricho made the effort to ask," I mumbled.

Nadya perked up. "What now?"

"We have an audience," I said, and handed her the letter. I caught her smile to herself as she read it, and she quickly fixed her hair as soon as she handed it back. I mentally kicked myself for not factoring Nadya's weakness—scratch that, pathological death spot—for good-looking Japanese men. Add that to the absence of Japanese men fawning over her at the club . . .

"Stop fixing your hair. We don't even know what Oricho is—"

She pursed her lips and gave me a derisive sniff. "He probably saved your life from the dragon. One of us should be nice," she said, closing her laptop and tucking her files into her bag. She stood up and headed towards the glass sliding doors, as I followed closely. "Besides, I figured out what he is," she added as the automatic door closed behind us. "He's a kami, a Japanese justice spirit."

Damn it, why hadn't I thought of that? I ran to catch up, Captain on my heels. I still had that mouse, after all.

"Everything I've read about them says they aren't dangerous to humans," she continued.

"Ummm, that's a relative statement. Oricho isn't as bad as the others, but he's dangerous; trust me on this—"

Nadya spun to face me, hands on hips. "You didn't even know what he was until I told you." She turned and stormed towards the lobby.

I rolled my eyes. Fantastic. She wasn't going to listen. She was counting Oricho as a good guy because he'd saved me—and he was cute. Nadya was better at spotting supernaturals, so she was blowing me off, but she didn't have my experience dealing with them. Well, this would be a learning curve. I slid Captain's leash back. "Why doesn't anyone ever listen to me?" I said to him. He blinked and yawned.

"Well, maybe you can convince Oricho to wrangle the private jet to take us to San Francisco." I really hoped Marie's plan was to head to LA and wait for the exhibit to arrive.

I caught up to Nadya in the lobby. A rush of lily of the valley overwhelmed me. I jumped and swore, garnering dirty looks from guests having breakfast. I spun around searching for the vampire . . .

My panic turned to anger, and I swore again. Two large pots of lily of the valley decorated the front of the restaurant. I glared at the flowers and contemplated tossing them in the pool. Of all the stupid, lousy ...

People were still looking at me. "Sorry. Wasp," I said, raising my voice. If you substituted *wasp* for *naga*, you weren't far off the mark. "I'm allergic," I added. Everyone stopped watching me and went back to their breakfast, a few people nodding with understanding. I stopped by the hostess booth while Nadya kept going.

"Excuse me, who does the flowers in the restaurant?" The hostess gave me an apprehensive look. I forced a smile and added, "They're so beautiful, I'd love to get some for my room."

The hostess relaxed. "Oh, Lady Siyu does all the flowers in the casino herself. I can leave a message for her, Miss ... ?"

I should have known. I fixed the hostess with another smile. "Ms. Owl, and you do that."

Nadya raised an eyebrow as I rejoined her, shaking my head. "It's nothing. Lady Siyu's bad idea of a joke."

We didn't have far to look for Oricho. He was sitting at a table in the corner of the restaurant, newspaper in hand. I noted that even though the restaurant was packed, everyone avoided the corner. My guess? The ink; even though Oricho wore business suits worth a small fortune, the tattoos threw people off. So they stayed away, nice and safe ... beside Mr. Kurosawa's casino slot machines ...

See, now this is exactly how I get my complexes. Not only couldn't I walk by a pot of flowers without having a panic attack but I'd never be able to hear a slot machine chime without breaking a sweat. Oh well, regardless of the reason—fear, confusion—Oricho's table was the only private place in the entire restaurant.

As I approached it, the background noise of casino chimes and voices faded to a dim murmur. I slid into the chair directly across from Oricho, not bothering to wait for an invitation.

Nadya took up a position behind me, standing. She's a survivor with an abundance of common sense. I'm not.

"Nice trick," I said.

Oricho didn't bother putting the newspaper down. "It is fascinating how you continue to place yourself into more and more precarious circumstances, even after experiencing the consequences. You are proving an interesting study of 'reckless abandon.'"

I leaned back and crossed my feet to make the point. "I thought you samurai types appreciated bravery in the face of certain death?"

"Bravery, yes. It is the lack of any forethought or direction I find disconcerting."

I shrugged. "Go ahead, beat me up and see how useful I am at finding your scroll."

The top of his paper snapped forward and he peered at me, the corner of his mouth turning down into the beginnings of a frown. "You brought that event upon yourself, despite my warnings to the contrary. I suggest you reflect on that detail, however small it may seem."

I sighed. Arguing and pressing Oricho's buttons weren't going to get me anywhere. While even I had to admit there was something gratifying about getting Oricho to break his deadpan, somehow I doubted playing the fly in his coffee was constructive to my well-being.

I held up the note. "We've been summoned. Why?"

"I *requested* you meet me so I could relay a message in person. Sabine's thralls were spotted at the Tokyo airport boarding a plane for Los Angeles. Neither of you are to leave casino grounds without Rynn as an escort."

My stomach turned. I doubted Marie knew exactly where the scroll was—otherwise she'd have sent her lackeys to San Francisco instead of the exhibit's next stop, meaning she would have had it by now. It was more likely the Berkeley exhibit was another box to tick off on her search list. I checked the clock on the wall. Rynn's flight would be landing at McCarran in less than an hour. "Listen, Oricho, it can't wait. Tell Rynn to wait at the airport, me and Nadya will meet him there—"

Oricho shook his head as he interrupted me and began to fold his paper. "Rynn's flight was delayed due to weather conditions. He will not arrive until late this afternoon. You may discuss your travel arrangements with him at that time."

I bit back the first response that popped into my head—*Like hell*—and put aside my irritation that Oricho expected me to defer to Rynn on how to do my job. "Can't you find someone else, or can't you come with us?" I said.

Something close to anger flashed across his face, not directed at me but . . . well . . . at everything. "Rynn is the only person I trust with this, and I am needed at Mr. Kurosawa's side."

Hunh. I hadn't expected that. He didn't look happy about it either. I filed that piece of information away for later. "Well, that's a problem, because we need to go to San Fran. *Now,* not tonight. I think we've found the scroll," I said, and filled him in. "I don't think Sabine knows *exactly* where it is, otherwise she'd have headed straight there, but I'm not taking the chance that she stumbles across it."

The corner of Oricho's mouth twitched and his frown deepened. "This does change things, but I cannot consciously send you without Rynn's protection. Especially if, as you say, Sabine is aware of the East India connection. I will arrange travel first thing tomorrow morning and watch Sabine."

"You don't understand. They'll start packing everything up into crates right after the museum closes today. Have Rynn meet us in San Francisco. I promise we won't do anything stupid," I said, and crossed my heart.

His brow furrowed, as if he was struggling with a choice between bad and worse. He was damned if he sent us and Marie showed up, and damned if he didn't send us and let her get the scroll first. I wanted to say, *Welcome to my world.*

Oricho excused himself. Phone in hand, he headed for the lobby, where he disappeared from view. I ordered a coffee.

Fifteen minutes passed before Oricho returned, as tense and

disturbed as when he'd left. "My sources say Sabine returned to Bali and sent her thralls in Los Angeles. It should be safe for you to go to San Francisco, but," he said, frowning at me, "under the condition that you wait to enter the museum until Rynn arrives. I've rerouted him to San Francisco International and made him aware of the situation. He will land at one p.m."

"Oricho, that's an awful idea. What if she shows up and gets the scroll first?" I said.

Oricho fixed his level stare on me. "There will always be a chance to regain the scroll if she reaches it first. The cost of your life is not so easily recouped. Wait for Rynn."

I nodded, bit my lip, and thought sincere thoughts as I rammed my hands into my jacket pocket and crossed my fingers, twice. For a supernatural, Oricho wasn't half bad. I hoped to hell I wouldn't have to break my word.

He turned to leave the cafe, newspaper in hand, looking more troubled than when we'd arrived.

"Good to know my effect on people is consistent," I whispered to Nadya.

She shot me a dirty look and took three steps after him. "One more thing," Nadya said, then stopped dead in her tracks as he turned and arched a tattooed eyebrow. It did not convey, *Please, continue talking.*

I tripped over my chair as I scrambled to catch up to her. When I did, I watched as her fantasy version of Oricho collided with the more accurate "only slightly less scary than the other monsters" Oricho.

She swallowed hard before continuing.

"There—there's a leak, from in here. That's how Sabine knows where Owl is," she said, choosing her phrasing carefully.

He turned his serious stare on her, the one that got me to shut up. "I do not appreciate the implication that one of my trusted staff is a traitor to myself or Mr. Kurosawa. Such accusations have serious consequences. Are you prepared to suffer the consequences should you be wrong?"

The color drained out of Nadya's face, her confidence shaken by his tone. I was just about ready to turn and run. For someone who'd been contemplating hitting on a monster . . . Nadya might know her monsters better than anyone else, but she didn't know them like I did.

"For Christ's sake, stop shaking," I whispered.

She glared at me, but it pushed her past her fear. She cleared her throat and shook her head. "I'm certain."

I couldn't bear watching Nadya negotiate with a supernatural. She didn't have my experience, or my lack of common sense. I stepped in.

"Oricho, we're positive. Sabine has to be getting inside information from here. There's no other way she could be following me so closely."

He placed me in his sights instead of Nadya. She let out a breath she'd been holding.

"You suspect Lady Siyu," he said.

I shrugged. "As we like to say, if the shoe fits . . ."

"I am aware that you do not communicate well with Lady Siyu. However, personal grudge matches are not justification for suspicion."

"I agree, and if it was just her winning personality, we wouldn't have brought it up, but they've known what I'm doing before I do."

"Lady Siyu is Mr. Kurosawa's most trusted advisor, more so than I." He glanced at Nadya. "It is more likely an infiltration on your end."

"Sure, if it was just Bali, but they knew I was at the casino and Nuroshi's office. Only you guys knew I was heading to see Nuroshi; Sabine was waiting for me. And now she just happens to have her flunkies in LA? The only thing that surprised them was Rynn. Did Lady Siyu know about that?"

Oricho didn't take his stare off me, but the righteous anger dissipated. After a moment, he looked out the garden window and said, "No. She was not apprised of Rynn. She was otherwise occupied."

I shook my head. "Either we can add mind reader to Sabine's repertoire, or you and Mr. Kurosawa have a leak. I can't prove it's Lady Siyu, but I think it warrants a look."

Oricho narrowed his eyes, his jaw drawn tight. He gave me curt nod and left.

Nadya let out another breath and slumped into a chair. "How often do they do that?" she said. I could see that sweat had started to accumulate on her lip.

"Switch from normal to bipolar at warp speed? Praise your ingenuity, then threaten to kill you? Try all the time. It's when they don't I start to worry. You done with your supernatural crush?"

She nodded and we headed upstairs to get ready for Berkeley. When we got into the elevator, Nadya asked, "Do you think he'll do anything about Lady Siyu?"

I shrugged. I wasn't completely unsympathetic to Oricho having his superior supernatural ideals burst, but it was his job to grow a pair and deal with Lady Siyu. "If I didn't, there'd be nothing we could do about it anyways. Let's get that scroll, translate it, and get the hell out of here."

16

BREAKING AND ENTERING

2:30 p.m., hippie coffee shop outside Berkeley

I hate B&E's, especially museums. It's a far cry from excavating out of dig sites. If it's already in a museum, I usually tell people to hire a thief. It's cheaper.

And no, they're not the same thing; I'm an archaeologist who likes cats, not a cat burglar who likes old stuff. I spent five years in grad school slaving away on dig sites, only to get thrown under the bus when the department needed a good scapegoat. Three months before I was supposed to graduate. Excuse me if I don't have a moral dilemma making a profit from under their noses.

I sighed. I may not like B&E's, but I'll do them in a pinch if I have to. "Thanks, keep the change," I said, and slid six bucks across the counter to the forty-something hippie manning the cash register. I retrieved the two coffees: mocha for Nadya and a latte with an extra shot of espresso for me. I held the cups above my shoulders and pushed through the sea of student backpacks to Nadya. We'd camped out at a round table right in front of the coffee shop's large, open storefront window. Not only did we have a panoramic view of the main campus entrance and museum, but Captain, tucked underneath my chair, would also smell any vampires in range.

I slid back into the wooden chair, spilling some of the coffee on the table as the uneven legs rocked under my weight. Captain complained but curled back up around my feet. I passed Nadya the mocha, garnering dirty looks from a group of students sitting beside us. One of them cleared his throat until I made eye contact with him.

"What's their problem?" Nadya said.

"Apparently we're in their seats." I shrugged at the guy and took a slow sip of my latte. The coffee burned my mouth, but I swallowed anyways. I needed the caffeine more than my comfort right now.

I checked my watch again. 2:30 p.m. Rynn's plane should have landed an hour and a half ago—where the hell was he? The museum would be closing at 4:00. I craned my head around the windowpane to glance towards the subway station.

"Staring down the sidewalk isn't going to make him show up any faster," Nadya said casually. "Neither is calling him," she added as I pressed redial for the third time.

"Come on, Rynn, pick up," I said after the third ring passed.

Rynn picked up. All I heard was the dull roar of a crowd. "What possessed you to tell the dragon to fuck off?" he said.

I winced. I recognized the sharp accent that Rynn let slip when he was pissed. "Shit, Oricho told you about that?"

"It came up in conversation. What were you thinking?"

That I'd get a translation, for starters. "It's a dragon. Nothing makes a supernatural feel big and strong like beating the shit out of a human—"

"Then for God's sake, stop volunteering!"

I crinkled my nose. There was a sliver of wisdom in there I should probably take. "Besides, Oricho handled it—he's not half bad for one of them."

I took another sip of coffee and glanced out the window at the museum. "Can we talk about this later? After I get the scroll—"

I trailed off as Captain lifted his head and gave a halfhearted growl under my chair. "Rynn, just a sec," I said, and put him on hold before he could answer.

I scanned the courtyard, my heart rate increasing. My chair rocked back as someone placed their hands on either side.

"Excuse me?" a guy said in my ear.

I jumped, and my pulse spiked two dozen more BPMs as I turned to see who it was. I frowned. It was the student who'd been glaring at us when we'd sat back down. He was way too close for comfort.

"Hey, do you guys think you could move to a smaller table and let us have the extra seats?" he said, exuding thinly veiled contempt as he invaded my personal space.

My temper flared. I hate patronizing politeness. "Get lost, we need the table," I said, and pushed one of three extra chairs towards him.

He flipped a strand of brown hair out of his face. "That's not what I meant—"

Nadya pushed the other two empty chairs towards him. "Take them and get lost."

He headed back to his friends and exchanged words with them, glaring and nodding back at me. I got a good look at their clothes—H&M—then snorted; they weren't even real hippies. I finished surveilling outside and put Rynn back on.

"How far away are you now? The museum is closing at four, and the natives are getting restless."

"I just got off the plane, I'm at least an hour away—"

Goddamn it, the plane had been delayed. Again. "We don't *have* an hour—"

"Listen to me, I'm getting in a taxi now. *Wait* for me."

Waiting another hour in the coffee shop was about the last thing I wanted to do. "Fine, but you better be on your way now. They'll stop letting people in, and we'll . . ."

Captain growled and stood up with a start. He hopped up on the windowsill and stuck his nose into the breeze. His ears pointed forward, and his lips curled up as he growled deeper.

Shit. I scanned the students for vampires and thralls and caught sight of Red standing under the shade trees that lined the pathway, with a woman in a black hoodie, the hood pulled far down over her face. I waited until she turned to the side. Bindi. They were arguing, or, more precisely, Bindi was yelling at Red and nodding towards the museum.

I dropped my binder as I scrambled out of the chair and pulled Captain off the windowsill. I turned my face away from the window on the off chance they were looking for me. Nadya lifted her head from her laptop and raised an eyebrow. I nodded towards Marie's thralls and mouthed, "*Vampire.*" She swore under her breath and started gathering up her papers.

"Owl?" Rynn said. "What's going on?"

Damn it, I'd almost forgotten he was still on the phone.

"You really aren't going to like this. Nadya and I need to get in there. Now. The psycho Bobbsey Twins just showed up. Meet us inside when you get here. We'll be careful." I shoved Captain into his carrier with minimal resistance.

"Wait for me. Getting the scroll is not worth your life," Rynn said.

I bit my lower lip. I wasn't crazy about it either, but what choice did I have? "I don't have a lot of options here. If I wait, they'll get the scroll first, and who knows what Marie will do with it?" I said, and hung up on him. I didn't feel good about blowing Rynn off, but what choice did I have?

We stepped out onto the sidewalk and into a crowd of students getting out of class. I hazarded a glance over towards where I'd seen Bindi and Red . . .

And they'd gotten closer to the museum entrance. I jabbed Nadya with my elbow. "They're on their way in—the redhead and the blond surfer chick in pink shorts and black hoodie. We need to get into that exhibit now." I picked up Captain's carrier and started after them. If I could just get past them and into the exhibit . . .

"Alix!" Nadya grabbed my arm before I could step out from under the coffee shop awning. She spun me so that I was facing the store window. "We need a plan."

In the window's reflection I watched them waltz right in, hand in hand. I squeezed my eyes shut and resisted the urge to bang my head against the glass. I should have headed in hours ago; why the hell had I listened to Oricho? I was the professional antiquities thief for Christ's sake, not him. "We don't have time for a plan—they're already inside. Stay here. I'll try to go in the back and beat them to the exhibit," I said.

"This is exactly why we need a plan. You can't steamroll through every job and expect to come out in one piece. Besides," she said, and nodded at Captain's carrier, "you won't be able to sneak up on them with him."

She had a point. He'd reduced his growl to a low rumble now that the psycho dynamic duo had slipped inside the museum, but he wasn't exactly inconspicuous . . . still, Nadya hadn't seen these two at work. My stomach churned thinking about it.

"Nadya, these two are a new shade of crazy—especially Bindi. They'll go straight for the exhibit and not give a flying rat's ass who they hurt. Yeah, a plan would be real nice, but do you really want to leave them in there? With people?"

"And say you storm in. What then?" Her eyes narrowed. "I may not have as many run-ins with the supernatural as you do, but I've seen my share of vampire thralls. And you running in the front door will only get them to kill more people faster."

I glanced over her shoulder into the window. No smoke and screams. Yet. Damn it, what the hell was I supposed to do? My gut told me to run interference as fast as possible.

Maybe that was my problem? I always go for the quick fix—try to run damage control, get in and out as soon as possible, especially when the stakes go up. Maybe Nadya was right, maybe this needed a little more finesse . . . or maybe I was just giving them the chance to kill everyone left in the museum. I'd feel real swell about that. I glanced at the reflection and back to Nadya, her arms crossed and mouth set in a hard line. She wasn't budging.

And she was right. We were supposed to be working as a team. If I didn't trust her judgment, then I might as well put her on a plane back to Tokyo.

"OK, we do it your way," I said. "What do you have in mind?"

She relaxed, like a weight was lifted off her shoulders. "The first thing we need to do is get people out. We'll trigger the fire alarm. Marie's thralls won't care, but it will get everyone else clear."

"After that?"

She shook her head. "Hope Rynn gets here before they find us?"

"That's your plan? Pull the fire alarm and hope they don't get their hands on us?"

"I didn't say it was perfect. We'll adapt as things happen. We'll go in separately. You through the back, me through the front. Less likely they know what I look like, especially without my red hair." She pulled two Bluetooth earpieces out of her pocket. "Put this on—we'll be able to keep in touch."

I turned the earpiece over. Secure frequency, decent range. High-tech. "Where did you get these?"

"Rynn gave them to me before we left Tokyo. He thought you might do something stupid. Don't frown, he thought you'd forget them in a drawer."

I kept frowning. Figured.

We split up; me around the back with my hoodie pulled up over my head, and Nadya towards the front entrance, looking every bit the grad student with her long brown hair tied in a ponytail and her thick, black-rimmed glasses. I stalled at the corner of the building, pretending to tie my nonexistent shoelaces. I don't know why, but I couldn't shake the feeling things were going to go to hell in a handbasket, which made no sense. On a bad day I wouldn't recognize Nadya.

She paid for her ticket and entered the museum with no hassle.

OK, my turn. I turned onto the nature path that wound around back. The brush on either side quickly thickened. I found a spot where it was dense enough to cover me, then ducked off the trail. As I approached the museum, I felt in my pocket for my UV flashlight and garlic water, just in case.

I hugged the wall until I found the heavy metal door all university buildings have. Bingo. The great thing about grad students is that they're lazy as hell, even the archaeologists. Someone had wedged a stick into the door so it wouldn't close completely, probably so they could go on a coffee break and get back in without having to go around to the front. I used the wedge to open it farther and peeked around the corner into a narrow hallway lit with blue floor LEDs. There was no one there, so I slipped through and eased the door shut.

The hallway ended in a pair of doors. The one to the right was ajar, fluorescent light ebbing out and a Top 40 music station playing in the background. I peeked in. A coffeepot burning coffee was housed in the corner of the closet-sized room, and two computer towers jerry-rigged together beside a thirty-two-inch monitor hummed away against the not-so-far wall, a plastic Guitar Hero guitar discarded on the desk under paperwork.

I'd stumbled into the grad student office.

There was no one around, so I slipped in to take a peek at what they were last working on. I slid a pair of gloves on first—I'm not stupid about my fingerprints.

It was the inventory list for the East India Company exhibit. I read through for the scrolls—they were on the second floor, cabinet five. I opened the file to see what kind of security they'd outfitted and breathed a sigh of relief. Level one glass cases with basic system rigged alarms. Nowhere near the security measures they'd normally put in place for supernatural or magic items. They had no idea what was sitting under their noses. Good—made my job a lot easier . . . There was a set of notes entered by the grad student in charge of the display, Mike Krascheck . . . now, why did that sound familiar?

"Who the hell are you?"

I recognized that voice. That's why the name sounded familiar. I spun around to find Mike standing in the doorway. He was wearing a yellow biohazard T-shirt covered in coffee stains and a pair of worn brown cords that sat just below a developing beer gut—think Shaggy from *Scooby-Doo* ten years after the Scooby snacks catch up.

Mike's angry indignation at finding someone snooping on his computer morphed into shock, then more anger as he recognized me. Mike and I had met a few times at conferences a few years back. He was one of Benji's buddies.

His face went bright red. I think there were more broken blood vessels along his nose than there had been a few years back. "I don't know what you want, Hiboux, but you can get the fuck right out of my office. *Now,*" he said.

I crossed my arms and slid my left hand inside my jacket, where I kept the bottle of chloroform and cotton. "Hi Mike, nice to see you too. What have I been up to, you ask? Not much since the department threw me under the bus, you know, just trying to make ends meet, keep myself out of trouble. What about you? I see you're working hard on the beer gut."

He sniffed. "Don't throw your sob story at me. You knew what would happen, same thing that happens to all of us when we don't stick with the program."

"You think that's what happened? I told them to fuck off three months before my defense?"

He slid his hand behind the coffeemaker stand and removed an aluminum baseball bat. "I'm giving you one more chance. Get the hell out of my office, or I'll use this—"

My foot connected hard with Mike's balls. Fair is great in video games and dojos, but not when I'm about to get my head split open like a watermelon at a frat party.

Mike crumpled to the floor, clutching his jewels. "Jesus fucking Christ—" His watering eyes went wide as I pinned him down and pushed a wad of chloroform-soaked cotton into his mouth.

"Yeah, about following the IAA program? Turns out you do what they say and they go ahead and fuck you over anyways. And tell Benji I'll be seeing him soon."

Mike passed out and I dragged his unconscious body into the closet.

My Bluetooth buzzed as I stepped out into the hall. "Alix? Where are you?"

I tapped the receiver. "I'm inside. Remember Mike Krascheck, Benji's friend?"

"The one who looked like Scooby-Doo?"

"Shaggy, actually—Scooby-Doo was the dog. Just put him out with chloroform after perusing through the exhibit files. The scroll is on the second floor, level one security."

"That's good. I'll head up and meet you there. Can you get to the second floor through the back?"

"Just a sec," I said, and cracked open the other door in the hallway, adjacent to the office. Behind it there was a storage room–sized alcove and a set of stairs leading up. Beside the stairs was a stage door with MUSEUM, EXHIBIT FLOOR ONE written across it.

"Shouldn't be a problem. Any sign of Bindi and Red?"

"Not since we saw them walk in. I'm going to pull the fire alarm in two minutes. Head upstairs and bolt the back door until people give up on that exit. We need it to get by the fire trucks and any IAA that show up. Whatever you do, don't come out until after I've set off the alarm, otherwise the cameras will catch you."

I cringed. Turning the cameras off was a fail-safe in case something supernatural caused the fire. I'd spent a lot of time—and money—wiping my picture off the university databases. I was in no hurry to stick myself back on their radar, especially after Mike woke up and told them I'd passed through. "Be careful on your end," I said.

"You too. I'll meet you at the case," Nadya said before my earpiece clicked off.

I took the stairs to the second floor, dead-bolted the door, and waited. I noted the red fire alarm bell above the door right before it went off.

"Son of a—" I dropped to my knees. Goddamn it, why are fire alarms always louder than I remember? I cupped both ears with my cargo jacket sleeves. It didn't help, especially the ear that held the Bluetooth.

The door rattled as people tried to get into the stairwell, followed by a lot of swearing when it wouldn't open . . . then the kicking started. Jesus Christ, how long does it take for someone to figure, *Gee, the fire escape won't open, maybe I should find another way out?*

My ears were ringing now—as in painfully. I needed to drown out the alarm, and fast. I fished around in my bag for my earplugs—thank God some grad school habits die hard—and clicked the earpiece on. "Nadya, the fire alarm is killing me out here—see you inside," I yelled into what I hoped was the mic. Before she could say anything—not that I would have heard—I pulled the earpiece out, shoved it in my pocket, and pushed in my grubby earplugs as fast as I could.

The idiots on the other side had stopped trying to kick the door down. I cracked the door open, easing the handle so as not to make a sound.

There was no sign of Bindi and Red. Maybe they'd thought the fire alarm was real and evacuated with everyone else . . . or maybe they were waiting around the corner with a baseball bat.

Damn it, I should have grabbed Mike's bat when I'd had the chance.

The exhibit room was dark, punctuated by strobing red lights along the floor and crown molding. I stepped out and tried to get my bearings. Now where the hell was the glass case with my scroll?

The first display I passed by was the front half of a clipper hull dredged off the bottom of the Caribbean, along with the water-soaked logbook . . . an interesting set of chests . . . I shook my head and pulled my eyes off the displays. Not shopping for inventory.

Two glass cases and another shipwreck later, I found the Bali items. They occupied a small room off from the main exhibit, the kind they stick the filler in so people can peruse something in between the big-ticket items.

The first and biggest case held ceramic pots and pans collected during the Dutch occupation. Trinkets really, and not worth much. The second and third cases held period clothing worn by the Dutch and the Balinese. From the smell of mothballs as I passed by, they were real. I swear mothballs have a supernatural origin—how the hell else can you smell them through an inch of sealed and climate-controlled glass?

And there were the scrolls. I put Captain's carrier down so I could get a closer look.

"Shit." There had to be thirty scrolls crammed into the two cases, and the red strobe lights made it near impossible to make any of the writing out. I started to rummage through my bag for my UV flashlight when I heard the closet door jostle. I dove behind the ship hull with Captain. The door jostled again as someone—or something—on the other side wrestled with the handle. Where the hell was that flashlight? I dumped the contents of my pack on the floor until my two flashlights rolled out. I readied one, aiming it at the closet door, and shoved the other one into my pocket. The door creaked open, and I turned the flashlight on.

"Alix, what the hell? Get that light off me."

I breathed a sigh of relief as Nadya stepped out. "Sorry, I thought it was Bindi or Red."

She stepped out, a frown etched on her face. "If you hadn't taken your earpiece out, you'd have known they left with everyone else. Apparently their madness and loyalty to Marie is still trumped by death by fire."

"You're sure? They're gone?"

Nadya nodded. "They were looking at logbooks downstairs in the glass cases and left out the front doors when the fire alarm went off. I think they were only doing reconnaissance. I don't think they even know it's here."

Well, thanks for small and infrequently spaced miracles.

Nadya did a quick scan of the room before glancing at her watch. "Not to nag, but have you found the scroll yet? A few minutes and this place will be crawling with firemen and IAA."

"Here," I said, and tossed her my extra UV flashlight. "Help me search through these. Look for the symbols." I hated exposing any of the scrolls to UV, but there was no other way we'd find the supernatural needle in the haystack. Besides, we couldn't take all of them and figure it out later—five maybe, not thirty.

Nadya caught my flashlight and started searching through the second case. "Rule out anything singed or damaged. The spell scroll is near indestructible," she said.

The first four in my case were an easy rule out. Singed from too much sun exposure over the years, probably in someone's private collection. The next four were covered in typical Balinese writing from the ninth century, also an easy rule out. Worth something, but not what I was looking for today.

I shook my head. "I think these are all a bust—"

"What about these two?" Nadya said.

I moved to the second case. Nadya had made it halfway through, and she shone her light on two scrolls near the center. My heart rate jumped; the writing was definitely not Balinese. I kept myself in check until I found something I recognized. I re-angled my flashlight to get a better look at three symbols in the bottom left-hand corner, like a signature. Both looked uncannily like the writing on the tablets. "Go figure, what are the chances two spell scrolls are sitting in the same place?" I stood on my toes and aimed the flashlight to get a better look . . . if I could just find a matching set of symbols, any matching set of symbols . . .

Sirens sounded in the distance and closed fast. Nadya ran to the window and peeked through the heavy blinds that protect the museum from sunlight.

"Hurry up. The fire department is here, along with an unmarked

SUV." Unmarked SUVs—the favorite transportation of IAA officials everywhere. My heart rate spiked.

"I'm going as fast as I can." But it was no use. I needed to take the scrolls out to figure which one was which. "Keep an eye on the firemen." I went for my tool kit, then changed my mind as I caught sight of a silver trash can sitting in the corner of the room. I ran for it; I didn't have time to be fancy and careful.

I hefted the trash can over my head and brought it down on the glass. It bounced off, sending a painful shock through my shoulder. Damned reinforced Plexiglas. I hit the cabinet again. This time it cracked.

"Alix, they've opened a metal box on the side of the building, and they're arguing with someone, looks like faculty."

"As long as they're outside," I said. I brought the trash can down for a third time and the Plexiglas broke. If breaking the display cabinet set off a second alarm, and I'd bet money it had, I didn't hear it over the fire alarm. That wouldn't last long though, with the firemen here now. I grabbed the two scrolls and unrolled them. *Come on, symbols, give me something I recognize . . .*

There it was, in the middle of the page, a set of three symbols that matched the blood ones from the first Bali temple. I shoved the scroll in my bag and shoved the second one inside my jacket. Just in case.

"Come on, time to run for it," I said, and bolted towards the exit I'd used to get in.

We'd reached the main exhibit display room when the fire alarm shut off. My ears were relieved, but my stomach turned as I heard the quieter, second alarm that said, "Intruders."

"Shit," I said.

"Alix! You set the alarm off."

"Didn't have time to disarm it." I slid into the back door and tried the handle.

The first drop of water hit my face. At first, I thought it had to be a mistake. What kind of an idiot rigs a museum with sprinklers?

Then the second and third drops hit, and Captain howled inside his carrier.

Behind me, Nadya swore. "That was what the faculty was arguing with the firemen about," she said.

I hesitated. The spell scrolls in my jacket and purse would be OK—magic is a real bitch that way—but everything else in the case I'd broken would be ruined in a matter of minutes.

"Here, take Captain and go," I said.

"Don't you dare—"

But I had already bolted. "One minute," I yelled back at Nadya. I skidded to a halt in front of the broken case, my sneakers squeaking against the linoleum. Maybe I could stash the scrolls under something . . . or at least save a few and sell them to interested buyers who knew not to install an automatic sprinkler system. I reached the case—some of the scrolls were already wet—and grabbed four that had ancient Balinese on them, pushing them into the other side of my jacket. The rest I could . . . Oh, hell, I didn't know what I was going to do with the rest of the scrolls. I couldn't fit all of them.

"Looky, looky what we got here," I heard a familiar, singsong voice say from the main stairway behind me.

Bindi.

With the sprinklers going, I'd missed any residual rotting lily of the valley wafting off them. I started to edge around the cabinet so I could make a run for it . . .

"Stop right there, birdbrain, or I'll shoot," Bindi said, making a show of the gun in her hand.

I did as I was told . . . holding a broken piece of Plexiglas.

"Now raise your hands up and turn around. *Slowly*."

"Sure thing," I said, and launched a piece of broken glass at her head.

She screamed and ducked out of the way. Leave it to a good old-fashioned California girl to protect her face. I ran for it.

"Nadya, run," I said, hoping to hell she'd left with Captain already.

Someone slammed into me from behind and knocked me to the floor, hard. I kicked and tried to scramble away, but they had a solid grip on my ankle. I managed to twist myself around so my face wasn't planted into the tile floors. Red had my legs pinned down and Bindi stood over me, hands on her hips and grinning. One look at Red's drawn and haggard face told me who'd been getting the better deal over the past few days. "I'd fold your cards now, Red. You won't last another week with Sabine," I said.

Shock flickered across his face, chased by a vicious snarl. His fist slammed into the side of my head. "Says the woman ruining the entire East India Company's collection."

It was my turn to be shocked. "*I'm* ruining it? The hell I am! I'm not the idiot who put a sprinkler system in—"

Red snorted and I sighed. There was no winning. And no use explaining it was an accident. Besides, he'd just hit me again.

Bindi knelt beside me, her wet hair brushing my face. There was something different about her . . . somehow she seemed less of an addict than she had a few days ago . . .

"You know, I really should thank you. We'd have never found the scrolls on our own. Good thing we knew you'd be here."

I closed my eyes. Oricho must have told Lady Siyu, or she'd found out where we'd been heading and let Marie know.

Why didn't anyone ever listen to me?

Bindi was still smiling as she leaned in until she was an inch from my face. Red had me pinned down so tight that I couldn't even twist my head away from her. She began to sniff my skin, and a fresh hit of rotten lily of the valley hit me.

Shit, she was a vampire. And she was drinking from the same pot of crazy juice Marie was.

"Let's see what you have in here, shall we?" she said, and pulled open my jacket. She grew enraged as she pulled the Balinese scrolls out. She waved them in my face. "Which one is it?" she said.

Poker face, don't fail me now. I tried to look pissed. Bindi slugged me.

"Give me that," Red said, and shifted his weight so his legs were pinning me. He held out his hand for the scroll. After a moment he frowned. "These aren't them, they're Balinese. Check her again."

Bindi glared at Red before reaching into the other side of my jacket. I could tell she was supposed to be the dominant one in this relationship and didn't like Red questioning her, even when he was right.

Instead of going for my bag, Bindi found the spell scroll hidden under my shirt. "What about this one?" she said, handing it off to Red. I started to struggle.

"That's not it—" I started, but Bindi slugged me again. It had the desired effect; she stopped looking.

Red tried to shelter the scrolls in the remnants of the broken case. He frowned. "I can't tell for sure. The symbols aren't distinct enough. I think this is it," he said.

Bindi snatched the scroll back from Red. I cringed, half expecting it to explode.

While Bindi struggled to read the scroll, I caught a shadow move behind the clipper hull. It was Nadya, with something slung over her shoulder, moving undetected under the sounds of the sprinklers and the arguing. Without alerting Red, I strained to see what she was carrying. It was an old musket with a bayonet from the armory display. "What do we do with her?" Red asked.

Bindi smiled and I felt my heart race, but not out of fear. Bindi had been lying on me now for a few minutes. I'd been careful with my breathing, but pheromones were still hitting my system.

"Sabine wants her alive, but that doesn't mean we can't play with her first." Bindi showed me her fangs. "Now tell me, little birdy, where's your friend and the cat? Sabine's been asking about them too."

"Eat garlic, bitch," I said, and spat in her face, fighting the pheromone pull.

She just smiled wider, not the least bit fazed. "Keep it up, canary. As soon as I bite you, you'll be begging to tell me everything."

I made a face at her, trying not to glance over and give Nadya away. She was almost behind Bindi and Red now. A few more steps and she'd be in striking range . . . I'd need to give her a distraction.

"I think I'll make you skin your cat. For kicks," Bindi said.

"Wonder what the Paris boys will do when they catch you? Not too much of a worry, I guess, since Sabine will have eaten you by then."

Rage took over her otherwise pretty features. "Why you little— How *dare* you speak about Sabine that way—"

Nadya stepped out from behind the ship hull and drove the bayonet through Bindi's chest. She jerked forward, and Red loosened his grip on me. It was all the chance I needed. I drove my elbow into his face and connected hard with his nose. "I'll take those, thank you very much," I said, and grabbed back the scrolls. No sense breaking the ruse now. I scrambled out from under him and ran for the door.

"Nadya, run! She's a vampire now," I yelled. Nadya swore and dodged as Bindi lunged for her. The bayonet did little more than piss Bindi off, but lucky for us it was giving her logistical problems; she couldn't maneuver fast enough.

Nadya slipped by her and was a few steps behind me when Red recovered enough to trip her. She fell with a yelp and started to drive her boot into his face. He yelled as she connected with his already broken and bleeding nose.

But by that point Bindi had pulled the bayonet out and was heading straight for Nadya. "Sabine told me about you," she said, as she closed in.

I slid to a stop behind the clipper hull. Nadya could handle Red on her own; it was Bindi I was worried about. I glanced around the exhibit for something to distract her with.

Captain's carrier was sitting by the black stairwell door, where Nadya must have left it. I did a double take. Captain was almost through the mesh. I *pss't* to get his attention as quietly as I could. He saw me and chewed through the last bit of mesh keeping him inside. He bunched himself, ready to charge the vampire. I help up my hand and hoped to hell he'd stay. He wasn't happy, but he waited.

OK, now I needed another distraction. *Come on, think, Owl, think* . . . I noticed the fluorescent light flickering behind Bindi. The bayonet was a foot or two away. I hoped the grad students here never bothered checking for ammo either, then dove for it.

"Hey, Bindi. The name's Owl," I said. I raised the musket and pulled the trigger, but it didn't fire.

Shit.

Bindi smiled. "Missed me," she said, exposing her fangs.

Well, so much for that idea. OK . . . time for another one.

I hurled the bayonet at the fluorescent lights. Bindi kept smiling until the bayonet cracked the casing and the bare UV light registered on her skin.

Bindi started to smoke. She screamed, but I wasn't anywhere close to done with her yet. I whistled. On cue, Captain came barreling out from behind the display case and launched himself onto Bindi in a white and brown ball of Mau cat fury. He growled and bit into the back of her neck.

Bindi's screams reached a new high, as if she'd never imagined something so painful in her wildest dreams. She reached for Captain, who was making short work out of her back.

Red, stunned and not sure what to do with Bindi screaming, still held Nadya's leg.

"Let go of her," I said, running over and driving my foot into his stomach. He let go of Nadya and rolled out of the way. I jumped onto his back and sank my arm around his throat.

Bindi was still screaming.

"You know what happens to Sabine's thralls, don't you?" I whispered in his ear as I pulled the choke tight, cutting the blood supply to his brain.

He grunted. "Every minute in Sabine's service is worth it. I get to be a vampire, just like Bindi."

Man, Marie gave these guys a ride down to rock bottom at warp speed. I was guessing from Red's happy and sane demeanor that he had a lot of vampire pheromones coursing through his system. Didn't mean I wasn't going to try and get it through his thick skull. "Who the hell do you think Sabine is getting her meals from, moron? It's only a matter of time before she drains Bindi dry. You're next on the menu. You're not her subject, you're just the duck she's stuffing to make pate—Ow!"

Red bit down on my hand, the one holding my choke in place. I shook my head and straightened out. Some people just don't want to be helped. Red gurgled, but I didn't let go until I was certain he was out cold.

I brushed the water out of my eyes and stood to see where Nadya and Bindi had gotten. I was soaked and had a hard time getting my wet hair out of my face.

"Owl!" Nadya yelled.

It took me a minute to realize they'd headed back into the scroll room where I'd smashed the display cabinet. I ran after them, but not before grabbing my pack and tossing my gas mask on. I reached them in time to see Bindi madly trying to dislodge Captain as Nadya stabbed her with the bayonet, again and again. Then Nadya stumbled. She shook her head, as if trying to focus. She tried to lift the bayonet up again but failed. Vampire pheromones are not water soluble, so the sprinklers did nothing to dull the effect. And despite, or maybe because of, Captain, Bindi was giving her the full effect. Nadya would be out cold soon.

"Nadya" I yelled. She saw me and stumbled over. I handed her my pack. "There's another gas mask in there," I said. She got it out and fastened it around her face. She'd be OK, but there was no way she'd be able to fight.

"Time to get the hell out of here," she said.

I couldn't have agreed more.

Bindi almost had Captain, so I whistled him off. He shot me a dirty look, growled, and bit down harder.

Shit, Bindi had too much vampire blood.

With a last scream she latched onto the scruff of Captain's neck and pulled him off. She held him out at arm's length and shot me a look of pure murder. I had my flashlight and gas mask, but if I lost that . . . I shook my head. If I couldn't pull this off, we'd all be dead. I readied my UV flashlight. "Drop my cat, bitch."

"Make me," Bindi said with a smile. The fact that she was soaking wet and sashaying towards me made her look even more the crazy surfer chick than when she'd been alive.

"Happy to," I said, and turned my flashlight on her eyes. She snarled and covered them with her free hand. But even as smoke began to rise off her, she kept hold of Captain and started towards me.

I was out of ideas. "Nadya, run," I said.

"No," she said.

I started to argue, but the look on her face told me there was no point. She wasn't leaving.

I swore as Bindi staggered towards me, hate on her face and Captain a vicious ball of fury in her hand. She'd kill me, take the scrolls, and then kill Captain and Nadya, or worse. It dawned on me that this was all my fault. I'd been stupid not to wait for Rynn and now, hell, now he'd show up and they'd probably kill him too.

Marie had set the bait, and I'd strolled right into her trap.

"I—am going to slice—you—into a thousand pieces—and—stitch—you—back—together—so—I can do it—again," Bindi said, now no less than three feet away. The purple welts from Captain's bites made her look like living death.

I swore. I was out of tricks and ideas. Not only was I going to pay for it with my life but so were my friends. Someone should give me an award—worst friend ever.

Bindi's face contorted into a mask of rage, then surprise. She let go of Captain, who started his attack again, then she dropped to her knees and reached behind her before falling forward. Three darts were lodged in the back of her ruined hoodie. Rynn stood behind her in a fireman's jacket, holding a crossbow.

I ran and threw my arms around his neck. "I've never been so glad to see someone." He squeezed back, but only briefly. He put me at arm's length, not bothering to hide that he was furious.

"Get your cat, I'll get Nadya. I've locked the doors to the second floor from the inside, but they'll be through with axes soon."

Even I know when to keep quiet. Captain had latched back onto Bindi and was trying to pull chunks out of her. After a lot of growling and hissing, I managed to pull him off. I held him up, a piece of Bindi's skin in his mouth. "So not cool, Captain. So not cool."

"Come on," Rynn said, and headed towards the stairwell.

"What are we going to do with these two?" I said.

Rynn and Nadya both frowned.

"Well, we can't leave them here," I said. "They'll just find their way back to Marie."

"What do you suggest? We're not taking them with us," Rynn said.

He was right. Still . . . I remembered Charles's phone and dialed. "Come on, come on," I said, as the fifth ring came and went.

"To what do I owe this pleasure?" Alexander said, a cheerful tone to his voice I didn't like. There were birds in the background.

"Hey, you guys finally got out of the tunnel," I said.

"Oh yes, in fact, I'm in North America as we speak. Care to guess where?"

"Can't touch me, Alexander."

"Of course, but accidents always happen, *ma chérie.*"

I heard the first axe fall on the second-floor entrance doors and voices shouting on the other side.

"Owl, now—" Rynn said.

"Hey Alexander, I'm in a real hurry here, but I've got a present for you."

"And what would that be? A light bomb? Your mercenary friend with the toys? You've found an entire pack of Mau cats, maybe?"

"Well, look. If you think it's a trap, don't take it. But if you want some evidence to hand over to the Contingency, proof someone is being a very naughty vampire, then I'd get your vampire ass over here as fast as possible."

Alexander paused. "Where would I find this . . . *present?*"

"Follow the cell phone." I hung up and dropped it in Bindi's front jacket pocket.

"Rynn, help me hide them."

Rynn shook his head in disgust, but he helped me drag them into the air vent—somewhere the firefighters wouldn't look. I hoped. Otherwise they were in for a big surprise.

We all heard the door crack at the same time. An axe tip was poking through. I took one last look at the soaked scrolls and grabbed what I thought I could salvage.

Rynn frowned at me. "You almost get killed by a vampire, and you have time to steal?"

"Look, you can return all of it after I fix it up," I said, grabbing my ruined carrier and shoving the scrolls inside. "I don't trust these idiots not to do more harm than good. Automatic sprinkler system, my ass."

We ran for the exit and followed Rynn through the crowd of faculty and firemen. Lucky for us, there wasn't much attention paid to a good-looking fireman escorting a couple of grad students out of the labs. I kept my head down and my hoodie up, just in case the IAA was watching. Time to lose ourselves in the crowd.

"This way," Rynn said, and veered towards a collection of IAA jeeps.

"You can't be serious," I said when he hopped into the front seat.

"Dead serious. Both of you get in now."

I crawled in before an IAA agent decided to look our way. "I thought you hate stealing."

"The IAA strikes me as real assholes. Besides, it's not stealing if they leave the keys in the ignition."

I didn't get the chance to argue his wisdom, because Rynn was already peeling out of Berkeley.

Once we were well on the highway—me in the front with an

icy Rynn, and Nadya lying down in the back with Captain—I called Oricho.

"Good news and bad news. Bad news is Sabine's brats are in town."

Oricho drew in a sharp breath.

"Good news is we have the scroll. How quickly can you get the plane in the air?"

"I will notify the pilot. You are en route?"

"Oh yeah, and we need out of here, now. We ran into Marie's thralls—correction, vampire and thrall. It didn't end up being a very covert operation," I said.

Rynn shot me a dirty look. "That was about the worst covert operation I've ever seen—"

I glared back.

"I understand," Oricho said, "though with Sabine's thralls involved, I am not the least bit surprised. The pilot will leave as soon as you arrive." He paused. "Owl, I am very pleased with your progress. You have lived up to my expectations."

Coming from him, that praise was about as high as I figured I was going to get. As far as supes went, Oricho at least made the attempt to treat me with respect. I glanced back at Nadya to see how she was doing—worse for wear—and checked that the scrolls were still in my bag. "Listen, just answer one question. Your kind of kami . . . you can't lie, right? I mean, the whole justice thing?"

He drew a breath. "That is . . . a simple but accurate definition."

"Just tell me Mr. Kurosawa really doesn't plan on using this thing to wipe out a few cities."

"I swear to you that Mr. Kurosawa will not use this weapon. Some arms carry too high a price."

"See you in a few hours," I said, and hung up. I felt more assured. Handing it over to Mr. Kurosawa still worried me, but Oricho I could deal with.

My reprise was short-lived though, given the look on Rynn's face as he drove.

"Look—" I started.

"Not now," he said, keeping his eyes on the road. "I'm too angry to talk to you."

If there is one thing I understand, it's needing space. I hopped into the backseat with Nadya, who was still coming down from the phero-mones and nursing the black eye Red had given her.

"Don't you think you should have mentioned we can't read the scroll?" she said.

I shrugged. "No one can. I figured let them be happy for a few hours. At least we have it." Besides, maybe not being able to translate it was a good thing. If I could swing it and get out with my life, that was exactly what I planned on doing.

"Here," Nadya said, and pressed her Bluetooth into my hand. "Give that back to Rynn for me, would you?"

I felt around in my back pocket for mine and pulled out one bro-ken piece of expensive electronics, exposed wires and all. I shrugged. "I must have landed on it."

She shook her head. "And you wonder why Rynn won't give you nice things."

Thinking back to the fifteen one-of-a-kind sopping wet scrolls, I was starting to think no one should give me nice things. Ever.

17

OUBLIETTE; A DEEP, DARK, DOORLESS PIT

9:45 p.m., the Japanese Circus

"The good news, Mr. Kurosawa, is I've got the scroll. The bad news is I've got no idea how to read it. How 'bout we call it even and go our separate ways?" I tried.

Rynn didn't look at me, but he shook his head.

"Yeah, that's what I thought." I pulled my hair back and tried to fix it into a ponytail for the fourth time since we'd stepped into the casino elevator. Nadya was still in the car and would wait there until we were out of my meeting.

No matter how I ran the scenario over in my mind, rephrasing it didn't help. Great, I had the scroll. Somehow I didn't think handing over a nonfunctional weapon would appease the dragon. So much for my budding career as a supernatural arms dealer.

The elevator door opened onto the second floor of the Japanese Circus, and Rynn exited ahead of me straight into the crowded mezzanine. He hadn't said much on the trip back, and I was giving him space until he was ready to talk. Me. Waiting to talk to him. That was a role reversal.

"Come on, Captain," I said. Since he'd ruined his carrier eating his way out, I had him on a leash. He took one step out of the elevator, nose in the air, and a few curious vacationers and gamblers gave us a passing glance. He ducked back behind my legs and tried to pull me back into the elevator. Whereas most cats would balk at the sheer volume of people, Captain was balking at the same thing I was. The sheer smell. Vegas's own patented "Eau de twenty-four-hour blackjack and slot machine marathon."

"Come on," I said, and dragged him out. "Across the bridge is a building dedicated to fresh fish." He got the hint and followed. I got a dirty look and a grunt from a very Rubens-esque woman—oh screw it, she wearing a muumuu and enough blue eye shadow to scare a drag queen, with the kind of body only a diet of mimosas and french fries can build. I pushed by, ignoring her.

Resigning himself to the idea that, like it or not, he was along for the ride, Captain stuck his tail in the air and trotted after me.

I caught sight of Rynn waiting by the bridge to Samurai, Vegas's premier sushi restaurant. I pushed through the crowd to reach him and glanced down at my watch. 9:50 p.m. In time for my meeting with Oricho.

Even though it was late, Samurai still had a line running from the bamboo doorway looking over the Zen gardens all the way to the elevator. I was amazed that the bridge, a series of ropes and planks stretched over the garden, held under the mass of people crammed onto it. Why do people always think crowding around the door equates moving up the line? Squeezing your two-hundred-pound frame as close as possible doesn't get you inside any faster.

"Rynn, I don't think I'm getting across that bridge. Maybe I should try tomorrow?"

"Watch," he said, and nodded at the entrance. Sure enough, one of Oricho's tattooed henchmen came out and began to clear the crowd, not caring that disgruntled patrons clamored to shove past. Two more henchmen on either side of the bridge made them think twice. The first henchman strode right up to Rynn and bowed.

"I'll wait here," Rynn said, taking up a post by the bridge.

"Wait a minute, why aren't you coming inside?"

"Because Oricho didn't invite me."

I glanced over at the three henchmen. "Is it safe to go in? By myself?"

Rynn frowned. "It's a little late to be worried about 'safe.'"

I bit my lower lip. "OK, bad choice of words, but I'm serious. Are you going to be OK out here? By yourself? Oricho is OK, but I trust the goons about as far as Lady Siyu."

Some of the anger dissipated from his face. "I'll be fine, so will you. If anything happens, I'll come in and find you." Something else flickered across his face, something I hadn't seen before, like he was hiding something but felt guilty about it at the same time.

I told myself to stop reading into things. I was projecting because I had screwed up our arrangement at the museum. Rynn was my friend—maybe more—and had pulled me out of trouble not once but several times now. Even if he was hiding something . . . well, I had my secrets, I'm sure he had his too.

I nodded. "Let's hope this is fast," I said, and accompanied Oricho's henchman—I started to call him "Bob" in my head to distinguish him from the other henchmen—across the bridge, under the watchful eye of disgruntled patrons who looked like they wanted to lynch me.

Get in line, folks.

As Bob led me past tables towards the back of the room, the noise and smell of people who'd spent too long sweating at the slot machines gave way to the expensive, heavy perfumes favored by trophy wives and high-end call girls everywhere. This was where the serious gamblers hung out, the ones with money.

Bob led me to a table, where only one person sat. Lady Siyu. "Oh, you've got to be kidding me," I said. Bob shook his head.

"Goddamn it, just shoot me now," I said, sliding into the opposite chair.

"You're late," Lady Siyu replied, glancing up from her tea.

"Clearly you didn't see the line up all the way to the elevator."

She frowned. "Clearly I do not care." She took the cup of tea in her hands and turned it clockwise before taking another sip and placing it back on the table.

"Where's Oricho?" I said.

"He is detained with other business and will be late."

"So he sent you instead? And I thought the ghosts were torture."

Her perfectly painted red lips tilted down at the corners. "Believe me when I say I tried to get out of this as well," she said, and held a menu up. A waiter appeared at her side, though I didn't see where he'd come from. There was a quick exchange of Japanese I didn't even bother trying to follow. The waiter bowed, then disappeared.

"Is it true you retrieved the scroll?"

"Why don't you ask Oricho?"

"I am asking you."

"So, what's good?" I said, changing the subject.

Lady Siyu's frown deepened. "I've already gone to the trouble of ordering. Your human palate would taint the art of selection." She narrowed her eyes and extended her arm across the table, hand up. "The scroll," she said.

I laughed. "If you think I'm just going to hand over the scroll to *you,* you've got another think coming."

Her eyes narrowed. "I will not ask again."

"Good, because I'll only hand it over to Oricho."

Lady Siyu's eyes shifted to a pair of black slits set in gold as she lost some of her control. "I am Mr. Kurosawa's right-hand servant," she snarled. "Refusing to give me the scroll is refusing to give it to Mr. Kurosawa."

"I'm not giving you the scroll because I don't trust you as far as I can throw you."

"How dare you—"

"Sabine knew *exactly* where I was in Bali and Japan, and yesterday her goons were waiting for me to head into the museum—they almost got my friends killed. Someone in here told them exactly where I'd be and what I was doing. I'm betting it was you."

Lady Siyu stood up and leaned across the table. Her tongue forked, and two long fangs extended down from her mouth. "You ungrateful *insect*—I am Mr. Kurosawa's most loyal servant, not Oricho. He should have handed you over to the vampires."

"You know, for all your bitching about how evolved you all are, to this lowly human you look exactly like one of us trying to climb a social ladder. My guess? You figure you're better off with the scroll— maybe Sabine's a better bet, or maybe you figure you can take her out and keep the scroll for yourself. Me? I couldn't care less about your sadistic games, but if you think I'm going to hand over the scroll to you and forfeit my life for some stupid, inane etiquette misstep, you got another think coming. You want the scroll so bad? Take it from your boss or Oricho. Oh no wait, that would be hard. It's so much easier to beat it out of a no-good, lousy human—stop me when I've covered all the bases."

Lady Siyu grabbed the front of my collar and pulled me close. "I will rip out your throat for that insult."

I was so pissed, so angry I'd had to work while this bitch had been trying to kill me, that I laughed in her face. "Have fun finding the scroll without me—"

Oricho cleared his throat. Lady Siyu turned her rage-filled eyes on him.

"Lady Siyu, thank you for entertaining the human Owl. I will take it from here."

For a second I thought Lady Siyu was going to ignore him and rip my throat out anyway, but then she got her face back under control, put me down, and gave Oricho a forced smile. "She's all yours," she said and strode out, her heels clicking against the bamboo tiles.

Oricho waited until she was out of the building before turning to me. "Angering Lady Siyu was unwise. Her kind is known for their pride."

I rubbed my throat. "She's trying to kill me."

His eyebrow arched. "Can you prove it? Beyond the shadow of a doubt? Because I cannot, regardless of what I believe."

I sat back in the chair. "So what? I'm supposed to roll over and die?"

"I expect you to use your wits and intelligence."

I snorted. "Keep showing up late and you'll see just how far my wits and intelligence take me—"

"For example," Oricho continued, "you say Lady Siyu wants to kill you, yet you are not dead. In fact you sat here this evening and angered her to the point of attack." He shook his head. "Jeopardizing Mr. Kurosawa's interests in such a way is unacceptable. She knows the . . . provocative nature of humans. I will have to ask her to excuse herself from the rest of this project, since she is unable to control herself in your presence."

What Oricho had done seeped in. "You tricked her into this—I didn't know you had it in you."

Ever so slightly he inclined his head in agreement. "I will admit that is an unfortunate side effect of Lady Siyu's loss of control this evening." He gave me a slight smile. "You see, we are not always so different in our behavior as you humans. Now, I believe you have something that belongs to Mr. Kurosawa?" he said, and held out his hand.

I passed him the scroll.

"And the translation?"

"Ahh, yeah. That I can't do. We have no idea how to translate it. It's ancient magic, so it has to be supernatural. Even if it was safe for me to read it, the codex is gone from history." I shrugged. "If Mr. Kurosawa doesn't recognize it, I don't know whether any human will be able to help. Sorry."

Oricho frowned. "Then we have a 'kink,' as you would say. Mr. Kurosawa is very insistent that the scroll be accompanied by a translation."

"Well, I can't. You'll have to find someone else to do it," I said, and shrugged.

He shook his head and glanced warily towards the restaurant's entrance. "It is not so simple. As part of your agreement, you need to translate the scroll. Anything else would be considered in breach."

"Why you—I agreed to get it for you. If your dragon boss doesn't know what it says, how the hell do you expect me to do it?"

Oricho glanced again at the entrance. "We suspect it is encrypted, and ancient encryption is your specialty, not my master's." He struggled with whether to part with more information. "We suspect it is mixed with mortal writing in order to better hide the spell, and we have almost as much difficulty with mortal writings as your kind has with ours." He held up his hand as I started to protest. "We have had hundreds, in some cases thousands, of years to learn the current mortal forms of communication, but it is not an easy task. Mastery of mortal concepts and ways are a sign of great accomplishment."

I sat back in my chair. Alexander's obsession with human phrases, Lady Siyu's with fashion, Oricho's with global communication, hell, even the casino. I nodded.

Oricho frowned. "What I tell you is not common knowledge, and I trust you will keep it in confidence. I would not have parted with that information if I had not thought it necessary. Will you attempt to translate it?"

I thought about it. I still didn't think there was a snowball's chance in hell I'd be able to do it. Humans can't read supernatural text. But, then again, this was a supernatural and, if Oricho was to be believed, human code . . . Oricho had gone out on a limb for me, I could go out on a limb for him. I nodded. "OK. Now that I know the scroll is human made, I'll give it one last shot, but no promises." I got up and noticed that the restaurant was empty. "One of these days you are going to have to tell me how that trick works—the emptying rooms thing."

He smiled, or the expression I associated with Oricho smiling. "Translate the scroll, and it will be my honor."

We were on a roll, so I kept going. "And we have got to keep the lines of communication open. You need to tell me what's going on, otherwise I jump to the wrong conclusion."

"I will take that into consideration. Anything else?"

I swear he was developing a sense of humor. "Yeah. Humans, like my friend Nadya? Just try smiling every now and again, OK?" He raised an eyebrow and I added, "Just chalk it up to crazy human tendencies, but try it out, OK?"

The confusion was still there, but he nodded and we made our way outside, where Rynn was still waiting for me. He glared when he saw me, and I realized Lady Siyu must have stormed past half changed.

"Look, I can explain—Lady Siyu, that really wasn't my fault this time."

"She performed as planned," Oricho said. "Lady Siyu will no longer be working with us on the scroll."

Rynn scrutinized Oricho, then me. Then he said something to Oricho in that damned language the two of them spoke—Eastern European something. One of these days I needed to remember my recorder. I could check it on Google.

Oricho shrugged and replied. Rynn shook his head and headed to the elevator.

"What did he say?" I asked Oricho.

He thought about it for a moment. "The closest translation is 'She couldn't plan her way out of a lit and unlocked closet,' or something to that effect." He gave me a small bow. "Let me know as soon as you have a translation."

Oricho left, and I ran after Rynn, who was standing by the elevator.

"I can't plan my way out of a lit closet?"

"You forgot unlocked. And you can't," he said. In the elevator, he did his best not to look at me, and an awkward silence passed between us. It wasn't until the elevator chimed that he turned to me and said, "Next time tell me when you plan to bait a naga. I almost shot her when she came out, and if Oricho hadn't just gone in, I would have."

I stared at my shoes, feeling Rynn's eyes on my back, scrutinizing me . . .

"Despite that, I have to admit I'm impressed. I didn't realize you could be that subtle; manipulating a naga is no small feat—"

Damn it, I'm a lousy liar. "Fine, Oricho planned it and I played the witless wonder, happy?"

Rynn smiled, satisfied, as the elevator door slid open. "Train wreck."

"Whore."

We stepped outside and signaled Nadya. She pulled around in my Winnebago. "Are we ready to blow this Popsicle stand yet?" she said.

I shook my head. "They're insisting on the translation."

She groaned but slid out of my van with Captain and handed the keys to the valet. "Somehow I knew this would happen," she said. She pulled out our bags, tossed me mine, and headed back into the hotel. Yeah, I wasn't happy we weren't leaving either. I was less happy about being handed over to the vampires.

The four of us made a beeline for the elevator. Nadya was awfully quiet on the ride up.

"What?" I said.

She bit her lip. "First they say if you found the scroll you'd be free. Then when they realize they can't read it, they tell you they need the translation. Forgive me for suspending disbelief, but all it looks like to me is they tell you to do whatever the hell they want. I'll believe they're letting you go when I see it. That's all."

"Yeah, that thought crossed my mind too."

"Well?" she said.

"Well what? Do you have any brilliant ideas?"

Nadya shook her head.

We stepped out onto the twenty-third floor, where our rooms were. "Regroup in my room in ten and come up with a plan for tackling the translation?" I asked.

Nadya took one look at me, glanced over at Rynn, and let out a big yawn. "Not me, I need sleep. You want to come with me, Captain?" she said.

Captain mrowled and followed her.

"Traitor," I said as my cat disappeared into Nadya's room. I turned to Rynn. "So, where are you staying?"

He shook his head and opened the door to my suite. "I don't trust you out of my sight," he said. He headed through the living space into the bedroom and tossed his bag on the bed.

Considering this afternoon, it wasn't exactly what I was expecting. I knew he was still pissed at me for heading into the museum . . .

"Are we going to talk about this afternoon?" Rynn said, stepping out of the bedroom. With his jacket off now he looked more like the Rynn I knew from Tokyo and less like mercenary Rynn. "Where should we start?" I asked.

He held up his hand and started to count down. "In the last twenty-four hours, you've mouthed off to a dragon, a naga, a couple vampires," he said, getting angrier as he went.

I started to correct him. "One vampire, one thrall—"

"*Two* vampires, one thrall. You forgot about Alexander. Though you've told so many people off today I can see how you'd lose track." Rynn threw up his hands and looked at me with disbelief. "You have a death wish," he said finally.

OK, well, at least we were talking about it now. That was better than Rynn being pissed at me. I think. "I had to think on my feet, and I think we can both agree thinking on my feet is not my strongest skill set—"

Rynn snorted. "And then you ran into the museum. What if Marie had been waiting for you? Or Alexander?"

"I couldn't let them get the scroll. I didn't know they were waiting for me to lead them to it. If I had, I would have waited."

"That's just it, you make decisions without any information, you stumble blind into every situation. Half the time I wonder if you're even capable of learning from your mistakes." His anger dissipated, but he didn't bother to hide his disappointment as he sat in the chair by my desk. "You realize the dragon would have killed you if Oricho hadn't stepped in?"

I took a deep breath. "Nadya says the scroll is the equivalent of a magic bomb. Do you know what Marie could do with it?"

He tilted his chin down and glared at me. "And a dragon holding your life over your head has nothing to do with it?"

"Of course it does, hell, I don't even know if I made the right choice. I don't know if I can trust Mr. Kurosawa to not use it, but I know people will get killed if Marie gets ahold of it."

Rynn leaned back in the chair, closed his eyes, and ran his fingers through his cropped blond hair.

"Rynn—"

"What? Are you going to tell me to fuck off too? Because if you are, I don't think I can take this anymore."

"I'm sorry," I said.

He stared up at the ceiling for a minute then looked straight at me.

"You're right," I said. "I should have waited, I shouldn't have run in. I shouldn't be telling every supernatural creature I run into to fuck off. I'm listening. *But,*" I added, "do you think I want people's deaths on my hand? I made a judgment call. Maybe it was the wrong one, but I wasn't about to risk Marie getting ahold of the scroll. And I did OK this time. I got the scroll, I took Bindi and Red out of the game—"

Rynn shook his head. "You're going to be the death of me," he said, and stood up.

My heart sank. He'd had enough and was leaving. "Rynn, I mean it, I'm sorry—"

I didn't have a chance to finish my sentence as he wrapped his arm around me. He picked me up and pushed me up onto the desk. Sitting on the desk made up for the height difference, and we were eye level. It had to be the angle or trick of the room's lighting, because I don't think I'd ever seen Rynn's eyes that blue before.

"I'm not on board with what you're doing, but I'm not angry anymore either," he said, and kissed me.

I drew in a breath as he tightened his grip around my waist and leaned in to nuzzle me just below my ear. Having Rynn so close was intoxicating, and a shiver ran through me as he kissed my neck. My computer chimed with a message from Carpe. I reached back and gently slammed the lid shut.

"Besides, I've got a particular apology in mind," he said, coming back to lean his forehead against mine. I looped my fingers around his neck and pulled him in to kiss me. Kissing Rynn had always been good, but this time a wave of euphoria hit me.

Then his phone rang. He broke off to glance at it.

I wrapped my boot around the back of his leg to get his attention. Rynn growled and slid his cell onto the desk. He bit my neck and slid a hand under my T-shirt against the small of my back. I shivered at the touch and leaned back against the wall.

His phone rang again. This time he swore and opened it.

"What?" he said, but it sounded more like a growl. He barked something I didn't catch before closing it.

My body protested as Rynn took a step back.

"That was Lady Siyu," he said, the crisp accent seeping in that meant he was frustrated or annoyed. "Oricho needs to speak with me. Now."

I touched the back of my head against the expensive, textured wallpaper and closed my eyes. Of all the lousy, stupid times for Lady Siyu to call. "She did that on purpose," I said.

"Probably wants to talk strategy. Sabine knows by now we have the scroll. She'll be desperate to get it."

"Fine, then Oricho has lousy timing," I said.

That got me a laugh. Rynn kissed me, bringing my sex drive right back to the forefront of my brain.

"That's not helping," I said.

He slid his jacket on and winked. "I'll be back soon. Don't go anywhere. And we still need to talk."

"Yeah right. Talk. Whatever you want to call it."

"Train wreck," he said.

"Whore."

I heard the door click shut behind him. I got up and slid the dead bolt in. I'd blown it off, but Rynn was right. Marie was going to want the scroll back, and she was crazy enough to try to grab it. I needed a cold shower. Very, very cold.

My stomach growled, and I realized I'd only had coffee since before Nadya and I had touched down in San Francisco. I called room service and ordered a bottle of red, more Corona, and one of those fancy hamburgers hotels love. As long as it came with fries, I could care less what they called it. Then I stepped into the washroom and took that cold shower I needed.

—⁓—

Still drying off my hair, I grabbed my last Corona and opened my laptop to see what Carpe wanted.

Where have you been? popped up in our chat box.

I snorted and wrote back, *Busy not being eaten by a dragon. Now go away.* But I slid into the chair and put my headset on. It had been almost twenty-four hours since my Byzantine Thief had fallen down the temple trap and blacked out. It was time to see how bad the damage was. I'd had a resurrection charm on me, so regardless, it wasn't game over. Yet. Still, dying by trap chute was humiliating . . . and a waste of a resurrection charm. Think of it this way: imagine you were a highly trained assassin who had to use a rare antidote because you accidently poisoned yourself with your own tools. That's how this felt.

I took a deep breath and a big sip of beer as the screen loaded. I couldn't take it. I closed my eyes and counted to ten.

My play screen came alive with the familiar blue I preferred, my stats displayed along the bottom. My life bar was down to half, but it was there.

"Holy shit, I'm not dead," I said into my headset. My elation disappeared a moment later when I didn't teleport out. "Oh no."

"What's wrong now?" Carpe said.

I hit the button again that should have activated the teleport spell

Carpe had sold me. Nothing. "Hey, did you sell me a faulty teleport scroll?"

"Umm, no—that's below my standards threshold."

"Then why the hell isn't it working?"

"Give me three," Carpe said.

While I waited, I flipped open my inventory and equipped myself with my prized possession: a pair of dragon goggles, two steampunk-ish green orbs that sat on Thief's face like a pair of fly eyes. Dragon goggles are few and far between in World Quest. Not only do they let you see in the dark but they also let you see magic, infrared, heat—basically anything a dragon can see. I won't go dungeon crawling without them. Why waste a torch when you can slide on these babies? Come to think of recent events, I wonder how accurate these are . . .

The room was small and circular, providing just enough space to stand. I made my avatar walk the entire way around. No doors, no cracks. I started tapping sections of the wall, looking for weak spots. All I heard was solid brick.

"A perfect replica of the Ah Puch Mayan temple, fourth set of catacombs down," I said.

"Hey Byz, that room you're in is magic blocked. Any spell Level fifteen or lower won't work. Is there a door?"

"No, nothing—no writing, no doors, no seams, no cracks." I looked up. There was only the thin chute I'd fallen down. "Oh for the love of God, I'm in an Oubliette."

"What's that?"

"It's French for a deep, dark, doorless pit."

"OK. How do you get out?"

"You don't. That's the point. No doors or windows means they can forget about you," I said.

"I'm up top, can I pry the trapdoor open—"

"No! Not that I don't appreciate it, it's just a really bad idea. Liable to set off another trap." I tried shooting at the trapdoor with my crossbow. Not even a dent.

"Owl, try Reveal Magic. It's a Level nineteen spell. It should work in there," Carpe said.

"That's a brilliant idea. Why the hell didn't I think of that?" I said, and set the Byzantine Thief casting.

"By the way, I have some bad news about Paul."

I snorted. "Can't possibly be bad enough."

A message appeared in my inbox. I opened it, and a Wanted poster unfolded on my screen. It was for Paul and promised a reward of a rare spell book, one out of Carpe's stash, and better than gold. I checked the view rate. One hundred thousand and counting. It put a smile on my face. Paul wouldn't last the week. "Carpe, you never cease to impress. Remind me never to get on your bad side."

I watched the Reveal Magic spell set as gold-orange writing covering the walls started to solidify. I zoomed the screen camera in to get a better look at the ones on the ceiling.

"It's going to take me a while to puzzle through this—Oh, you got to be fucking kidding me," I said as the symbols came into focus. They were the same kind of symbols and ring series as the Balinese inscriptions.

"What?"

I folded my head against my keyboard. "Nothing. Just the universe screwing me over. Again. Look, there's no sense in you sticking around. I've got an alarm set if anyone attacks, but honestly, I don't even think a rat could find me here."

"All right. Shout if you need help. I'm playing for the next few hours."

"Roger Wilco," I said.

—⁂—

I was still working through the puzzle when I heard the knock at the door.

"Room service," I said to Carpe and took my headset off.

I checked the door peephole. It was the same scared girl I'd seen before. "Just a minute," I yelled as pleasantly as I could and threw on a T-shirt and sweats. I checked my reflection and pulled my wet hair into a respectable ponytail. I was dead set not to scare the crap out of her for the second time in a row. I looked very all-American this time, not one bruise, not even a little black eye. I practiced a quick smile and answered my door.

"Hi there," I said.

Instead of looking scared out of her wits, the girl gave me a shy smile. "Can I bring this in?" she said.

It worked! Point and match for a friendlier, more personable Owl. I nodded and held the door open as she pushed the tray in.

My laptop chimed, twice. Carpe.

"You can put it over there," I told the girl, pointing to the dining room as I went to check what he'd said. I smelled urea and wondered if Captain had peed somewhere, although he was with Nadya. *Owl, whatever you do, do not open the door. It's not safe, there's someone trying to kill you, right now. Run. Get out of there, and call me, I can help—*

I turned around. Too late.

The girl was right behind me, leaning against the wall. "You know this one is terrified of you. She's convinced you're some kind of hit woman, or spy. Her essence is shaking, even now as I stand here," she said with a strong Russian accent, just like Nadya when she was angry or smashed.

I wrapped my hand around the empty Corona bottle and swung at her head. I was too slow. She leapt at me and in a moment had me pinned to the plush carpet. "It" grinned, and I saw the serrated yellowed teeth.

Skin walker.

Skin walkers are the kind of monster nightmares are made of. They don't possess you like a genie or demon, they rip your skin off and wear it. It gets worse; before you die, they steal your essence so they can do a passable job pretending to be you.

"I'll have fun wearing you around I think," the girl-wearing skin walker said. It had lost the Russian accent in favor of the girl's mid-American. That made things worse.

"Really doubt that," I said and bridged up, arching my back and throwing all my weight into it. This close I could really smell the urea seeping out from under its skin, a natural disinfectant that keeps the stolen hides preserved a few days longer.

The skin walker was lighter than me and growled as I tossed it off. I reached for the beer bottle, broke it against the table leg, and rammed it into its face as hard as I could.

It screeched and covered its face, giving me some space to back up. I ran for the door, but not fast enough.

My hand was on the handle when it snarled. I glanced back as it readied to pounce, moving the girl's legs like a cat's hindquarters. "You'll regret that," it said and leapt for me.

I grabbed its wrist as it slammed me into the floor for a second time. I cringed; its skin looked normal from the outside but was clammy to the touch, and I could feel its spindly bones underneath. I struggled even more to get it off me. I started to scream, but it clamped its hand down over my mouth and breathed yellow gas in my face before I could make a sound.

The wooziness hit me. Damn it, how come there was no mention about yellow gas in the textbooks?

As the skin walker leered over me, it dawned on me that the reason there was nothing written about the yellow gas in textbooks was that no one had ever lived to tell the tale.

—〰—

My head hurt. And I was cold.

And the bathtub was running.

I opened my eyes, or at least the one I could. The one that wasn't swollen. I was handcuffed to the corner of the antique wrought-iron bathtub I'd been enjoying ... whenever that was.

The girl's skin was discarded over the back of the chair. Yet another person who'd ended up dead because of a passing association with me. Who needs an end of the world when all I have to do is look at you? I was turning into the angel of death.

The skin walker was kneeling over the running water, humming a pop song I'd heard on the radio. Probably stolen it from the girl's head before it killed her. I'd read something about skin walkers needing water to get in and out of the skins, one of the reasons they'd never spread outside Russia until after the Industrial Revolution, when trains had been invented. It was also something I'd never hoped to see in practice.

"I know you're awake," the skin walker said, its voice no longer high and feminine but low and raspy, like a car running over loose gravel.

"I suggest you listen," it continued. It moved around the tub and sat on its haunches in front of me. Its thin yellow hide covered its bones like plastic wrap, probably evolved to better slip into other creatures' skins. And its face, well, it was like a skull wrapped under cured leather. And the *smell*. I coughed as I choked on the ammonia.

"If you tell me where the translation is, I will kill you quickly. I won't even wear your skin like I did this girl's. However, the clock is ticking."

It picked up the girl's skin and held it over the bathtub. I realized the ammonia wasn't just the urea from the bare skin walker. It had filled the tub with lye, something that could dissolve a body.

"I need to walk out of here in something. It can be this skin or yours. It makes no matter to me which it is."

I coughed. "What? No 'I'll let you live'? Just die bad or die worse? What kind of choice is that?"

Its smile widened. "An honest one. Consider it respect paid a worthy adversary. Or more worthy than this girl at any rate. I do hate it when humans freeze up, so much better when they struggle."

I don't think I've ever been more scared in my life. My coping mechanism? Run my mouth off. "Get rid of the handcuffs and I'll show you just how much trouble I can be," I said.

"Before you make your decision, think on this. If I leave in your skin, I'll know every secret, every heart's desire, every fear. I'll hunt down those you love and torture them. Then I'll wear their skins and do it all over again. Why? Because it's in my nature." It leaned in and smelled my skin. "Now, where is the translation?"

Somehow, I didn't think this was the situation Rynn had had in mind when he'd suggested I stop mouthing off to supernaturals. "Go to hell," I said.

It slammed the back of my head into the bathtub. My ears started to ring.

"You think your friends would know?" It smiled and shook its head. "They won't. No one ever does, not after I rip your mind apart. Otherwise I wouldn't be in business."

"Who sent you?" I said. I could barely hear myself with my ears ringing.

It smiled. "No one of any consequence."

I kicked at it and it grabbed my neck, squeezing. "Where is the translation?"

Lady Siyu or Marie. It had to be. The dragon would have just tortured me. "Joke's on you, I don't have one."

It turned my head from side to side and sniffed my skin. I cringed as a pink, wormlike tongue flicked out and tasted my cheek. It sat back and laughed, more gravel.

"I believe you are telling the truth," it said. "I can smell it on you, you know. A lesser-known trait of ours. Pity. You do realize I will have to eat your soul now? Just to be on the safe side." It let the girl's skin slip into the lye-filled tub. It hissed, and smoke rose in a fog of ammonia.

Think, brain, think, what hurts skin walkers . . . I glanced around the bathroom, looking for something, anything.

It twisted my neck until I was looking it in the eyes, black and pupil-less. "Now be a good girl and look at me."

I closed my eyes and spit in its face. It slapped me. Hard. On a hunch the skin walker was male, I kicked up.

I guessed right.

It crumpled over and grabbed its crotch as soon as I connected. I worked on the handcuffs, trying to slip my hands through.

He grabbed my wrist. "I'm done playing nice," he said and twisted.

"Funny, I'm not done telling you to fuck off yet—" I screamed as I heard a snap and a sharp pain travelled from my wrist up to my shoulder.

"You know you don't need to be conscious to have your soul stolen?" he said. I grimaced as my thoughts, memories, things I hadn't thought of in years flooded to the front. My dad leaving for Mexico, my mom's death, friends I'd forgotten about, Rynn, Nadya—everything flowed out of me, every personal detail. I tried to hold back, stop it . . . It was like an ice pick was being driven into my thoughts, again and again. I couldn't stop it.

I heard a door kick in somewhere, and the skin walker growled.

I couldn't be bothered to open my eyes. Maybe whoever it was would help me die a little faster.

"Stay here, little Alixandria the Great," the skin walker said, using a name only my father ever called me. "I'll be back in but a moment. Perhaps I'll take a skin for the road."

I couldn't do or say a thing—not even yell a warning—as it opened the door on Rynn. I was too empty. I could watch though. Maybe that was what the skin walker wanted.

The skin walker grabbed Rynn by the neck and dragged him to the ground. It pinned him down and crawled onto his chest, but not before glancing over at me and smiling.

I didn't even have the strength to look away.

"Now, look into my eyes, mercenary—No!"

The skin walker jumped off Rynn in surprise and clutched its head, shocked and hurt. Rynn got up, unharmed, and walked towards it. The skin walker held up its leathery hands in defense, backing towards the bathroom as Rynn followed.

What the hell was going on?

"No, I was tricked, I was not told about you, you sneaky, vile—"

The skin walker never finished its sentence. Rynn hit it across the face, and its head cracked into the porcelain of the bathroom sink. It dropped unconscious to the floor beside me. Rynn checked the skin walker first, then knelt beside me. He frowned when he touched my broken arm. I couldn't blame him. It was bent at an awful angle.

I swallowed. It was hard, as my mouth was dryer than I expected. "Told another supernatural to fuck off," I said. It was a bad joke. Rynn didn't laugh.

"I hate skin walkers," he said. "Bottom feeders." I heard the bathtub drain, and I was glad the ammonia would be gone. He was on the phone, Nadya maybe, it sounded like Russian . . .

"How did you know?"

"Oricho was delayed by a disturbance on the casino floor. Skin walkers. They almost always travel in packs. I tried to get hold of you, and when I couldn't, I worried."

I tried to lift my arm but couldn't. I was light-headed and didn't like the way it jutted out at an angle, like a rag doll's. I closed my eyes so I wouldn't have to look at it.

"It didn't break your arm, only dislocated it," Rynn said, his voice soothing.

"I'm pretty sure it's broken," I said. He touched my face and pried my eyes open with cool fingertips.

"No, it's just twisted. The poison is making you see things." I heard water running and the lye in the bathtub drain away. Good riddance.

Part of me wanted to believe it, it made so much sense . . .

His blue eyes flared. "Stop being so pigheaded. Your arm isn't broken."

I shook my head.

Rynn gave up and fetched a set of keys from the unconscious skin walker. I winced as the cuffs were pulled off. He checked my hands where I'd tried to pull them through and swore under his breath. "You made a mess of your wrists. They're too small to slip handcuffs."

He lifted me, and I protested.

"I'm putting you into the bathtub so I can ice it."

"Just put ice on it then," I said. He stuck me in the tub anyways. I yelped as ice-cold water hit me from the tap, but my eyelids were getting heavy. I wondered for a moment if having my clothes on or getting wet with my head this light was a great idea. In the end I couldn't be bothered. I started to drift off. Fine, if Rynn didn't want me to think my arm was broken before I passed out, so be it. "Fine, you win, my arm is fine." Even as I said it I started to feel better, and started to believe it. And drift off . . .

———— ⁓ ————

I woke aware of being carried. I was out of the tub, and though my hair was still wet and cold, sweats and a T-shirt had replaced my soaked clothes. I lifted my head and fought the dizziness. I lifted my arm. It was fine. Bruised, yes, but not broken.

"See, it's worthwhile listening to me sometimes," Rynn said and deposited me in my bed. Before I could force my slow mind to come up with something snappy, a knock at the door had Rynn's attention.

I knew I should probably get up and see who it was; I pushed myself to sitting and slid my legs over the side. My head revolted, and I had to lie back down.

"I gave you a sedative. You need to sleep the poison off," Rynn said, and threw the covers over me. They were heavier than I remembered, and I was in no condition to argue. I heard voices coming from the door outside the bedroom, and I strained to listen. They weren't familiar, but I tilted my head to get a better view through the crack left in the bedroom door.

Two of the nymphs I recognized from the pool came in and picked up the skin walker. For harmless supernaturals, I was finding it unnerving how often they disposed of dead bodies . . . I strained to hear some of the words, but I couldn't make them out . . .

The door closed, and I felt Rynn sit on the side of the bed.

"How often do those guys deal with dead bodies? And how the hell did you learn to take out a skin walker?" I said.

"Go to sleep," Rynn said.

His voice was enough to remind me how tired I was. "I need a hospital," I said, and stifled a yawn. I was losing the battle with sleep.

"Train wreck," Rynn said.

I think I called him a whore before drifting off.

18

I NEED TO STOP LETTING MONSTERS
BEAT THE SHIT OUT OF ME . . .

I'll be damned if I know what time it is.

I was handcuffed to a bathtub, a yellow-skinned monster driving an ice pick down towards my face. I pulled at the cuffs and heard the snap as my shoulder came out of its socket. The skin walker leaned in, breath reeking like rotting meat. A pink tongue licked my face . . .

I sat up with a start, and Captain howled as he toppled off the bed.

I took a quick inventory of my room as I wiped cat saliva off my cheek. Besides Captain, my room was empty. I was still dressed in sweats. The blinds were drawn, but sunlight peeked through the slats.

At least a night had passed, maybe more.

Damn it.

I swung my legs over the side of my bed. OK, maybe not such a good idea, considering the head rush. I braced myself before I slid off, and I pulled my injured arm back in delayed reflex . . .

It felt fine. I even checked the bone, and sure enough there wasn't even a sore spot. Using the vanity by the bed for balance, I stood up and got a good look at myself in the mirror. My makeup had been washed off, which didn't bother me—I rarely wear any unless I'm out with Nadya—but where I should have had a black eye and a swollen lip, my face looked completely normal. I could have sworn I'd just had the shit kicked out of my by a Russian skin walker.

What the hell had happened?

I checked the washroom. There was a dent in the wall where the skin walker had slammed me, and the sink was broken. I shook my head. I hadn't imagined it; I'd almost died. My head swam as I tried to remember . . . Rynn had said something about poison. Had I been hallucinating?

Captain hopped back up on the bed and mewed.

I shook my head at him. "I so need to stop letting monsters beat the shit out of me."

And where the hell was my cell phone? And laptop? I checked the nightstand, the bedsheets, the desk. I hate not having my stuff. A hair away from full-on panic, I checked my jacket pocket and breathed a sigh of relief as my fingers felt the leather of my wallet.

"Come on, Captain," I said as I slid on a pair of slippers—no way was I trying heels, considering how woozy I was—and headed for the door. "You can help me sniff out my stuff."

I opened the door to my room. A bodyguard blocked the way, his back to me. I almost tripped over my own feet scrambling back. "Hey, just what the hell is going on? Where are Rynn and Oricho?"

The bodyguard turned towards me. It was Oricho.

I leaned against the doorframe. "Jesus, I don't care if you are a kami, don't ever scare me like that again."

A frown spread over his face as he took in my slippers and sweats. "Though I am glad to see you are awake, I do not think it wise to venture out just yet."

"I'm fine," I said.

Oricho glanced at the door frame I was leaning against.

"OK, I'm not 'fine,'" I said, "but I can walk." I noticed the chair beside the door. "How long was I out?"

"Twelve hours at most," he said.

"Then why don't I look like I had the shit kicked out of me?" I said.

Oricho took me by the arm, gently, and steered me back into the living room. I tried to anchor my feet to the floor, but I wasn't in the best shape to accomplish it.

"Where most humans would be grateful to wake up unharmed after a battle, your first thought is to ask why. Does that insight not concern you?"

I pulled my arm away and beelined for the kitchen, struggling to catch my balance. I needed a coffee. I turned the coffee machine on and waited. The gods didn't hate me that much. Today. As soon as my cup was filled, I took a long sip. "No, because I'm well aware I had the shit kicked out of me by a skin walker twelve hours ago." I raised my arm. "*This* should be broken," I said, "so why isn't it?"

Oricho shook his head and passed me a chair. "Skin walkers are known to produce a powerful hallucinogen."

I glared at the chair, but it's hard to have pride when you're about to face-plant. I sat down, and my head rush subsided. "Yeah, I know, Rynn told me. Trust me, I'm feeling the effects."

Oricho's brow furrowed. "What did it want?"

I took another sip of my coffee and shrugged. "The translation. It was convinced I had it—What?" I said as the furrow in his brow deepened.

"Lady Siyu is looking into the security breach."

I snorted. "I'll bet she is," I said. I'd eat cat food if Lady Siyu wasn't behind this.

Oricho frowned but continued. "Though severe, using a skin walker was a . . . sound strategy."

"Ripping my brain into shreds is a sound strategy?" I said.

"Better to get the translation and dispose of you in one move so we stand little chance of deactivating the scroll." He paused, then added, "Lady Siyu is very powerful. And determined. *If* it is her, she will not accept failure."

I shook my head. "Same goes for Marie. The skin walker was

convinced I had it, and it killed that girl just to get to me. One more person whose death I'm responsible for. I should start keeping count," I said, and combed my fingers through my hair. I didn't get far with the tangles.

"If you count yourself responsible for every death that crosses your path, you will soon drown under the guilt."

"Old kami words of wisdom?"

"No, just logical advice."

I sighed. "Look, I know my arm was broken—badly—so just tell me what you did. I have the right to know. No more hiding information, remember?"

Oricho's eyes narrowed. "You truly do not recall anything past the attack?"

I shook my head. "Just foggy hallucinations. Rynn fighting with it, being thrown in a bath of ice water." I shrugged. "It slammed my head pretty hard against the sink. I was probably passing out."

Oricho is one of those creatures that can stand perfectly still while he watches you. To say the least, it's a little unnerving, especially when he tries to stare you down. I crossed my arms and stared right back.

His nostrils flared. "You are most trying. The incubus was able to heal your wounds, though he had little effect on the hallucinogen. It is powerful, and you have yet to sleep off the poison, so I suggest—"

A chill went down my spine. "An incubus? You let an incubus near me? Oricho, what the hell were you thinking?" Goddamn it, there were incubi in Vegas. Note to self, warn Nadya no picking up men at the bar.

"I assure you he had no intention of harming you—"

"And where the hell was Rynn? He just let you sic an incubus on me? You realize it could have killed me? Where is he? I'm going to kill him."

The corner of Oricho's mouth twitched, something I'd never seen him do before.

"Goddamn it, you think this is funny?" I swore. "I should have known Vegas was crawling with incubi and succubi. Let me guess, you've got them working the casino strip joint?"

Oricho bowed his head this time. "I am afraid—I was not aware you did not know, please forgive me—" And it hit me.

Damn good thing I was sitting down already, because hallucinogen or not I would have needed a seat. It's not every day you get your heart smashed into a million pieces while someone watches.

"Where's Rynn?" I said, my voice a whisper, even to me.

Oricho waited until I looked up at him. I swear to God, I think for once I scared him. "He is downstairs. We were taking turns watching you—"

I stood up and made for the door. Oricho held out his arm to block my path. "Perhaps it is not wise for you to seek him out just yet, as angry as you are. The hallucinogen's effects are still strong—"

"Out of my way," I said.

He paused for a moment, then bowed his head and stepped out of my way. "As you wish."

I headed for the elevator.

"Owl," Oricho called.

"What?" I forced back tears. Goddamn it, I was not going to cry. It was my own goddamned fault for letting someone in . . .

"You are angry with what you perceive to be a deception, but I caution you to think about your actions. You are fortunate . . . It is not often we choose—"

"Choose what? Choose to trick humans? Choose to use humans? Choose to manipulate humans? 'Cause to me that looks like just about all you bastards do."

He bowed his head. "Choose to care about humans," he said.

I closed my eyes. Goddamn it. Remind me never to let Oricho talk to me when I'm angry ever again. "I'll call you when I have a translation . . . and I want my laptop and cell phone back," I said as the elevator door closed.

The elevator door opened on the ground floor. If I hadn't seen him, if he hadn't been right there at the bar . . . well, maybe I would have stepped back into the elevator and taken Oricho's advice and slept the rest of the poison off.

Instead, I rolled everything over in my skin walker–addled brain. The club, Rynn's familiarity with the supernatural world . . . How could I have been so stupid, blind, idiotic . . .

I walked by a table where someone had left an empty Corona bottle. Fitting. I grabbed it by the neck and carried it into the Japanese Circus bar.

Rynn looked up. "Owl—" he said, surprised.

I launched the bottle at his head. He dodged, and it crashed into the top shelf, amidst startled bar staff and patrons. Everyone turned to look at me.

I'm not proud of it. It really seemed like the best idea at the time. Yet another phenomenal display of my decision-making skills.

Before the bouncers could figure out what had happened, I headed back to the elevator. Rynn chased after me. He caught me as I was pressing the Up button.

"What is *wrong* with you?" he said, pinning my shoulder to the wall.

"That hurts. *Let go,*" I said. I wrenched away and hit the elevator call button again.

"You threw a beer bottle. *At my head.*"

I couldn't decide if I wanted to kill him or scream at him. "When were you going to tell me you're a goddamn incubus?" I whispered so onlookers wouldn't hear.

His eyes widened and his expression softened. His surprise was evident enough. I was bad at spotting supernaturals; there was no reason for him to think I'd ever figure it out. The elevator opened.

"Alix, I can explain," he said, and followed me inside.

"Really? Because I'd love to hear it. Please, explain to me why the hell you never once bothered to mention you were an *incubus.*"

"I knew you'd overreact. Exactly like you are."

"What did you expect me to do? You've been lying through your teeth—"

He held up a finger to stop me. "I never once lied, I left out a detail." His eyes narrowed. "You do it all the time."

I rolled my eyes. The elevator opened on the twenty-third floor. Rynn followed me out.

"Please, Alix—"

I spun on him. "How often have you used magic on me? Honestly?"

"Twice."

My eyes went wide. I hadn't really expected him to admit it.

"Once in Bali—you were about to leave the temple and would have run into the police at the airport. I suggested that you stay until the luck demon could get us out. Then I couldn't let you fall asleep after your run-in with Marie in Tokyo, and Nadya was mad at you, so I suggested you come home with me . . ."

"You what?"

"In all fairness, I didn't talk you into bed with me. That was you."

"So what? You got to feed off me as a bonus prize?"

He frowned. "I deserve a little more credit than that, and it doesn't exactly work like that. I feed enough off the overflow from working in bars and clubs. Besides, I wouldn't do that to you."

I stared up at the hall lights. Rynn grabbed me and pulled me in close. I refused to look into his blue eyes; I'd bet half my stockpile they had something to do with the mind influence . . . or whatever he called it. Instead I stared down at my slippers.

"Alix, please don't walk away from me. You make bad decisions when you're scared and angry."

"I run away," I said.

"Bad decisions," he said simply.

"What do you want?"

"You."

I closed my eyes, took a deep breath, and pushed him away,

shaking my head. I didn't have a clue what I wanted. What I didn't want was to end up like a vampire junkie . . . but I also had a hard time throwing Rynn and Oricho in the same class as vampires . . . Somewhere my lines in the sand with the supernatural world had gotten real murky.

"Look at me." He put his hand on my face and lifted my chin. "See, I can touch you without hurting you. I won't force you to do anything you don't want. I promise. See?" he said, then he let go of me and took two steps back.

I opened the door to my room. "Rynn, I need to think—and deal—with everything."

"I care about you."

I kept my eyes on the floor and closed the door.

The problem was—if I was completely honest with myself—I cared too. That was the part I was worried about.

I got in and found that Oricho had returned my cell and laptop. Captain was sleeping on them. He slid off only after I opened the lid. While my laptop started up, I checked my messages. There were five missed calls on my phone from Rynn, and I remembered he'd been madly trying to warn me about the skin walker. I shoved that away for later and read the text message from Nadya: *Call me.* I did.

"Alix? I thought you were dead. I've had one of Oricho's goons guarding my door, and they won't let me out or tell me what happened, they only keep insisting you're still alive. I've tried everything short of throwing a punch and coming to find you myself. What happened?"

"Skin walkers," I said.

Nadya drew in a sharp breath.

"I'm OK," I said, and filled her in on everything, minus Rynn being an incubus. I wasn't ready to talk about that yet. "I think the guards are just a precaution. I'll talk to Oricho and ask him to call them off." I took a deep breath. "There are going to be more supernatural things coming after us until we get this thing translated and get the hell out of here."

I could hear Nadya pursing on the other end. "What?" I asked.

"It's nothing," she started tentatively.

"Nadya, what?"

"Look, I can't place my finger on it, but my nose tells me there's something not right with all this."

"Yeah, hunting season just opened. On us. Speaking of which, I'm opening the files as we speak. I'll take another crack at them, and I suggest you do the same before the next monster Marie's cooked up comes crawling."

Nadya sighed. "It's something more than just being targets. There's something we're missing. But I'll get back on the scrolls as well, if just to buy us breathing room so I can think things through."

I checked the clock. It was 8:00 p.m. "All right, gimme a couple of hours to look through everything again and see if there's another angle we can take," I said.

"I'll do the same. I have a few more ideas, but I want to check them first. I'll call you then."

"One more thing," I said. "You're human, right? I mean, you're not some, I don't know, succubus or demon, or something pretending to be human, right?"

There was a long pause. "Alix, what happened that you're not telling me?"

"Forget I asked. I'll tell you later. Four hours or so, OK?"

"All right, fine. Four hours, but call as soon as you think you have something," she said, and hung up.

I opened up the files, the whole shooting match: the inscriptions from the Balinese temple, the scroll I'd scanned, even the tablets. They all matched, they all fit together as a matching set, but the more I looked at them, the more I had no idea what to do with them or how to read them. A perfectly coherent jumbled mess.

After an hour of staring at the screen I wasn't getting anywhere and I knew it. As much as I tried pushing Rynn and the skin walker to the back of my mind, that wasn't working either. I wasn't in a state to be translating anything.

I did what I always did when I was this stressed and confused.

I grabbed a Corona from my fridge and logged into World Quest. Time to get out of that goddamn pit and go kill me some monsters.

As the screen went live though, somewhere in the back of my mind I knew killing monsters wasn't going to make me feel any better tonight.

19

THROWING IN THE GAME CONTROLLER

11:00 p.m., three beers, two hours later, and I'm still stuck in a goddamn pit in World Quest . . . please someone shoot me now . . . or better yet, shoot whoever designed this level . . .

I slid the control arrow over the green line on the Oubliette's wall . . . careful, oh so careful . . . it slid into place, and before it could move out of alignment, I hit the left click button and held my breath as I waited. It had to be the faint green line, it was the only thing left in the chamber to try . . .

Nothing. Absolutely nothing happened.

I groaned and folded my head onto the keyboard. My computer chimed in protest. I'd scoured the room, pixel by goddamn pixel. There was no hidden lever, no secret entrance, and no magic button. If I ever found the person who designed this level, I might make a habit of throwing empty beer bottles.

My phone buzzed on the table with an incoming text message. I stared at it for a few seconds before flipping it over. It was from Rynn. I turned the message alert off and put the phone back on the table, facedown. I couldn't bring myself to open his message, let alone text back.

Not right now, anyways . . . Maybe after I got out of the pit and killed a few orcs, I'd be ready to talk to him.

Captain butted my leg with his head. I reached down and gave him a quick pat before looking back up at the screen and the inscribed walls. "Things were a lot easier when we were living out of the Winnebago," I told him.

He mewed back. Actually, things hadn't been simple since we'd had to abandon my condo in Seattle. Three months was all I'd had at that place before my first run-in with the vampires. Everything since had been downhill.

"All right, thinking things through isn't doing anything. Let's try brute force, shall we?" I pulled up the Byzantine Thief's inventory and scrolled through the pages until I found the right scroll. It was one I'd gotten off Carpe a few months back. Exploding missile. The spell specs made me think it'd have the same effect as localized dynamite, but if I boosted up my health with potions right before setting it off, I might only lose half my health bar . . .

My laptop chimed, and an unsolicited message box popped up in the lower left corner of my screen. *Owl? What the hell are you doing?* Carpe wrote.

I frowned. First Rynn and now Carpe. "Great. Another person I'm not ready to talk to right now," I said to Captain. I knew there was no way I'd be able to have a civil conversation with Carpe. He'd known there'd been a skin walker after me. Yes, the warning had probably helped saved my life, but he'd known there'd been a skin walker after me . . . He was starting to intertwine with my real, messed-up life, and I wasn't comfortable with it. World Quest was supposed to be my retreat, not a recruiting ground for my life's weirdness.

I closed the text box as I made the Byzantine Thief down the health boost before I cast the spell. Another text box piped up in its place.

I mean it. You really don't want to fire that missile, Carpe wrote.

Why the hell not?

It won't work. Even if it manages to break through the stone wall, and that's still a big but, the explosion will kill you.

I took another sip of my Corona, then typed back, *I say it won't.*

Owl—will you just put your headset on? Please?

No, I wrote, and tried to close the dialogue box. When it wouldn't close, I minimized it and locked my screen. Carpe didn't stop though. My screen shook like it was having an epileptic seizure. I frowned and tried to click the Cast button, but I couldn't lock onto it with my mouse. It kept shaking out of reach.

"Goddamn it." I threw my headset on and flipped the mic open. "See, now this is exactly why I hate hackers. Just because you can bypass my security doesn't mean you're invited."

"What is with the cold shoulder?"

"You're my World Quest partner, yet you keep interjecting yourself into my real life—you're not even trying to keep our agreement," I yelled.

"Seriously? You're mad about our agreement? Geez, how about 'Hey Carpe, thanks for saving me from the skin walker'? I might appreciate it, you know."

"Yeah, about that. How the hell did you know that was going to happen?"

"I'm the Sojourn Hacker," he said, a little too full of himself for my liking. "You realize these kinds of hit jobs are posted online? Besides, the Japanese Circus only has an OK security system. Took me fifteen minutes to access the cameras."

"Great. So now you're spying on me remotely too? Has anyone ever told you you might be a cyber stalker?"

"Only once. But she fundamentally misunderstood what I was doing—"

"Jesus, as soon as this job is done I'm diving right back off the grid. And for the record, you didn't save me—you warned me. Completely different. A warning just means I had a heads-up someone is trying to kill me. Now, my friend who showed up and kicked the skin walker's ass 'saved me,' if you care for distinctions."

Carpe laughed. "Who do you think called your boyfriend?"

I clenched my jaw. This was exactly why I hadn't wanted to talk to Carpe right now. All he was doing was pissing me off. "Why does everyone think he's my boyfriend?" I paused. "And how did you get Rynn's number?"

"Easy. When you didn't answer my message, I hacked into your phone and went through your texts," he said matter-of-factly.

"I don't believe you. It's bad enough you take over my computer, now you hack into my cell too?"

"Ummm, it was an emergency? If I hadn't, you'd be dead. And for the record, as a friend, I really think there's a lot left to be desired in that guy, I mean, if you knew half the things—"

"Get the hell out of my game screen. And stay out of my love life!"

"So you admit he's your boyfriend?"

I sighed. "Carpe, I'm warning you—I'm not in the mood for this."

"I'm not leaving you alone until you listen to me. I don't care if he's your friend, there are a few things you should know about that guy."

I swore. "Look, I don't want to hear it. All I want is to spend a few hours playing World Quest. *By myself.* And to do that, I need out of this goddamned hole. Which brings me back to my first point. *Go away.*"

"Owl, he's an incubus."

I leaned back in my chair and ran my hand through my hair. "Yeah, I know."

There was a pause. "You do?"

"Yeah—and why is that so surprising?"

There was another pause. "Don't take this the wrong way, but you aren't exactly known for spotting supernaturals. More like blindly crashing into them."

"*Good-bye,* Carpe—and I mean it this time." I turned off my mic and pulled up a firewall that blocked out everything short of essential World Quest transmissions. Hopefully Carpe got the message.

I went back to the game and pulled up my equipped items. Funny, I could have sworn I'd equipped the scroll. Next, I checked my inventory. The scroll was gone. "Son of a bitch," I said, and started to write a nasty letter to Carpe telling him to return my scroll or I'd put up a Wanted poster in the Dead Orc and have every first-level World Questing treasure whore hounding him. Before I could hit Send, there was a hard knock at the door. I didn't move. Maybe if I was quiet, they'd go away.

The banging got louder. "Owl. Open this door now," Nadya said. I got up and peered through the eyehole. Sure enough, there was Nadya. I was about to open the door when a gut-wrenching thought struck me.

"How do I know it's really you and not another skin walker?" I said.

Nadya tsked and shook her head. "You don't."

I ran her answer over in my head. If it really was a skin walker, it'd be more concerned with convincing me to let it in, not validating my fears . . . then again, if it had all Nadya's thoughts . . . I shook my head. Overanalyzing is not a virtue.

Captain was sitting at my feet, in front of the door. "What do you think?" I asked him. "Do we let her in?"

He mewed, stood on his hind legs, and started scratching the door.

I swung the door open. Pissed, Nadya stood with her arms crossed and laptop bag slung over her shoulder.

She pushed past me and dropped her bag and purse on my coffee table. "Why the hell haven't you been answering your phone? I've been texting and calling you for the last twenty minutes."

I winced. "Sorry, I turned it off. I wanted to avoid, well, everyone."

"Spill."

"No. I don't want to talk about it yet."

"Alix. *Now.*"

I took a deep breath. I could tell from her tone this wasn't open to negotiation. "Remember when I asked if you were human?"

"Yes. And why would you ask me such a stupid question? Of course I'm human. I think the skin walker hit your head too hard—"

It probably had . . . "Well, it's not that stupid of a question, because Rynn sure as hell isn't," I said.

Her eyes widened, and she sat back into the hotel couch. "There has to be some kind of mistake—"

"No. No mistake," I said, and filled her in.

"I can't believe it never occurred to me—" She shook her head. "I mean, it makes sense. The Tokyo club, knowing Oricho, familiarity with supernaturals . . . Alix, I have a better eye than you, and I never even thought . . ." She looked up at me. "What are you going to do?"

I laughed. "Well, let's see. I can't sleep with him anymore, so that's done. Other than that," I shrugged, "I don't know. I'm still cooling off."

Nadya pursed her lips. "Why do you need to stop seeing him?"

"Were you not listening? Rynn is an *incubus*. By definition, sleeping with him could, and probably would, kill me."

Nadya crossed her arms. "I agree it would be stupid to chase after an incubus if we were talking about a stranger. Rynn is my friend *and* yours. The only thing that has changed in the last twenty-four hours is that you now know he's an incubus. And you said he was confident he wouldn't hurt you."

"Those weren't my exact words," I said. "And you believe everything a supernatural tells you? I have a lovely bridge for sale, you could put in a nice tollbooth and everything."

Nadya tsked. "I've known him for two years now and I still trust him with you, even if he is an incubus. I know you're upset about him not telling you, but how many times has he pulled you out of trouble in the last week since this mess began?"

I sat up. "Are you not listening? He's not human . . ."

Her frown deepened. "All the humans you know, except for me, have tried to sell you to the vampires."

She had a point. One that wasn't lost on me . . . But still, this was way outside my realm of comfort.

"Rynn is your friend, and he cares about you. Otherwise he wouldn't keep pulling you out of fires. What if it turned out I was a nymph?"

"Or a vampire?" I added.

She frowned. "Not a fair comparison. Vampires are different. They secrete a narcotic, even if they can't help it. Hanging out with a vampire is an addiction sentence, but it isn't their fault. This is different. Not all supernaturals have that kind of an effect on humans."

"Incubi feed off humans—or did you miss that class?"

"No, but you did. Otherwise you'd know they feed off energy, not humans specifically—"

"But they *can*."

Nadya made an exasperated noise. "So what? If it turned out I was a succubus, you'd be convinced it was only a matter of time until I killed you? That would be the end of our friendship?"

I slumped back into my chair. "Can't you just let me be angry for a few more hours? He lied to me—"

"You've already had hours to be angry. Now what are you going to do?"

I ran my hand through my hair. "I don't know. I said I was going to stay away from supernaturals; *you* said I needed to stay away from supernaturals. You now changing your mind is not helping me."

"Yes, and I still think you need to stay away from the supernaturals that are trying to kill you—and let's face it, with your mouth, that's almost all of them. Rynn is the one who seems hell-bent on keeping you alive—" She shrugged. "Do what you want, but if you want an excuse to keep running, don't look at me, I'm not going to give it to you."

I glanced at my cell, still lying facedown on the coffee table. Goddamn it, why did I always get left with these kinds of decisions? Why didn't I ever get to make easy decisions, like what color to wear?

"Nadya, it's not that simple. I mean, I have trust issues."

She snorted. "I am well aware of your trust issues. And it *is* that simple, but go ahead and keep telling yourself that if it lets you sleep at night." She shook her head and headed over to the fridge. "But if this is how you treat your friends . . ." She swore in Russian when she opened it. "No beer? You are losing your touch."

"I was beaten up by a skin walker," I said.

"Yes, the one Rynn saved you from," she said as she slid back onto the couch.

"Nadya, friend of supernaturals everywhere."

"Just the ones willing to put up with you. Keeping you alive is turning into a full-time job. I make more money and get shot at less working the bar. Besides, I think he's good for you. He cares about you, and God knows how, but he's patient with you too." Nadya opened my laptop and made a derisive noise at World Quest on the screen. "Working hard on the translation, I see?" She shot me a dirty look.

"You know it helps me think," I said. Nadya had never really understood the symbiotic bond I had with the game. It helped me problem solve, and I was one of the necessary millions of players needed to fill its code with witty adventure.

She snorted and pulled up one of the files I'd been working on before we'd left for Berkeley.

"Look here," she said, and pointed to one of the rings we'd found in the dragon temple—the one written in blood and set with magic, the one I'd thought had been the translation key.

"I've been playing with this," she said, and rotated the first ring. "It looks like one kind of inscription from the top, but when you turn it on its side, see how some of the symbols change?" She highlighted a symbol that reminded me of a sword. Sure enough, as she rotated the ring, the sword took on a different configuration until it looked more like a heart symbol.

"It's like an optical illusion," I said, not bothering to hide my excitement. "How many more are like that?"

"From what I've seen so far, they all carry these kinds of hidden symbols."

I took a closer look at the rotated ring. As I scanned through the symbols, every one showed a second form, and I recognized at least one from the scroll. "Have you ever seen anything like this before?"

She shook her head. "I'm trying it with the other rings to see what

I get. I've got a program running through them all and isolating every symbol that has two orientations." She shrugged. "We still have to figure out the arrangement and correlate them with the scroll. It might be something, it might be nothing."

I rocked back on the couch and looked up at shadows cast on the ceiling by the hotel chandelier. I'd cracked a lot of ancient codes over the years—they were my thing. When people hide things, whichever millennium or century they were from, they try to make it as hard as possible for people like me to find them. In the circle of archaeology— or grave robbing, depending what perspective you're coming at it from—I was a first-rate decoder, but even I'd missed the symbol rotation. And the level of complexity the layer of rotation suggested . . .

I'd worry about that though when we had something more. Like an actual key or concrete pattern to go on. At this point we were pulling at straws, even if it was a hell of a lot more than I'd found in the last twenty-four hours. We either solved it or would spend the next few months dodging Marie and Mr. Kurosawa's attempts to kill us. Considering how well that had gone so far . . .

I nodded and opened the scroll file on my laptop. "Send me the symbols as you find them and I'll start pulling them out of the scroll. We'll know in a few hours if we're actually making headway or playing our own special version of tic-tac-toe."

Nadya started to pack up her own laptop.

"Where are you going?" I asked.

"Back to my room, where, unlike you, I have a bottle of champagne. Call me when you restock your fridge." She stopped to grab my empty Corona bottles, including the one in my hand. "And I think I should take these, just so you're not tempted to weaponize them again."

"Nadya?" I said as she was reaching for the door.

She turned and raised an eyebrow.

"Thanks."

She nodded and gave me a wry smile. "Anytime. It's really

self-preservation. If it wasn't for me, you'd have made many more stupid decisions by now and would probably be living off my couch."

I went back to my laptop and the new set of symbols.

"Owl?"

I looked back up at Nadya.

"Whatever you decide to do with Rynn, make up your mind soon, or at least hear him out. I don't care if he's an incubus—you're being cruel," she said, and closed the door behind her.

I sighed. She was right. I was still pissed, but I was assuming the worst, and I was starting to feel guilty about it. Rynn hadn't done anything except be my friend.

Every time I ran into someone from the archaeology grad school circuit, without fail they assumed the worst, even after they called me to save their asses. Like Benji. Granted, the university archaeology heads hadn't helped with the rumors they'd spread about my dismissal, and I do in fact take things they would rather I didn't from their dig sites. But I'd never hurt anyone. And until the last week at the temple in Bali, I'd never damaged anything either, and that had been the guards' and naga's fault. Even Benji, whose career and life I'd gone out of my way to save, had had no problem going back on our deal just because it was me and I was Owl, the bad thief. I knew what it felt like to have people judge you by a name. I turned my cell phone over and opened Rynn's message.

Train wreck was all he'd written.

I typed in *Whore* and pressed Send. Then I went back to the scroll and started highlighting the two new symbols Nadya had found.

I don't know if it was the right or wrong call, but I owed it to Rynn to hear him out.

I logged out of World Quest. It's not like the Byzantine Thief was going anywhere. I'd hit a stalemate with the Oubliette wall now that Carpe had stolen my missile scroll. Might as well puzzle through the other, real scroll. "Let's see just what you're hiding in there," I said and got back to work.

—⚊—

An hour later Nadya and I had five more symbols to add to the heart and sword: a cross with a loop, a sun (or moon, depending on how you looked at it), a river, what I was convinced was a tree of life, and a skull, which Nadya kept calling a doubloon. Apparently "skull" was too ominous for her. I pointed out this entire job was ominous, but there you have it. We settled on "doubloon."

In the first line of the scroll, I'd found the heart, sword, and doubloon, overlaid with individual words in the script, like an ancient version of 3-D, but in no specific pattern or order. In the following scroll lines, I'd managed to find all the other symbols as well. The sword and heart were the most common; I'd found ten of each, with the sun, cross, and river following a distant second, at four, three, and five respectively. There was only one tree of life and one doubloon. The tree of life I'd found in the beginning of the second line, and the doubloon was on the last word of the last line. Though what that meant was beyond me.

If I wasn't looking at the codex to activate the damn thing, it was time to retire. Reading it, however, was an entirely different matter. I tried isolating the words, then the letters the symbols were overlaid with. When that didn't give me anything, I tried isolating the individual letters. Then I tried removing the words and letters from the script, to see if that made a difference. Last, I tried changing the order based on the symbols and still came up with nothing.

My phone rang. It was Nadya.

"I found all the symbols in the scroll and I still have no idea how to read it. Any luck on your end?" I said.

"No more than you. I've checked all the rings. There are only the seven symbols hidden in it. I've been isolating the words—"

"Let me guess: then the letters, then removing the words and letters, and rearranging the words and letters—"

"And still nothing. I've got one or two more ideas, but I need to access the Moscow archives again. I want to see if any of these symbols are in there."

"Just be careful. That'll make twice in one week. Somehow I don't think you want the Moscow archaeology department at your front door."

She snorted. "They're so understaffed I don't think anyone bothers monitoring it anymore. All the old passwords still work. Couldn't be bothered changing them."

"All right, let me know how it goes. I'm at a dead end—I'm going to take a break." There was a knock on my door, soft, but I caught it. "Call me as soon as you find anything," I said. I closed my cell phone and checked to see who was there.

Rynn was leaning against the doorframe and looked right at me as I peered through the peephole. Damn it, he could probably see me. How the hell had I missed that he was supernatural? I swung the door open.

He raised an eyebrow. "Because swinging the door open is the smartest idea."

I stepped back and let him in. "Somehow, I get the impression skin walkers can't steal your skin."

He nodded begrudgingly and scanned the room.

"What are you looking for?"

"Beer bottles," he said.

"Nadya took them away already."

That at least got a smile out of him, and he headed for my room. "I left my bag here. And we never got the chance to talk."

All right, time to be a grown-up, Owl.

"I'm sorry about the beer bottle. It was uncalled for."

He came back into the living room, his pack slung over his shoulder, and stopped an arm's reach in front of me. "I'm not entirely surprised. You don't think when you get scared or upset."

I leaned against the desk table and rubbed my eyes. "Yeah, and it was stupid and uncalled for and I should have more control by now."

He watched me for a moment, then said, "I was going to come by sooner, but after healing you, I had to recoup. The bar and the nightclub downstairs is the best place to do it. Nowhere near as good as Tokyo, but," he shrugged, "decent enough in a pinch."

"Why didn't you just tell me?"

He focused on a spot on the wall behind me. "Remember in Bali? I mentioned I'd gone through Kuta."

Yup, that one had already come back to me. I'd given him a lecture on succubi. Who looked like the genius now?

"OK, but just going to Kuta doesn't mean you're an incubus," I said.

"If I'd told you right there and then, you wouldn't have been able to get out of the jeep fast enough. I understood what you'd been going through with the vampires, then Mr. Kurosawa and Oricho, so I decided to wait until you got to know me better."

I wanted to deny it, but he was right. It was the same damn mistake I always make—running from what scares me.

"You're bad with people. I'm selfish," Rynn continued. "Was it wrong to hide it? Yes. But I never lied. As soon as you confronted me, I admitted what I was. That has to count for something."

He had a point. He'd done exactly what I do all the time. And now he was standing in front of me asking for, or maybe giving me, a second chance.

I was starting to really regret that beer bottle.

Somewhere between talking to Nadya and Rynn coming to see me, I'd stopped being angry. I wanted to fix things. That scared the hell out of me, and not just because Rynn was an incubus. Not letting people in was my best defense, the only one I had complete control over. How's that for pop psychology?

Rynn took my silence while I mulled over my thoughts as rejection. Without one more word, he was heading out my door. And I was the idiot letting him.

"Rynn, stop." When he closed the door and turned back to face me, I said, "How does it work . . . exactly? I mean, feeding?"

He closed his eyes for a brief moment, then said, "I feed off attraction mostly, and 'feed' is a poor word choice, more like absorb. It works best if the attraction is directed at me, but attraction amongst others works as well. Humans release adrenaline and an onslaught of emotions and energy: I pick it up out of the air, like breathing in oxygen."

He narrowed his eyes before dropping his pack and leaning in to smell my neck, just short of touching me. I held my breath.

"Kind of like now. It's rising off your skin, attraction mixed with fear—but with you, I find those always go hand in hand. It's a peculiar quality." His eyes changed from gray to the bright blue I always noticed but never recalled until they were right in front of me. He lifted his hand and traced the outline of my face without touching my skin.

"Touch works even better, but if you don't know what you're doing, or don't care, you can—"

"Kill someone?" I said as my heart raced.

He stood very still, his face a hairsbreadth away from mine. Damn it, I wasn't going to step back. Rynn wasn't going to hurt me. He hadn't even touched me yet.

"I was going to say damage, but in extreme circumstances, yes, I suppose that's possible too. If it makes you feel better, I've never met a succubi or incubi who would kill someone. I don't think I could, I've never wanted to try. And to answer your other question, no. I've absorbed the energy you release naturally, I can't help it, but I've never actively pulled it from you. To do that, I'd have to push your attraction to an unnatural state through suggestion, and I find it about as invasive and unpleasant as it sounds."

I made myself let go of the breath I was holding. "What about the mind control? How did you block me from remembering that your eyes change color? And how did you heal me?" I said. Now that I was getting control of my fear, the questions were pouring out. It's not every day a supernatural plays twenty questions.

But Rynn shook his head. "Oricho told you there were rules when dealing with humans we have to abide by. I can't tell you everything you want to know." He raised his hand as I started to protest. "I'm sorry, but I can't. There are consequences I have no intention of triggering."

"But you can control my thoughts? No offense, but that scares the hell out of me, more than anything else."

He shook his head again. "I can suggest things, like ignoring details or directing a choice, but that only goes so far. I can't make you do anything you don't want to do, like walk over burning coals. The other night I had a hell of a time convincing you your arm wasn't broken because it was and you're very stubborn when you want to be. I can't wipe or alter your memory."

I nodded. No real mind control, just manipulation. No more than what a good con artist could do . . .

What was I doing here? An hour ago, two hours ago, there was no way I'd have lasted this long without backing into a corner. Maybe it was the amount of time I'd spent dealing with supernaturals over the past year, but I was almost OK with this. I started to ask another question, but Rynn broke our stalemate and touched my face, running his fingers along my cheek. A shiver went down my spine. "You're not using suggestion on me now, are you?" I asked.

He shook his head. "Not for something like this. I'd never be able to enjoy getting you that way." With his free arm he reached around my waist and stopped just short of pulling me in. "Owl, you need to make up your mind. Can you deal with what I am or not?"

I closed my eyes. I wanted this, but there was one more question I needed answered to put my mind at ease. "Why me?"

He lifted my chin with a finger and searched my face. "Why what?"

"I'm stubborn, I rarely listen, I have trust issues, you've seen my intimacy issues, and even though you'll never hear me admit this again, I'm a thief . . . You could have just about any girl in Tokyo. So why me?"

Rynn glanced down with a thoughtful expression. "You're very broken, more so than most people, but you've never relinquished your potential. You blind yourself to it and pretend it isn't there, but you refuse to let go. You wear your damage and heart on your sleeve, though you pretend not to. I think it's very beautiful. The thieving I can overlook. Did I mention I like a challenge?"

He was so close I felt his breath on my skin. It was now or never. I leaned in and twined my fingers around the back of his neck. He tilted his head towards me, but this time I kissed him. One thing about incubi is they don't need much encouragement. Before I knew what was happening, I was back on the desk where we'd left off before the skin walker had attacked me.

"I'll make you a deal," Rynn said. "I put down my bag and bail on my meeting with Oricho, and you close your laptop and forget we're here for the rest of the evening."

I nodded. I could deal with tonight. One small step at a time.

The corner of Rynn's mouth turned up. "Train wreck," he said.

"Whore."

He picked me up off the desk and headed for my bedroom. I didn't even bother putting up a fight. Sometimes there are things more important than finding scrolls and digging stuff up.

20

WHAT YOU SEE IS WHAT YOU GET

8:00 a.m., my room at the Japanese Circus

I woke up by myself, with a vague memory of Rynn getting up while I was too groggy to say or do anything except roll over and bury myself under the covers. As much fun as I'd had with him last night, I needed sleep. Badly. Four days running on empty had caught up, and I'd needed the rest, both physically and mentally. I was still adjusting to the idea of having Rynn around, let alone the incubus factor . . . I pulled the duvet over my head. Dear God, what the hell was I doing?

I reached over to the nightstand and checked my cell. No messages from Nadya, Rynn, or anyone else wanting to yell at me. I stretched out with every intention of sleeping for another hour or two when I heard the first scratch on the door—light . . . probing. I closed my eyes and buried my face in the pillow, but Captain's scratching kept coming. Damn it, he'd heard me pick up my cell phone from the other room.

I pushed the covers off and swung out of bed. I had no intention of seeing what kind of damage bill Lady Siyu was gonna give me if Captain scratched the paint.

I opened the door just as he started a second run of scratching. "It's amazing how much noise you make when you want something," I said. He slid through to complain in person. Instead of mewing, he stood on his hind legs, begging for food.

I headed into the kitchen, Captain hard on my heels. Was I caving? Yeah, but trust me, it was better this way.

On the living room table, beside my laptop, stood a folded piece of white paper. It was from Rynn.

Meeting with Oricho. Text me if you do anything stupid.

Yeah, right. Like I'd have the chance to text him first.

As soon as I got close to the kitchenette, the aroma of warm coffee hit me. I made a beeline straight for the coffeepot, ignoring Captain's protests as I breezed by his empty food bowl.

I poured a cup and had a sip—still warm, dark but not burned . . . OK, maybe I could get used to having Rynn around some mornings.

I deposited Captain's wet food in his bowl—so that he'd shut up, not that he actually deserved it—and headed back into the living room. Coffee in hand, I slid into the desk chair, opening my laptop and a text window to Nadya.

Just got up. Taking another crack at the codex. Please say you're doing better than I am.

A few seconds later Nadya rang me. I answered but didn't even get the chance to say hello.

"I hope you have a backup plan. One that involves running." You'd think if anyone would have a backup plan that hinged on running, it'd be me. "Uhh, yeah. Don't count on it," I said. Nadya swore. "Look, let's meet here in five hours and compare notes again. These symbols are the codex—I'm sure of it. We just have to figure out how to read it."

"Fantastic. The American woman tells me all we have to do is decode a three-thousand-year-old encryption, then translate it."

I ignored her tone. "If anyone can translate it, it's you. In the meantime, don't open the door for anyone, and call if you get anywhere. And let me worry about cracking it."

"Vice versa. See you in five hours. And Alix?"

"Yeah?"

"Tell Rynn to have his clothes on," she said.

"Oh come on—" But she'd already hung up. I shook my head and hunched back over my laptop.

The one thing I was sure of was that the symbols, not the actual written words, were meant to be read off the scroll. The words themselves, illegible to both humans and supernaturals, were only there to hide the symbols like a very sophisticated mask. How did I know? I'd run into it before in ancient texts out of Russia, though they'd been much less sophisticated. No 3-D rotations, only pictures hidden in the paper. This was on another level entirely. The symbols could only be seen in a 3-D rendering of the text.

I just wish I had a hint as to what the symbols meant. I wasn't delivering an incomplete spell scroll and entering into round two with the dragon.

I am capable of learning from some mistakes.

I ran a few translation programs from the International University archives on pairs and groups of symbols, and then again on each of the individual symbols against all the known supernatural languages on file. Zip, nada, all roads lead to a dead-end nothing.

"Maybe I should just package it up in a zip file, send it to Mr. Kurosawa, and run before he can open it," I said to Captain after my translation program finished comparing images from a Peruvian university. It'd been a long shot, but you never know—in their heyday, those South American civilizations got around a lot more than you might have thought. Apparently it pays to worship a demigod.

About 12:00 p.m. the lock to my room jostled and the door caught on the chain. I'd set it and the dead bolt. I had a sneaking suspicion the next supernatural goon Marie sent wouldn't bother trying to trick me into letting them in.

Rynn's face scowled at me from the small crack. "Do you mind?" he said and pointed at the chain.

"You told me to be more careful," I said as I unlocked the door.

"That isn't safe, it's annoying. Do you have any idea how easy it is to break one of those chains?" he said.

"Well, what would you suggest? Since you're the professional on all things supernatural and mercenary," I said.

Rynn removed two bottles of bleach and a water gun from a plastic bag. "These, for starters. Bleach burns skin walkers, accelerates their chemical preservatives to dangerous levels, and stops them in their tracks."

The mention of skin walkers, I figure, drained the color right out of my face. "Please say there aren't any more running around the casino."

"We found two more in the casino kitchens. Came looking for the rest of their pack. I'm fairly certain it's the last of them."

"Then what's the bleach for?" I said.

He glanced over his shoulder. "Precaution. Skin walkers are bottom feeders, but they get hired for this kind of work a lot."

I took a deep breath and suppressed the urge to go and hide under my comforter. I pulled up the scroll again and tried rearranging the symbols for the fifth time that afternoon.

I felt Rynn come up behind me and lean on the back of my chair to look over my shoulder.

"Making any progress?" he said.

I shrugged and zoomed in on the symbols. Maybe Rynn would recognize them. "Yes and no. Nadya and I found these symbols hidden in the scroll and the inscriptions. It's slick—three-dimensional encryption without a computer. Whatever supernatural wrote this knew what they were doing. Ever seen them before?"

He narrowed his eyes at the screen. "Seen what?" he said.

"These," I said, and highlighted the sword symbol with my cursor, drawing a circle around it. "The one that jumps off the page like a picture. It was hidden underneath the writing. You just have to take the writing off and rotate it," I said, and set my program running again. The writing lifted off the page and rotated at 180 degrees, uncovering the symbols.

"Alix, there's nothing there except for the writing."

There was no way. "Have you ever watched a 3-D movie?"

He shook his head. "Tried once. I didn't like all the colors. I'm not entirely sure what the appeal is, no offense."

"Holy shit," I said, and reached for my phone. There was no way, it could not be this easy—how the hell had no one picked up on this before? I called Oricho.

"Hey," I said as soon as he picked up. "You study humans—ever seen a 3-D movie?"

There was a pause before Oricho said, "I fail to see why you would call to ask my opinion on human entertain—"

"It's important—just answer the stupid human's question."

Like always, Oricho paused, then said carefully, "I've seen one before but did not like the blurred motion and colors. I fail to see the appeal."

"I'll bet you do," I said, imagining what Oricho and Rynn must have seen. "Look, I need to run one more test. Don't go too far from your phone. I might have just figured out how to read the scroll," I said, and hung up.

Rynn was looking at me as if I'd gone nuts. I bit my lip and tried to figure out the best way to explain it. I pulled out a piece of paper and pencil and started to draw a cube. "What do you see on the paper?" I asked him.

He looked down at it, then back at me. "Poorly drawn squares and triangles," he said.

I nodded. No wonder supernaturals thought we were so stupid. "OK, technically you're right. On the piece of paper I've drawn a bunch of uneven lines. But to humans that looks like a cube. Our brains take in the angles and translate them into a familiar three-dimensional shape." I wondered what film and pictures looked like to Rynn. I pointed to a painting across the room of a group of ballet dancers. A Degas reprint, or, knowing Mr. Kurosawa, an original. "What do you see in the painting?"

"A picture, colors, like a snapshot." He shrugged. "Well done, but a flat representation of ballet dancers."

"OK. So in order for you to recognize it, it has to be done well. For whatever reason, your brain is harder to trick than mine—or slower, depends how you want to think about it. Human eyes and brains work independently of our consciousness. Our eyes see the shape of a box and translate it into the three-dimensional cube, without me even noticing they're doing it. If it's convincing, like a film, a photograph, or even a painting, you and Oricho can tell what it's supposed to be, even though you know it's a two-dimensional representation. We just have a . . ." I reached for the right word. ". . . call it a lower threshold, an ability to recognize three-dimensional objects from something as simple as angles. When it comes to TV and 3-D, you guys are back to seeing the lines and blurred colors—it's not convincing to your eyes, or brains, or whatever. To us though, it looks like we're not just watching the film; we're in it."

Rynn stared at the cube I'd drawn and back at the scroll on my screen. He shook his head. "I still don't see it, but I believe you."

I nodded. "I don't think a supernatural could have made this. I think a human did." We exchanged a glance as both of us realized what this was. Shit, I was looking at human written magic. Something that hadn't been around since . . . well, think the legends of King Arthur's court and ancient Egypt and you get the picture. We sure as hell didn't have any reliable written records of it.

Rynn pulled out his cell phone. "I'd better call Oricho back. This is not going to go over well with Mr. Kurosawa."

I stopped him. "Let me run one more test." I went into my essentials bag—ever since the skin walker, I didn't like having it too far out of reach—and pulled out a scrambling device I'd picked up in Japan for my cell phone.

I headed back to my laptop, and Rynn frowned as I attached it to my cell. "Alix, what are you doing?"

"I want to see if I can get confirmation about the 2-D, better than you and Oricho just not being able to see it."

"How do you plan on doing that?" he said, still frowning.

"There's only one supernatural I know of that starts off human," I said, and punched in Alexander's number.

"H-hello?" a timid female voice said after the third ring.

I frowned. I'd never had someone else pick up Alexander's phone. "Umm, yeah, is Alexander there?"

"Who should I say is calling?"

Wait a minute, I knew that voice. "Bindi?" I said, not quite believing.

"Y-yes—who is this?" she said, taking on that unmistakable, petulant tone.

Damn, I'd have figured Alexander would have just killed them. Oh well, vampires are a fickle lot. "Alexander has you answering his phone now? Jesus Christ. It's Owl—put him on. Now."

She placed her sleeve on the receiver, and I could hear her muffled voice say, "Alexander? Owl is requesting an audience—"

"Oh for Christ's sake, Bindi," I said as loud as I could, hoping Alexander would hear. "Grow a backbone. Just tell him to fuck off and answer the goddamn phone before I ha—"

"Owl." Alexander's clear, smooth voice came across the line. "To what do I owe this distinct displeasure?"

"You've seriously got them answering phones for you? I thought you'd have turned them in or killed them or something."

"Who says I won't? I can still change my mind. And I only use the girl for answering the phone. I found other uses for the boy."

I rolled my eyes. "Listen—I need to know something. You remember way back when you were a human? Three-dimensional boxes drawn on paper; can you still see them?" I asked.

He paused. "A very interesting academic question. One I believe should have a price."

"Just answer the question, vampire boy—can you still see a 3-D object out of a 2-D rendition or not? Yes or no?"

"You have still not addressed what's in it for *me*," he said.

I sighed. "Next time you try to kill me, I'll count to five before sicing my cat on you. Hey!" I said as Rynn snatched my phone away.

He glared at me before holding it up to his ear and speaking French to Alexander. Damn it, times like this I wish I had an ear for languages.

"Here," Rynn said, giving the phone back. "He'll tell you what you need to know."

"How did you do that?"

"Easy. I told him I'd do worse than light a grenade if he didn't stop flirting with you."

I cringed and covered the mic. "Please don't tell me that was vampire flirting."

Rynn shrugged and smiled. "Fine. I won't," he said and headed into the kitchen. I cringed again.

"All right, Alexander. Can you see 3-D or not?"

His voice came on like a purr. "Why, Owl, you surprise me. I wonder if you know half the things I do about your new companion. Shall we see? A game of twenty questions, perhaps?"

I closed my eyes and just about hung up. "Just answer the goddamn question—"

"Yes. Though it is much more difficult than when I was alive. My mind remembers, but my eyes do not want to see."

"Finally. We're getting somewhere. Could you still draw or write a 3-D object?"

I thought I heard paper crinkling and pencil scratches on the other side.

"I regret to inform you that it gives me a headache, much like watching a 3-D movie, even in short increments," he said. I even thought I caught a slight sigh in his voice.

I snorted. Alexander could reminisce about being alive on his own time. He was drawing this out, and my call scrambler wasn't foolproof. Given enough time, someone could track it.

"So is that a 'no, you couldn't draw it' or 'you could, but you'd get a bad headache and take it out on some poor human'?" I said.

"Much as it pains me to say so, I would not be able to draw such a thing anymore."

"Finally. *Thank you*," I said and hung up the phone. "Goddamn it, I hate vampires."

I heard Rynn laugh from the kitchen. "Maybe you should stop calling them then?" he said.

"If I had a non-vampire vampire expert, I would."

He came back into the living room with one of my Coronas and leaned against the doorway. "Sounded like you got what you needed."

I nodded. "Yeah. A vampire maybe could have written it, but doubtfully. Alexander couldn't even draw a box, let alone something this detailed, and he's a couple hundred years old. It's gotta be human made." Damn, if it was human made, that meant we could translate it—really translate it. "Do you know what this means?"

Rynn gave me a half smile and took a pull off his beer. "Yeah. My evening plans are shot," he said and pulled a chair up beside me.

I called Nadya and gave her a rundown on what I'd discovered.

"I know just what archive to run it through," Nadya said. "It'll take an hour or two, at most."

Next I called Oricho. "You are not going to believe this, but the scroll isn't supernatural. It's human. Nadya is running the symbols through her databases."

"You will be able to read it?" he asked.

"Let's hope so." A thought occurred to me, and I needed to test it immediately. "We should have more for you in another hour. I'll give you a shout then," I said and hung up.

"Anything I can do?" Rynn asked, leaning further over my shoulder. I got the distinct impression he was squinting at the computer screen, still trying to see the symbols.

I shook my head. "No offense, but human eyes only."

"None taken." He headed into the kitchen and returned with his jacket in one hand and the bleach-filled water gun in the other. "I'm heading to the bar—the skin walkers took a hit out of me and, let's face it, I'm the last thing on your mind right now."

I looked over my shoulder at him. He did look tired. Damn, I hadn't even thought to ask him how he was; I'd gone straight into my problems. "Sorry. I've just finally gotten somewhere with this mess—"

"Don't worry about it," he said. He leaned in and kissed my cheek. "Keep the bleach gun close," he added.

I logged into World Quest. There was one more thing I had to do before working on the scroll; get rid of my Achilles' heel. I made the Byzantine Thief get up, light a torch, and place it in a holder. Then I made her take off her dragon eye goggles.

Son of a bitch.

The same inscription rings that had been there all along flared with the three-dimensional symbols, just like they appeared on the scroll. The far wall was what really got me though.

Rows of symbols, maybe thirty or so, lined the walls in a grid pattern, four across the top, six down the side. I'd noticed etchings before but had brushed them off as graffiti, since I hadn't been able to see the full three-dimensional shapes with my dragon eye goggles on. A trap for supernaturals. Guess Ah Puch didn't play nice with his brethren.

Damn, the guys who designed this game were good.

All I had to do was hit the right symbols in the grid, laid out in the inscription rings overhead. In no time I had a series of symbols from the inscription rings dashed in the dirt. I started with the first in the sequence, guessing it had to be the symbol that followed a small gap in the outer inscription ring. I tried not to think of what would happen if I got the order wrong.

After I pressed the last symbol the room shook slightly, and there was a flash that knocked me onto my backside and made everything go dark. For a second I thought I'd entered them wrong and killed myself.

Then the Byzantine Thief came to with a tunnel stretched out in front of her.

Jackpot.

I gave Carpe a call. "The Byzantine Thief is back in play," I said. And to be honest, I wasn't feeling too shabby about me, Owl, either.

21

I HATE SNAKES

5:00 p.m., Japanese Circus main-floor lounge

By five o'clock Nadya and I both had cabin fever, so we headed downstairs to the bar. I wasted no time ordering a Corona from the rotund, red-faced bartender with a nametag that read, HI, MY NAME IS SYOKO. He stopped midpour and narrowed his eyes at me as I slid onto the barstool. He'd been on staff when I'd thrown the beer bottle. I shrugged; if I spent time dwelling on all my mistakes . . .

Nadya ordered a fancy drink that included champagne as one of many ingredients. Tomorrow was the start of a long weekend, and the bar was packed. I couldn't take my eyes off Syoko. His eyes were big—too big—and seemed to sit on his face like strange gold orbs. "Frog demon?" I asked Nadya.

She shook her head and took a sip of her champagne cocktail. "No, he'd have a more yellow or green undercast," she said, and squinted. "Japanese radish demon. I'd put money on it."

I nodded. Yup, radish demon fit—and yes, there are plantlike supernaturals out there. I think even with the noise he overheard us.

He shot me a glare, and when I passed him bills for our drinks, he stared at them as if I'd been offering him kryptonite.

"Do you think any humans work here?" I asked Nadya after the radish demon snatched my money away with a grunt and didn't bother bringing back change.

"Please focus for a minute. I finished the translation. *Wait*—" she added as I opened my mouth. "The symbols refer back to a Cyrillic precursor, a very old dialect. And it's a curse, a bad one."

"We already knew that from the genie text, didn't we? The priest Cervac? The great equalizer?"

Nadya started to answer but was interrupted by her phone chiming with a new message. She glanced down, and I noticed a ghost of a frown cross her face as she read. She put the phone away and returned her attention back to me, but now her words spilled out fast, as if she was worried about running out of time.

"Yes, but I think Cervac was wrong. I don't think he had a very good translation. By the time he wrote this book, the dialect had been out of use for three centuries. We know now that Cervac couldn't have read it himself, even with a human body. He'd have needed a human translator, and they would only have had a remedial understanding of the language."

"So what does it really say?"

She shook her head. "I can't be sure, but I think it's a wasting disease. Remember the old children's rhyme 'Ring around the rosy, a pocket full of posies'?"

" 'Hush a hush a, we all fall down'?" I finished. "Of course I do. It signaled the black plague. The original one, not the bacterial bubonic. People thought singing kept it at bay."

"Yes, well, not quite. When the goblin clans found themselves in the middle of land disputes in old Europe, instead of going to war they'd solve them by sending their young into human villages, masquerading as small children. They'd sing the song and start the curse. The village would die out, and they'd come in to split up the land and fill their salt pantries."

I hadn't heard that one before, but I wasn't surprised. Goblin clans weren't known for scruples. I cringed at the thought of what they'd filled their salt pantries with.

"So if this thing gets read, it won't blow up a block, it'll release the next black plague?" Nowadays with international travel it wouldn't just wipe out a town; it'd cause a global pandemic.

"Not the black plague exactly, but I think something similar."

"OK, but it can't be a goblin curse. For one, they can't write." Goblins came from the same school of thought as skin walkers when it came to written records. If it didn't include fingerpainting with entrails, what was the point?

"Now that we have the order of symbols, that's what it reads like," Nadya said.

I pinched the bridge of my nose. Vampires, dragons, and now deadly magic plagues—goddamn it, why had I taken that egg job? I knew I'd had a bad feeling about it, I just knew it . . .

Nadya continued, "My translation's not exact. Some words got lost over the centuries. It can't be helped, but the emphasis in the scroll is placed on the tree of life and the doubloon—"

"Skull," I corrected her. I couldn't help myself. It was a damn skull, not pirate treasure.

She tsked. "I could care less what you think it is. Let me finish. The two together with the sword and heart mean that the strong will fall, and the great and powerful will crumble. Worse though, there is one more way to interpret the scroll. I think Mr. Kurosawa plans to use it as a weapon—Oh for the love of God, what now?" Nadya said as her phone buzzed again. This time she didn't bother to hide the frown as she read. "What's wrong?" I asked.

She shook her head, still distracted. "Nothing. Just wait here, will you? There's something I need to deal with."

From the way her brow furrowed, I wasn't buying it. "Nadya?" I started, but she silenced me with a shake of her head.

"I just need to check on a detail—it pertains to the scroll, and I can't do it from here."

"What detail?"

"It's not important," she said. Whatever had been on the phone, though, had her distracted. I tried to get a glimpse, but she hid the screen by slipping it back in her pocket.

"Yeah, forgive me if that doesn't instill confidence. Spill. *Now.*"

She glanced up and shook her head. "I do not wish to say until I am certain. It will only prove a distraction—"

"Nadya—"

"Alix, trust me on this one. Don't worry, it is probably nothing, but I have a very short server window. I won't be more than ten minutes. It's important," she added.

I capitulated and watched Nadya head into the lobby, then disappear into the elevator. If it was nothing, why did I have such an awful feeling about it?

I turned my attention to the people crowding the casino floor and shook my head. If they knew a quarter of the things going on in this place . . . a murderous naga, ghoulish nymphs, a couple of hired skin walkers, the odd vampire looking for a weekend lunch mixed in there . . . let alone the fact that a dragon owned this casino, one who had a penchant for collecting ghosts in his private slot machines.

I shook my head and went back to my drink. Who was I kidding? Most of the time I wasn't any better off with the supernatural than they were. I just knew they existed.

Fifteen minutes slipped by while I people-watched and worked on my Corona. I began to tap my foot against the bar. Nadya should have been back by now. It never fails that this close to the end of a job I get antsy, like if something is going to go wrong, it'll be now . . .

My phone rang and Nadya's number flashed across the screen. "What happened to ten minutes tops?"

"Listen to me carefully," she whispered. "Get the scroll. I don't care how, just get it and don't let anyone read it."

I heard banging in the background.

"What the hell is going on?" I said. "Where are you?"

She swore. "Locked in my bathroom. I ducked in right before the room door gave out."

I grabbed my jacket. "Get on the toilet and cram yourself into the vent. You just need to hide until I get there with Rynn—"

"I'm out of time. Check your left pocket," she said, and I heard the door crash.

"Nadya?!" I yelled. "Nadya?!" But there was no answer.

Shit.

I jumped out of my chair and ran for the elevator. An impatient crowd hovered around the two gold elevator doors. I skidded to a stop. They'd been shut down.

I ducked into a corner and called Rynn. "Something's happening to Nadya," I said.

"What?"

"Someone kicked her door in and shut down the elevator." I scanned the crowded hotel floor. The stairs were out; our rooms were on the twenty-third-floor penthouse, and there was no way I'd reach Nadya in time . . .

I saw the ropes before I saw the bench. Window washers. I ran out the front door. Lucky for me they'd taken off for the day. I stepped on and grabbed the control switch. I'd seen these worked before. How hard could it be?

One of the hotel bellboys was running flat out towards me, his hand raised. "Miss! Miss! You can't use that!"

"Lady Siyu can bill me," I said, and hit the Up switch. The bench jolted up faster than I'd anticipated. I involuntarily sat down as it sky-rocketed up the side of the building. I grabbed the switch hanging above me. Yellow meant slow down, right? I pressed the yellow button. To my relief, it slowed to a pace where I could stand up—and look down at the pavement and people so very far below me . . . I forced my eyes back on the building. Probably a good thing my fear of heights doesn't kick in until I look down . . .

Finding the twenty-third floor was easy; the building only had twenty-six, and I knew firsthand that Mr. Kurosawa's private ghost casino took up three floors. I stopped the bench when it reached the penthouse floor. There were only four suites, so, lucky me, I ended up outside mine.

I tapped on the window twice. Captain bolted from the other room and jumped up onto the glass. I pointed at the window lever. Captain swished his tail, grabbed the lever with his teeth, and pulled. Yes, we've done this before—Oh hell, I don't need to explain why I've trained my cat to let me into locked windows.

As soon as I was in, I dropped my laptop bag, grabbed the bleach gun, and ran for the door.

Barred shut.

I tried my shoulder against it. Nothing.

I looked around the room for something to break it down with.

I grabbed one of the ornate Louis XIII chairs and hefted it over my head. I was going to get a hell of a lot of pleasure out of breaking one of Lady Siyu's precious antiques. I slammed it into the door as hard as I could. It shattered into four pieces, the paint on the door barely scratched. Lousy wooden antiques. Why couldn't she have furnished the hotel with some nice, metal industrial furniture?

I hoped Rynn was having better luck than I was. I called Oricho.

He answered on the second ring. "You have the translation?"

"No, Nadya is being attacked and my door is barricaded. Get up here to help her and get me out," I yelled. I couldn't talk fast enough.

Oricho didn't reply immediately, but I could hear him typing. "The rooms are on an automatic lockdown. Someone has accessed the hotel's security system and shut all the doors on your floor. I regret that I cannot open it from here."

"Shit. Just find some way to help her," I said and hung up. Could things possibly get any worse?

As if the universe was listening in on my thoughts, just so it could screw me over, a text from Rynn came in:

Power to the elevator was cut as well— STAY—

Whoever orchestrated this had thought of that, too.

I grabbed another antique chair. Like the first, it shattered without making a dent. I glanced around the room for another piece to ram the door with. Something in here had to be able to break it . . .

My laptop.

I pulled my laptop out, raised a chat screen with Carpe, and put my headset on. "Think fast, can you hack into the hotel security system?"

"What? Why?" he said, sounding as if he'd just rolled out of bed.

"It's an emergency."

"Yeah, sure—" he said, his fingers rapidly clicking against his keyboard. "Whoa—whoever hacked this knew what they were doing. They put a firewall in, a decent one—"

I heard a scream. Nadya. "Carpe, get my door open!"

"It'll take me a minute," he said.

"I don't have a minute—"

The door's lock clicked open.

"Thanks, I owe you one," I said.

"That wasn't me—" Carpe started.

But I had my headset halfway off before he could finish. I grabbed the bleach-filled water gun and made a dash straight for Nadya's room.

My stomach sank as I turned the corner. The door hadn't been kicked down so much as split in two warped halves.

I didn't think. I just ran into the room. It was empty. Whoever had been here was gone . . .

And left Nadya lying on the floor, halfway out of the bathroom.

"Nadya?" I yelled. She didn't move; she was out cold. I stopped panicking when she breathed, until I noticed the two bloodstains on her white shirt over her left shoulder. I pulled the collar down to reveal two large puncture wounds, larger than a vampire bite. The skin around them had turned dark purple, and it was spreading.

Venom.

I heard footsteps coming down the hallway. "Alix?" Rynn yelled.

"In here," I said.

Like the professional he was, Rynn assessed the situation at the door before coming in. To his credit he didn't say a goddamn thing this time about me ignoring his "Stay."

He crouched down and pressed gently against Nadya's wound. Yellow liquid came out, which he then raised to smell. After a moment he looked up at me. "Naga," he said.

More footsteps fell on the carpet and Oricho stepped through the door. He almost looked like he'd broken a sweat, and I wondered if he'd run up the twenty-three flights of stairs. He glanced down at Nadya, a shadow crossing his face. "I regret to inform you that Lady Siyu is no longer in her chambers. I can no longer account for her whereabouts," he said, and dropped his chin in apology, something I'd never seen him do before.

I shook my head. "I was too late—and she knew what we'd do, she even trapped Rynn in the elevator," I said. "Can't you help her?" I asked Rynn. "You know, like the skin walker?"

He shook his head. "Sorry, injuries I can work with. Not poison."

"Two supernaturals in the goddamn room and sorry, thanks for playing, game over?"

Rynn lifted the hotel phone from the desk. "I'll get Dylan to come up. He's a nymph at the pool downstairs. One of his relatives owes me a favor."

"Nymphs heal people too?"

Rynn considered that. "No and yes. Nymphs feed on decaying flesh. Evolutionary offshoot of the ghoul family."

"I'm sorry, did you just say nymphs eat rotting flesh?"

He shrugged. "Or the chemicals coming off it. This kind of snake venom rots the flesh. It's why the skin around it is turning black. It's similar enough he should be able to pull it out of her system and get a meal in the bargain."

Eww, gruesome. And they were all so damn pretty; talk about evolving under the radar. Well, it explained why they always seemed to show up when there was a corpse to be taken care of . . .

After calling Dylan, Rynn surveyed the room again. "Oricho, something isn't right."

Oricho nodded. "This was not the attacker's intended target. This is a distraction."

"That was my thought," Rynn said.

My stomach churned. "The scroll. Lady Siyu needed a distraction so she could steal the scroll." I'd been right all along; in spite of Mr. Kurosawa's and Oricho's insistence she was loyal, she'd been working with Marie. At times like this, I hate being right. "Oricho, does she know where Mr. Kurosawa keeps it?"

He nodded. "Who would know more about a red dragon's treasure than his trusted naga?" He pulled out his phone and issued commands to his men. "Lady Siyu will try to reach the vault in Mr. Kurosawa's private casino," Oricho said to us.

"If we're quick, we can block the exits before she can escape," Rynn added. "But what if she plans on using the scroll?"

"I fear she intends to use it as soon as she has it, and with the number of people in the city . . ."

I couldn't believe it—this was the first goddamn break we'd had. "She can't read it," I said. Both Rynn and Oricho looked at me. "She needs a *human* to read it. Nadya and I figured that out last night—and they'd have to be able to figure out the pronunciation, properly, not some hashed-up version like modern Egyptian or Latin."

Oricho wasn't convinced. "But if she reaches you, Owl, surely—"

I shook my head. This was too good to be true. There was no way Lady Siyu knew she couldn't read the scroll. She'd probably grabbed Nadya's translation off her computer and figured that was all she needed. "Are you kidding? I can *read* it, sure, but I suck at speaking modern languages, let alone ancient ones. Nadya's the one with the knack for figuring out pronunciation, and Lady Siyu just poisoned her. Unless she has some human stowed away somewhere who's an expert on ancient dialects—" I shrugged. "Considering her disdain for humans and Sabine's general level of psychosis, I highly doubt that."

"I still do not wish her to obtain the scroll—or you, which she may still attempt. It is not safe for you—"

"Owl can come with me to block the main elevator exit to the lair," Rynn said.

Oricho frowned. "Is that wise? What if Lady Siyu wishes to take vengeance on her next, or believes she can translate the scroll?"

Rynn shrugged. "Better that she should be with me." Oricho was less than thrilled, but he conceded with a curt nod.

We ran right smack into Dylan exiting the elevator. I stared up into his perfect white teeth, chiseled jawline, and bare bronze chest . . . It was the same nymph who'd picked up the skin walker from my room. I took a step back, two steps back in fact. I could see the ghoul family similarities now: waxy skin, glassy eyes, lack of facial expression due to rudimentary nerve development . . .

Rynn took hold of my arm and steered me into my room. "I need to get my things. Bring your vampire kit as well."

"I've got an extra UV flashlight, chloroform, plus my gas mask and the bleach gun," I said.

He nodded. "Get those as well."

I ran into my bedroom and started assembling my bag. I tossed on my cargo jacket for good measure. Not armor, but better than my T-shirt if a vampire or Lady Siyu tried to bite me. Ready, I grabbed my loaded backpack. Rynn was standing by my door, arms crossed.

I dropped my bag as it dawned on me what was really going on. "Rynn?" The warning was implied.

"What?" he said, raising an eyebrow. He didn't move away from my bedroom door.

"Not fair, you manipulated me."

The corner of his mouth turned up. "Manipulation one, human reckless abandon zero," he said.

"Oh come on. So help me—"

The trace of a smile vanished. "I'm serious, something isn't right."

"Yeah. A rabid naga just attacked my best friend."

"That's what worries me. There is no way a naga or a vampire got up to this floor without Oricho or myself knowing. It's not possible."

"Well, we know it wasn't you. What about Oricho? I mean, his warriors are trapped in slot machines—"

Rynn shook his head. "It can't be Oricho. Believe me, there's no love lost between him and Mr. Kurosawa, but once a kami swears loyalty—" He shrugged. "It is not physically possible for Oricho to disobey or betray Mr. Kurosawa. That's why Mr. Kurosawa wanted him."

"But—"

"He's kami and sworn to serve as a servant. That's just the way it is. There is nothing Oricho can do. Believe me, we've tried."

I sighed. I did not want to be locked in my room, leaving my life in the hands of supernaturals. No matter how much I trusted Rynn, I wasn't OK with it. "What about a human thrall?" I tried.

Rynn placed both hands on my shoulders. "Give me an hour."

"How do you know they can't get in here too?"

"Easy. I'm booby-trapping the door."

"Then I can't get out."

"That was the idea." Rynn unceremoniously picked up a sleeping Captain off the floor. I don't think I've ever seen that cat look more shocked in my life.

"What the hell are you doing with my cat?"

"I trust him about as much as I trust you right now. Less so, because he might figure a way out."

"This isn't OK. You can't keep doing this to me—"

He turned on me, his eyes verging on blue. They shifted back to gray before I had to say anything. Reflex, I was betting. "Do what? Every other instance so far I've let you make your own choice, even when I knew you were in over your head. I can't let you stumble through and learn for yourself this time. It's too dangerous, and chances are you'll succeed in getting yourself killed."

"Why? Because I'm a lousy human?"

"No, because whoever got to Nadya fooled me, and I've had a hell of a lot more practice than you." His eyes stayed gray. At least he was keeping his word and not using the incubus eye thing—that counted for a lot. "I'm sorry, but even I'm not sure what the hell is going on, and I don't want you caught in the middle of a supernatural blood-bath."

I stepped back. This was bodyguard/mercenary Rynn talking. I was pissed, but he was doing his job.

As much as it pained me, I sat down in the chair. "Go," I said.

His face softened. "One hour, I promise. And keep your cell on you."

"I thought no one could get in?"

"I thought that about Nadya too."

Rynn closed the door behind him. I heard Captain howl as he was deposited in the bathroom.

I sat on the bed. It dawned on me that for once Rynn hadn't called me a train wreck and I hadn't called him a whore . . . somehow I didn't think that boded well.

I lay there for a few more minutes. I hated the idea that things might be decided while I was locked in this damn room, just like when I'd been a grad student . . .

I remembered Nadya had told me to check my pocket before I'd run full tilt out of the bar. Inside was a slip of napkin, and on it was the same skull symbol from the scroll. Which I now knew was a precursor to Cyrillic, and could be read.

Under the skull she'd written in her impeccable penmanship, "Not what it seems."

Not what it seems? I still had no idea what the skull meant in the first place, though my first guess was still something to do with death. Damn it, leave it to Nadya to leave me a cryptic message and expect me to figure it out. The last thing Nadya had said to me was to make sure I got the scroll back . . .

Something scuffed against metal above me. Adrenaline up, I jumped off the bed and scanned the ceiling. The air vent—something was coming through the air vent. I grabbed the bleach water gun and UV flashlight and ducked behind the antique sofa chair. I had a flash of anger at Rynn for leaving me here. It was small consolation that he'd been wrong about things getting in—especially since chances were real good I wouldn't be able to tell him, *I told you so.* Well, I'd be damned if I wouldn't put up a fight.

Something was kicking the grate loose. I readied the water gun and turned the flashlight on. I heard the meow before the grate fell and Captain stuck his head through. He gauged the distance to the bed before launching onto it. He had my black makeup brush roll I'd left in the bathroom in his mouth. My lock-pick kit. Anyone who says cats aren't trainable . . .

Captain close on my heels, I let myself out of the bedroom and headed for the main window, where I'd left the window washer bench. I wasn't planning on taking it all the way up to the roof; too good a chance someone would see me. But I bet the adjacent room wasn't locked.

I stepped through the window and closed the glass behind me. Captain howled and began scratching the glass. "Dude, no way. There'll be vampires," I said.

He meowed balefully through the window.

I went to the far edge of the bench and stepped over onto the wide ledge that ran along the wall. I found finger holes and started to inch my way across. I could still hear Captain howling.

When I reached the adjacent room's window, I made my first mistake: I looked down.

Shaking, I pried the window open with one of my blunter tools and slid through. As suspected, the door was unlocked. I checked the hallway before heading to the service elevators.

I was back in the game.

It dawned on me as the gold elevator doors slid shut that I was about to do what I'd sworn I wouldn't. Break into a red dragon's treasure room.

22

WE ALL HAVE OUR GHOSTS

6:00 p.m., happy hour at the Japanese Circus

The service elevator took its sweet time going up, chiming like the bells on Mr. Kurosawa's slot machines. I was glad I had the water gun under my jacket. I removed it and aimed it at the unopened doors, just in case, hoping that snakes liked bleach about as much as skin walkers did.

Something nagged me as I waited for the doors to open. Marie was this stupid, sure, but Lady Siyu? She was egotistical, aloof, bigoted against humans, and elitist, but not stupid. She had access to Mr. Kurosawa's treasure room; why hadn't she just grabbed the scroll and then killed me and Nadya? She could have been on the private jet by now, scroll in hand. Or maybe the lack of plan was her plan? *Come on, Owl, think. That's what you're supposed to be good at.*

The elevator doors slid open to a mirrored hall covered in the black lotus design. "You!"

I raised my hands. Slowly.

A very transformed and very angry Lady Siyu stood at the end of the hall. Unlike the naga I'd met in Bali, Lady Siyu's skin and tail were mottled green and gold, instead of white, and she was half the size. Her black hair framed her face in a plaited crown that reminded me of a pharaoh's headdress. Confirming my suspicion, Lady Siyu raised her tail. The bone rattle echoed off the mirrors.

A chill ran down my spine. Only one type of Naga had a rattle. Viper Queens. Worse temperament, more venom.

And in her hand was the scroll.

"You?" Lady Siyu snarled again, as if I were the devil itself. Then she lunged at me with a lightning-quick strike.

I dove back inside the elevator and slammed the Close Door button, then pressed the emergency button for good measure. Where the hell were Oricho and his kami? My stomach sank; if Lady Siyu had had no problem taking out two of Oricho's kami, she must have reached him first.

I called Rynn. It went straight to voice mail. "Oh, you have got to be kidding me—" I swore and waited for the message chime. "Rynn?" I said, and covered the receiver as the elevator doors rattled.

I pressed the mezzanine button repeatedly. Nothing happened. Lady Siyu must have damaged the elevator when she'd hit it with her tail.

Heavy . . . solid metal doors. They locked down in emergencies, right?

In answer, the entire elevator swung on its suspension as Lady Siyu crashed against the doors again, this time leaving a serpent tail–shaped dent.

I pulled my hand off the receiver. "Rynn! Get up to Mr. Kurosawa's casino now. Lady Siyu has the scroll—"

That was as far as I got before two sets of red lacquered claws broke through the elevator seal and began to pry the doors apart. I swallowed hard as they slid open a few centimeters and I caught a glimpse of a fang set in red lips. I lifted my foot and rammed my boot heel into the claws. One broke, and I was rewarded with a screech as Lady Siyu withdrew them, clipping another one against the metal.

"Try a can opener, bitch snake," I yelled.

Me taunting the naga through the partially opened elevator door was premature.

I heard the warning rattle and jumped back as her tail crashed into the doors again, deepening the dent. Lady Siyu wedged her claws back through, but this time she worked them back and forth in a disjointed unity, like the spines of a sea urchin. The door slid open another few centimeters until she could reach a hand through, her scales glinting under the fluorescence. She pressed her face against the crack, and drops of black venom collected on her fangs as she snarled, "I will feast on your bones, little thief."

Double shit.

I texted as fast as my fingers would let me. *Rynn, get your ass up here now. Naga—angry naga—*

I hit Send as the doors opened. They screeched with every inch gained as only shearing metal can do.

Most of Lady Siyu's black hair had come loose by now, and thick strands hung in her face, making her parted red lips that much more sinister. She growled, and the rattle sounded to my right. I couldn't help but look. A clear misdirection, which I didn't realize until her tail whipped from the left.

At my head.

I ducked and dove out of the way, but the elevator was too confining. The bone rattle smashed into my hand, sending my cell phone into the elevator's glass wall. It dropped to the floor in three pieces. So much for calling for help. Lady Siyu smiled, raised her tail, and hissed as she readied another blow. Seeing no reason to stay in this elevator death trap, I waited until her tail was arched in the air and baseball-slid under it. As soon as I was past, I tucked my feet under and came up in a run. I heard her snarl as I bolted down the hall. There was a crash that sounded like collapsing drywall; I presumed it was her coming after me, since there was no way in hell I was looking over my shoulder.

On a good day, snakes—let alone a three-hundred-pound

naga—were faster than me. I needed interference, and fast, so I darted into the first set of open doors I came across . . . and skidded to a halt in front of Mr. Kurosawa's maze of slot machines.

Goddamn it, I can pick them.

I bolted to my left down the first row of slots. With my first step, on cue, the chimes and bells started to ring.

I heard Lady Siyu scream amid the whine of crunching metal and sick, mistuned chimes. I ducked in beside a green slot machine flashing four-leaf clovers and peeked around the edge in time to see a slot machine two rows away catapult into the air and take out two more on the way down. Snakes in general are sensitive to vibration and sound. With all the slot machines going off, she wouldn't be able to hone in on me.

Well, score one for the ghosts—though I doubt Mr. Kurosawa had had quite this in mind when he'd trapped them here. I stayed where I was.

"Get back here, *thief*," Lady Siyu screamed.

"What did you do to Oricho?" I yelled back.

She growled and swayed her head from side to side, trying to pinpoint my voice through the slot vibrations. Her eyes glinted more gold than green under the lights. "You humans are all alike, thieves with no honor," she screamed, and took out three more slot machines not that far away from my hiding spot.

Damn it, I should probably run—now . . .

I was timing Lady Siyu's outbursts to make another run for it when I caught movement in the hallway behind the open doors.

Rynn.

He slipped in just as Lady Siyu's back was turned, then ducked into the shadows.

I switched gears; I needed to keep her occupied, and pissing her off seemed like the best way to do it.

"You've got a really strange definition of stealing," I yelled back. "If I was holding Mr. Kurosawa's scroll in one hand, that would be one thing—Oh no, wait, that's you."

Lady Siyu spat and lunged not far from where I was hiding, taking out another machine. I couldn't help wondering what happened to the ghost when its house was smashed to smithereens—did it piggyback with a buddy? Disappear into some netherworld? A sickening thought struck me as an old Japanese pot toppled on its side and rolled across the floor. Just how long had Mr. Kurosawa been collecting ghosts?

Bad timing for contemplation, I know, especially since Lady Siyu had stopped her tantrum.

The picture of calm and serene, she swayed back and forth on her tail, lifting herself to full height. She tilted her face up, and her red forked tongue flicked up into the air.

I held my breath. Damn it, I wished I could remember whether nagas smelled with their tongues, like snakes. From the way she turned and smirked right at me, I guessed she could smell where I was just fine.

In two sinuous slides she was in front of my lucky charm slot machine. She gripped the sides and wrapped her tail completely around it. "I will not entertain your lies. I claimed the scroll first to protect it from *you*," she said.

"As if," I said. I threw my jacket in her face and dodged to the side, but she was faster and tripped me with a tail sweep, knocking me flat on my ass. She came in for the kill at lightning speed, pinning me down. Her jaws extended and opened to strike. Black venom ran down her fangs and collected at the tips.

What the hell was Rynn doing? Checking email? I needed to buy myself time. I wriggled underneath Lady Siyu, making it next to impossible for her to strike.

"Why—the hell would I go to the trouble of finding and handing the scroll over if all I wanted to do was steal it back?" I said.

With a hiss, she pinned my arms down. "Humans are all the same. Liars, cheats, greedy, destructive—not fit to walk the earth." Her tongue flicked out, smelling and tasting my cheek.

Now that she had me pinned, I was having trouble breathing

under the weight of her tail. "Destructive? I'm not the one trashing the whole goddamn casino," I said.

"You plan on using the scroll," she said, accusation dripping from each syllable.

I choked down a scream.

Anytime now, Rynn, anytime.

"Why the hell would—I want to kill—argh—everyone?" I strained to say.

"I'll send slivers of your corpse back to the treacherous incubus," she said. She bent her head back and opened her jaws wide, wider than should have been possible. Her fangs arched out, gleaming with black venom.

The quip about Rynn pissed me off. I set my jaw and tried one last time, using every last bit of adrenaline to wriggle out from under her. It was as if she had a sixth sense for injury—she shifted her weight and drove her hand into my dislocated rib. I screamed, and a wave of nausea hit me as I experienced a new kind of pain. A single drop of venom fell on my face, numbing and burning my cheek at the same time.

Someone whistled from behind Lady Siyu.

The pressure eased off my chest. Lady Siyu swiveled her torso around to see who was behind her.

"I hate being talked about behind my back," Rynn said, holding a harpoon with a jagged spear tip.

Lady Siyu bolted for Rynn. Shit, he'd never get out of the way in time.

He waited until she'd almost reached him. "Owl, catch," he said and launched the harpoon—at me.

What did he expect? That I was going to catch it midair? Shit, that's exactly what he had in mind . . . I scrambled back, as fast as my rib let me. The jagged spear tip lodged itself inches from my feet. I swore and dove for it. I'd have to have a long talk with Rynn about how he passed humans weapons.

Seeing this, Lady Siyu one-eighty'd and hurtled back towards me, fangs bared, like she was at the center of some sick and twisted version of monkey in the middle.

Well, I wasn't about to throw it back. I tucked it under my arm and hoped Lady Siyu was too enraged to notice.

I don't know if it was because Lady Siyu was furious or didn't think much of humans in the first place, but she didn't slow down.

Fine by me. I fixed my grip on the harpoon shaft.

"You know what, Lady Siyu?" I said. She snarled. Ten feet away, five feet away . . . now.

I raised the harpoon as she glided the last few feet towards me and extended her torso, teeth bared. "Life's a real bitch, and so am I," I said.

Shock, or the closest thing I'd ever seen to it on her face, registered as she impaled herself on the harpoon. I skidded back against the floor with the impact but held on. Lady Siyu grasped the tip with both red-clawed hands and shrieked.

Rynn headed over.

"Next time you pass me a weapon, don't send the pointy end first," I said.

"It worked, didn't it? Nagas tend not to think the more enraged they get. Do you mind," he asked me, nodding at the spear I was barely managing to hold onto. Saying Lady Siyu was strong was an understatement, and she was already trying to work the spear tip out.

"Be my guest," I said, and let him take it. I figured let the supernatural deal with each other one-on-one.

"Now, you were saying something about dismembering Owl and sending the pieces through the mail? Please," Rynn said, twisting the harpoon until Lady Siyu growled in pain, "continue."

She hissed and wrapped her tail around the length of the spear, reminding me of a worm on a fishing hook. "Lowliest trash of the ethereal world—"

I shook my head and took a big step back. Supernaturals.

"The scroll, Alix," he said.

Oh, yeah, right. She'd dropped it on the floor a few inches out of reach. I edged forward. My fingers brushed the edge of the scroll as Lady Siyu's rattle tip struck. I scrambled back and almost fell flat on my face.

"You get it!" I said.

"I'm a little busy," he said.

"I was lucky that wasn't my head," I yelled back.

Rynn grimaced and shifted his weight as Lady Siyu twined and retwined her tail. She wasn't hurt, only immobilized—and really, really pissed off. It was only a matter of time until she torqued the harpoon out of Rynn's grip. I really didn't want either of us to be around for that part . . .

"Damn it, where the hell is Oricho when you need him?" I said.

"I believe here would be the correct answer," Oricho said.

I turned around. I hadn't believed my ears, and I didn't quite believe my own eyes, but there he was, stepping over the top half of a ruined slot machine.

"Has anyone ever told you you have lousy timing?" I said.

He arched his tattooed eyebrow. "I wouldn't say that."

"Are you kidding? You missed just about everything we could have used you for."

Lady Siyu spat as he walked up to where the scroll still lay. She hissed and thrashed at him with the tip of her tail, but he evaded it as if it had been no more than a gust of wind. He retrieved the scroll, then did something that caught me off guard—he bowed to her. Not that I claim to even begin to understand supernatural culture, but even Rynn looked taken aback, and he understood the etiquette and nuances.

Lady Siyu said something I had no hope of understanding.

Whatever it was though got Rynn's attention. "Oricho, what's she talking about?" he said, more tense than he had been a moment before.

Oricho stood no less than a foot away from me, his face the emotionless mask I'd grown used to. Real fast I was aware that Lady Siyu and the spear were standing between me and Rynn. "Oricho . . .

answer Rynn's question, preferably in English so I know what the hell is going on too."

"Snakes always did have a hard time controlling their tempers," he said.

Lady Siyu called him something in the strange language again.

Oricho replied, "And yet, as you flail on the end of a stick, incapable of upholding your honor, you still can't bring yourself to speak in a common tongue. It is a failing, Lady Siyu. A mortal one."

Rynn pulled the spear out and circled with it to keep Lady Siyu at bay as he took a step closer to me. He was frowning at Oricho, and I realized it wasn't Lady Siyu he was pointing the harpoon at. Oricho strode over and grabbed Lady Siyu by the neck. He twisted it, and her tail went limp as she crumpled into a heap on the floor.

"Owl, move," Rynn said as I stared at Lady Siyu's dead body.

"What the hell just happened?" I said. "Oricho?"

He stepped towards me. Shit. I looked into the same ice-cold eyes I remembered from the first day I met him. They scared the shit out of me then, and they still did.

I made for Rynn, but Oricho was faster. He grabbed me around the waist and lifted me off the ground. "I don't care what private war you had with Lady Siyu," I said, "let me go and leave me out of it."

"If only it were that simple." He shook his head, and for a moment I thought I saw a flicker of regret—maybe even sadness. But it was gone before I really knew what I'd seen. "You've acted honorably. I am sorry you are here. Unlike many of my kind, I prefer not to involve humans in our spats."

"Alix, duck," Rynn said. I didn't exactly have a hell of a lot of mobility, and the only version of "duck" I could come up with was burying my face in Oricho's shirt. Idiotic moment of relief; it smelled like cherry blossoms, not some version of supernatural BO.

I felt something stir my hair as it passed by. Whatever it was, Oricho breathed out fast and loosened his grip as he was thrown back. I slid out and ran, reaching Rynn before turning around to see what had happened. The harpoon was sticking out of Oricho's shoulder. Something wet was trickling down my neck, and I reached to wipe it away. My hand came back with blood—my blood. I swore and slapped Rynn. "Will you stop throwing harpoons at me?"

"I missed."

I held up my bloody hand. "This is not 'missed.'"

He frowned. "Fine. I didn't hit anything vital—"

"It's my head."

"Oh for the love of— Will you stop arguing and run?" he said, and pulled me after him.

"Oricho has the scroll—" I started.

"I don't know about you, but I stopped caring about five minutes ago."

He had a very good point. Let the supernaturals kill each other while I sent a nice little email to Mr. Kurosawa from a safe distance on a Mediterranean beach—or better yet, on the other side of the planet, like Australia's Gold Coast.

"If we move fast, we should be able to get Nadya and Captain and get the hell out of here before—" Rynn added when we were mere footsteps away from the casino exit.

Oricho spoke in an old-sounding Japanese dialect, and a gust of air came up around us. The doors to the casino slammed shut, and both of us crashed into them.

The ghosts.

Rynn swore, or I think he swore, since I couldn't understand what he said as he pulled me back down the first row of slot machines . . . or what was left after Lady Siyu's tirade.

"There is no escape that way, old friend," Oricho said as the chimes started and all the machines spewed coins over the floor. They piled up fast, blocking our way.

Rynn stopped and spun, removing a hunting knife from inside his jacket. Oricho smiled as he strode towards us and reached behind his head. His hand came back holding the hilt of a very sharp and polished samurai sword.

That scared me. Rynn might survive a fight with Oricho, but considering the short work Oricho had made of Lady Siyu, my chances were slim, at best. That meant my best hope was to talk my way out . . . shit. Here went everything.

"I thought you kami cared about honor? What the fuck is this supposed to be?"

"Dishonor to an honorable end," Oricho said.

"Let's see, you're working for Sabine to help her steal a weapon she really shouldn't be in possession of, and then you snapped Lady Siyu's neck after Rynn harpooned her—I'm not up on supernatural death rules, but I *doubt* that was an honorable fight, and for what? To steal the magic version of a localized nuke from your boss? I get you hate him, but I don't get this."

Oricho was taking his time but still getting closer.

Rynn stepped in front of me. "Oricho, don't do this—it's not worth stealing from Mr. Kurosawa, whatever Sabine is offering you. You can't do this, you're kami—"

Oricho stopped a few feet away, a sad, uncharacteristic smile on his face. "Who said anything about working for Sabine? She is under my employ. Honorable unto death," he said, and undid the collar of his crisp white shirt to reveal a thick, angry red welt, never properly healed and still oozing.

Rynn's eyes went wide in shock. Oricho nodded at him and raised his sword back up.

"You are right, old friend. A kami would serve as duty dictates. When I found out the true purpose of the scroll a few months back, I paid Sabine to take my life."

Oricho had died. Some supers can do that—but when a kami dies, it becomes something else.

"You're onryo," I said. A spirit of vengeance.

He gave me an eerie smile, showing a completely different side, one I hadn't even suspected lay beneath the surface.

"Honor for my samurai in vengeance," he said.

The pieces began to fall into place. Lady Siyu hadn't been the target, and neither were Rynn and I really. Hell, he wanted to take out his boss. A personal nuke with enough explosive power to take out a kilometer of Las Vegas just might do it. And take everyone else with it . . .

Lady Siyu had just been guarding it until I'd run in looking for Oricho, and Rynn had come looking for me . . . "Lady Siyu didn't poison Nadya—you did," I said.

Oricho removed a pair of incisors from his pocket. "My associate was able to retrieve these from the Balinese temple after you incidentally killed the naga guarding the catacombs. I suspected they might come in handy—naga venom is so difficult to come by. I am sorry your friend had to be poisoned. I had no other way to steer you towards this path."

I nodded. If I'd been less pissed at Lady Siyu and not so convinced she was guilty, I would have stopped and wondered what the hell she'd been doing waiting for me outside the elevator. "And you told her a thief was on its way down to steal the scroll, didn't you?"

He inclined his head.

Which was why Lady Siyu had been more than happy to try and kill me. My strengths and weaknesses had all been used to get me here to distract Lady Siyu so Oricho could steal the scroll. And I'd been stupid enough to not only wander in headfirst but also drag Nadya and Rynn along for the ride.

Still stupid, reckless Owl.

"You have everything that you want—*everything*. Let us go," I said.

"If it is any consolation, I assure you Nadya was not given a lethal dose. Unlike most of my kind, I abhor killing innocents."

"Some fucking consolation," I said.

He nodded. "I do not begrudge you your anger. I wish there were another way," he said, and his eyes turned a ghostly white. Almost as one, the ghosts from the slot machines rose up in a hazy fog and gathered around him. Onryo could absorb energy from the dead. He didn't though; he just sent them at us.

"I wished you'd not insisted on taking this job, Rynn," Oricho said before the ghosts descended.

They brushed me to the side as if I'd been nothing, feather fingers holding me in place. They collected around Rynn's head in a dense fog, and his face turned gray as he gasped for breath. "Rynn!" I yelled, but the ghosts held me back. When he fell to his knees, they let me go.

I knelt down beside him; he didn't look good. "If incubi can do that whole energy stealing thing, now would be a good time," I said.

Rynn shook his head and mouthed, "*Sorry.*" His eyes turned bright blue, and then he passed out.

"Incubi are hard to kill, but they do require air to function," Oricho said.

I stood up, balled my fists, and faced him. "What the *hell* did you do that for?"

"So I need not hurt him any more than I have to." He nodded at the back of the casino and raised his voice. "Bring her out. Owl will not fight now. She gambles with her own life, but refreshingly not with the lives of others."

Great. Someone finally believes I'm not the bad guy, and it's going to get me killed.

I did what I do best. Ran. Oricho's expensive Italian shoes clipped against the tiled floor behind me. I darted behind the pool table and into the dark lounge with the white couches where I first met Mr. Kurosawa. The door to the roof had to be around here somewhere.

But where did that leave Rynn . . . and Nadya, and Captain? I stopped and looked for another door or route—one that might lead me to Mr. Kurosawa. Oricho was gaining, so I jumped behind the bar and grabbed the Bacardi 151. Maybe flammables would put a dent in an onryo.

"We're on the same side, you and I," Oricho said.

"Bullshit," I yelled. I felt for the lighter in my left pocket. It wasn't there. Goddamn it. I checked my other pockets . . . it had to be here somewhere . . .

"Believe it or not, it makes no difference," he continued. From the clip of his shoes, I could tell that he'd reached the edge of the lounge. I started opening drawers, looking for a lighter.

"Does that include a skin walker almost ripping my brain apart?" I yelled.

"Believe me when I say I regret its use, but I had to know whether you were withholding the scroll's translation. Sometimes the ends justify the means. I learned that lesson one thousand years ago."

I hid under the bar as Oricho's footsteps grew closer.

"I can smell the fear rising off you, Owl. It is an interesting insight into the workings of a human mind. Still, your kind has not moved past your fear of the dark," he said.

Damn it. "Not the dark, just what I can't see. I'm guessing your kind has no trouble seeing in the dark." No point in hiding anymore; I stood up and continued rifling through the drawers.

Oricho inclined his chin in acquiescence. "Yet the two are often one and the same. Let us say a fear of the unknown then."

I'd opened the last drawer. No lighters or matches. I sat back; there wasn't much time left before Oricho reached me, and I was out of options. I was going to die. Either Oricho was going to make me try and read the scroll, which I couldn't, so I'd blow us up, or he'd slit my throat for not trying. Either way, things turned out the same—me dead.

I don't know if it was a reflection in the mirrored glass, or the angle at which I turned my head as I looked for a last-minute escape route, but behind the white couch in the corner was a stray shadow that shouldn't have been there. It was a second before I realized it was a smoke and mirrors trick. There was a hallway, and I was willing to bet my life it led right to Mr. Kurosawa's chamber. I vaulted over the bar and ran, hoping to hell he had some kind of fail-safe in there for intruding humans.

"There is no help for you that way," Oricho said, but he didn't step up his pace. I ignored him and turned into the passageway, skidding to a halt at the sharp corner.

Rotting lily of the valley hit me full force right as I made the ninety-degree turn, but it was too late to stop. I slammed right into Marie, dragging a bound and gagged Nadya. I swore. Nadya lifted her head and her eyes widened—she was on her feet but looking worse for wear, partly from the venom, partly from vampire pheromones.

Marie smiled, showing me her fangs.

"I told you there was no help for you that way," Oricho said.

Marie pushed Nadya ahead of her, her cloaked jacket swirling around her heels. "This something of yours?" she said to Oricho. "Because this looks like mine," she added, grabbing my arm.

Nope. Not a chance in hell the universe was done screwing with me yet.

"You do not see it now, but you will. I am helping you," he said, taking Nadya and leading the way back to the casino main floor.

Marie dragged me along. I winced as she dug her fingers into my arm. The vampire pheromones were starting to hit me too. From now on I was going to keep a gas mask around my neck. With my free hand I pulled my shirt over my face—not much, but better than nothing.

"You think killing all of us humans while blowing up your boss is protecting us? What kind of sick, twisted monster are you?"

In honorable samurai fashion, Oricho didn't respond. Didn't say one goddamn thing.

"Go to hell," I said.

"That's exactly where I've been these last thousand years."

"Yeah, and I just bet this is exactly the kind of revenge samurai would appreciate—lie and cheat until everyone who pissed you off is dead." I was bluffing. I had no idea what samurai would want; if they were anything like ancient ninja, I probably just succeeded in talking myself into an early grave.

Marie jabbed me in the back. "Quiet," she said.

We reached the destroyed slot machines. Rynn was still slumped in the corner, though he was looking less gray. Lady Siyu was still a mess on the floor.

"Bring Owl here," Oricho said.

But Marie stopped just short of the wreckage. "We agreed she was my payment for helping retrieve the scroll," she said, tightening her grip. Yeah, blood circulation was definitely cut off now.

Oricho frowned. "That is an artistic interpretation of our deal, vampire. You will exact your vengeance on her after my task is completed."

"Son of a bitch—"

Marie cut me off with a blow to the kidney, and I doubled over. "Why, so you can screw me over again? I was supposed to have her in Bali, until you sent a rescue party," Marie snarled.

"And I explained I could not hand her over without raising Mr. Kurosawa's suspicions," Oricho replied as if lecturing a petulant child.

"I helped you get the scroll. I'm taking Owl. Now."

Oricho frowned. "*In spite* of your efforts, I obtained the scroll. At best you provided a distraction."

Marie's face twisted, making her look even more like the supernatural monster she'd become. "I will not be cheated out of my vengeance. She made me this—"

"You made your own bargains," Oricho said, and glanced at me with a hard, calculating set to his eyes.

"Please don't do this," I said to Oricho. "I get the whole wanting to kill Mr. Kurosawa, I do, really, but you can't hand me over to Sabine. Just kill me now, it'll be kinder."

He shook his head. "She has a debt of vengeance against you. It is not something I can ignore—"

"Coward," I said.

"Perhaps." He inclined his head and the ghosts swarmed around us, pulling me out of Marie's grip and throwing both of us in opposite directions. I landed on a broken slot machine, a glass jar of coins rolling back and forth at my feet. Marie screamed as she landed a few feet away. She was on her feet and snarling at Oricho.

"Here is your opportunity for vengeance, Sabine. I suggest you do not waste it, for I doubt you will get another," he said.

She clenched her hands until they turned whiter than they already were. "I won't forget this—" she started.

"My debt to you is paid. I would move quickly, as I do not know how much longer her friend will stay unconscious." Then Oricho turned his back on her. He pulled Nadya up off the floor and handed her the scroll. Shit. Oricho knew Nadya was the one who could read it because I'd told him.

"Nadya, don't read it, whatever he says or does, don't," I yelled as Marie circled around me like a rabid cat.

"Alix—" Nadya started, but Oricho silenced her with a shake of his head while he gripped the side of her neck, applying pressure to her carotid artery.

My attention was divided between them and Marie, but I saw the color drain from Nadya's face as Oricho leaned in and whispered in her ear. She looked down at the scroll and nodded.

She began to read.

I glanced and saw that Rynn was on his knees now, shaking his head and trying to get up—

Well, at least Oricho hadn't been lying about that part. Marie only had a few minutes at most to kill me or turn me. I did a double take as my eyes passed over the slot machine wreckage. Where the hell was Lady Siyu's corpse? For a moment I thought the ghosts had taken her, but then I caught a glimpse of yellow and gold sliding behind the slot machines.

Damn, nagas weren't easy to kill either.

If anyone here knew how to wake a sleeping dragon, it was her.

Oricho must have noticed the missing body about roughly the same time I did, because he left Nadya and stalked away, samurai sword in hand.

"Rynn, I can't believe I'm saying this, but keep Oricho from Lady Siyu," I yelled as loud as I could, dodging to the side as Marie made her first lunge.

I was slow; vampire pheromones were slipping through my

shirtsleeve. I stumbled over my own feet, and her fingernails grazed my face.

She smiled.

Out of the corner of my eye I saw Rynn stand and take an unsteady step towards me. I swore. Not the time to play hero. "I can handle Marie, Lady Siyu can't handle Oricho, and we need Mr. Kurosawa— right now."

I dodged another slash. Marie was playing with me. I glared and picked up the jar of coins; she'd regret not taking Oricho's advice. I bashed them against her face and sent her reeling back with an inhuman yelp.

Rynn and I locked eyes for a moment, and I mouthed, "*Go.*" I must have looked damn convincing, because he nodded, but not before taking a knife from inside his jacket and launching it towards me.

I swore as it sailed right over my shoulder.

Marie screeched again, the knife buried to its hilt in her collarbone.

By the time I glanced back to frown at Rynn, he'd already headed after Oricho. Marie pulled the knife out, but she'd taken on the clammy, emaciated appearance I associate with young vampires. She wasn't smiling anymore.

I had to hand it to Rynn; he'd evened the playing field.

"So how's it feel to not even rate a backup plan?" I said.

"Oricho hired me to find the scroll," she said. The clamminess gave her face a feral edge.

It was my turn to smile and shake my head. "No, you were hired to distract me so I'd be thrown off guard and not ask the right questions. Oricho never for one second thought you'd actually find it. Why do you think he didn't fork me over in Bali? Face it, you were a half-rate thief when you were alive, and vampirism hasn't done you any favors."

I launched a handful of gold coins at her head, turned, and bolted. If I could keep her busy until Lady Siyu did her job—

Marie slammed into my back and knocked me to the ground. My makeshift filter slid off my face, and I didn't have the chance to pull it back on before Marie was all over me. "I've waited over a year to sink my teeth in your neck. You did this to me." She pinned my collarbone down and lunged for my neck.

I rammed my forearm in her face instead and winced as her teeth punctured my skin. An onslaught of pheromones coursed through me. Still, better my forearm than right into a major artery. I looked around; we'd landed beside a broken shelf. A Japanese vase depicting a scene from *The Tale of Genji* was lying on its side next to me; eleventh-century Heian period, one hundred grand easy, maybe close to a million, depending on who'd painted it . . .

I wrapped my hand around the handle. Here's hoping Mr. Kurosawa agreed it was a hundred grand well spent. "Just keep telling yourself that," I said, and slammed the pot into the side of her head.

She reeled from the blow and let go of my wrist, but she didn't return the punch.

Even with the loss of blood, she should have . . . Hell, I'd removed her Bindi and Red power food supply. She hadn't had a vampire to feed off in days, not without sounding alarm bells all over the vampire world. She was back to being a regular vampire—more crazy, but normal.

I pushed myself up and scrambled back, but the mainlined pheromones were really slowing me now. I only got a few feet before she pinned me under her again.

Shit, normal vampire or not, I couldn't keep this up much longer.

Something scratched against metal overhead, insistent and irritating as hell while I wrestled with Marie, trying to keep her teeth out of my neck. I glanced up, wondering . . . hoping . . . oh yeah. Latte-colored fur poked through the grates.

Captain.

I don't know how the hell he'd done it, but he was in the air vent above, working his hind legs and bulky midsection to kick the cover off. It was loose, but he'd need another second to squeeze himself through. Note to self: fewer cat treats from now on.

Marie lifted her head to see what the noise was, so I elbowed her in the face. I felt her nose crack as I connected with cartilage. She screamed. I was 0 for 2 in the running department, so I threw all my weight into a roll. She was off-balance enough that she rolled with me, and I hung on for dear life and came up on top. I delivered a few punches to her face, working on the broken nose until she recovered her wits enough to snatch my wrist. I wrenched it back, but I was no match for a vampire's viselike grip.

She smiled. "Being locked in a tomb is the least of your worries," she said.

I got angry. Yet again someone blaming me for all their problems.

I hit her in the throat with my free hand. "I used to feel guilty about leaving you in that tomb, but you're the one who's screwed up every last chance you've ever had, not me."

That didn't go over well. She rammed my forearm across my throat and pressed down, cutting off the air. "I didn't have choices," she said, pinning me back down. "I was surviving."

"Hell, I made a bad choice I'm not proud of, but you? You keep saying being a vampire is my fault when the unifying link between all your disasters isn't me, Marie, it's *you*. And now you're taking stupid kids and turning them so you can eat them? How's that for vicious cycle?"

She snarled, flashing her fangs. I spat. That earned me a slap, and the next thing I knew Marie pushed my face to the side and held it down. I felt her warm breath on my neck as bits of glass cut into my flesh.

Out of the corner of my eye, I saw the grate crash to the floor. Captain hopped down and slid behind a slot machine, just within my peripheral view, waiting.

"Last chance, Marie, and I mean it this time. Get up and walk away," I said.

Rotting lily of the valley stuck to my skin like rancid perfume. Any much longer and I'd be done for; time to play my last card.

"Say whatever you want, Owl, you won't be alive much longer," she said.

I couldn't help smiling. "There's one thing I do that you don't," I said.

"And what's that?" she said.

"Learn from my mistakes." I whistled. "I trained my cat." It was almost worth breathing in vampire pheromones to see the look on her face as Captain leapt at her, claws first. She screamed and fell back, writhing on the floor as he went to work.

I looked around the room for something to knock Marie out with and caught sight of Rynn's pack near the door. Inside I found a UV flashlight and a syringe. I ran back, dropping the flashlight twice, woozy from the pheromones.

I needn't have bothered.

For whatever reason, whether it was Marie's newborn vampire status or her steady cannibal diet, Captain's bites and scratches were doing one hell of a job. She was out cold, her eyes no longer dilated, her face and arms red and swollen. Captain walked over her, leaping and attacking imaginary twitches, hoping his prey would get back up. He mewed when he saw me, then bit deep into Marie's hand. Immediately the surrounding skin turned a purplish red. One hell of an allergic reaction.

I pulled Captain off just as her body started to shrivel. Vampires don't turn to ash; it's a myth. Their cells feed off each other when they stop getting food, and the net effect is similar to burning up. I looked away as her body withered. It was a nasty way to go—I wouldn't wish it on anyone, even someone like Marie.

And it didn't have to be this way.

As soon as she was gone and I was certain she wasn't going to get back up and try to kill me, I grabbed Captain and Rynn's pack. "Time to see what everyone else is up to," I told him and headed into the back of the casino, where the rest of the party had migrated.

I stopped short as I rounded the turn into Mr. Kurosawa's private lounge. I'd been expecting the gunfight at the O.K. Corral; what I'd stumbled into was more along the lines of a Mexican drug cartel blowout. It was that unrecognizable. The polished white leather couches and mirrored coffee table were overturned and in pieces. Oricho was holed up, with a bound and gagged Nadya stuffed under an overturned couch behind him. The elegant bar with more top-shelf booze than I could count was on fire. I glanced over in time to see Rynn grab another bottle and douse the bar. A wall of fire shot up, turning the ghosts back. He managed to get a shot off at Oricho with a crossbow through the flames. Oricho parried with the sword . . . and a bolt came sailing at me. I dodged behind the wall but heard the telltale thwack as it lodged into the expensive wood. I peeked; the bolt had landed a few inches from my head. OK, note to self: never, ever walk into a supernatural battle ever again. I grabbed Captain by his collar and pulled him back before he could join the fray.

There was no way I was getting between Rynn and Oricho's supernatural death match. For one thing, I still had the element of surprise. I picked up a stray coin, aimed it at Nadya under the couch, and threw. Her head whipped around as it struck her forehead, and she searched for the source until she spotted me. I held my finger to my mouth in the age-old signal for "shut the fuck up"—not that she could have said much, gagged as she was, but it never hurts to clarify.

Well, at least there was no sign of Lady Siyu; I just hoped she'd made it to Mr. Kurosawa and had been able to wake him.

Wake him, that is, before Rynn and Oricho burned the place down.

Another flame shot up from the bar, blocking another flank of ghosts from reaching Rynn. The delicate, hand-painted Japanese wallpaper went up in flames.

I watched and waited for a chance to get to Nadya . . . and saw it. Now used to the wall of flame, Oricho's ghosts tried flanking the bar to get to Rynn. He'd either figured it out beforehand or was damn fast on the fly, because the fire extinguisher came out. Did you know you could turn one into a flamethrower? Another gust of flame shot up, and this time even Oricho had to shield his eyes. I ran, Captain close on my heels, and vaulted over the makeshift barricade. I undid Nadya's gag, then untied her as fast as I could.

As soon as her hands were free, she grabbed my shoulders. "We made a mistake—the scroll, it's not what we thought. The symbol I left before Oricho attacked me?"

"Yeah, your skull? FYI—come up with something *useful* next time. Now let's get out of here," I said, and peeked over the couch. If I could get Rynn's attention . . . The door to the roof was right near here. A fast run, and we could be outside. I couldn't fly the helicopter, but Rynn might be able to. If we were lucky, we'd clear the perimeter before Oricho could chase us. He'd have the scroll, but it'd take him months to find someone as good as Nadya to read it.

Nadya grabbed my arm, breaking my train of thought. "Will you listen to me? I was wrong. I figured it out last night, and when I couldn't get in touch with you, I called Oricho." She shook her head. "I thought I was warning him, but he already knew—"

"Not that I don't care, but can't this wait until we hot-wire Mr. Kurosawa's helicopter? Otherwise, whatever you have to tell me about the scroll is not going to matter one goddam, minuscule bit," I said, and passed her a handful of the coins I'd found. I fished through Rynn's bag until I found a light grenade—or at least I hoped it was a light grenade. "I don't know about you, but I'm done with this party."

Nadya shook her head, tears forming in her eyes. "You're not listening, Oricho—"

"On the count of three, you aim for Rynn and get his attention. As soon as this goes off, bolt for the stairs. Rynn will get the idea. One, two"—damn, I really hoped this worked—"*three.*"

Nadya hit the top shelf with the coins, and Rynn glanced over at us. Fantastic, one down. I hefted the grenade and readied to throw . . . where was Oricho? He'd been right there—

An arm reached around my waist, and I felt the sharp tip of a sword at my throat as I was lifted over and away from the couch. "Our arrangement has not changed, Nadya," Oricho said. "Please. Continue reading the scroll, or I will slit Owl's throat myself."

My eyes widened. "Nadya, what have you done?" She wouldn't look at me.

Oricho pushed the tip into my throat. "I tire of your protests, and my patience is not infinite. She can and she will, or I will slice your throat open in front of her."

My heart sank. Oricho had leveraged my life against Nadya's conscience. There was no way she could say no. Didn't mean I wasn't going to try. "Nadya, don't do it—it's not worth it—"

She shook her head at me and cast her eyes down at the scroll, defeated. "I'm sorry," she said, and began to read.

The pronunciation was beyond me, but I followed the word repetition as she read out each symbol and conjugated it to the next. She read the first line, then the second—I counted each symbol off in my head. She reached the fifth line, midway through. Captain stayed at my feet, growling uncertainly at Oricho. The worst part about this whole mess was that I had no way to tell Captain what was about to happen. *Hey cat, you followed the wrong damn human out of those Egyptian ruins you were squatting in.* Despite the sword, I grabbed my cat. I closed my eyes tight and waited for the end.

The ghosts screamed first. I looked over at Rynn. His face was white, a look of pure shock as he braced himself against the bar. A streak of red ran down from his nose. Blood. He grabbed his midsection and screamed. Somewhere out of sight I heard a woman's voice, what had to be Lady Siyu's, lend a sharp, piercing shriek to the mix.

It was nothing though compared to the bellow that made me cover my ears and sounded like some long-extinct prehistoric monster being dropped in molten lava.

Mr. Kurosawa.

I waited another heartbeat for the pain to rip through me, imagining being ripped apart at the molecular level.

Nothing happened. I opened my eyes. Nadya was fine, and Captain, struggling and moderately pissed I was holding him, was also fine.

Something wet ran down the back of my neck, and Oricho grunted. The sword stayed steady at my artery, but he loosened his grip on my throat. I hazarded a glance. Blood trickled out of the corners of his eyes and nose.

Son of a goddamn bitch . . . the scroll was never intended to kill humans. It was made by humans to kill everything else . . .

And Oricho had known that all along. Mr. Kurosawa had probably known too, which was why he'd wanted to get his own hands on it instead of letting some scared human get it.

Oricho gritted his teeth, but the corner of his mouth turned up in a smile. "The scroll will kill every supernatural in Vegas. Once word gets out, the others, such as Alexander and the Paris Contingency, will be wary of venturing here for a long while. Especially knowing the human holding the scroll hates supernaturals as much as you do," he added.

The pieces started to fall into place The great equalizer, a scroll made by humans that could only be read by humans. A scroll that could wipe out supernaturals. All of them, including a dragon.

No more vampires, no more Mr. Kurosawa, and no more Lady Siyu. All major plusses in my world. Hell, without being charged with keeping the supernatural world under wraps, the IAA would lose their stranglehold on the universities . . . I could go back. I wouldn't even have to use the scroll again; I'd only have to let people know I had it and threaten to use it if they got within a square mile of me.

When Nadya got to the last line, all my problems would be gone . . .

But there's a part of my brain that isn't hardwired for instant gratification. Rynn would be dead, along with the nymphs who kept clearing away my trail of corpses, and probably a lot of others in the hotel who'd never done a damn thing to me. All gone. Even Oricho—though he'd gone a little crazy on me—was trying to avenge a handful of humans. He was well and clear out of my good books for this mess, but he didn't deserve to die either—or at least die again.

And if I was being really honest with myself, none of my problems would be gone. They'd turn into new ones.

Just like Marie's problems had every single time she'd tried the easy way out.

"Nadya, stop!" I screamed. I felt the tip of the samurai sword drive into my throat and a trickle of blood run down my neck.

"Stop reading, and Owl dies. It is your choice," Oricho said through clenched teeth. Rynn had stopped screaming—I didn't think that was a good sign.

Nadya glanced up from the scroll. Like most active magic, it created a dim veil around her, like heated air over your barbecue. She glanced at Rynn and then back at me. Her lip quivered and she said sorry with her eyes, her lips never skipping a beat of the scroll's incantation. I couldn't fault her; Oricho had put her between a rock and a hard place. Read the scroll and kill one friend, or don't read the scroll and kill your best friend.

As if he could read my thoughts, Oricho said, "It is the only thing either of our kind understands. You will see in the end I am right."

"If there's one thing you ought to know about me by now, it's that I'll be damned if I'm going to do what some supernatural tells me. And this isn't the way to get back at Mr. Kurosawa," I said, and kicked up hard with my boot.

Oricho wasn't ready for it. No male of any species ever is, which is why it's so damn useful. To his credit, he barely flinched. In his weakened state, though, it was enough. The sword tip slipped to my collarbone and I dropped down. As soon as I was free, Nadya ran for me. I grabbed the scroll from her and shoved it in my jacket pocket. Both of us jumped behind the bar.

"Light it back up," I said. "Fire is about the only thing that stops him."

Nadya doused the bar in liquor while I ran to Rynn, who was doubled over on the floor.

I turned him over. That he was a hell of a lot worse off than Oricho was an understatement. The whites of his eyes had hemorrhaged red, and welts had formed on his face where skin looked as if it had boiled.

"Shit."

"It looks worse than it is," he said, but he winced as he sat up.

"Owl, lighter!" Nadya yelled. "He's getting back up."

"Please say you have a lighter on you," I said to Rynn.

"Left jacket pocket."

I tossed the lighter to Nadya. She set the bar ablaze, and Oricho bellowed.

"Can you run?" I asked Rynn.

"Please say we're not running."

"Well, that depends. Somehow I don't think Mr. Kurosawa will go back to sleep. You really want to be here for the finale?"

He grunted and used the wall for support to push himself to standing. "Running's good," he said, and indicated I should fork his pack over. I was more than happy to. Explosives make me nervous.

Passing out halfway up the stairs didn't seem too far-fetched, considering the shape he was in. "Umm, just so you know, this plan hinges on you being able to hot-wire and fly a helicopter . . ."

He snorted but leaned on my shoulder, using me for balance.

"What's the plan?" Nadya said.

"On my signal, light up the bar," Rynn said, "as high as it will go—he won't risk the flames—then run for the stairs." Rynn was about to add something else but ducked instead, pulling me down with him. Three crossbow bolts, the tips covered in a black tar, lodged into the wall where his head had been. A dark look crossed his face. He yelled something at Oricho in what I now thought of as "common supernatural." Oricho yelled right back.

"What the hell was that about?" I said.

"I told him to grow a pair instead of shooting me with my *own weapons*," he said, yelling the last two words.

Fantastic, Oricho had Rynn's crossbow. Rynn fixed one of the liquor bottles with a rag, lit it, and launched it towards his old friend. I was starting to see how they'd trashed the place in no time fast.

"OK, short run to the stairwell using an uncontrolled bar fire as cover with a mad supernatural trying to pick us off with a crossbow. What could possibly go wrong?" I asked.

"Not helping, Alix," Rynn said.

"Owl!" Oricho shouted over the roaring fire. "You are trying my patience and making this more dangerous than need be. Hand over the scroll so I can end this quickly."

"Go back to hell," I said.

Nadya had doused the bar with one bottle and moved on to the next. We needed the flames high. Rynn fished through his bag and tossed her a yellow bottle. "Use this—it's an accelerant." Nadya dropped the booze and emptied the bottle. She got the lighter ready and waited for my signal.

"Oricho, let us leave. Now, with the scroll."

"And what should I tell Mr. Kurosawa? That you stole the scroll, you and Nadya?" he said.

"You can tell him I disappeared down a rabbit hole for all I care," I shouted back.

Oricho laughed, and I caught sight of his silhouette through the flames tempered by the emergency sprinklers. Good thing we were leaving, because I didn't know how much longer the room would last. I heard sirens outside and fire alarms throughout the casino now—I had no doubt the fire was spreading.

"Rynn," Oricho shouted. "Do you think the dragon will care she stopped me? Or just put her ghost to work like all the others? Will you be able to live with yourself?"

"Let us pass and we won't have to find out. One dragon isn't worth an entire city, you've said it yourself."

"Even we change," Oricho said. "Nadya, read the scroll, and after all the supernaturals in Vegas are dead, you and Owl can walk out, unharmed."

"I'm not killing one of my friends for your psychotic plan," she said.

"The ghosts went with the first few lines of the scroll," I told Oricho. "They're free. Isn't that what started this whole mess? You wanted them freed? Well, they're about as free as they get. Now let us go."

For a second I thought, hoped, he might go for it. "What's it going to be?" I yelled, then held my breath and waited.

Another crossbow bolt lodged into the bar.

Sometimes people just don't want to be helped. I nodded at Nadya, and she dropped the lighter. The flames shot up to the ceiling, which we expected, the heat singeing the hairs in my nose and scorching my throat, but I didn't expect the flames to shoot outwards as much as they did.

Neither did Oricho, judging from his scream.

Rynn shoved me in the back before I could look, but I glanced through the curtain of flames engulfing the room as we ran. Oricho clasped the tattooed side of his face. As we ran past, he removed his hand. The tattoos were a scorched, burned mess.

"Door, now," I said.

I ran, Rynn still leaning on me, and Nadya close enough behind that I could hear her breathing, Captain on our heels. The smoke thickened as we climbed the stairs. I coughed, and my muscles started to complain under Rynn's weight. He stumbled, and both of us stumbled onto the stairs, but I wasn't about to stop or look behind me.

The red lacquered door to the roof came into view. A few more feet and we were home free. I grabbed the door handle and pulled.

It stuck. The adrenaline coursing through my veins did a one-eighty to panic. "Rynn, get the door open," I said.

He gripped the handle, but it wouldn't turn. "I can't, magic seal—"

"The ghosts are gone, how the hell can it be sealed?" Nadya said, adding to my own panic. Stuck at the top of a burning building. Smoke rises.

To top it all off, a deep rumble sounded from below, shaking what remained of the supports in the private casino. A beam or wall crashed below.

Mr. Kurosawa.

I didn't care if it was magic; I shoved past Rynn and really started working on the door. I had my lock pick kit out in two seconds flat.

"Turn around," Rynn said.

"Not until I get this damned door open."

"Now—"

"Will you just wait—" I thought the door was giving a little. The barrel was stuck and the smoke was killing me, but I swore I heard the click.

Rynn placed his hand on the top of my head and forced me to look back down the stairwell. "Because there's a three-story red dragon behind us."

At the bottom, peering up at us with narrowed red eyes, was a fifteen-foot-tall red dragon, reminiscent of the ones you'd see on old Japanese and Chinese paintings. I dropped my lock pick.

Mr. Kurosawa smiled. There were a lot of teeth—lots and lots of teeth.

Blackened lips curled up as out of his nose he blew white smoke that filled the stairwell with sulfur. He made a noise somewhere between a growl and a laugh.

He looked right at me with a large red eye, glowing in the firelight. "I smell thieves," he said.

I hoped to hell one of the coins hadn't lodged itself in my boot.

23

I HATE DRAGONS

Saying we didn't have a choice about returning downstairs was an understatement. Back on the casino floor, I helped Rynn along slowly, Captain hanging back a few feet with Nadya. The sprinklers were still going, bathing everything in a damp haze, but the fires were out.

Mr. Kurosawa watched us from the charred remains of the casino floor as we descended. He was an extremely large dragon, the head and neck offset not by a mane of hair but by things more like ribboned tendrils like you'd see on a deep-sea fish. They were a mix of red and gold, and offset the red and gold scales. Up close, I could see now that there were in fact pupils housed in the red eyes, gold in color and highly reflective. I also noted the ruined wall on the far side of the casino. Mr. Kurosawa was pissed enough at this point to forgo niceties like human-sized doors.

"Japanese red," Nadya said under her breath, just loud enough that Rynn and I would hear.

"I know that," I said. Japanese reds are known for treasure hoarding, but they're also known for bad tempers and short attention spans when it comes to humans. Those two personality traits did not work well in our favor.

Mr. Kurosawa lowered his head so he was eye to eye with us, so to speak, and I cringed, imagining what being shredded alive by razor-sharp teeth felt like. A quick glance around the room showed no sign of Oricho. At all.

Instead of opening his jaws to eat us in one bite, he started to shrink. The ribboned mane grew and turned from gold and red to black. It swathed the red scale hide in mad swirls, consuming the dragon completely. Out of the storm of black and red walked the Japanese businessman I'd grown to fear about thirty times over, complete with expensive black suit and Italian shoes.

"And to think I almost slept through the entire show," he said.

He stopped just short of me and held out his hand, an unpleasant smile on his face. Every time I had the pleasure of meeting him, I liked the look on his face less and less.

"My scroll, if you please," he said.

I'd forgotten about that little detail. I fumbled it out of the inside of my jacket, almost dropping it as I handed it over.

He turned it over and raised an eyebrow at me. The scroll was wet and covered in my sooty fingerprints.

I cleared my throat. "Those will wipe clean off, and it dries better than you'd think. We put it over a heater last time—oomph." I glared at Rynn and then Nadya. Both of them had jabbed me in the side at the same time. Well, so much for making small talk with the dragon.

Mr. Kurosawa watched me, his eyes glittering under the sprinklers and light. I don't think he had any trouble reading through my façade of confidence. I was quaking in my proverbial boots, and he knew it. Though even I had to admit that I was doing a damn good job of not fidgeting.

Not taking his eyes off me for a second, his face an unreadable mask of geniality, Mr. Kurosawa snapped his fingers. From the ruined arcade of slot machines I heard the unmistakable heels clicking against the soot-covered, ruined, wet floor.

Lady Siyu was back in her business suit and dragging a scarred and burned Oricho. Well, the dragon hadn't eaten him, but knowing these two, I didn't think that was a good sign.

"Look, Mr. Kurosawa, there has been a huge misunderstanding—" I started.

Oricho lifted his head and straightened the charred sleeves on his ruined shirt. "No misunderstanding, Owl. Mr. Kurosawa is apprised of the situation."

Mr. Kurosawa's lip turned up, exposing a residual fang. He lingered on me a moment before turning towards Oricho. "And here I thought I had won myself a loyal kami, sworn to my service. All this time I had an onryo in hiding, waiting and plotting to kill me. Well played, Oricho." He glanced over at the ruined slot machines. "Though your warriors are free, you have failed to avenge them."

I stood there and waited for Oricho to throw the rest of us under the bus. Blame us, blame Marie, blame Lady Siyu for Christ's sake. I'd almost consider backing him if he said Lady Siyu was behind it— especially the way she was looking at me . . .

"Mr. Kurosawa and Lady Siyu are aware that I acted alone, and that you and your associates were as much victims of my plot as they," Oricho said, looking at both Lady Siyu and Mr. Kurosawa evenly.

Mr. Kurosawa turned to me. "Yes. Much to my surprise, little thief, you have kept your end of the bargain." The main door swung open. "You three are free to go."

I waited. There had to be something more to this. No argument, no double-crossing—they were letting us walk out alive?

"No catches. The vampires will leave you alone and you are free to go, with payment we agreed upon."

I turned to go, but I couldn't leave without knowing. "What are you going to do with Oricho?" I asked.

Mr. Kurosawa frowned, at the end of his patience for humans. His eyes glinted as he glanced at the slot machines. "I do not take betrayal lightly."

I stood there and exchanged looks with Rynn and Nadya. I didn't like this one bit. Mr. Kurosawa had the scroll; what was the point of torturing Oricho to death?

"You've won," I said.

"Don't worry, little thief. I intend to give him a sporting chance."

The way Mr. Kurosawa and Lady Siyu were circling Oricho like a pair of sharks, I doubted that very much.

Oricho removed what was left of his jacket and, as if sensing my reluctance to leave, said, "I appreciate the sentiment, but I am ready to accept the consequences. My warriors are now at peace." A smile crossed his face. "The same thing cannot be said for Mr. Kurosawa's treasure room."

Great, now Oricho gets a sense of humor.

Don't get me wrong, Oricho wasn't a good guy. The skin walker, Marie, almost being burned alive—all of this would be giving me nightmares for a long, long time. But he wasn't exactly evil either. His methods were nuts, and I think he took a step off the deep end a few hundred years ago, but it's not like he was out to kill people for kicks. Mr. Kurosawa and Lady Siyu, on the other hand . . . well, let's just say I got the distinct impression they'd enjoy punishing Oricho, not to mention us if we didn't hightail it out of there . . . Goddamn it, there was no right or wrong here. Just a lot of very angry monsters who'd had a few centuries to stew.

"This whole thing sucks," I said to Nadya and Rynn.

After a nod from Mr. Kurosawa, Lady Siyu broke off and sashayed towards us. "Leave now," she said, and flashed me her fangs. "If I have to throw you out of our casino, odds are not good you will survive."

"Fine, we're going," Rynn said, turning both of us around. "Owl, there's nothing we can do. I wish it were different, but it's within Mr. Kurosawa's rights. I'm sorry, I'm not happy about it either. Oricho's been a good friend—"

"Even though he tried to kill you?" I said, surprised, to say the least. Oricho hadn't planned on killing us, but Rynn? He'd been a calculated casualty.

He shook his head and looked back. "I've known him a long time. A few hundred years with his guilt, and maybe I'd be pushed to a breaking point as well."

We'd won. We should have been celebrating. So why did I feel so sick to my stomach?

I stopped in my tracks and grabbed Rynn's sleeve. I knew damn well why I felt sick to my stomach; I was better than this. Yeah, my conscience had gotten me thrown out of the university, but I was the one who had to live with it.

I stopped and turned to face Lady Siyu and Mr. Kurosawa.

"Alix, what are you doing?" Nadya said.

"Something really, really stupid," I said. But it was worth it if I could walk out of this without the guilt. I raised my voice to address Mr. Kurosawa. "What can we do?" I said.

Mr. Kurosawa and Lady Siyu turned their gazes on me, not even making a pretense this time at geniality. I was interrupting their dinner.

Rynn grabbed my arm. "This isn't your fight. Oricho knew what he was getting into when he concocted this plan."

I ignored him. "There has to be something, Mr. Kurosawa," I hissed. "What? What would be worth more than the satisfaction of killing Oricho?"

Lady Siyu looked as if she wanted to flay me alive, but Mr. Kurosawa eyed me with an even, thoughtful expression. "Not even you have enough treasure stashed away to buy Oricho's life from me," he said.

I nodded and turned back towards the door. I'd tried. I'd failed, but I could sleep at night with that.

"But you might be able to steal enough."

I turned back. Mr. Kurosawa's murderous stare had turned

thoughtful. "I'm branching out into antiquities," he added. "And I'm in the market for an acquisitions and appraisals agent. Interested?"

It took me a second to realize what he was proposing. "You want me to find more treasure for your hoard?" I said.

"What you humans would call an employee/employer arrangement. A three-year contract," he continued as I balked. "I pass jobs your way, and you fetch the items. Why, I'll even allow you to pursue other projects on your own time. Think of it as a mutually beneficial agreement."

I highly doubted there was anything mutually beneficial about it.

"Owl—" Rynn tried, but Lady Siyu silenced him with a hiss.

"I agree to work for you and you'll what? Just let Oricho go?"

"No, but as a sign of good faith, I'd be obliged to give him a running start. He might even live."

I ran it over in my head. It was the only chance Oricho would get.

"Seventy/thirty," I said. "And you pay the expenses."

"Sixty/forty, and that's me being very generous," he said. The teeth were back, and I took that as "negotiations are over."

"If he gets out?" I asked, desperately trying to think my way out of any loopholes.

"Then Oricho is free to try and kill us another day."

"And what about her?" I said, nodding at Lady Siyu.

She smiled. "I'll kill him if I ever see him again."

Considering the position I was in, that was probably the best I could do.

I looked at Oricho, who had a frown on his ruined face. "You have no obligation to indenture yourself to their service," he said.

"Oh, it's a contract. Three years, and I plan to make one hell of a profit out if it."

Not to mention I'd be able to hide from the IAA for the rest of my life. Make no doubt about it, this last week's series of disasters put me well back on their radar. The difference was in three years I could afford to hide without having to steal antiquities. Ever again . . . Did I mention the money?

He bowed his head.

"And for the record, Oricho, if you make it out of here alive, I never want to see you, *ever* again," I said, and turned back to Mr. Kurosawa. "We have a deal," I continued, as Rynn drew in a sharp breath beside me.

Mr. Kurosawa laughed. "Lady Siyu will be in touch."

All I wanted to do was get the hell out. I turned to leave, Nadya, Rynn, and Captain close on my heels. "And consider me on vacation for the next month," I told him.

We were almost out the doors when Oricho called my name. I made the mistake of glancing back in time to see him darting through what was left of the casino. "I owe you a debt and a life. I always repay them."

I kept walking. Why did Oricho have to be the bad guy? Or maybe just the bad guy who lost? No . . . Killing Mr. Kurosawa was one thing, killing Rynn and dragging a damaged, hapless vampire like Marie into it . . . besides, I'd made my bet with the dragon. For now.

"I hope you know what you're doing," Nadya said.

I shook my head. "I'm pretty sure I don't."

We got the hell out of there. With the firefighters and patrons roaming around the main floor, no one paid us any mind. I thought about leaving without my computer—I was this close to doing it but decided to grab what I could.

I don't think I've ever driven the Winnebago that fast before in my life; even Rynn opted to sleep in the back instead of watching me drive.

Maybe hanging around me is a death sentence. I really seem to attract trouble.

Then again, I've gotten some interesting friends out of it too.

Epilogue

I'M ON VACATION

11:00 a.m., Saturday, April 10, my place, Seattle

I grabbed a coffee before heading to my favorite window seat overlooking Elliott Bay. It was April and gray and raining—it's always raining—but I couldn't have cared less. Damn, it felt good to be home—and have my apartment back—without the vampires. Hardly seemed like I'd been out of Vegas almost a month.

I'd closed the bedroom door so Rynn could sleep in. Usually he was up before me, but last night we'd been out, and I'd been learning about the Seattle supernatural underworld. Apparently this city wasn't quite as free of supernaturals as I'd thought. Vampires, yes, but there was a whole other layer I'd never realized was here.

I liked having the odd morning to myself. Rynn usually left me alone first thing—he seemed to think it helped me cope, or whatever psychoanalysis crap he was reading and bouncing off me.

Little-known fact: supernaturals know less about humans than you'd think. Rynn had thrown himself into learning. It had unnerved me at first, until we'd come up with an arrangement—I'd put up with the psychoanalysis hobby if he'd start giving me lessons on the supernatural world. The arrangement was working and eased some of the—I don't know what you'd call it. Interspecies tension?

I wasn't used to having any roommates except Captain, albeit Rynn was a roommate with his own place in Tokyo. But Captain seemed fine with it, which was good enough for me. I was even starting to trust my own judgment about people as well.

Despite the rain, the view from up here looked awesome. Not even one goddamned vampire.

Then the phone rang, breaking my Saturday morning peace and quiet. I dreaded looking at the caller ID, knowing who it would be.

Lady Siyu.

Again.

Goddamn, it'd only been a month and I already missed Oricho. Soooo much easier to deal with over the phone. Still, neither one of the bastards would tell me if they'd eaten him or not. Between you and me, I was guessing Oricho had gotten away. Why? I'm positive Lady Siyu would have bragged if she'd caught him. A lot.

Wherever Oricho was, I hoped he'd stay the hell out of trouble. And far, far away from me.

"What?" I said.

"Vacation is over. You are to meet Mr. Kurosawa with your companions tomorrow at noon. I have made flight arrangements."

"You could have *emailed*," I said.

I could just imagine her eyebrow and a corner of her lacquered red mouth lifting in contempt. "You have an uncivilized habit of not answering your messages on time."

"Oh come on, I have to sleep. Besides, I just saved you and your boss—"

"I expect prompt responses. You have yet to deliver on that expectation."

I ground my teeth. "Nadya is in Japan. She'll be hard-pressed to get here by next week, let alone tomorrow—"

"See that the two of you are presentable," she said, and hung up.

I closed my eyes. Damn it, I did not make a friend there. No sirree.

I picked up the phone and called Nadya.

"Hello?" she said. I could tell she'd been asleep.

"We've been summoned to Vegas. Tomorrow."

Nadya swore.

I didn't blame her. She'd insisted on helping me with the contract, though with a phone call in the middle of the night I suspected she was rethinking it.

We set travel arrangements just as Rynn came out of the bedroom.

"Who was that?" he asked as I hung up.

"We're being summoned. Mr. Kurosawa has a job for me and Nadya. And I don't think they've eaten Oricho yet," I added.

He nodded. "I'll come with you—"

"I thought you said you weren't back to normal yet?" Rynn was still recovering from the scroll's effects.

"Better than I was."

"Wait here until we have the job. I doubt much will happen while we're there."

"I'm fine," he said.

I let out a breath and stopped myself from saying the first thing out of my mouth: *No, you aren't*. Rynn, who'd spent years working as a club host, had pride. Who knew?

"I'm not suggesting otherwise, I'm suggesting you might as well take the rest."

He came up beside me and touched his forehead to mine. "I'm fine. Besides, I've reached a deal with Mr. Kurosawa."

"You what? Please tell me you're not the new Oricho. Toadying is not something I see you doing well."

He winked. "I'm taking over the casino bar."

I groaned. Not what I wanted to hear.

He kissed me on the forehead "Alix, I'll be fine. The bar was running a deficit. If there's one thing dragons hate more than insults to their pride, it's losing treasure. I've even got staff coming from Tokyo, and I've got a mind to put some of the nymphs to work as servers."

"Why is this the first I'm hearing of this?"

"Because you're a train wreck and never tell me anything."

"Whore," I said as Rynn disappeared into the shower. I wasn't sure if it was an incubus thing or not, but Rynn sure as hell loved his showers. Though mine was pretty luxe. Two nozzles, large stone walls. I'd gone all out.

I opened up my laptop. It'd been days since I'd logged into World Quest. Carpe opened up a chat window as soon as I was on. I'd been limiting our conversations to chat lately, trying to curb his stalker instincts.

I need your help was all the message said.

Sure, I have a couple hours to kill, I messaged back.

I need to talk to you in person, he wrote.

Not a chance in hell. I closed the chat function and headed into my game.

My phone rang. Lady Siyu. Goddamn it. "What?" I said.

But it wasn't Lady Siyu.

"Owl, I need your help. I'm serious," Carpe said.

"Why you little toad. How dare you trick me into answering the phone?"

"I wouldn't be contacting you if it wasn't a matter of life and death. It's supernatural. I need you to find something."

Crap.

"Listen real good. I don't do supernatural."

"No offense, but that's not what I hear."

"I don't care what you hear, I'm not doing it."

There was a slight pause. "Please don't make me go through Mr. Kurosawa."

I don't think I've ever been that floored in my entire life. Here I am trying to keep what's left of my subnormal life normal . . . I did something I haven't done in my entire gaming career. I flipped on the camera and dropped his firewall with a worm I'd been keeping stashed for a rainy day.

Yeah, I was that pissed.

A man in pajama bottoms, with a slight build—more sinuous than muscular—and long brown hair tied in a ponytail, sat across from me. There was a window behind him, looking out on a forest somewhere. It was morning, roughly the same time of day—Northwest, from the look of it . . . His jaw dropped as he realized what I'd done.

"What kind of an asshole spies on his friends and then threatens them? I mean, who does that?" I said.

He recovered fast, I'll give him that. He set his jaw and looked straight at me. "Sorry, but you weren't leaving me any choice."

"Fantastic. Is there anything you couldn't find out about me behind my back I can help you with?"

He swore under his breath. "Yes, as a matter of fact. The one thing I need to know and I couldn't find out was whether you were familiar with Egyptian spell books, Old and Middle Kingdom."

I just about fell out of the chair. "Pardon?"

"I know you've been to Egypt a number of times. You even came back with a Mau cat. What I don't know is whether you've dealt with any Egyptian mummies, or if you've come across the spell books—"

I closed my eyes and buried my head on my desk. I attract trouble, I work for a dragon, my go-between is a naga, and I date an incubus. But even I know when to run in the other direction, and if I was going to draw the line somewhere, Egyptian mummies were it.

"Hell no," I said. "Now listen good. I'm turning you off and forgetting we ever had this conversation. If you know what's good for you, you'll stay out of my personal life and also forget we ever had this conversation."

Carpe frowned. He was good-looking in a feminine, geek chic kind of way. Not my type, but even I had to admit he wasn't the fat, acned kid I'd pictured. He was still a royal jerk however.

"Owl, if it's a question of money, I can pay—"

"Yeah, and if I become suicidal, I'll let you know."

"You're overreacting, and I don't think you realize how serious this is. I'm not kidding when I say it's a life-and-death matter."

Do one supernatural job and start working for a dragon . . .

"Do I really look that stupid? Oh, don't look so put out. Look at it this way. If you're not dead by this weekend, I'll see you on World Quest. By the way, nice pajamas." I tried to close the screen, but Carpe had gotten in and locked it.

"Son of a bitch—Carpe, get out of my laptop."

"It's one spell book. That's all I need—"

"Yeah, and I'm pretty sure the dead guy is still using said spell book, so the answer is still no."

"Please, I'm begging you—"

Rynn got out of the shower just as Carpe pleaded with me. He'd been headed for the kitchen and coffee machine, but he stopped at the sound of Carpe's voice.

"Owl, who are you talking to?" he said, making a beeline for my laptop, a deep frown etched on his face.

"My World Quest friend, Carpe. And we're done talking—Rynn, do you mind? I'm finishing an argument," I said as he leaned over my shoulder and took over my keyboard, zooming in on Carpe's face. Rynn's lip curled, and I noticed Carpe's smile drop.

Rynn turned to me, his brow furrowed. "When the hell did you start talking to elves?"

Acknowledgments

I'd like to thank my husband, Steve, and my friend Leanne Tremblay, who read each and every chapter. I don't know if I would have finished the book without their feedback and encouragement.

I also have to thank my agent, Carolyn Forde, who picked my manuscript out of the slush pile; Alison Clarke and Adam Wilson from Simon & Schuster, who both saw something in Owl; and my editor, Sean Mackiewicz, for his keen eye and hard work. There are many other people who have mentored and encouraged me in my writing career over the past few years, but this space is small. Thank you all!

Finally, there is one non-human without whom this book would never have been written, and that is my cat Captain Flash, on whom the character Captain is absolutely based.

About the Author

Kristi Charish is a scientist and science fiction/fantasy writer who resides in Vancouver, Canada, with her spousal unit, Steve, and two cats named Captain Flash and Alaska. She received a BS and MS in molecular biology and biochemistry from Simon Fraser University, and a PhD in zoology from the University of British Columbia. Kristi writes what she loves: adventure-heavy stories featuring strong, savvy female protagonists.

Get email updates on

KRISTI CHARISH,

exclusive offers,

and other great book recommendations

from Simon & Schuster.

Visit **newsletters.simonandschuster.com**

or

scan below to sign up: